Praise for *New York Times* bestselling author Fern Michaels

"An action-packed plot . . . Michaels's fans will be satisfied."
—*Publishers Weekly* on *Late Bloomer*

"Michaels's snazzy tales reveals the ups-and-downs of friendship and small-town life."
—*Booklist* on *Late Bloomer*

Praise for *New York Times* bestselling author Lisa Jackson

"No one tells a story like Lisa Jackson. She's headed straight for the top!"
—Debbie Macomber

"Provocative prose, an irresistible plot, and finely crafted characters make up Jackson's latest contemporary sizzler."
—*Publishers Weekly* on *Wishes*

Praise for *New York Times* bestselling author Linda Lael Miller

"Pure delight from the beginning to the satisfying ending . . . Miller is a master craftswoman at creating unusual storylines and charming characters."
—*Rendezvous* on *Springwater Wedding*

"A fun read, full of Ms. Miller's simmering sensuality and humor, plus two fabulous brothers who will steal your heart."
—*Romantic Times* on *Two Brothers*

Praise for *New York Times* bestselling author Virginia Henley

"A master storyteller . . . With each new novel, Virginia Henley tests her powers as a writer, and as readers, we reap the splendid rewards."
—*Romantic Times*

"A brilliant author whom we've come to rely on for the best in romantic fiction."
—*Rendezvous*

Praise for *New York Times* bestselling author Marcia Evanick

"Light, funny and full of heart, a book by Marcia Evanick is always a satisfying read."
—Kasey Michaels

"Marcia Evanick's stories are charming and fun."
—*Rendezvous*

Books by Fern Michaels

About Face
Annie's Rainbow
Celebration
Charming Lily
Dear Emily
Finders Keepers
The Future Scrolls
The Guest List
Kentucky Heat
Kentucky Rich
Kentucky Sunrise
Listen to Your Heart
Plain Jane
Sara's Song
Vegas Heat
Vegas Rich
Vegas Sunrise
What You Wish For
Weekend Warriors
Whitefire
Wish List
Yesterday

Books by Lisa Jackson

See How She Dies
Intimacies
Wishes
Whispers
Twice Kissed
Unspoken
If She Only Knew
Hot Blooded
Cold Blooded
The Night Before
The Morning After

Books by Marcia Evanick

Catch of the Day
Christmas on Conrad Street
Blueberry Hill
A Berry Merry Christmas

Published by Kensington Publishing Corporation

DECK THE HALLS

FERN MICHAELS

LISA JACKSON * LINDA LAEL MILLER

VIRGINIA HENLEY * MARCIA EVANICK

KENSINGTON BOOKS
http://www.kensingtonbooks.com

KENSINGTON BOOKS are published by

Kensington Publishing Corp.
850 Third Avenue
New York, NY 10022

All Kensington titles, imprints and distributed lines are available at special quantity discounts for bulk purchases for sales promotion, premiums, fund raising, educational or institutional use.

Special book excerpts or customized printings can also be created to fit specific needs. For details, write or phone the office of the Kensington Special Sales Manager: Kensington Publishing Corp., 850 Third Avenue, New York, NY 10022. Attn. Special Sales Department. Phone: 1-800-221-2647.

Kensington and the K logo Reg. U.S. Pat. & TM Off.

ISBN 0-7582-1047-7

First Kensington Trade Paperback Printing: November 2004
10 9 8 7 6 5 4 3 2 1

Printed in the United States of America

Contents

Merry, Merry

Fern Michaels

Andi Evans stared at the light switch. Should she turn it on or not? How many kilowatts of electricity did the fluorescent bulbs use? How would it translate onto her monthly bill? She risked a glance at the calendar; December 14, 1996, five days till the meter reader arrived. The hell with it, the animals needed light. She needed light. Somehow, someway, she'd find a way to pay the bill. On the other hand, maybe she should leave the premises dark so Mr. Peter King could break his leg in the dark. Breaking both legs would be even better. Like it was really going to happen.

Maybe she should read the letter again. She looked in the direction of her desk where she'd thrown it five days ago after she'd read it. She could see the end of the expensive cream-colored envelope sticking out among the stack of unpaid bills. "Guess what, Mr. Peter King, I'm not selling you my property. I told that to your forty-seven lawyers months ago." She started to cry then because it was all so hopeless.

They came from every direction, dogs, cats, puppies and kittens, clawing for her attention, their ears attuned to the strange sounds coming from the young woman who fed and bathed them and saw to their needs. They were strays nobody wanted. This was what she'd gone to veterinarian school for. She even had a sign that said she was Andrea Evans, D.V.M. Eleven patients in as many months. She was the new kid on the block, what did she expect? Because she was that new kid, people assumed they could just dump unwanted animals on her property. After all, what did a vet with only eleven patients have to do?

Andi thought about her student loans, the taxes on her house and three acres, the animals, the bills, the futility of it all. Why was she even fighting? Selling her property would net her a nice tidy sum. She could pay off her loans, go to work for a vet clinic, get a condo someplace and . . . what would happen to her animals if she did that? She wailed louder, the dogs and cats clambering at her feet.

"Enough!" a voice roared.

"Gertie!"

Tails swished furiously; Gertie always brought soup bones and catnip. Andi watched as she doled them out, something for everyone. She blew her nose. "I think they love you more than they love me."

"They love what I bring them. I'd like a cup of tea if you have any. It's nasty out there. It might snow before nightfall."

"Where are you sleeping tonight, Gertie?"

"Under the railroad trestle with my friends. Being homeless doesn't give me many choices."

"You're welcome to stay here, Gertie. I told you the cot is yours anytime you want it. I'll even make you breakfast. Did you eat today?"

"Later. I have something for you. Call it an early Christmas present. I couldn't wait to get here to give it to you." Gertie hiked up several layers of clothing to her long underwear where she'd sewn a pocket. She withdrew a thick wad of bills. "We found this four weeks ago. There it was, this big wad of money laying right in the street late at night. Two thousand dollars, Andi. We want you to have it. We watched in the papers, asked the police, no one claimed it. A whole month we waited, and no one claimed it. It's probably drug money, but them animals of yours don't know that. Better to be spent on them than on some drug pusher. Doncha be telling me no now."

"Oh, Gertie, I wouldn't dream of saying no. Did you find it in Plainfield?"

"Right there on Front Street, big as life."

Andi hugged the old woman who always smelled of lily of the valley. She could never figure out why that was. Gertie had to be at least seventy-five, but a young seventy-five as she put it. She was skinny and scrawny, but it was hard to tell with the many layers of clothing she wore. Her shoes were run-down, her gloves had holes in the fingers, and her knit cap reeked of moth balls. For a woman her age she had dewy skin, pink cheeks, few wrinkles and the brightest, bluest eyes Andi had ever seen. "Did you walk all the way from Plainfield, Gertie?"

Gertie's head bobbed up and down. "Scotch Plains ain't that far. I left my buggie outside."

Translated, that meant all of Gertie's worldly possessions were in an Acme shopping cart outside Andi's clinic.

"Here's your tea, Gertie, strong and black, just the way you like it. It's almost Christmas; are you going to call your children? You should, they must be worried sick."

"What, so they can slap me in a nursing home? Oh, no, I like things just the way they are. I'm spending Christmas with my friends. Now, why were you bawling like that?"

Andi pointed to her desk. "Unpaid bills. And a letter from Mr. Peter King. He's that guy I told you about. His forty-seven lawyers couldn't bend me, so I guess they're sending in the first string now. He's coming here at four-thirty."

"Here?" Gertie sputtered, the teacup almost falling from her hand.

"Yes. Maybe he's going to make a final offer. Or, perhaps he thinks he can intimidate me. This property has been in my family for over a hundred years. I'm not selling it to some lipstick mogul. What does a man know about lipstick anyway? Who cares if he's one of the biggest cosmetic manufacturers on the East Coast. I don't even wear lipstick. These lips are as kissable as they're going to get, and his greasy product isn't going to change my mind."

"I really need to be going now, Andi. So, you'll tell him no."

"Gertie, look around you. What would you do if you were me? What's so special about this piece of property? Let him go to Fanwood, anywhere but here. Well?"

"Location is everything. This is prime. Zoning has to be just right, and you, my dear, are zoned for his needs. I'd tell him to go fly a kite," Gertie said smartly. "I hear a truck. Lookee here, Andi, Wishnitz is here with your dog food."

"I didn't order any dog food."

"You better tell him that then, 'cause the man's unloading big bags of it. I'll see you tomorrow. Greasy, huh?"

"Yeah. Gertie, I wish you'd stay; it's getting awfully cold outside. Thanks for the money. Tell your friends I'm grateful. You be careful now."

"Hey, I didn't order dog food," she said to the driver.

"Bill says it's a gift. Five hundred pounds of Pedigree dog food, sixteen cases of cat food and two bags of birdseed. Sign here?"

"Who sent it?"

"Don't know, ma'am, I'm just the driver. Call the store. Where do you want this?"

"Around the back."

Andi called the feed store to be sure there was no mistake. "Are you telling me some anonymous person just walked into your store and paid for all this? It's a fortune in dog and cat food. No name at all? All right, thanks."

A beagle named Annabelle pawed Andi's leg. "I know, time for supper and a little run. Okay, everybody *SIT!* You know the drill, about face; march in an orderly fashion to the pen area. Stop when you get to the gate and go to your assigned dishes. You know which ones are yours. No cheating, Harriet," she said to a fat white cat who eyed her disdainfully. "I'm counting to three, and when the whistle blows, *GO!* That's really good, you guys are getting the hang of it. Okay, here it comes, extra today thanks to our Good Samaritan, whoever she or he might be."

"Bravo! If I didn't see it with my own eyes, I wouldn't have believed it. There must be thirty dogs and cats here."

"Thirty-six to be exact. And you are?" Andi looked at her watch.

"Peter King. You must be Andrea Evans."

"Dr. Evans. How did you get in here? The dogs didn't bark." Andi's voice was suspicious, her eyes wary. "I'm busy right now, and you're forty-five minutes early, Mr. King. I can't deal with you now. You need to go back to the office or come back another day." The wariness in her eyes changed to amusement when she noticed Cedric, a Dalmatian, lift his leg to pee on Peter King's exquisitely polished Brooks Brothers loafers.

The lipstick mogul, as Andi referred to him, eyed his shoe in dismay. He shook it off and said, "You might be right. I'll be in the waiting room."

Andi raised her head from the sack of dog food to stare at the tall man dwarfing her: Thirty-six or -seven, brown eyes, brown unruly hair with a tight curl, strong features, handsome, muscular, unmarried: no ring on his finger. Sharply dressed. Pristine white shirt, bold, expensive tie. Very well put together. She wondered how many lipsticks he had to sell to buy his outfit. She debated asking until she remembered how she looked. Instead she said, "You remind me of someone."

"A lot of people say that, but they can never come up with who it is." He started for the waiting room.

"It will come to me sooner or later." Andi ladled out food, the dogs waiting patiently until all the dishes were full. "Okay, guys, go for it!" When the animals finished eating, Andi let them out into their individual runs. "Twenty minutes. When you hear the buzzer, boogie on in here," she called.

Andi took her time stacking the dog bowls in the stainless steel sink full of soapy water. She'd said she was busy. Busy meant she had to wash and dry the dishes now to take up time. As she washed and dried the bowls, her eyes kept going to the mirror over the sink. She looked worse than a mess. She had on absolutely no makeup, her blond hair was frizzy, her sweatshirt was stained and one of her sneakers had a glob of poop on the heel. She cleaned off her shoe, then stacked the dishes for the following day. "When I'm slicked up, I can look as good as he does," she hissed to the animals and let the dogs into their pens. The beagle threw her head back and howled.

"I have five minutes, Mr. King. I told your forty-seven lawyers I'm not selling. What part of no don't you understand?"

"The part about the forty-seven lawyers. I only have two. I think you mean forty-seven letters."

Andi shrugged.

"I thought perhaps I could take you out to dinner . . . and we could . . . discuss the pros and cons of selling your property." He smiled. She saw dimples and magnificent white teeth. All in a row like matched pearls.

"Save your money, Mr. King. Dinner will not sway my decision. You know what else, I don't even like your lipstick. It's greasy. The colors are abominable. The names you've given the lipsticks are so ridiculous they're ludicrous. Raspberry Cheese Louise. Come *onnnnn.*" At his blank look she said, "I worked at a cosmetic counter to put myself through college and vet school."

"I see."

"No, you don't, but that's okay. Time's up, Mr. King."

"Three hundred and fifty thousand, Dr. Evans. You could relocate."

Andi felt her knees go weak on her. "Sorry, Mr. King."

"Five hundred thousand and that's as high as I can go. It's a take it or leave it offer. It's on the table right now. When I walk out of here it goes with me."

She might have seriously considered the offer if the beagle hadn't chosen that moment to howl. "I really have to go, Mr. King. That's Annabelle howling. She has arthritis and it's time for her medication." She must be out of her mind to turn down half a million dollars. Annabelle howled again.

"I didn't know dogs got arthritis."

"They get a lot of things, Mr. King. They develop heart trouble; they get cancer, cataracts, prostate problems, all manner of things. Do you really think us humans have a lock on disease? This is the only home those animals know. No one else wanted them, so I took them in. My father and his father before him owned this kennel. It's my home and their home."

"Wait, hear me out. You could buy a new, modern facility with the money I'm willing to pay you. This is pretty antiquated. Your wood's rotten, your pens are rusty, your concrete is cracked. You're way past being a fixer-upper. You could get modern equipment. If you want my opinion, I think you're being selfish. You're thinking of yourself, not the animals. The past is past; you can't bring it back, nor should you want to. I'll leave my offer on the table till Friday. Give it some thought, sleep on it. If your decision is still no on Friday, I won't bother you again. I'll even raise my price to $750,000. I'm not trying to cheat you."

Andi snorted. "Of course not," she said sarcastically, "that's why you started off at $200,000 and now you're up to $750,000.

I didn't just fall off the turnip truck, Mr. King. Let's cut to the chase. What's your absolute final offer?"

It was Peter King's turn to stare warily at the young doctor in front of him. His grandmother would love her. Sadie would say she had grit and spunk. Uh-huh. "A million," he said hoarsely.

"That's as in acre, right? I have a little over three acres. Closer to four than three."

King's jaw dropped. Annabelle howled again. "You want three million dollars for this . . . hovel?"

"No. Three plus million for the *land*. You're right, it is a hovel; but it's my home and the home of those animals. I sweated my ass off to keep this property and work my way through school. What do you know about work, Mr. Lipstick? Hell, I could make up a batch of that stuff you peddle for eight bucks a pop right here in the kitchen. All I need is my chemistry book. Get the hell off my property and don't come back unless you have three million plus dollars in your hand You better get going before it really starts to snow and you ruin those fancy three-hundred-dollar Brooks Brothers shoes."

"Your damn dog already ruined them."

"Send me a bill!" Andi shouted as she pushed him through the door and then slammed it shut. She turned the dead bolt before she raced back to the animals. She dusted her hands dramatically for the animals' benefit before she started to cry. The animals crept from their cages that had no doors, to circle her, licking and pawing at her tear-filled face. She hiccupped and denounced all men who sold lipstick. "If he comes up with three million plus bucks, we're outta here. Then we'll have choices; we can stay here in New Jersey, head south or north, wherever we can get the best deal. Hamburger and tuna for you guys and steak for me. We'll ask Gertie to go with us. I'm done crying now. You can go back to sleep. Come on, Annabelle, time for your pill."

Andi scooped up the pile of bills on her desk to carry them into the house. With the two thousand dollars from Gertie and the dog and cat food, she could last until the end of January, and then she'd be right back where she was just a few hours ago. Three million plus dollars was a lot of money. So was $750,000. Scrap that, he'd said a cool million. Times three. At eight bucks a tube, how many lipsticks would the kissing king need to sell? Somewhere in the neighborhood of 375,000. Darn, she should have said two million an acre.

It might be a wonderful Christmas after all.

Peter King slid his metallic card into the slot and waited for the huge grilled gate to the underground garage of his grandmother's high-rise to open. Tonight was his Friday night obligatory dinner with his grandmother. A dinner he always enjoyed and even looked forward to. He adored his seventy-five-year-old grandmother who was the president of King Cosmetics. He shuddered when he thought of what she would say to Andrea Evans's price. She'd probably go ballistic and throw her salmon, Friday night's dinner, across the room. At which point, Hannah the cat would eat it all and then puke on the Persian carpet. He shuddered again. Three million dollars. Actually, it would be more than three million. The property on Cooper River Road was closer to four acres. He had two hard choices: pay it or forget it.

Who in the hell was that wise-ass girl whose dog peed on his shoe? Where did she get off booting him out the door. Hell, she'd pushed him, shoved him. She probably didn't weigh more than one hundred pounds soaking wet. He took a few seconds to mentally envision that hundred-pound body naked. Aaahh. With some King Cosmetics she'd be a real looker. And she hated his guts.

"Hey, Sadie, I'm here," Peter called from the foyer. He'd called his grandmother Sadie from the time he was a little boy. She allowed it because she said it made her feel younger.

"Peter, you're early. Good, we can have a drink by the fire. Hannah's already there waiting for us. She's not feeling well." Sadie's voice turned fretful. "I don't want her *going* before me. She's such wonderful company. Look at her, she's just lying there. I tried to tempt her with salmon before and she wouldn't touch it. She won't even let me hold her."

Peter's stomach started to churn. If anything happened to Hannah, he knew his grandmother would take to her bed and not get up. He hunched down and held out his hand. Hannah hissed and snarled. "That's not like her. Did you take her to the vet?"

Sadie snorted "He went skiing in Aspen. I don't much care for all those fancy vets who have banker's hours and who don't give a damn. Hannah is too precious to trust to just anybody. Let's sit and have a drink and watch her. How did your meeting go with Dr. Evans?"

"It was a bust. She wants a million dollars an acre. She means it, too. She booted my ass right out the door. I have a feeling she's a pretty good vet. Maybe you should have her take a look at Hannah. One of her dogs squirted on my shoe."

"That's a lot of money. Is the property worth it?"

"Hell yes. More as a matter of fact. She ridiculed my low-ball offer. Hey, business is business."

"We aren't in the business of cheating people, Peter. Fair is fair. If, as you say, Miss Evans's property is the perfect location, then pay the money and close the deal. The company can afford it. You can be under way the first of the year. I know you had the attorneys do all the paperwork in advance. Which, by the way, is a tad unethical in my opinion. Don't think I don't know that you have your contractor on twenty-four-hour call."

"Is there anything you don't know, Sadie?"

"Yes."

Peter eyed his grandmother warily. God, how he loved this old lady with her pearl white hair and regal bearing. It was hard to believe she was over seventy. She was fit and trim, fashionable, a leader in the community. She sat on five boards, did volunteer work at the hospital and was an active leader in ways to help the homeless. Her picture was in the paper at least three days a week. He knew what was coming now, and he dreaded it. "Let's get it over with, Sadie."

"Helen called here for you about an hour ago. She quizzed me, Peter. The gall of that woman. What do you see in her? I hesitate to remind you, but she dumped you. That's such an unflattering term, but she did. She married that councilman because she believed his PR campaign. She thought he was rich. The man is in debt over his ears, so she left him. Now, she wants you again. She's a selfish, mean-spirited young woman who thinks only of herself. I thought you had more sense, Peter. I am terribly disappointed in this turn of events."

He was pretty much of the same opinion, but he wasn't going to give his grandmother the pleasure of knowing his feelings. She'd been matchmaking for years and was determined to find just the right girl for him.

"We're friends. There's no harm in a casual lunch or dinner. Don't make this into something else."

"I want to see you settled before I go."

"You can stop that right now, Sadie, because it isn't going to work. You're fit as a fiddle, better than a person has a right to be at your age. You can stay on the treadmill longer than I can. You aren't going anywhere for a very long time. When I find the right girl you'll be the first to know."

"You've been telling me that for years. You're thirty-six, Peter. I want grandchildren before . . . I get too old to enjoy them. If you aren't interested in Helen, tell her so and don't take up her time. Don't even think about bringing her to your Christmas party. If you do, I will not attend."

"*All right,* Sadie!"

Sadie sniffed, her blue eyes sparking. "She just wants to be your hostess so she can network. Men are so stupid sometimes. Tell me about Dr. Evans. What's she like?"

Peter threw his hands in the air. "I told you she kicked me out. I hardly had time to observe her. She has curly hair, she's skinny. I think she's skinny. She had this look on her face, Sadie, it . . . Mom used to look at me kind of the same way when I was sick. She had that look when she was with the animals. I was sizing her up when her dog squatted on my shoe. The place is a mess. Clean, but a mess."

"That young woman worked her way through school. She worked at a cosmetic counter, did waitressing, sometimes working two jobs. It took her a while, but she did it. I approve of that, Peter. That property has been in her family for a long time. Both her parents were vets, and so was her grandfather. No one appreciates hard work more than I do. Take a good look at me, Peter. I started King Cosmetics in my kitchen. I worked around the clock when your grandfather died and I had three children to bring up. I read the report in your office. I can truthfully say I never read a more comprehensive report. The only thing missing was the color of her underwear. I felt like a sneak reading it. I really did, Peter. I wish you hadn't done that. It's such an invasion of someone's privacy."

"This might surprise you, Sadie, but I felt the same way. I wanted to know what I was up against, financially. For whatever it's worth, I'm sorry I did it, too. So, do we buy the property or not?"

"Are you prepared to pay her price?"

"I guess I am. It's a lot of money."

"Will she hold out?" Sadie's tone of voice said she didn't care one way or the other.

"Damn right. That young woman is big on principle. She's going to stick it to me because she thinks I tried to cheat her."

"You did."

"Why does it sound like you're on her side? What I did was an acceptable business practice."

"I'm a fair, honest woman, Peter. I don't like anything unethical. I wish this whole mess never happened. Why don't you invite Dr. Evans to your Christmas party. If you got off to a bad start, this might shore up things for you. I think you're interested in the young woman. I bet she even has a party dress. And shoes. Probably even a pearl necklace that belonged to her mother. Girls always have pearl necklaces that belonged to their mothers. Things like pearl necklaces are important to young women. Well?"

"Before or after I make the offer?" Jesus, he didn't just say that, did he?

"If you're going to make the offer, call her and tell her. Why wait till Monday? Maybe you could even go over there and take Hannah for her to check over. That's business for her. Then you could extend the invitation."

Peter grinned wryly. "You never give up, do you?"

"Then you'll take Hannah tomorrow."

"For you, Sadie, anything. What's for dinner?"

"Pot roast," Sadie said smartly. "I gave the salmon to Hannah, but she wouldn't eat it."

"Pot roast's good. We settled on the three million plus then?" His voice was so jittery-sounding, Sadie turned away to hide her smile.

"I'd say so. You need to give Dr. Evans time to make plans. Christmas is almost here. She'll want to spend her last Christmas at her home, I would imagine. She'll have to pack up whatever she's going to take with her. It's not much time, Peter. She has to think about all those animals."

"Three million plus will ease the burden considerably. She can hire people to help her. We're scheduled to go, as in *go*, the day after New Years. I hate to admit this, but I'm having second thoughts about the contractor I hired. I think I was just a little too hasty when I made my decision, but I signed the contract so I'm stuck. Time's money, Sadie. If the young lady is as industrious as the report says, she'll have it under control."

Sadie smiled all through dinner. She was still smiling when she kissed her grandson good night at the door. "Drive carefully, Peter, the weatherman said six inches of snow by morning. Just out of curiosity, do you happen to know what kind of vehicle Dr. Evans drives?"

"I saw an ancient pickup on the side of the building. It didn't look like it was operational to me. Why do you ask?"

"No reason. I'd hate to think of her stranded with those animals if an emergency came up."

"If you want me to stop on my way home, just say so, Sadie. Is it late? Why don't I call her on the car phone on the way?"

"A call is so impersonal. Like when Helen calls. You could tell Dr. Evans you were concerned about the animals. The power could go out. She might have electric heat. You could also mention that you'll be bringing Hannah in the morning. If she doesn't like you, this might change her mind."

"I didn't say she didn't like me, Sadie," Peter blustered.

"Oh."

"Oh? What does oh mean?"

"It means I don't think she likes you. Sometimes you aren't endearing, Peter. She doesn't know you the way I do. The way Helen did." This last was said so snidely, Peter cringed.

"Good night, Sadie." Peter kissed his grandmother soundly, gave her a thumbs-up salute, before he pressed the down button of the elevator.

As he waited for the grilled parking gate to open, he stared in dismay at the accumulated snow. Maybe he should head for the nearest hotel and forget about going home. What he should have done was bunk with Sadie for the night. Too late, he was already on the road. The snow took care of any visit he might have considered making to Scotch Plains. He eyed the car phone and then the digital clock on the Mercedes walnut panel. Nine o'clock was still early. Pay attention to the road, he cautioned himself.

In the end, Peter opted for the Garden State Parkway. Traffic was bumper-to-bumper, but moving. He got off the Clark exit and headed for home. He could call Dr. Evans from home with a frosty beer in his hand. When the phone on the console buzzed, he almost jumped out of his skin. He pressed a button and said, "Peter King."

"Peter, it's Helen. I've been calling you all evening. Where have you been?"

He wanted to say, what business is it of yours where I was, but he didn't. "On the road," he said curtly.

"Why don't you stop for a nightcap, Peter. I'll put another log on the fire. I have some wonderful wine."

"Sorry, I'm three blocks from home. The roads are treacherous this evening."

"I see. Where were you, Peter? I called your grandmother, and she said you weren't there."

"Out and about. I'll talk to you next week, Helen."

"You're hanging up on me," she said in a whiny voice.

"Afraid so, I'm almost home."

"I wish I was there with you. I didn't get an invitation to your Christmas party, Peter. Was that an oversight or don't you want me there?"

Peter drew a deep breath. "Helen, you aren't divorced. I know your husband well. We play racquetball at the gym. He's a nice guy and I like him. He's coming to the party. It won't look right for you to attend."

"For heaven's sake, Peter, this is the nineties. Albert and I remained friends. We're legally separated. He knows it's you I love. He's known that from day one. I made a mistake, Peter. Are you going to hold it against me for the rest of my life?"

"Look, Helen, there's no easy way to say this except to say it straight out. I'm seeing someone on a serious basis. You and I had our time, but it's over now. Let's stay friends and let it go at that."

"Who? Who are you seeing? You're making that up, Peter. I would have heard if you were seriously seeing someone. Or is she some nobody you don't take out in public? I bet it's somebody your grandmother picked out for you. Oh, Peter, that's just too funny for words." Trilling laughter filled Peter's car.

Peter swerved into his driveway just as he pressed the power button on the car phone, cutting Helen's trilling laughter in mid-note. He waited for the Genie to raise the garage door. The moment the garage door closed, Peter's shoulders slumped. Who *was* that woman on the phone? Jesus, once he'd given serious thought to marrying her. He shook his head to clear away his thoughts.

How quiet and empty his house was. Cold and dark. He hated coming home to a dark house. He'd thought about getting an animal, but it wouldn't have been fair to the animal since he was hardly ever home. He slammed his briefcase down on the kitchen counter. Damn, he'd forgotten the report on Andrea Evans. Oh, well, it wasn't going anywhere. Tomorrow would be soon enough to retrieve it.

Peter walked around his house, turning on lights as he went from room to room. It didn't look anything like the house he'd grown up in. He leaned against the banister, closing his eyes as he did so. He'd lived in a big, old house full of nooks and crannies in Sleepy Hollow. The rug at the foot of the steps was old, threadbare, and Bessie, their old cocker spaniel had chewed all four corners. She lay on the rug almost all her life to wait for them to come home, pooping on it from time to time as she got older. When she died, his parents had buried her in the backyard under the apple tree. Jesus, he didn't think there was that much grief in the world as that day. He thought about the old hat rack with the boot box underneath where he stored his boots, gloves and other treasures. The hat rack and boot box were somewhere in the attic along with Bessie's toys and dog bones. He wondered if they were still intact.

Peter rubbed at his eyes. He'd loved that house with the worn, comfortable furniture, the green plants his mother raised, and the warm, fragrant kitchen with its bright colors. Something was always cooking or baking, and there were always good things to eat for his friends and himself after school. The thing he remembered the most, though, was his mother's smile when he walked in the door. She'd always say, "Hi, Pete, how's it going?" And he'd say, "Pretty good, Mom." They always ate in the kitchen. Dinner hour was long, boisterous and memorable. Even when they had meat loaf. He tried not to think about his younger brother and sister. He had to stop torturing himself like this. He banged one fist on the banister as he wiped at his eyes with the other. He looked around. Everything was beautiful, decorated by a professional whose name he didn't know. Once a week a florist delivered fresh flowers. The only time the house came alive was during his annual Christmas party or his Fourth of July barbecue. The rest of the time it was just a house. The word nurture came to mind. He squeezed his eyes shut and tried to imagine what this perfectly decorated house would be like with a wife, kids and a dog. Maybe two dogs and two cats.

"Five thousand goddamn fucking square feet of *nothing.*" He ripped at his tie and jacket, tossing them on the back of a chair. He kicked his loafers across the room. In a pique of something he couldn't define, he brushed at a pile of magazines and watched them sail in different directions. Shit! The room still didn't look lived in. Hell, he didn't even know his neighbors. He might as well live in a damn hotel.

On his way back to the kitchen he picked up the portable phone, asking for information. He punched out the numbers for the Evans Kennel as his free hand twisted the cap off a bottle of Budweiser. He wondered if her voice would be sleepy sounding or hard and cold. He wasn't prepared for what he did hear when he announced himself.

"I don't have time for chitchat, Mr. King. I have an emergency on my hands here and you're taking up my time. Call me on Monday or don't call me on Monday." Peter stared at the pinging phone in his hand.

Chitchat. Call or don't call. *Emergency.* Sadie's dire warnings rang in his ears.

Peter raced up the steps. So there was a sucker born every minute. Sadie would approve. He stripped down, throwing his clothes any which way as he searched for thermal sweats, thick socks and Alpine boots. His shearling jacket, cap and gloves were downstairs in the hall closet.

Emergency could mean anything. She was handling it. Oh, yeah, like women could really handle an emergency. Maybe his mother could handle one, or Sadie, but not that hundred pound prairie flower. He raced to the garage where all his old camping gear was stored. Blankets and towels went into the back of his

Range Rover. He threw in two shovels, his camp stove, lanterns, flashlights. The last things to go in were Sterno lamps and artificial fire logs. What the hell, an emergency was an emergency.

It wasn't until he backed the 4 by 4 out of the garage that he questioned himself. Why was he doing this? Because ... because ... he'd heard the same fearful tone in Dr. Evans's voice that he'd heard in his mother's voice the day Bessie couldn't get up on her legs anymore.

Driving every back street and alley, over people's lawns, Peter arrived at the Evans Kennel in over an hour. Every light appeared to be on in the house and the kennel. There were no footprints in the snow, so that had to mean the emergency was inside the house. Even from this distance he could hear the shrill barking and high-pitched whine of the animals that seemed to be saying, intruder, intruder.

Peter walked around to the door he'd been ushered out of just hours ago. His eyebrows shot up to his hairline when he found it unlocked. He felt silly as hell when he bellowed above the sound of the dogs, "I'm here and coming through!"

In the whole of his life he'd never seen so many teeth in one place—all canine. "You need to lock your goddamn doors is what you need to do, Dr. Evans!" he shouted.

"You!" She made it sound like he was the devil from hell making a grand entrance.

"Who'd you expect, Sylvester Stallone? You said it was an emergency. I react to emergencies. My mother trained me that way. I brought everything. What's wrong?"

Andi, hands on hips, stared at the man standing in front of her, the dogs circling his feet. She clapped her hands once, and they all lay down, their eyes on the giant towering over them.

"I had to do a cesarian section on Rosie. Her pups were coming out breach. Come here. Mother and puppies doing just fine, all eight of them. God, eight more mouths to feed." Andi's shoulders slumped as she fought off her tears.

"I'll take two. Three. I love dogs. It won't be so hard. I'm going to meet your price. Three million plus, whatever the plus turns out to be. It's fair. You'll be able to do a lot if you invest wisely. I can recommend a pretty good tax man if you're interested. You might even want to give some thought to taking payments instead of one lump sum. You need to talk to someone. Am I getting girls or boys? Make that four. I'll give one to my grandmother. That's another thing, her cat Hannah is sick. I was going to call you in the morning to ask if you'd look at her. Their regular vet is away on a winter vacation."

"Oh, my. Listen, about this afternoon . . ."

"You don't have to apologize," Peter said.

Andi smiled. "I wasn't going to apologize. I was going to try and explain my circumstances to you. I appreciate you coming back here. It's the thought that counts. Are you serious about the pups?"

Was he? "Hell yes. Told you, I love dogs. Isn't it kind of cold out here for the new mother and my pups?"

"No. Actually, dogs much prefer it to be cooler. I was going to take Rosie into the kitchen, though. I leave the door open, and if the others want to come in, they do. At some point during the night, when I'm sleeping, three or four of them will come in and sleep outside my door. There's usually one outside the bathroom when I shower, too. They're very protective; they know when you're bathing and sleeping you're vulnerable. It's really amazing."

"Bessie was like that. Do you want me to carry the box?"

"Sure. Can I make you some coffee? I was going to have a grilled cheese sandwich. Would you like one or did you have your dinner?"

Peter thought about how he'd pigged out on his grandmother's pot roast. "I'm starved. Coffee sounds good, too. I brought a lot of blankets and towels with me. I thought maybe your heat went out."

"I could really use them. My washer goes all day long, and like everything else in this house, it's getting ready to break down. My furnace is the next thing to go."

Peter's face turned ashen. "Your furnace? Don't you check it? You need to call PSE&G to come and look at it. My parents . . . and my brother and sister died from carbon monoxide poisoning. Turn it off if it's giving you trouble. Use your fireplace. I can bring you electric heaters. Is the fireplace any good?"

Andi stared at the man sitting at her table, a helpless look on her face. "I . . . I'm sorry. I don't know the first thing about the furnace except that it's very old. The fireplace is in good condition; I had it cleaned in September. I'd probably be more at risk using electric heaters; the wiring and the plumbing are ... old. I guess I just have to take my chances. It's only another two weeks. You said you wanted to ... start ... whatever it is you're going to do right after the first of the year."

"Tomorrow when I bring Hannah I'll bring you some of those detectors. I have one in every room in my house. I was away at school when it happened. All you do is plug them in."

"I appreciate that. I won't charge you for Hannah, then."

"Okay, that's fair." He wasn't about to tell her each detector cost eighty-nine dollars. She would need at least four of them for the sprawling house and kennel.

"Want some bacon on your sandwich? Ketchup?"

"Sure."

"I made a pie today. Want a piece?"

Peter nodded. "Your house smells like the house I grew up in. It always smelled like apples and cinnamon. At Christmastime you could get drunk on the smell. Speaking of Christmas, I give a party once a year, would you like to come? I think you'll like my grandmother. It's next Thursday."

"I don't know ... I hate to leave the animals. I haven't been to a party in so long, I don't think I'll remember how to act. Thank you for asking, though."

"Don't you have a pair of pearls?" he asked, a stupid look on his face.

"What do pearls have to do with it?"

"Your mother's pearls." Jesus, he must have missed something when Sadie was explaining party attire. She was staring at him so intently he felt compelled to explain. "You know, pearls to go with the dress. Your mother's pearls. If you have that, you don't have to worry about anything else. Right? Can I use your bathroom?"

"Upstairs, third door on the right. Don't step on the carpet at the bottom of the steps. Annabelle lies there all the time. She pees on it and I didn't have time to wash it. She chewed all the fringe off the corners. She's getting old, so I can't scold her too much."

Peter bolted from the room. Andi stared after him with puzzled eyes. She scurried into the pantry area where a mirror hung on the back of the door. She winced at her appearance. She didn't look one damn bit better than she had looked earlier. "What you see is what you get," she muttered.

Andi was sliding the sandwiches onto plates when Peter entered the room. "This must have been a nice house at one time."

Andi nodded. "It was a comfortable old house. It fit us. My mother never worried too much about new furniture or keeping up with the neighbors. It was clean and comfortable. Homey. Some houses are just houses. People make homes. Did you know that?"

"Believe it or not, I just realized that same fact today. Every so often I trip down memory lane."

"I don't do that anymore. It's too sad. I don't know how I'm going to walk away from this place. My mother always said home was where your stuff was. Part of me believes it. What's your opinion? By the way, where do you live?"

"In Clark. It's a new, modern house. Decorated by a professional. Color-coordinated, all that stuff. I don't think you'd like it. My grandmother hates it. I don't even like it myself. I try throwing things around, but it still looks the same."

"Maybe some green plants. Green plants perk up a room. You probably need some junk. Junk helps. I'll be throwing a lot away, so you can help yourself."

"Yeah? What kind of junk? My plants die."

"You need to water plants. Get silk ones. All you have to do is go over them with a blow dryer every so often. Junk is junk. Everybody has junk. You pick it up here and there, at a flea market or wherever. When you get tired of it you throw it away and buy new junk."

Peter threw his head back and laughed until his eyes watered. "That's something my grandmother would say. Why are you looking at me like that?"

"I'm sorry. You should laugh more often. You take yourself pretty seriously, don't you?"

"For the most part, I guess I do. What about you?" He leaned across the table as though her answer was the most important thing in the world. She had beautiful eyes with thick lashes. And they were her own, unlike Helen's.

"I've been so busy scrambling to make a go of it, I haven't had the time to dwell on anything. I guess I'm sort of an optimist, but then I'm a pessimist, too, at times. What will be will be. How about some pie? I can warm it up. More coffee?"

"Sure to everything. This is nice. I haven't sat in a kitchen . . . since . . . I left home. We always ate in the kitchen growing up."

"So did we. Are you married?"

"No. Why do you ask? Do you have designs on me?"

"No. I just want to make sure Rosie's pups get a good home. Who's going to take care of them when you work?"

"I already figured that out. I'm going to hire a sitter. I'll have her cook chicken gizzards and livers for them. My mother used to cook for Bessie. She loved it. You're very pretty, Dr. Evans. Why aren't you married?"

"Do you think that's any of your business, Mr. King?"

"As the owner of those dogs, of which I'm taking four, I should know what kind of person you are, marital status included. Well?"

"I was engaged, not that it's any of your business. I wanted to come back here; he didn't. He wanted to work in a ritzy area; I didn't. He was in it for the money. I wasn't. I don't know, maybe he was the smart one."

"No, you were the smart one," Peter said quietly. "It's rare that the heart and mind work in sync. When it does happen, you know it's right."

"Your turn."

Peter shrugged. "I run my grandmother's business. She tells me I'm good at it. She's the only family I have left, and she's up in years. I always . . . take . . . introduce her to the women I, ah, date. I value her opinion. So far she hasn't approved of anyone I've dated. That's okay; she was on the money every single time. Guess I just haven't met the right girl. Or, maybe I'm meant for bachelorhood. Would you like to go out to dinner with me to celebrate our deal?"

"Under other circumstances, I'd say yes, but I have too much to do. I also want to keep my eye on Rosie and the pups. If you like, you can come for dinner tomorrow."

"I'll be here. I'll bring in the towels and blankets and shovel you out before I leave."

"I'll help you. Thanks."

It was one o'clock in the morning when Andi leaned on her shovel, exhaustion showing in every line of her face. "I'm going to sleep like a baby tonight," she panted.

"Yeah, me, too. Tell me, what's it like when you operate on one of the animals, like you did tonight?"

"Awesome. When I saw those pups and when I stitched up Rosie, all the hard years, all the backbreaking work, it was worth every hour of it. Guess you don't get that feeling when you label Raspberry Cheese Louise on your lipsticks."

Suddenly she was in the snow, the giant towering over her. She stretched out her foot, caught him on the ankle and pulled him down in an undignified heap. He kissed her, his mouth as cold and frosty as her own. It was the sweetest kiss of her life. She said so, grinning from ear to ear.

"Sweet?" he asked.

"Uh-huh."

"Didn't make you want to tear your clothes off, huh?"

"You must be kidding. I never do that on a first date."

"This isn't a date." He leered at her.

"I don't do that on pre-dates either. I don't even know you."

"I'll let my hair down tomorrow, and you can *really* get to know me."

"Don't go getting any ideas that I'm easy. And, don't think you're parading me in front of your grandmother either."

"God forbid."

"Good night, Mr. King. You can call me Andi."

"Good night, Dr. Evans. You can call me Peter. What are we having for dinner?"

"Whatever you bring. Tomorrow is bath day. I'm big on fast and easy. What time are you bringing Hannah?"

"How about ten? Our attorney will be out bright and early for you to sign the contract. Is that all right with you?"

"Okay. Good night."

"I enjoyed this evening. Take good care of my dogs."

"I will." Suddenly she didn't want him to go. He didn't seem to want to go either. She watched the 4 by 4 until the red taillights were swallowed in the snow.

He was nice. Actually, he was real nice. And, he was going to give her over three million dollars. Oh, life was looking good.

* * *

The following morning, Andi woke before it was light out. She threw on her robe and raced down the stairs to check on Rosie. "I just want you to know I was having a really, that's as in *really,* delicious dream about Mr. Peter King." She hunched down to check on the new pups, who were sleeping peacefully, curled up against their mother.

While the coffee perked, Andi showered and dressed, taking a few more pains with her dress than usual. Today she donned corduroy slacks and a flannel shirt instead of the fleece-lined sweats she usually wore in the kennel. Today she even blow dried her hair and used the curling iron. She diddled with a jar of makeup guaranteed to confuse anyone interested in wondering if she was wearing it or not. A dab of rouge, a stroke of the eyebrow pencil and she was done. She was almost at the top of the steps when she marched back to her dressing table and spritzed a cloud of mist into the air. She savored the smell, a long-ago present from a friend. She told herself she took the extra pains because it wasn't every day she signed a three-million-plus deal. As she drank her coffee she wondered what the plus part of the contract would net her.

Andi thought about Gertie and her friends under the railroad trestle. Where did they go last night during the storm? Were they warm and safe? As soon as everything was tended to and she checked out Hannah the cat, she would drive into Plainfield and try to locate Gertie and her friends. Now that she had all this money coming to her, she could rent a motel for them until the weather eased up, providing the manager was willing to wait for his money.

The notebook on the kitchen table beckoned. Her list of things to do. Call Realtor, make plans to transport animals. Her friend Mickey had an old school bus he used for camping in the summer. He might lend it to her for a day or so. She could pile Gertie and her friends in the same bus.

Andi's thoughts whirled and raced as she cleaned the dog runs and hosed them out. She set down bowls of kibble and fresh water, tidied up the kennel, sorted through the blankets and towels. The heavy duty machines ran constantly. Her own laundry often piled up for weeks at a time simply because the animals had to come first. She raced back to the kitchen to add a note to her list. Call moving company. She wasn't parting with the crates, the laundry machines or the refrigerator. She was taking everything that belonged to her parents even if it was old and worn-out. The wrecking ball could destroy the house and kennel, but not her *stuff*.

She was on her third cup of coffee when Peter King's attorney arrived. She read over the contract, signed it and promised to take it to her attorney, Mark Fox. Everything was in order. Why delay on signing. The plus, she noticed, amounted to $750,000. That had to mean she had three and three-quarter acres. "Date the check January first. I don't want to have to worry about paying taxes until ninety-seven. Where's the date for construction to begin? Oh, okay, I see it. January 2, 1997. We're clear on that?"

"Yes, Dr. Evans, we're clear on that. Here's my card; have Mr. Fox call me. Mark is the finest real estate attorney in these parts. Give him my regards."

"I'll do that, Mr. Carpenter."

The moment the attorney was out of her parking lot, Andi added Mark Fox's name to her list of things to do. She crossed her fingers that he worked half days on Saturday. If not, she'd slip the contract, along with a note, through the mail slot and call him Monday morning.

Andi's eyes settled on the clock. Ten minutes until Peter King arrived with his grandmother's cat. She busied herself with phone calls. Ten o'clock came and went. The hands of the clock swept past eleven. Were the roads bad? She called the police station. She was told the roads were in good shape, plowed and sanded. Her eyes were wet when she crouched down next to Rosie. "Guess he just wanted my signature on the contract. My mother always said there was a fool born every minute. Take care of those babies and I'll be back soon."

At ten minutes past twelve, Andi was on Park Avenue, where she dropped the contract through the slot on Mark Fox's door. She backed out of the drive and headed down Park to Raritan and then to Woodland, turning right onto South Avenue, where she thought she would find Gertie and her friends. She saw one lone figure, heavily clad, hunched around a huge barrel that glowed red and warm against the snow-filled landscape. Andi climbed from the truck. "Excuse me, sir, have you seen Gertie?" The man shook his head. "Do you know where I can find her? Where is everyone?" The man shrugged. "I need to get in touch with her. It's very important. If she comes by, will you ask her to call me? I'll give you the quarter for the phone call." She ran back to the truck to fish in the glove compartment for her card, where she scrawled, "Call me. Andi." She handed the card, a quarter and a five-dollar bill to the man. "Get some hot soup and coffee." The man's head bobbed up and down.

Her next stop was Raritan Road and her friend Mickey's house. The yellow bus was parked in his driveway next to a spiffy hunter green BMW.

Mickey was a free spirit, working only when the mood struck him. Thanks to a sizable trust fund, all things were possible for the young man whose slogan was, "Work Is A Killer." She slipped a note under the door when her ring went unanswered. Her watch said it was one-thirty. Time to head for the moving company, where she signed another contract for her belongings to be moved out on December 22nd and taken to storage on Oak Tree Road in Edison. Her last stop was in Metuchen, where she stopped at the MacPherson Agency to ask for either Lois or Tom Finneran, a husband/wife realty team. The amenities over, she said, "Some acreage, a building is a must. It doesn't have to be fancy. I'm going to build what I want later on. Zoning is important. I was thinking maybe Freehold or Cranbur. You guys are the best, so I know you can work something out that will allow me to move in with the animals the first of the year. Have a wonderful holiday."

There were no fresh tire tracks in her driveway and no messages on her machine. "So who cares," she muttered as she stomped her way into the kennel. The kitchen clock said it was three-thirty when she put a pot of coffee on to perk. When the phone shrilled to life she dropped the wire basket full of coffee all over the floor. She almost killed herself as she sprinted across the huge kitchen to grapple with the receiver. Her voice was breathless when she said, "Dr. Evans."

"Andi, this is Gertie. Donald said you were looking for me. Is something wrong?"

"Everything's wrong and everything's right. I was worried about you and your friends out in the cold. I wanted to bring you back

here till the weather clears. I signed the contract this morning.
For a lot of money. Oh, Gertie, what I can do with that money.
You and your friends can come live on my property. I'll build you
a little house or a big house. You won't have to live on the street,
and you won't get mugged anymore. You can all help with the
animals, and I'll even pay you. I'll be able to take in more animals. Oh, God, Gertie, I almost forgot, Rosie had eight puppies.
They are so beautiful. You're going to love them. You're quiet, is
something wrong?"

"No. I don't want you worrying about me and my friends. I'll
tell them about your offer, though. I'll think about it myself. How
was . . . that man?"

"Mr. King?"

"Yeah, him."

"Last night I thought he was kind of nice. He came back out
here later in the evening and shoveled my parking lot. He was
starved, so I gave him a sandwich and we talked. I invited him to
dinner tonight. He was supposed to bring his grandmother's cat
for me to check and he was a no-show. I even let him kiss me after
he pushed me in the snow. You know what, Gertie, I hate men.
There's not one you can trust. All he wanted was my signature on
that contract. He had this really nice laugh. We shared a few
memories. As far as I can tell the only redeeming quality he has is
that he loves his grandmother. Oh, oh, the other thing was, he
was going to bring me some carbon monoxide things to plug in.
He was so forceful I agreed and said I wouldn't charge for Hannah.
That's the cat's name. He even invited me to his Christmas party,
but he never even told me where he lived. Some invitation, huh? I
should show him and turn up in my rubber suit. He acted like he
thought I didn't know how to dress and kept mumbling about my
mother's pearls. You're still coming for Christmas, aren't you?
You said you'd bring all your buddies from the trestle. Gertie, I
don't want to spend my last Christmas alone here in this house
with just the animals. If they could talk, it would be different.
Promise me, okay?"

"I can't promise. I will think about it, though. Why don't you
hold those negative thoughts you have for Mr. King on the side. I
bet he has a real good explanation."

Andi snorted. "Give me one. Just one. The roads are clear.

Alexander Bell invented this wonderful thing called the telephone, and Mr. Sony has this machine that delivers your messages. Nope, the jerk just wanted my signature. I'll never see him again and I don't care. Do you want me to come and get you, Gertie? It's supposed to be really cold tonight."

"We're going to the shelter tonight. Thanks for the offer. Maybe I'll stop by tomorrow. Are the pups really cute?"

"Gorgeous. That's another thing; he said he was taking four, three for him and one for his grandmother. On top of everything else, the man is a liar. I hate liars as much as I hate used car salesmen. You sound funny, Gertie, are you sure you're all right?"

"I'm fine. Maybe I'm catching a cold."

"Now, why doesn't that surprise me? You live on the damn streets. I'll bet you don't even have any aspirin."

"I do so, and Donald has some brandy. I'll talk to you tomorrow, Andi. Thanks for caring about me and my friends. Give Rosie a hug for me."

"Okay, Gertie, take care of yourself."

Andi turned to Rosie, who was staring at her. "Gertie was crying. She's not catching a cold. She's the one who is homeless, and she's the one who always comes through for us. Always. I can't figure that out. She's homeless and she won't let me do anything for her. I hope somebody writes a book about that someday. Okay, bath time!"

Andi ate a lonely TV dinner and some tomato soup as she watched television. She was in bed by nine o'clock. She wanted to be up early so she could begin going through the attic and packing the things she wanted to take to storage. If her pillow was damp, there was no one to notice.

Less than ten miles away, Peter King sat on the sofa with his grandmother, trying his best to console her. He felt frightened for the first time in his life. His zesty grandmother was falling apart, unable to stop crying. "I thought she would live forever. I really did. My God, Peter, how I loved that animal. I want her ashes. Every single one of them. You told them to do that, didn't you?"

"Of course I did, Sadie. I'm going to bring them by tomorrow. Do you want—"

"Do not touch anything, Peter. I want all her things left just the way they were. I wish I'd spent more time with her, cuddled her more. Sometimes she didn't want that; she wanted to be alone. She was so damn independent. Oh, God, what am I going to do without Hannah? She kept me going."

"It can't be any worse than when Bessie died. I still think about that," Peter said past the lump in his throat.

"She just died in her sleep and I was sleeping so soundly last night. What if she needed me and I didn't hear her?"

"Shhhh, she just closed her eyes and drifted off. That's how you have to think of it."

"Don't even think about getting me another cat. I won't have it, Peter. Are you listening to me?"

"I always listen to you, Sadie."

"Did you call Dr. Evans?"

"No. She'll understand. She loves animals. She's nice, Sadie. I really liked her. She forced a sandwich on me and I ate it to be polite. I shoveled her parking lot and pushed her in the snow." At Sadie's blank stare, his voice grew desperate. "I kissed her, Sadie, and she said it was a sweet kiss. Sweet! It's too soon to tell, but I think she might be *the one*. Did you hear me, Sadie?"

"I'm not deaf."

"I invited her to the party, but she doesn't want to come. I screwed up the pearl thing. She thought I was nuts." Sadie's eyes rolled back in her head. "Okay," Peter roared, "that's enough, Sadie, pets die every day of the week. People and children grieve, but they don't go over the edge. You're teetering and I won't have it."

Sadie blinked. "Oh, stuff it, Peter. This is me you're talking to. I need to do this for one day, for God's sake. Tomorrow I'll be fine. Why can't I cry, moan and wail? Give me one damn good reason why I can't. I just want to sit here and snivel. You need to make amends to that young veterinarian, and don't go blaming me. I didn't ask you to stay here with me. You didn't even like Hannah and she hated you. Hannah hated all men. I never did figure that out. Go home, Peter. I'm fine, and I do appreciate you coming here and staying with me. It might be wise to send the young lady an invitation. I'd FedEx it if I were you."

"Do you want me to call that guy Donald you're always talking about?"

"Of course not. He's . . . out and about . . . and very hard to reach."

"Why don't you get him a beeper for Christmas."

"Go!"

"I'm gone."

Peter had every intention of going home, but his car seemed to have a mind of its own. Before he knew it he was on the road leading into the driveway of Andi's clinic. What the hell time was it anyway? Ten minutes past ten. It was so quiet and dark he felt uneasy. Only a dim light inside the clinic could be seen from the road. The rest of the house was in total darkness. If he got out to leave a note, the animals would start to bark and Andi would wake up. Did he want that? Of course not, his mother had raised him to be a gentleman. He felt an emptiness in the pit of his stomach as he drove away. He couldn't ever remember being this lonely in his entire life. Tomorrow was another day. He'd call her as soon as the sun came up, and maybe they could go sleigh riding in Roosevelt Park. Maybe it was time to act like kids again. Kids who fell in love when they were done doing all those wonderful kid things. One day out of their lives, and it was a Sunday. Just one day of no responsibilities. He crossed his fingers that it would work out the way he wanted.

Andi rolled over, opening one eye to look at the clock on her nightstand. Six o'clock. How still and quiet it was. Did she dare stay in bed? Absolutely not. She walked over to the window and raised the shade. It was snowing. Damn, her back was still sore. Maybe she could call one of the companies that plowed out small businesses.

She was brushing her teeth when the phone rang. Around the bubbles and foam in her mouth, she managed to say, "Dr. Evans."

"This is Peter King. I'm calling to apologize and to invite you to go sleigh riding. Hannah died in her sleep. I spent the day with my grandmother. I'm really sorry. Are you there?"

"Wait." Andi rushed into the bathroom to rinse her mouth. She sprinted back to the phone. "I was brushing my teeth."

"Oh."

"You should have called me. It only takes a minute to make a phone call." Hot damn, he had a reason. Maybe . . .

"I came by last night around ten, but everything was dark, and I didn't want to stir up the animals so I went home."

He came by. That was good. He said he was sorry. He was considerate. "I went to bed early. It's snowing."

"I know. Let's go sledding in Roosevelt Park. My parents used to take me there when I was a kid. I have a Flexible Flyer." He made it sound like he had the Holy Grail.

"No kidding. I have one, too. Somewhere. Probably up on the rafters in the garage."

"Does that mean you'll go? We could go to the Pancake House on Parsonage Road for breakfast."

"Will you pull me up the hill?"

"Nope."

"I hate climbing the hill. Going down is so quick. Okay, I'll go, but I have things to do first. How about eleven o'clock?"

"That's good. What do you have to do? Do you need help?"

This was looking better and better. "Well, I have to clean the dog runs and change the litter boxes. I was going to go through the things in the attic. You could see if you can locate someone to plow my parking lot and driveway. Don't even think about offering. I know your back is as sore as mine, and my legs are going to be stiff if we climb that hill more than once. It's going to take me at least two hours to find my rubber boots. Is your grandmother all right? I have some kittens if you're interested."

"It was a real bad day. She doesn't want another cat. Hannah is being cremated so she'll have the ashes. She'll be okay today. Sadie is real gutsy. I know she'll love it when I give her one of Rosie's pups. She'll accept the dog but not a cat. I understand that."

"Yes, so do I."

"What did you have for supper last night? I'm sorry about standing you up. I mean that."

"Tomato soup, a TV dinner and a stale donut. If you do it again, it's all over." She was flirting. God.

She was flirting with him. Peter felt his chest puff out. "Bundle up."

"Okay. See you later."

"You bet. Don't get your sled down; I'll do that."

"Okay." A gentleman. Hmmnn.

* * *

Peter kicked the tire of his Range Rover, every curse known to man spitting through his lips. How could a $50,000 year-old truck have a dead battery? He looked at his watch and then at the elegant Mercedes Benz sitting next to it. The perfect vehicle to go sledding. "Damn it to hell!" he muttered.

He was stomping through the house looking for his keys when the doorbell rang. Expecting to see the paperboy, he opened the door, his hand in his pants pocket looking for money. "Helen!"

"Peter! I brought breakfast," she said, dangling a Dunkin' Donuts bag under his nose, "and the *New York Times*. I thought we could curl up in front of a fire and spend a lazy day. Together."

He wanted to push her through the door, to slap the donut bag out of her hand and scatter the paper all over the lawn. What did he ever see in this heavily made up woman whose eyelashes were so long they couldn't be real. "I think one of your eyelashes is coming off. Sorry, Helen, I have other plans. I'm going sledding."

"Sledding! At your age!" She made it sound like he was going to hell on a sled.

"Yeah," he drawled. "Your other eyelash is . . . loose. Well, see you around."

"Peterrrrr," she cried as he closed the door.

He was grinning from ear to ear as he searched the living room, dining room and foyer for his keys. He finally found them on the kitchen counter right where he'd left them last night. She really did wear false eyelashes like Sadie said. He laughed aloud when he remembered the open-toed shoes she had on. "My crazy days," he muttered as he closed the kitchen door behind him.

In the car, backing out of the driveway, he realized his heart was pounding. Certainly not because of Helen. He was going to spend the whole day with Andrea Evans doing kid things. He was so excited he pressed the power button on his car phone and then the number one, which was Sadie's number. When he heard her voice he said, "Want to go sled riding? I'll pull you up the hill. I'm taking Dr. Evans. You won't believe this, but she has a Flexible Flyer, too. So, do you want to come?"

"I think I'll pass and watch a football game. Don't forget to bring Hannah's ashes. I don't want to spend another night without her. I don't care, Peter, if you think I'm crazy. Be sure you don't break your neck. Are you aware that it's snowing outside? I thought people went sled riding when it *stopped* snowing."

"I don't think you're crazy at all. I know it's snowing. I think there's at least three inches of fresh snow. You know how you love a white Christmas. I'll be sure not to break my neck, and I think you can go sledding whenever you want. Mr. Mortimer said I could pick up the ashes after five this afternoon. I'll see you sometime this evening."

"Peter, does this mean you're . . . interested in Dr. Evans?"

"She's a real person, Sadie. Helen stopped by as I was leaving—I'm talking to you on the car phone—and she had open-toed shoes on, and both her eyelashes were loose at the ends. How could I not have seen those things, Sadie?"

"Because you weren't looking, Peter. Do you think Dr. Evans is interested in you?"

"She agreed to go sledding. She wasn't even mad about yesterday. I like her, Sadie. A lot."

"I love June weddings. Six months, Peter. You have to commit by six months or cut her loose. Women her age don't need some jerk taking up their time if you aren't serious."

"How do you know her age?"

"Well . . . I don't, but you said she put herself through vet school and the whole education process took ten years. That should put her around thirty or so."

"I don't remember telling you that."

"That's because you were rattled over Helen. It's all right, Peter, I get forgetful, too, sometimes. Now, go and have a wonderful time."

Peter pressed the end and power buttons. He decided his grandmother was defensive sounding because of Hannah. He wished the next eight weeks were over so he could present her with one of Rosie's pups.

Peter was so deep in thought he almost missed the turnoff to the Evans Kennel. He jammed on his brakes, the back end of his car fishtailing across the road. He took a deep breath, cursing the fancy car again. Shaken, he crawled into the parking lot and parked the car. He wondered again if the Chevy pickup actually worked.

"I saw that," Andi trilled. "It's a good thing there was no one behind you. Where's your truck?"

"Dead battery."

"We can take my truck. It's in tip-top shape. Turns over every time. No matter what the weather is. It was my dad's prized possession. The heater works fine and we can put our sleds in the back." Andi dangled a set of car keys in front of him. She was laughing at him, and he didn't mind one damn bit. "Those boots have to go. When was the last time you went sled riding?"

"Light-years ago. These boots are guaranteed to last a lifetime."

"Perhaps they will. The question is, will they keep your feet dry? The answer is no. I can loan you my father's Wellingtons. Will you be embarrassed to wear yellow boots?"

"Never!" Peter said dramatically. "Does the rest of me meet with your approval?"

Andi tilted her head to the side. "Ski cap, muffler, gloves . . . Well, those gloves aren't going to do anything for your hands. Don't you have ski gloves?"

"I did, but I couldn't find them. Do you have extras?"

"Right inside the yellow boots. I figured you for a leather man. I'm a mitten girl. I still have the mittens my mother knitted for me when I was a kid. They still fit, too. When you go sled riding you need a pair and a spare. I bet you didn't wax the runners on your sled either."

"I did so!"

"Prove it." Andi grinned.

"All right, I didn't. It was all I could do to get the cobwebs off."

"Come on," Andi said, dragging him by the arm into the garage. Neither noticed a sleek, amber-colored Mercury Sable crawl by, the driver craning her neck for a better look into the parking lot.

"Here's the boots. They should fit. I'm bringing extra thermal socks for both of us, extra gloves and mittens. There's nothing worse than cold hands and feet. I lived for one whole winter in Minnesota without central heat. All I had was a wood-burning fireplace."

"Why?"

"It was all I could afford. I survived. Do they fit?"

"Perfectly. You should be very proud of yourself, Andi."

"I am. My parents weren't rich like yours. Dad wasn't a businessman. There's so much money on the books that was never paid. He never sent out bills or notices. I'm kind of like him, I guess."

"My parents weren't rich. My grandmother is the one with the money. My dad was a draftsman; my mother was a nurse. You're right, though; I never had to struggle. Did it make you a better person?"

"I like to think so. When you're cold and hungry, character doesn't seem important. You are what you are. Hard times just bring out the best and worst in a person. Okay, your runners are ready for a test run."

"Do you ski?"

"Ha! That's a rich person's sport. No. I'm ready."

"Me, too," Peter said, clomping along behind her.

"You look good in yellow," Andi giggled.

"My favorite color," Peter quipped.

"That's what my mother said when she presented my father with those boots. The second thing she said was they'll never wear out. My dad wore them proudly. How's your grandmother today?"

"Better. I promised to stop by this evening with Hannah's ashes. My grandmother is a very strong woman. She started King Cosmetics in her kitchen years ago after my grandfather died. I'd like you to meet her."

"I'd like that. Do you want to drive or shall I?"

"I'll drive. Sleds in the back," he said, tossing in both Flexible Flyers.

An hour later they were hurtling down the hill, whooping and hollering, their laughter ringing in the swirling snow.

On the second trek up the hill, Peter said, "Have you noticed we're practically the only two people here except for those three kids who are using pieces of cardboard to slide down the hill?"

"That's because we're crazy. Cardboard's good, so is a shower curtain. You can really get some speed with a shower curtain. A bunch of us used to do that in Minnesota."

Peter clenched his fists tightly as he felt a wave of jealousy river through him. He wanted Andi to slide down a hill on a shower curtain with him, not some other guy, and he knew it had been a guy on the shower curtain next to Andi. He asked.

"Yeah." He waited for her to elaborate, but she didn't.

"Hey, mister, do you want to trade?"

Peter looked at Andi, and she looked at him. "The cardboard is big enough for both of us to sit on. Wanna give it a shot?" he asked.

"Sure. You sit in the front, though, in case we hit a tree."

"Okay, kid." He accepted their offer, then turned to Andi. "Did you notice they waited till we dragged these sleds to the top of the hill?" Peter hissed.

"I don't blame them. I think this is my last run. My legs feel numb."

"Sissy," Peter teased. "Cardboard's easy to drag. We've only been here two hours."

"It seems like forever," Andi said. "I can't feel my feet any-more. How about you?"

"Hey, mister, Where'd you get them yellow boots?" one of the kids asked.

"Macy's. Neat, huh?"

"They look shitty," the kid said.

"That, too. You kids go first and we'll follow."

"Nah, you go first. You might fall off and we'll stop and pick you up. You might break a leg or something. You're old."

Peter settled himself on the slice of cardboard that said Charmin Tissue. "Hang on, Andi, and sit up straight."

They were off. Andi shrieked and Peter bellowed as they sailed down the steep hill. Midway down, the cardboard slid out from under them. They toppled into the snow, rolling the rest of the way down the hill. The kids on the sleds passed them, waving and shouting wildly. Andi rolled up against Peter, breathless, her en-tire body covered in snow.

"Now *that* was an experience," Peter gasped as he reached for Andi's arm to make sure she was all right.

"I feel like I'm dead. Are we?"

"No. Those little shits are taking off with our sleds!" Peter gasped again.

"Who cares. I couldn't chase them if my life depended on it. Every kid needs a sled. Let them have them."

"Okay. Are you all right?"

"No. I hurt. This wasn't as much fun as I thought it would be. God, I must be getting old. My eyebrows are frozen to my head. They crunch. Do yours?"

"Yep. C'mon, let's get in the truck and go home. The first run was fun. We should have quit after that." He was on his feet, his hand outstretched to pull Andi to her feet. "Ah, I bet if I kissed your eyebrows they'd melt."

"Never mind my damn eyebrows, kiss my mouth, it's frozen."

"Hmmmnn. Aaahhh, oh, yes," Andi said later.

"Was that *sweet?* I have a kiss that's a real wake-up call."

"Oh, no, that one . . . sizzled. Let's try it out," Andi said.

"Oh, look, they're kissing. Yuk. Here's your sleds, mister."

"I thought you stole those sleds. Your timing is incredible. Go away, you can have the sleds."

"My mother ain't never gonna believe you gave us these sleds. You gotta write us a note and sign your name."

"Do what he says." Andi giggled as she headed for the truck, and Peter hastily penned a note.

"Guess you're gonna have to wait for my wake-up call," he said when he caught up to her.

"How long?"

Peter threw his hands up in the air. "I have all the time in the world. You just let me know when you're ready."

"Uh-huh. Okay. That sounds good. I had a good time today, Peter, I really did. I felt like a kid for a little while. Thanks. Time to get back to reality and the business at hand."

"How about if I drop you off, go pick up Hannah's ashes, take them to my grandmother and come back. We can have dinner together. I can pick up some steaks and stuff. I want to get those carbon monoxide units for you, too."

"Sounds good."

"It's a date, then?"

"Yep, it's a date."

"I'll see you around seven-thirty."

Inside the kennel the animals greeted their owner with sharp barks and soft whines, each vying for her attention. She sat down on the floor and did her best to fondle each one of them. "I smell worse than you guys when you get wet," she said, shrugging out of her wet clothes. "Supper's coming up!"

With the door closed to the outside waiting room, Andi paid no mind to the excessive barking and whining from the animals; her thoughts were on Peter King and spending the night with him. She had at least two hours, once the animals were fed, to shower and change into something a little more *romantic*.

Outside, Helen Palmer watched the dinner preparations through the front window. When she was certain no one else was in attendance, her eyes narrowed. She walked back to the office, a manila folder in hand, the detective's report on one Dr. Andrea Evans that she'd taken from Peter King's car when she'd backtracked from Roosevelt Park where she'd spied on her old lover.

She eyed the messy desk with the pile of bills. On tiptoe, she walked around the back of the desk to stare down at the piles of bills. With one long, polished nail, she moved the contract to the side so she could see it better. Three million, seven hundred and fifty thousand dollars! For this dump! She tiptoed back to the door and let herself out. Miss Girl Next Door would know there was no manila envelope on the desk. Better to drop it outside where Peter's car had been parked. "She'll think it fell out when he got out of the car. Perfect!" she muttered.

Her feet numb with cold, Helen walked out of the driveway to her car parked on the shoulder of the road in snow up to her ankles. She'd probably get pneumonia and all of this would be for naught. One way or another she was going to get Peter King for herself.

Inside the house, Andi climbed the stairs to the second floor to run a bath. She poured lavishly from a plastic bag filled with gardenia bath salts. It was the only thing she consistently splurged on. She tried to relax, but the dogs' incessant barking set her nerves on edge. What in the world was wrong with them today? Maybe they were picking up on her own tenseness in regard to Peter King. And she was tense.

"I hardly know the man and here I sit, speculating on what it would be like to go to bed with him." The bathtub was the perfect milieu for talking to herself. She loved this time of day when she went over her problems, asked questions of herself aloud and then answered them in the same manner. She wondered aloud about what kind of bed partner he would make. "Shy? No way. Lusty? To a degree. Wild and passionate? I can only hope. Slam, bam, thank you, ma'am? Not in a million years. A man with slow hands like the Pointer Sisters sang about. Oh, yeahhhhh."

Puckered, hyped and red-skinned, Andi climbed from the tub, towel dried and dressed. She fluffed out her hair, added makeup sparingly. The gardenia scent stayed with her.

Andi eyed the bed. When was the last time she changed the sheets? She couldn't remember. She had the bed stripped and changed inside of eight minutes. "Just in case."

Downstairs, the dogs milled around inside the house, running back and forth to the waiting room and her tiny office area. Susy, a long-haired, fat, black cat, hissed and snarled by the door, her claws gouging at the wood. "Okay, okay, I get the message, something's wrong. Let's do one spin around the parking lot. When I blow this whistle, everyone lines up and comes indoors. Allow me to demonstrate." She blew three short blasts. "Everybody line up! That's the drill. If you don't follow my instructions, you're out for the night. Let's go!" She stood to the side as the dogs and cats stampeded past her. She'd done this before, and it always worked because Beggin Strips were the reward when everyone was indoors. She waited ten minutes, time for everyone to lift their leg or squat, depending on gender. The floodlights blazed down in the parking lot, creating shimmering crystals on the piled-high snow. Now it was speckled with yellow spots in every direction.

Andi blew three sharp blasts on the whistle as she stepped aside. One by one, the animals fell into a neat line and marched to the door. "C'mon Annabelle, you can do it!" Andi called encouragingly. "You can't sit down in the middle of the parking lot. All right, all right, I'll carry you. Move it, Bizzy," she said to a cat with two tails. The cat strolled past her disdainfully. Andi gave one last blast on the whistle for any stragglers. Satisfied that all the animals were indoors, she walked over to Annabelle to pick her up. She noticed the folder then and picked it up. She stuck it under her arm as she bent to pick up the beagle. "I swear, Annabelle, you weigh a ton."

Inside, she did one last head count before she doled out the treats, the folder still under her arm. "My time now!"

Andi did her best not to look at the clock as she set the table and layered tinfoil on the ancient broiler. Candles? No, that would be too much. Wineglasses? She looked with disgust at the dust on the crystal. How was it possible that she'd been here almost a year and a half and hadn't used the glasses, much less washed them? That was going to change now. The wineglasses were special, and there were only two of them. She remembered the day her father had presented the Tiffany glasses to her mother and said, "When we have something special to celebrate we'll use these glasses." To her knowledge, nothing special had ever occurred. Well, tonight was special. She liked the way they sparkled under the domed kitchen light. Peter probably used glasses like this to gargle with every day.

He was late. Again. Her insides started to jump around. What should she do now to kill time? What if he didn't show up? "Oh, shit," she muttered. No point in letting him think she was sitting here biting her nails waiting for him. Only desperate women did things like that. In the blink of an eye she had the dishes back in the cabinet and the wineglasses in their felt sacks with the gold drawstrings. She refolded the tablecloth and stuck it in the drawer. She eyed the manila folder as she slid the drawer closed. It must have fallen out of Peter's car because it wasn't hers and no one else had been at the kennel today.

Eight o'clock.

Andi moved the folder. She moved it a second time, then a third time. She watched it teeter on the edge of the kitchen counter. She brushed by it and it slid to the floor. Now she'd have to pick up the papers and put them back in the folder. When she saw her name in heavy black letters on the first page, she sucked in her breath. Her heart started to pound in her chest as she gathered up the seven-page report. Twenty minutes later, after reading the report three times, Andi stacked the papers neatly in the folder. From the kitchen drawer she ripped off a long piece of gray electrical tape. She taped it to the folder and plastered it on the door of the clinic. She locked the doors and slid the dead bolt into place. She turned off all the lights from the top of the steps. Only a dim hall light glowed in the house.

She made her way to the attic. The small window under the eaves was the perfect place to watch the parking lot. Sneaky bastard. The report chronicled her life, right down to her bank balance, her student aid, her credit report, and her relationships with men. Her cheeks flamed when she remembered one incident where her landlady said Tyler Mitchel arrived early in the evening and didn't leave for three days. The line in bold letters that said *"The lady uses a diaphragm"* was what sent her flying to the attic. That could only mean someone had been here in her house going through her things. Unless Tyler or Jack or maybe Stan volunteered the information.

"You son of a bitch!"

Headlights arched into the driveway. Andi's eyes narrowed. Down below, the animals went into their howling, snarling routine.

Andi nibbled on her thumbnail as she watched Peter walk back to his car, the folder in his hand. Her phone rang on the second floor. She knew it was Peter calling on his car phone. She sat down on the window seat and cried. The phone continued to ring. Like she cared. "Go to hell, Mr. Lipstick!"

When there were no more tears, Andi wiped her eyes on the sleeve of her shirt. She had things to do. Empty cartons beckoned. She worked industriously until past midnight, packing and sorting, refusing to go to the window. Tears dripped down her cheeks from time to time. At one-thirty she crept downstairs for a soda. She carried it back to the attic and gulped at it from her perch on the window seat. He was still there. He was still there at four in the morning when she called a halt to her activities.

Andi curled herself into a ball on top of the bed with a comforter where she cried herself to sleep. She woke at seven and raced to the window. "We'll see about that!"

With shaking hands, Andi dialed the police, identified herself and said in a cold, angry voice, "I want you to send someone here right now and remove a ... person from my parking lot. He's been sitting there all night. You tell him he's not to dare set foot on my property until January. If I have to sign something, I'll come down to the police station. Right now. I want you to come here right now. My animals are going crazy. I have a gun and a license to use it," she said dramatically. "Thank you."

Her heart thundering in her chest, Andi raced back to the attic. She knew the dirt and grime on the window prevented Peter from seeing her. She clenched her teeth when she saw the patrol car careen into her driveway, the red and blue lights flashing ominously. She just knew he was going to give the officers a box of Raspberry Cheese Louise lipsticks for their wives.

Five minutes later the Mercedes backed out of her parking lot. It didn't look like any lipstick had changed hands. "He's probably going to mail them," she snorted as she raced down the steps to answer the door, the din behind her so loud she could barely hear the officer's voice.

"Do you want to file a complaint?"

"You're damn right I do," Andi screamed.

"All right, come down to the station this afternoon."

"I'll be there."

Andi closed the door and locked it. She tended to the animals, showered and ate some cornflakes before she resumed her packing. "You are dead in the water, Mr. Lipstick," she sniveled as she started to clean out her closet and dresser drawers.

At ten o'clock she called the Finnerans. "You really and truly found something in Freehold! . . . I can move in on Sunday? That's Christmas Eve! . . . Move-in condition! Fifteen acres! A heated barn for the animals. God must be watching over me. How much is fenced in? . . . Great. That's a fair price. . . . The owners are in California. . . . I knew you could do it. . . . Okay. I'll drive down this afternoon and look at it. . . . The last of their things will be out by Saturday. I'm very grateful, Tom." She copied down directions. Her sigh of relief was so loud and long she had trouble taking a deep breath.

Andi's second call was to her friend Mickey. "Can you bring the bus by today? Thanks, Mickey. I owe you one."

Her third call was to her attorney, who admonished her up one side and down the other for signing the contract before he had a chance to go over it. "You're lucky everything is in order. Congratulations. I'm going to set up a payout structure you'll be able to live with." Andi listened, made notes, gave the attorney her new address and told him to check with information for her new phone number.

The phone started to ring the moment she hung up from the attorney. The answering machine clicked on. If it was a patient she'd pick up. A hang up. Mr. Lipstick. "Invade my privacy, my life, ha! Only low-life scum do things like that. Well, you got your property, so you don't have to continue with this charade. It doesn't say much for me that I was starting to fall for your charms." Her eyes started to burn again. She cuddled a gray cat close to her chest, the dogs circling her feet. "So I made a mistake. We can live with it. We'll laugh all the way to the bank. The new rule is, we don't trust any man, ever again."

The elaborate silver service on the mahogany table gleamed as Sadie King poured coffee for her nephew. "You look like you slept in a barn, Peter. Calm down; stop that frantic pacing and tell me what happened. You've never had a problem being articulate before. So far all I have been able to gather is someone stepped on your toes. Was it Dr. Evans? I'm a very good listener, Peter."

"Yesterday was so perfect it scared me. She felt it, too, I could tell. Somehow, that goddamn investigative report fell out of my car and she found it. When I went back later for dinner, after I left you, she had it taped to the door. Obviously she read it. I called on the car phone, I banged on the door, but she didn't want any part of me. I sat in her parking lot all night long. This morning the police came and ran me off her property. Their advice was to write her a letter and not to go back or they'd run me off. I think I'm in love with her, Sadie. I was going to tell her that last night. I think . . . thought she was starting to feel the same way. My stomach tightens up when she laughs and her laughter shines in her eyes. She gave me her father's boots that were bright yellow, and his gloves. She's so down to earth, so real. I even started to wonder how our kids would look. What should I do? How can I make her understand?"

"A letter isn't such a bad idea. You could enclose it with the invitation to your Christmas party and send it Federal Express or have a messenger deliver it. I'd opt for the messenger because he could deliver it today. If you choose Federal Express she won't get it until tomorrow."

"What's the use, Sadie? I don't blame her. Jesus, the guy even . . . a diaphragm is pretty goddamn personal. I didn't want that kind of stuff. I didn't ask for it either. All I wanted was her financials and a history of the property. I have that same sick feeling in the pit of my stomach I used to get when I was a kid and did something wrong. I could never put anything over on my mother, and Andi is the same way."

"There must be a way for you to get her to listen to you. Apologies, when they're heartfelt, are usually pretty good. Try calling her again."

"I've done that. Her answering machine comes on. I know she's there listening, but she won't pick up. I told you, I don't blame her."

"Maybe you could disguise yourself and ride up on a motorcycle with . . . someone's animal and pretend . . . you know, it will get you in the door. She'll have to listen if you're face-to-face."

"Sadie, that's probably the worst idea you ever came up with. Andi Evans is an in-your-face person. She'll call the cops. They already gave me a warning. I don't want my ass hauled off to jail. They print stuff like that in the papers. How's that going to look?"

Sadie threw her hands up in the air. "Can you come up with a better idea?"

"No. I'm fresh out of ideas. I have to go home to shower and shave. Then I have to go to the office. I have a business to run. I'll stop by on my way home from the office." Peter kissed his grandmother goodbye, his face miserable.

Sadie eyed the urn with Hannah's ashes on the mantel. "Obviously, Hannah, I have to take matters into my own hands. Men are so good at screwing things up, and it's always a woman who has to get them out of their messes. I miss you, and no, I'm not going to get maudlin. I now have a mission to keep me busy."

Sadie dusted her hands before she picked up the phone. "Marcus, bring the car around front and make sure you have my . . . *things*. Scotch Plains. The weather report said the roads are clear." She replaced the receiver.

"They're meant for one another. I know this in my heart. Therefore, it's all right for me to meddle," Sadie mumbled as she slipped into her faux fur coat. "I'm going to make this right or die trying."

Andi had the door of the truck open when she saw Gertie picking her way over the packed-down snow. "Gertie, wait, I'll help you. If you tell me you walked all the way from Plainfield, I'm going to kick you all the way back. You're too old to be trundling around in this snow. What if you fall and fracture your hip? Then what? Where's your shopping cart?"

"Donald's watching it. I wanted to see Rosie and her pups. Can I, Andi?"

"Of course. Listen, I have some errands to run. Do you want to stay until I get back? I can drive you home after that."

"Well, sure."

"Rosie's in the kitchen, and the tea's still hot in the pot. Make yourself at home. I might be gone for maybe . . . three hours, depending on the roads. You'll wait?"

"Of course."

"Gertie, don't answer the phone."

"What if it's a patient?" Gertie asked fretfully.

"If it is, you'll hear it on the machine. Pick up and refer them to the clinic on Park Avenue. My offices are closed as of this morning. I called the few patients I have and told them."

"All right."

"I'll see you by mid-afternoon."

Ninety minutes later, Andi pulled her truck alongside Tom Finneran's white Cadillac. "Oh, it's wonderful, Tom! The snow makes it look like a fairyland. I love the old trees. Quick, show me around."

"Everything is in tip-top shape. Move-in condition, Andi. The owners' things are packed up ready for the mover. All the walls and ceilings were freshly painted a month ago. There's new carpet everywhere, even upstairs. Three bathrooms. A full one downstairs. Nice modern kitchen, appliances are six years old. The roof is nine years old and the furnace is five years old. The plumbing is good, but you do have a septic tank because you're in the country. Taxes are more than reasonable. I have to admit the road leading in here is a kidney crusher. You might want to think about doing something to it later on. Fill the holes with shale or something. It's a farmhouse, and I for one love old farmhouses. A lot of work went into this house at one time. Young people today don't appreciate the old beams and pegs they used for nails back then."

"I love it," Andi said enthusiastically.

"The owner put down carpeting for warmth. Underneath the carpeting you have pine floors. It was a shame to cover them up, but women today want beige carpets. The blinds stay, as do the lighting fixtures and all the appliances. You'll be more than comfortable. Take your time and look around. I'll wait here for you. The owner agreed to an end of January closing, so you'll be paying rent until that time."

"It's just perfect, Tom. Now, show me the barn."

"That's what you're really going to love. It's warm and there's a mountain of hay inside on the second floor or whatever they call it in barns. Good electricity, plumbing, sinks. There's an old refrigerator, too, and it works. The stalls are still intact. You can do what you want with them. There's a two-car garage and a shed for junk. The owner is leaving the lawn mower, leaf blower and all his gardening stuff. Any questions?"

"Not a one. Where do I sign?"

"On the dotted line. You can move in on Sunday at any time. I probably won't see you till the closing, so good luck. Oh, Lois took care of calling the water company, PSE&G and the phone company. Everything will be hooked up first thing Monday morning. You can reimburse us at the closing for the deposits."

Andi hugged the realtor. She had to remember to send him a present after she moved in.

The clock on the mantel was striking five when Andi walked through the doors of the kennel. "I'm home," she called.

Gertie was sitting at the kitchen table with three of the pups in her lap. "Rosie is keeping her eye on me. It almost makes me want to have a home of my own. Did you give them names?"

"Not yet. Did anyone call?" Andi asked nonchalantly.

"Mr. King called; his message is on the machine. He sounded . . . desperate."

"And well he should. Let me tell you what that . . . lipstick person did, Gertie. Then you tell me what you think I should do. I hate men. I told you that before, and then I let my guard down and somehow he . . . what he did . . . was . . . he sneaked in. I let him kiss me and I kissed him back and told him I liked it. Do you believe that!"

Gertie listened, her eyes glued to Andi's flushed face.

"Well?"

"I agree, it was a terrible thing to do. Andi, I've lived a long time. Things aren't always the way they seem. Everything has two sides. Would it hurt you to hear him out? What harm is there in listening to him? Then, if you want to walk away, do so. Aren't you afraid that you're always going to wonder if there was an explanation? You said he was nice, that you liked him. He sounded like a sterling person to me."

"Listen to him so he can lie to my face? That's the worst kind of man, the one who looks you in the eye and lies. That's what used car salesmen do. Sometimes lawyers and insurance men do it, too. I called the police on him this morning. He sat in my parking lot all night, Gertie."

"How do you know that?"

"Because I watched him. You know what else? I even changed the sheets on the damn bed because I thought . . . well, what I . . . oh, hell, it doesn't matter."

"Obviously it does matter. Your eyes are all red. You really sat up watching him sit in your parking lot! That's ridiculous!"

"I was packing my stuff in the attic. I looked out from time to time," Andi said defensively. "I guess he wasn't who I thought he was. I swear to God, Gertie, this is it. I'm not sticking my neck out, ever again."

"Don't businesspeople do things like that, Andi? I'm not taking sides here, but think for a moment; if the situation was reversed, wouldn't you want to get the best deal for your company?"

"Does that mean he and his company need to know about my love life, that I use a diaphragm? No, it does not. He had no damn right."

"Maybe it's the detective's fault and not Mr. King's. Maybe Mr. King told him to do a . . . whatever term they use, on you, and the man took it further than he was supposed to. That's something to think about," Gertie said, a desperate look on her face.

"Whose side are you on, Gertie? It sounds like you favor that war-paint king."

"I believe in giving everyone a fair hearing."

"Is that why you refuse to call your children and live in a ditch?"

"It's not the same thing, and you know it."

"There's no greater sin in life than betrayal. I could . . . can forgive anything but betrayal."

Gertie's tone turned fretful. "Don't say that, Andi. There's usually a reason for everything if you care enough to find out what it is. I've lived a long life, my dear, and along the way I learned a few things. An open mind is a person's greatest asset in this world."

"I don't want to hear it, Gertie, and my mind just shut down. I know his type; he was just playing with me in case I changed my mind about selling. I would have gone to bed with him, too. That's the part that bothers me. Then, one minute after the closing, it would be goodbye Andi."

"He's not like that at all, Andi. You're so wrong." At Andi's strange look she hastened to explain. "What I meant was . . . from everything you said, from what I've seen in the papers, Mr. King is a gentleman. You said so yourself. I really should be going. Someone's pulling into your driveway. I'm going to walk, Andi. I've been cooped up too long in the shelter." Gertie held up her hand. "No, no, I do not want a ride. You still have packing to do. Thanks for the tea and for letting me hold these precious bundles. When are you going to name them?"

"I was thinking of giving them all Christmas names. You know, Holly, Jingle, et cetera. Just let me get my coat; it's too cold, and there's ice everywhere. I refuse to allow you to walk home, wherever home may be today."

"I'm walking and that's final," Gertie said, backing out the door. "Besides, I have some thinking I have to do. I do thank you for caring about this old woman. I'll be fine. It's a messenger, Andi, with a letter. I'll wait just a minute longer to make sure it isn't an emergency."

Andi stared after her, a helpless look on her face. She knew how important it was for the seniors to feel independent. She reached for the envelope and ripped at it. "Ha!" she snorted. "It's an invitation to Mr. Lipstick's Christmas party."

"Guess that makes it official. Change your mind and go. Is there a note?"

"Yep. It says he's sorry about the report and all he had requested were the financials, none of the personal stuff. He said he meant to destroy it once he met me, but time got away from him. He also says he had more fun yesterday than he's had in twenty years, and he thinks he's falling in love with me. He's very sorry. Please call."

"So call and put the poor thing out of his misery. That certainly sounds contrite to me. Everyone makes mistakes, Andi, even you. I would find it very heartwarming to hear someone tell me they think they're falling in love with me. Think about that, Andi. Have a nice evening."

"Goodbye, Gertie. Be careful walking."

"I will, my dear."

Andi read the note and the invitation until she had them both memorized. She ran the words over and over in her mind as she finished packing up the attic. At one point, as she descended the attic steps, she put the words to music and sing-songed her way through her bedroom as she stuffed things in cartons.

Andi stopped only to feed the animals and eat a sandwich. The telephone continued to ring, the answering machine clicking on just as the person on the other end hung up. At eleven o'clock she carried the last of the boxes downstairs to the garage where she stacked them near the door. By three o'clock she had her mother's china packed as well as all the pictures and knickknacks from the living room sealed in bubble wrap. These, too, went into the garage.

At three-thirty, she was sitting at the kitchen table with a cup of tea, the invitation to Peter King's party in front of her and his letter propped up against the sugar bowl. Believe or not believe? Go to the party, don't go to the party? Call him or not call him? Ignore everything and maybe things would turn out right. Like thirty-year-old women with thirty-six animals were really in demand. Was Gertie right? Was she acting like some indignant teenager?

There were no answers in the kitchen, so she might as well go to bed and try to sleep. Was this how it felt to be in love? Surely love meant more than a sick feeling in the stomach coupled with wet eyes and a pounding headache.

Andi felt as old as Gertie when she climbed the stairs to the second floor. She blubbered to herself as she brushed her teeth and changed into flannel pajamas. She was asleep the moment she pulled the down comforter up to her chin.

Even in her dream she knew she was dreaming because once before, in another lifetime, she'd slid down the hill on a plastic shower curtain with a colleague named Tyler. The same Tyler she'd had a two-year relationship with.

She fell sideways, rolling off the frozen plastic, to land in a heap near a monstrous holly bush. The wind knocked out of her, she struggled to breathe.

"You okay, Andi?"

"Sure. Bet I'm bruised from head to toe, though. How about you?"

"I'm fine. You really aren't going with me tomorrow, are you?"

"No. I'll miss you. Let's stay in touch, okay?"

"People promise that all the time; they even mean it at the time they say it, but it rarely happens. I'll be in Chicago and you'll be in New Jersey. I want the big bucks. I could never be content living in some rural area counting my pennies and practicing veterinarian medicine for free. Right now you're starry-eyed at taking over your family's old practice, but that's going to get old real quick. You're gonna be the new kid on the block. Who's going to come to your clinic? Yeah, sure, you can board dogs, but how much money is there in that? Not much I can tell you. Let's go home and make some magic. We're probably never going to see each other again. We'll call at first and even write a few letters, and then it will be a Christmas card once a year with our name printed on it. After that it will be, Tyler who? Andi who?"

"Then why do you want to go to bed with me?"

"Because I think I love you."

"After two years you think you love me? I want to go home and I want to go by myself. I don't want to go to bed with you either because you remind me of someone I don't like. He makes greasy lipstick. I changed the sheets and everything, and then he found out, probably from you, that

I use a diaphragm. That was tacky, Tyler, to tell him something that personal."

"I never told him any such thing"

"Liar, liar, your pants are on fire. Get away from me and don't think I'm going to your stupid Christmas party either. Take this damn shower curtain with you, too."

"All right, all right. You came with me, how are you going to get home?"

"I have two feet, I'll walk. When you're homeless that's how you get around; I hope you make your three million plus. Goodbye, Peter."

"My name isn't Peter, it's Tyler."

"Same thing, birds of a feather flock together. All you're interested in is money. You don't care about me. The fact that you're taking this so well is suspect in my eyes. And another thing, I wouldn't let you see me wear my mother's pearls even if you paid me my weight in gold. One more thing, don't for one minute think I'm giving one of Rosie's pups to you to give your grandmother. She'll sneeze from all of that Lily of the Valley powder."

Andi rolled over, her arm snaking out to reach the phone. She yanked it back under the covers immediately. Six-thirty. She'd only had two and a half hours of sleep, and most of that had been dream time. Damn.

Andi struggled to remember the dream as she showered and dressed.

The animals tended to, Andi sat at the table sipping the scalding hot coffee. She frowned as she tried to remember what it was in her dream that bothered her. It didn't hit her until she finished the last of the coffee in the pot. Lily of the Valley. Of course. "When you're stupid, Andi, you're stupid." A moment later the phone book was in her hands. She flipped to the Ks and ran her finger down the listing. She called every S. King in the book until she heard the voice she was expecting. She wasn't sure, but she thought her heart stopped beating when she heard Gertie's voice on the other end of the line. *Sadie King, Peter King's grandmother, was the homeless Gertie.*

Blind fury riveted through her. Shaking and trembling, she had to grab hold of the kitchen counter to steady herself. A conspiracy. If the old saying a fool is born every minute was true, then she was this minute's fool. Of all the cheap, dirty tricks! Send an old lady here to soften me up, to spy on me so I'd spill my guts. You son of a bitch!

Andi fixed another pot of coffee. Somewhere in this house there must be some cigarettes, a filthy habit she'd given up a year ago. She rummaged in the kitchen drawers until she found a crumpled pack pushed way in the back. She lit one, coughed and sputtered, but she didn't put it out.

Promptly at nine o'clock she called King Cosmetics and asked to speak to Peter King. "This is Dr. Andrea Evans and this call is a one-time call. Tell Mr. King he doesn't get a second chance to speak with me. It's now or never."

"Andi, is it really you? Listen I'm sorry—"

"Excuse me, I called you, so I'm the one who will do the talking. Furthermore, I'm not interested in any lame excuses. How dare you send your grandmother to spy on me! How dare you! Homeless my ass! She said her name was Gertie and I believed her. I didn't get wise till this morning. It was that Lily of the Valley. *That always bothered me.* Why would a homeless lady always smell like Lily of the Valley? She should have had body odor. All those good deeds, all those tall tales. Well, it should make you happy that I fell for it. You have to sink pretty low to use an old lady to get what you want. Don't send her back here again either. My God, I can't wait to get out of here so I don't ever have to see you or your grandmother again. She actually had me feeling sorry for her because her children, *she said,* wanted to slap her in a nursing home. This is my R.S.V.P. for your party. I'll leave it up to you to figure out if I'm attending or not."

"What the hell are you talking about. Who's homeless? My grandmother lives in a penthouse, and she works to help—"

Andi cut him off in mid-sentence, slamming down the phone. She zeroed in on Rosie, who was watching the strange goings-on with puzzlement. Her owner rarely raised her voice. It was rarer still that she cried. "Do I care that his grandmother lives in a penthouse? No, I do not. Do I care that she sneaked in here and ... took care of us? No, I do not. I bet that old lady came here in a chauffeur-driven limousine and parked it somewhere, and then she trundled over here in her disguise. I am stupid, I admit it. Well, my stupid days are over."

Andi cried then because there was nothing else for her to do.

"Sadie!" The one word was that of a bellowing bull.

"Peter! How nice of you to come by so early. Did you come for breakfast?"

"Sadie, or should I call you Gertie? What the hell were you trying to do, Sadie?"

"So you found out. I only wanted to help. Who told you?"

"Guess!"

"Not Andi? Please, don't tell me Andi found out. So, that was who called this morning and hung up without speaking. I thought it might be Donald."

"Who the hell is Donald?" Peter continued to bellow.

"He covered for me. He's a homeless man I befriended. How did she find out?"

"I have no idea. She said something about you always smelling like Lily of the Valley."

"Yes, I guess that would do it. Was she very upset?"

"Upset isn't quite the word I'd use. She thinks I put you up to it. She thinks we had a conspiracy going to get her property."

"Well, I certainly hope you explained things to her. I'll go right over there and make amends."

"I wouldn't do that if I were you. I couldn't explain; she hung up on me. Don't meddle, Sadie. I mean it."

"She's so right for you, Peter, and you're perfect for her. I wanted you two to get together. When the men found homeless animals, I had them take them to Andi. They told me how nice and kind she was. I wanted to see for myself what kind of girl she was. I want you to get married, Peter, and I don't want you marrying someone like Helen. That's why I did it."

"Couldn't you trust me to find out for myself, Sadie? Why couldn't you simply introduce me or in this case leave me to my own devices? I met her on my own."

"No, I couldn't trust you. Look how long it took you to figure out Helen wore false eyelashes." She watched her grandson cringe at her words. "I just wanted to help so you would be happy. I'm sorry, but I'm not taking all the blame, Peter. You screwed it all up with that report."

"That's another thing. That report was on the backseat. The day we went sledding I didn't have anything in the backseat. I didn't even open the back door. All my stuff was in the trunk. How'd it fall out?"

"It doesn't matter now how it fell out. It did, and Andi found it and read it. End of story," Sadie said.

"I'm not giving up. I like her spunk."

"She hates your guts," Sadie said. "By the way, she isn't going to your party. I was there when the messenger brought your invitation. Peter, I'm so sorry. I just wanted to help. Where are you going?"

"To correct this situation."

"Peter, Andi is very angry. Don't go on her property again unless you want to see yourself and this company on the six o'clock news."

"Then what the hell am I supposed to do?"

"Does that mean you want my advice?"

"Okay, I'll try anything."

"Go to the police station and increase your Christmas donation to the Police Benevolent Association. Then ask them if they'll loan you one of their bullhorns. Talk to her from the road. She'll have to listen, and you aren't breaking any laws. I'm not saying it will work, but it's worth a try."

"Sadie, I love you!" Peter said as he threw his arms around his grandmother.

Peter King, the bullhorn next to him on the front seat, pulled his car to the curb. He felt stupid and silly as he climbed from the car. What to say? How to say it? Apologize from the heart. You know Spanish and French and a smattering of Latin. Do it in four languages. That should impress her. Oh yeah.

Peter took a deep breath before he brought the horn to his mouth. "Dr. Evans, this is Peter King. I'm outside on the road. I want you to listen to me. When I'm finished, if you don't want me to bother you again, I won't, but you need to hear me out. You can't run and hide, and you can't drown this out."

Peter sensed movement, chattering voices and rock music. Disconcerted, he turned around to see a pickup truck full of skis, sleds, and teenagers, pulling a snowmobile, drive up behind his parked car. "Shit!" Like he really needed an audience. Tune them out and get on with it.

"Andi, listen to me. Don't blame my grandmother; she only wanted to help. She wants to see me married with children before she . . . goes. I didn't know she was pretending to be a bag lady, I swear I didn't. As much as I love her, I wanted to strangle her when I found out."

"That's nice, mister," shouted a young girl in a tight ski suit and hair that looked like raffia. "You should always love your mother and grandmother. You're doing this all wrong. You need to appeal to her basic instincts."

"Shut up, Carla," a pimple-faced youth snarled. "You need to mind your own business. Yo, mister, you need to stand tall here and not beg some dumb girl for . . . whatever it is you want out of this scene."

"Listen, Donnie, don't be telling me girl stuff. You're so ignorant you're pathetic. Listen to me, mister, tell her she has eyes like stars and she's in your blood and you can't eat or sleep or anything. Tell her all you want in life is to marry her and have lots of little girl kids that look just like her. Promise her anything, but you better mean it because us women can spot a lie in a heartbeat."

Peter turned around. "She thinks I cheated her or tried, and then I did something really stupid, but I didn't know it was stupid at the time. Well, I sort of knew, but I didn't think anyone would ever find out. How do I handle that one?" he asked the girl with the three pounds of makeup and raffia hair.

"Tell her what you just said to me. Admit it. It's when you lie and try to cover up that you get in trouble."

"Don't listen to Carla, man; that chick in there is gonna think you're the king of all jerks."

"You're a jerk, Donnie. Listen to me, mister, what do you have to lose?"

Peter cleared his throat. "Andi, I'm sorry for everything. I was stupid. I swear to God, I'll never do another stupid thing again. I tried to explain about the business end of things. I want to marry you. I'll do anything you want if you'll just come out here and listen to me or let me come in and talk to you. Sadie says we're meant for each other. She's hardly ever wrong. What's ten minutes out of your life, Andi? I admit I'm dumb when it comes to women. I don't read *Cosmo,* and I don't know diddly squat about triple orgasms and such stuff but I'm willing to learn. I'll use breath mints, I'll quit smoking, I'll take the grease out of the lipstick. Are you listening to me, Andi? I goddamn well love you! I thought I was falling in love with you, but now I know I love you for real."

"Mister, you are a disgrace to the male race," Donnie said.

"Oh, mister, that was beautiful. You wait, she's coming out. Give her five minutes. No woman could resist that little speech. You did real good, mister. My sister told me about triple orgasms. I can explain . . ."

"Oh, jeez, look, she's coming out. That's who you're in love with?" There was such amazement in the boy's face, Peter grinned.

"Oh, she's real pretty, mister. I know she loves you. You gonna give her something special for Christmas?"

"Yeah, himself," Donnie snorted.

"You know what, kid, they don't come any better than me. You need to get a whole new attitude. Carla, we're looking for teenage models at King Cosmetics. Here's my card; go to personnel and arrange a meeting with me for after the first of the year. Dump that jerk and get yourself a real boyfriend. Here's the keys to my car. My address is in the glove compartment. Drop it off for me, okay? That way she'll have to take me home or else allow me to stay. Thanks for your help. Can you drive?"

"Now you got it, mister. I can drive. Remember now, be humble, and only the truth counts from here on in."

"Got it," he said as he moved toward the house.

Inside the kennel, Andi said, "You got the dogs in a tizzy. I'm in a tizzy. You're out of your mind. I never heard of a grandmother/grandson act before."

"It wasn't an act. Everything I said was true. I do want to marry you."

"I hardly know you. Are you asking me so the three million plus stays in the family?"

"God, no. I feel like I've known you all my life. I've been

searching for someone like you forever. My grandmother knew you were the one the moment she met you. She adores you, and she feels terrible about all of this. Can we start over?"

"Well . . . I . . . we're from two different worlds. I don't think it would work. I'm not giving up my life and my profession. I worked too hard to get where I am."

"I'm not asking you to give up anything. I don't much care for the life I move around in now, but it's my job. I can make it nine-to-five and be home every night for dinner. If you're busy, I can even cook the dinner or we can hire a housekeeper."

"I'm moving to Freehold Christmas Eve."

"Freehold's good. I like Freehold. It's not such a long commute. Sunday's good for me. I'm a whizbang at putting up Christmas trees. Well?"

"Were you telling me the truth when you said you couldn't eat or sleep?"

"Just look at the bags under my eyes. How about you?"

"I cried a lot. I would have cried more, but the animals got upset so I had to stop."

"So right now, this minute, we're two people who are starting over. All that . . . mess, it never happened. Your money will always be your money. That was a business deal. What we have is personal. So, will you marry me? If you don't have pearls, Sadie will give you hers. This way they'll stay in the family. That kid who took my car knows more than I do. I'll tell you about her later. Was that a yes or a no?"

"It's a maybe. We haven't even gone to bed yet. We might not be compatible."

"Why don't we find out."

"*Now?* It's morning. I have things to do. How about later?"

"Where we're concerned, later means trouble. Now!"

"Okay. Now sounds good. I put clean sheets on the bed on Sunday. You were a no-show. That didn't do anything for my ego," Andi said.

"I dreamed about it," Peter said.

"You said you didn't sleep."

"Daydreamed. There's a difference. In living color."

"How'd I look?"

"Wonderful!" Peter said. "Want me to carry you upstairs?"

"No. I'm the independent type. I can be bossy."

"I love bossy women. Sadie is bossy. People only boss other people around when they love them. Sadie told me that."

"You are dumb." Andi laughed.

"That, too. I sleep with my socks on," Peter confided.

"Me, too! I use an electric blanket."

"You won't need it this morning." Peter laughed.

"Pretty confident, aren't you?"

"When you got it you got it."

"Show me," Andi said.

"Your zipper or mine?"

"On the count of three," Andi said.

Zippppppp.

He showed her. And was still showing her when the sun set and the animals howled for their dinner. And afterward, when the kennel grew quiet for the long evening ahead, he was still showing her. Toward midnight, Andi showed him, again and again. He was heard to mutter, in a hoarse whisper, "I liked that. Oh, do that again."

She did.

"I hate to leave. Oh, God, I have to borrow your truck, do you mind?"

"Of course I mind. You sport around in a fifty-thousand-dollar truck and a ninety-thousand-dollar car and you want to borrow my clunker!"

"I'll have someone drive it back, okay? Is this going to be our first fight?"

"Not if I can help it. I do need the truck, though. I have some errands to do, and I'm not driving that bus."

"Are you going to call Sadie?"

"Not today. She needs to sweat a little. Are you going to tell her?"

"Not on your life. Well, did that maybe turn into a yes or a no? What kind of ring do you want?"

"I don't want an engagement ring. I just want a wide, thick, gold wedding band."

"Then it's yes?"

Andi nodded.

"When?"

"January. After I get settled in."

"January's good. January's real good. Jesus, I love you. You smile like my mother used to smile. That's the highest compliment I can pay you, Andi. She was real, like you. I don't know too many real people. When you stop to think about it, that's pretty sad."

"Then let's not think about it," Andi said as she dangled the truck keys under his nose.

"I can't see you till tomorrow. I'll call you tonight, okay? Some clients are in town, and the meetings and dinner are not something I can cancel. You're coming to the party?"

"Yes."

"What about the pearls?" Peter asked fretfully "You have to explain that to me one of these days."

"I have my mother's pearls."

"God, that's a relief."

He kissed her then until she thought her head would spin right off her.

"Bye."

Andi smiled, her eyes starry. "Bye, Peter."

Thursday morning, the day of Peter King's Christmas party, Andi climbed out of bed with a vicious head cold. Her eyes were red, her nose just as red. She'd spent the night propped up against the pillows so her nasal passages would stay open. If she'd slept twenty minutes it was a lot. The time was ten minutes to eight. In her ratty robe and fleece-lined slippers she shuffled downstairs to make herself some hot coffee. She ached from head to toe. Just the thought of cleaning the dog runs made her cringe. She shivered and turned up the heat to ninety. She huddled inside the robe, trying to quiet her shaking body as she waited for the coffee to perk.

Cup in hand at fifteen minutes past eight, she heard the first rumblings of heavy duty machinery in her parking lot. The knock on the door was louder than thunder. She opened the door, her teeth chattering. "What are you doing here? What's all that machinery? Get it out of here. This is private property. Is that a wrecking ball?"

He was big and burly with hands the size of ham hocks, the

perfect complement to the heavy duty monster machinery behind him. "What do you mean what am I doing here? I'm here to raze this building. I have a contract that says so. And, yeah, that's a wrecking ball. You gotta get out of here, lady."

"Come in here. I can't stand outside; I'm sick as you can see, and I'm not going anywhere. I, too, have a contract, and my contract says you can't do this. Mine, I'm sure, supersedes yours. So there. I have thirty-six animals here and no place to take them until Sunday. You'll just have to wait."

"That's tough, lady. I ain't comin' back here on Sunday; that's Christmas Eve. I have another job scheduled for Tuesday. Today is the day for this building."

"I'm calling the police; we'll let them settle it. You just go back outside and sit on that ball because that's all you're going to do with it. Don't you dare touch a thing. Do you hear me?" Andi croaked. She slammed the door in the man's face. She called the police and was told a patrol car would be sent immediately.

Andi raced upstairs, every bone in her body protesting as she dressed in three layers of clothing. She had to stop three times to blow her runny nose. Hacking and coughing, she ran downstairs to rummage on her desk for her contract to show the police. While she waited she placed a call to both Peter and Sadie and was told both of them were unavailable. Five minutes later, her electricity and phone were dead.

Two hours later, the electricity was back on. Temporarily. "I don't know what to tell you, ma'am. This man is right and so are you. You both have signed contracts. He has every right to be here doing what he's doing. You on the other hand have a contract that says he can't do it. Nobody is going to do anything until we can reach Mr. Peter King, since he's the man who signed both these contracts."

"Listen up, both of you, and watch my lips. I am not going anywhere. I'm sick. I have thirty-six animals in that kennel, and we have nowhere to go. Based on my contract, I made arrangements to be out of here on Sunday, not Saturday, not Friday and certainly not today. Now, which part of that don't you two men understand?"

"The part where you aren't leaving till Sunday. This is a three-day job. I can't afford to lose the money since I work for myself.

It's not my fault you're sick, and it's not my fault that you have thirty-six animals. I got five kids and a wife to support and men on my payroll sitting outside in your parking lot. Right now I'm paying them to sit there drinking coffee."

"That's just too damn bad, mister. I'm calling the *Plainfield Courier* and the *Star Ledger*. Papers like stories like this especially at Christmastime. You better get my phone hooked up again and don't think I'm paying for that."

The afternoon wore on. Andi kept swilling tea as she watched through the window. The police were as good as their word, allowing nothing to transpire until word came in from Peter King. Her face grew more flushed, and she knew her fever was creeping upward.

Using the police cell phone, Andi called again and again, leaving a total of seven messages on Sadie's machine and nine messages in total for Peter at King Cosmetics. The receptionist logged all nine messages, Mr. King's words ringing in her ears: "Do not call me under *any* circumstance. Whatever it is can wait until tomorrow. Even if this building blows up I don't want to know about it until tomorrow."

At five o'clock, Andi suggested the police try and reach Mr. King at his home. When she was unable to tell them where he lived, the owner of the wrecking equipment smirked. It wasn't until six o'clock that she remembered she had Peter's address on the invitation. However, if she kept quiet she could delay things another day. Besides, his party was due to get under way any minute now. He would probably try and call her when he realized she wasn't in attendance.

The police officer spoke. "You might as well go home, Mr. Dolan. We'll try and reach Mr. King throughout the evening and get this thing settled by morning."

Cursing and kicking at his machinery, Dolan backed his equipment out of the parking lot. The officer waited a full twenty minutes before he left. Andi watched his taillights fade into the distance from the kitchen window. The yellow bus was like a huge golden eye under her sensor light. Large, yellow bus. Uh-huh. Okay, Mr. Peter King, you have this coming to you!

"Hey you guys, line up, we're going to a party! First I have to get the location. Second, you need to get duded up. Wait here."

The Christmas box of odds and ends of ribbon and ornaments was clearly marked. Spools of used ribbon were just what she needed. Every dog, every cat, got a red bow, even Rosie. The pups, smaller, skinnier ribbons. "I'm going to warm up the bus, so don't get antsy. I also need to find my mother's pearls. I don't know why, but I have to wear them." Finally, wearing the pearls, wads of tissue stuck in the two flap pockets of her flannel shirt, pups in their box in hand, Andi led the animals to the bus. "Everybody sit down and be quiet. We're going to show Mr. Peter King what we think about the way he does business!"

Thirty-five minutes later, Andi swung the bus onto Brentwood Drive. Cars were lined up the entire length of the street. "This indeed poses a dilemma," she muttered. She eyed the fire hydrant, wondering if she could get past it and up onto the lawn. Loud music blasted through the closed windows. "It must be a hell of a party," she muttered as she threw caution to the wind and plowed ahead.

Andi grabbed the handle to open the door. "Ooops, wait just one second. Annabelle, come here. You, too, Cleo." From her pocket she withdrew a tube of Raspberry Cheese Louise lipstick and painted both dog's lips. Annabelle immediately started to lick it off. "Stop that. You need to keep it on till we get to the party. Okay, you know the drill, we move on three. I expect you all to act like ladies and gentlemen. If you forget your manners, oh, well." She blew her nose, tossed the tissue on the ground and gave three sharp blasts on the whistle. "We aren't going to bother with the doorbell, the music's too loud."

"Party time!"

"Eek!" "Squawk!" "Oh, my God! It's a herd!" "They're wearing lipstick! I don't believe this!"

"Hi, I'm Andrea Evans," Andi croaked. "I think I'd like a rum and Coke and spare the Coke." Her puffy eyes narrowed when she saw her intended lounging on a beautiful brocade sofa, his head thrown back in laughter. He laughed harder when Cedric lifted his leg on a French Provincial table leg. Not to be outdone, Isaac did the same thing. Annabelle squatted in the middle of a colorful Persian carpet as she tried to lick off the lipstick.

"Now, this is what I call a party," Peter managed to gasp.

"Ladies and gentlemen, stay or go, the decision is yours. It ain't gonna get any better than this! Wait, wait, before you go, I'd like to introduce you to the lady I'm going to marry right after the first of the year. Dr. Andrea Evans, meet my guests. I don't even want to know why you did this," he hissed in her ear.

"You said you wanted a lived-in house. Myra is going to get sick from all that pâté. Oh, your guests are leaving. By the way, I parked the bus on your lawn."

"No!"

"Yep. Don't you care that your guests are leaving? I'm sick."

"And you're going right to bed," Sadie said, leaning over Andi. "You can forgive me later, my dear. Oh, my, you are running a fever. Isn't this wonderful, Peter? It's like we're a real family. Your furniture will never be the same. Do you care?"

"Nope," Peter said, wrapping his arm around Andi's shoulders. "Do you want to tell me what prompted this . . . extraordinary visit?"

Andi told him. "So, you see, we're homeless until Sunday."

"Not anymore. My home is your home and the home of these animals. Boy, this feels good. Isn't it great, Sadie? That guy Dolan is a piece of work. It's true, I did sign the contract, but it was amended later on. I don't suppose he showed you a copy of that."

"No, he didn't. It doesn't matter. I thought you'd be angry. I was making a statement."

"I know, and I'm not angry. You did the right thing. You really can empty a room. Look, the food's all gone."

"Do you really love me?"

"So much it hurts."

"I'm wearing my mother's pearls. I think I'd like to go to bed now if you don't mind. Will you take care of Rosie and her pups?"

"That's my job," Sadie chirped. "Peter, carry this child to bed. I'll make her a nice hot toddy, and by tomorrow she'll be fine. Trust me."

Andi was asleep in Peter's arms before he reached the top of the steps. He turned as he heard steps behind him. "Okay, you can all come up and stand watch. By the way, thanks for coming to the party. I really like your outfits and, Annabelle, on you that lipstick looks good."

Peter fussed with the covers under Sadie's watchful eye. "I meant it, Sadie, when I said I love her so much it hurts. Isn't she beautiful? I could spend the rest of my life just looking at her."

"Ha! Not likely, you have to work to support all of us," Andi said sleepily. "Good night, Peter. I love you. Merry Christmas."

"Merry Christmas, Andi," Peter said, bending low to kiss her on the cheek.

"Ah, I love it when things work out," Sadie said, three of Rosie's pups cradled against her bony chest. "I think I'd like five grandchildren. Good night, Peter."

"Thanks, Grandma. It's going to be a wonderful life."

"I know."

A Baby for Christmas

Lisa Jackson

Prologue

December 1995
Boston, Massachusetts

I'll have a blue Christmas without you . . .

"Oh, no, I won't!" Angrily, Annie McFarlane snapped off the radio. She wasn't about to let the sad lyrics of that particular song echo through her heart. It was the Christmas season, for heaven's sake. A time for merriment and joy, not the dull loneliness that caused her to ache inside.

She unwound a string of Christmas lights and plugged it into the socket. Instantly the dreary living room of her condominium was awash with twinkling bright color. Red, blue, yellow, and green reflected on the carpet and bare walls, giving a hint of warmth to a room littered with half-filled boxes and crates, evidence of the move across country she was planning. Pictures, mementos of her life as a married woman, clothes, knickknacks, everything she owned was half-packed in the boxes strewn haphazardly through the condo.

Her throat tightened and she fought back another attack of hot, painful tears. "Don't do this," she reprimanded herself sharply. "He's not worth it. He never was."

So what if David had left her for another woman? So what if this was the first Christmas she would spend alone in her entire life? So what if she was truly and finally divorced, a situation she'd never wanted?

Women went through it all the time. So did men. It wasn't the end of the world.

But it felt like it. The weight on her shoulders and pain deep in her heart wouldn't listen to the mental tongue-lashings she constantly gave herself. "Get over it," she said aloud and was surprised that her words nearly reverberated in the half-empty rooms. Her dog, a mutt who looked like he had his share of German shepherd hidden somewhere in his genes, thumped his tail against the floor as he lay, head on paws, under the kitchen table.

"It's all right, Riley," she said, her words sounding as hollow as she felt.

Sleet slashed against the windows, the old Seth Thomas clock still mounted over the fireplace ticked off the seconds of her life, and the gas flames in the grate hissed steadily against ceramic logs that would never burn. Outside, the city of Boston was alive with the festivities of the holiday season. Brilliant lights winked and dazzled on garland-clad porches while bare-branched trees were ablaze in neighboring yards. Wreaths and pine-scented swags adorned doors and electric candles burned in most of the windows. Children in those other houses were too excited to sleep. Parents, frazzled but happy, sipped mulled wine, planned family dinners, and worried that their hastily bought, last-minute presents wouldn't bring a gleam of gladness to their recipients' eyes.

And here she was, stringing a single strand of lights over a potted tree she'd bought at the local grocery store, knowing that tomorrow she would eat alone, put in some hours down at the local women's shelter, and come home to pack the rest of her things. She only wished that she'd been able to move before the holidays, but her timing—or, more precisely, David's timing—hadn't allowed for Christmas.

Three months ago she'd called her real estate agent about selling the condo, watched through her tears as David had carried his half of their possessions out the door, smiled bravely when he'd casually mentioned that Caroline, his girlfriend, was pregnant, and then had fallen apart completely as she'd reluctantly signed the divorce papers.

Annie had never felt more alone in her life. Her mother and stepfather were spending the holidays cruising up and down the west coast of Mexico; her sister Nola, forever the free spirit, was again missing in action, probably with a new-found lover. Annie remembered Nola's last choice, a tall, strapping blond man by the name of Liam O'Shaughnessy, whom Nola professed to adore for all of two or three weeks. Since O'Shaughnessy, there had been others, Annie supposed, but none she'd heard of.

Then there was Annie's brother, Joel, and his wife. They were spending Christmas at home in Atlanta with their three kids. Though invited to visit them, Annie hadn't wanted to fly down south with her case of the blues and spoil everyone's Christmas so she'd decided to stick it out here, alone in the home that she and David had shared, until she moved to Oregon after the first of the year.

Thank God the condo had sold quickly. She couldn't imagine spending much more time here in this lonely tomb, which was little more than a shrine to a marriage that had failed.

She fished in a box of handmade ornaments she'd sewed and glued together only last year and placed a tiny sleigh on an already-drooping bough. As she finished looping a length of strung cranberries and popcorn around the little evergreen, she had to smile. The forlorn little tree looked almost festive.

There would be life, a more satisfying life, after David. She'd see to it personally. At least she still had Riley, who was company if nothing else.

With a glimmer of hope as inspiration, she walked to the kitchen, scrounged in a drawer for a corkscrew, and realized that, as she'd given the good one to David, she was forced to use the all-in-one tool they'd bought years before for a camping trip. The screwdriver-can opener-bottle opener was more inclined to slice the user's hand than open a can or bottle, but it was the best implement she could come up with at the moment.

She managed to open a bottle of chardonnay without drawing any blood, then found one of the wine goblets from the crystal she'd picked out seven years ago when she'd planned her wedding to David. She'd been twenty-three at the time, graduated from college as a business major and had met David McFarlane, a witty, good-looking law student, only to fall hopelessly in love with him. She'd never thought it would end. Not even during the horrid anguish and pain of her first miscarriage. The second loss—during the fifth month—had been no better, but the third, and final, when the doctor had advised her to think seriously of adoption, had been the straw that had broken the over-burdened back of their union. David was the last son of his particular branch of the McFarlane family tree and as such was expected, as well as personally determined, to spawn his own child, with or without Annie.

It was then, during the talks of surrogate mothers and fertility clinics, that the marriage had really started to crumble. Enter Caroline Gentry: young, nubile, willing, and, apparently, if David were to be believed, able to carry a baby to term.

"What a mess," Annie said to herself as she carried her bottle and goblet into the living room. On the hearth, she tucked her legs beneath the hem of her oversized sweater and watched the reflection of the colored lights play in her wine. "Next year will be better." She held up her glass in a mock toast and her dog, as if he understood her, snorted in disdain. "I'm not kidding, Riley. Next year, the good Lord willin' and the creek don't rise, things will be much, much better." Riley yawned and stretched, as if tired of her pep talks to herself. She took a long swallow and closed her eyes.

No matter what happened, she'd get over this pain, forget about David and his infidelity, and find a new life.

And a new man, an inner voice prompted.

"Never," she whispered. She'd never let a man get close enough to her again to wound her so deeply. "I'll make it on my own, damn it, or die trying."

Chapter One

December 1996

Oh, the weather outside is frightful . . .

"Damn." Liam snapped off the radio and scowling, settled against the passenger window of the battle-scarred Ford.

"Not in the spirit of the season?" Jake Cranston snorted as he stared through the windshield of his car. "I guess jail will do that to you."

Liam didn't respond, just clamped his jaw tight. He'd been through hell and back in the past few weeks; he didn't need to be reminded of it. Not even from a friend. Tonight Jake was more than a friend; he'd turned out to be Liam's goddamned guardian angel.

Liam glared out the window to the dark night beyond. Ahead of them, red taillights blurred through the thick raindrops that the wipers couldn't slap away fast enough. On the other side of the median, headlights flashed as cars screamed in the opposite direction. Christ, he was tired. He needed a good night's sleep, a stiff drink, and a woman. Not necessarily in that order.

It seemed as if Jake had been driving for hours, speeding through this rainy section of freeway without getting anywhere, but the city lights of Seattle were beginning to glow to the north.

"Want to stop somewhere?" Jake, while negotiating a banked turn, managed to shake a cigarette from his pack of Marlboros located forever on the dusty dash of his Taurus wagon. He passed the pack to his friend and shoved the Marlboro between his teeth.

He thought about lighting up. It had been six years since his last smoke and he could use the relief. He was so damned keyed up, his mind racing miles a minute even though he was dead tired. He tossed the pack onto the dash again. "Just get me home, Cranston."

"Why the devil would you want to go there?" Jake punched the lighter.

"Gotta start somewhere."

"Yeah, but if I were you I'd put this whole thing behind me and start over."

"Not yet."

"You're well out of it." The lighter clicked. Jake lit up and let smoke drift from his nostrils.

"Not until my name is cleared." Leaning back in the seat, Liam tried to forget the nightmare of the past few months and the hell he'd been through. But the days of looking over his shoulder and knowing he was being followed, watched by men he'd once trusted, still struck a deep, unyielding anger in his soul.

It had all started four months ago on a hot August night in Bellevue. In the early morning hours, there had been a break-in at the company offices where Liam worked. At first the police thought it was a typical burglary gone sour; the security guard on duty that night, old Bill Arness, had been unfortunate enough to confront the crook and had been bashed over the head, his skull crushed. Bill, a six-times grandfather with a wide girth and quick smile, had never awakened, but lingered in a coma for six weeks, then died before he was able to give the name of his attacker. His wife had never once left his side and the president of Belfry Construction, Zeke Belfry, had offered a twenty-five-thousand-dollar reward for anyone who had information that would lead to the arrest and conviction of the perpetrator. Zeke, a law-abiding, holier-than-thou Christian with whom Liam had never gotten along, was personally offended that his company had been singled out for any kind of criminal act and he wanted revenge.

Which he ultimately got.

Out of Liam O'Shaughnessy's hide.

Within a few months the police had decided the break-in was an inside job. Records had been destroyed. An audit showed that over a hundred thousand dollars was missing, all of the money skimmed from construction jobs for which Liam had been the project manager.

The police and internal auditors had started asking questions.

It had been nearly two months from the time of all the trouble until the police had closed in on him, slowly pulling their noose around his neck tighter and tighter while he himself was working on his own investigation. It was obvious someone had set him up to take a fall, but whom?

Before he could zero in on all of the suspects, one woman had come forward, a woman who held a personal grudge, a woman who had driven the final nails in his coffin. Nola Prescott, his ex-lover, had gone to the police and somehow convinced them that Liam was involved not only with the embezzling, but the death of old Bill Arness as well.

So here he was with his only friend in the world, trying to forget the sounds that had kept him awake at night. The clang of metal against metal, the shuffle of tired feet, shouts of the guards, and clank of chains still rattled through his brain. Prison. He'd been in prison, for Christ's sake. All because of one woman.

His teeth ground in frustration, but he forced his anger back. *Don't get mad, get even.* The old words of wisdom had been his personal mantra for the past few weeks. He'd known that eventually he'd be set free, that the D.A. couldn't possibly hold him without bail forever, that there wasn't a strong enough case against him because he hadn't done it.

"Okay, so what's the story?" he finally asked. "Why was I let go all of a sudden?"

"I thought you talked to your attorney."

"He just sketched out the details. Something about the prosecution losing their prime witness. Seems Nola chickened out. Didn't want to perjure herself."

Jake snorted and two jets of smoke streamed from his nostrils. "That's about the size of it. Nola Prescott recanted the testimony in her deposition."

Liam's guts churned. Nola. Beautiful. Bright. Secretary to one of the engineers at the firm. Great in bed, if you liked cold, unemotional, but well-practiced sex. No commitment. Just one body seeking relief from another. Liam had quickly grown bored and felt like hell after his few times in bed with her. Too much vodka had been his downfall. Their affair had been brief. "Why'd she change her mind?"

"Who knows? Maybe she got religion," Jake cracked and when Liam didn't smile, drew hard on his cigarette. He guided the Taurus onto the off-ramp leading to Bellevue, a bedroom community located north and east of Seattle.

"I think she might be protecting someone," Liam said, his eyes narrowing.

"Who?"

"Don't know. Maybe someone else she was involved with." He concentrated long and hard. "Someone at the company, probably. It would have been someone she was involved with six or seven months ago, before she left for her new job with that company in Tacoma."

"Christ, why didn't you tell this to the cops?"

"No proof. I'd look like I was just grasping at straws, but there's got to be a reason she set me up."

"You dumped her."

"So she accuses me of murder? That's even lower than Nola would go. She claimed to see me at the company that night. Why? She worked in another city."

"But still lived in the area."

"Too much of a coincidence, if you ask me." He stared at the streaks of raindrops on the windows. "It's just a matter of finding out who she was involved with." He drummed his fingers on the dash and thought of the possibilities—several names came to mind.

"Anyone you want me to check?" Jake offered.

"Yeah. Kim Boniface, one of her friends, but I wouldn't think she'd be covering for a woman. Then there's Hank Swanson, another project manager, Peter Talbott in accounting, and Jim Scorelli, an engineer who was always making a pass at her. Other than that,"—he shook his head, mentally disregarding rumors of financial difficulties of other friends and coworkers he knew at Belfry—"I can't think of anyone."

"I'll check."

"There's something else," Liam admitted, though he hated to bring up the subject. "I heard Nola was pregnant."

Jake's lips curled in upon themselves, the way they always did when he was weighing whether or not he should level with Liam. "So the rumor goes, but who knows? A woman like that—"

"Is it mine?"

The question hung in the smoky interior.

"How would I know?"

Liam squinted hard as the Taurus accelerated through the hills surrounding Bellevue. "Just tell me if the kid was born late in November or early December."

"Look, O'Shaughnessy, I wouldn't open that can of worms if I were—"

"Is it mine?" he repeated.

"For Chrissakes, Liam, who cares?" Jake growled.

"I do."

"Don't do this." He cracked his window and flicked his cigarette outside onto the pavement where the burning ember died a quick death in the gathering puddles.

"Do what?"

"Develop some latent sense of nobility. You had a fling with the woman. A *short* fling. Later she testified against you, tried to get you locked up for something you didn't do. She's no good. Leave her alone."

Liam's neck muscles tightened in frustration. "I just want to know if the kid's got O'Shaughnessy blood running through its veins."

"Right now, you should concentrate on getting a job. Just because you're exonerated doesn't mean that Zeke Belfry's gonna welcome you back with open arms."

That much was true. Ever since the old man had retired and his son Zeke had become president of the company, things had changed at Belfry Construction. Liam and Zeke had clashed on several occasions before all hell had broken loose. He'd already planned to sell his house, cash in his company stock, and start his own consulting firm. He didn't need Zeke Belfry—or anyone else, for that matter.

Jake nosed the Taurus into a winding street of upscale homes built on junior acres. Liam's house, an English Tudor, sat dark and foreboding, the lawn overgrown, moss collecting on the split shake roof, the windows black. The other houses in the neighborhood were aglow with strings of winking lights, nativity scenes tucked in well-groomed shrubbery, and illuminated Santas and snowmen poised on rooftops. The lawns were mowed and edged, the bushes neatly trimmed, the driveways blown free of leaves and fir needles.

Welcome to suburbia.

He fingered his keys.

"Your Jeep's in the garage. Mail on the table."

"Where's Nola?" Liam wasn't giving up.

Jake pulled into the driveway and let the car idle in the rain, the beams of his headlights splashing against Liam's garage. "Don't know."

"What?"

"No one does."

"Now, wait a minute—"

"Let it go, Liam." Suddenly Jake's hand was on his arm, his firm fingers restraining his friend through the thick rawhide of his jacket.

"Can't do it. Where is she?"

"Really. No one knows. Not even the D.A. She recanted her testimony and disappeared. A week ago. Your guess is as good as mine."

"She's got family," Liam said, remembering. "A brother in the south somewhere, folks who follow the sun, and a sister in Boston . . . no, she moved. To Oregon." Liam snapped his fingers.

"No reason to drag her into this."

"Unless she knows where Nola is and if the kid is mine."

"I knew I shouldn't have told you." Jake slapped the heel of his hand to his forehead.

"You had to," Liam said, opening the car door as a blast of December wind rushed into the warm, smoky interior. "Thanks."

"Don't mention it."

Liam slammed the door shut and saw his friend flick on the radio before ramming the car into reverse. Jake rolled down the window at the end of the drive and laughed without a trace of mirth. "Oh, by the way, O'Shaughnessy. Merry Christmas."

Feliz Navidad, Feliz Navidad . . .

Annie hummed along with José Feliciano as she sat at her

kitchen table and licked stamps to attach to her Christmas card envelopes. Marilyn Monroe, Elvis, and James Dean smiled up at her along with the more traditional wreaths, Christmas trees, or flags that decorated her rather eclectic smattering of stamps. Her home, a small cottage tucked into the low hills of western Oregon, was decorated with lights, fir garlands, pine cones, and a tree that nearly filled the living room. The cabin was warm and earthy from years of settling here in this forest. The pipes creaked, the doors stuck, and sometimes the electricity was temperamental, but the house was quaint and cozy with a view of a small lake where herons and ducks made their home.

Riley lay beneath the table, his eyes at half-mast, his back leg absently scratching at his belly.

Annie had been lucky to find this place, which had once been the home of the foreman of a large ranch. The main house still stood on thirty forested acres while the rest of the old homestead, the fields of a once-working farm, had been sliced away and sold into subdivisions that crawled up the lower slopes. The larger farmhouse, quaintly elegant with its Victorian charm, was empty now as the elderly couple who owned it had moved to a retirement center. It was Annie's job to see that the grounds were maintained, the house kept in decent repair, the remaining livestock—three aging horses—were fed and exercised and, in general, look after the place. For free rent, she was able to live in the cottage and run a small secretarial service from her home.

"I wanna wish you a Merry Christmas, I wanna wish you a Merry Christmas . . ." She sang softly to herself as the timer on the ancient oven dinged and she scooted back her chair to check the batch of Christmas cookies.

Outside, snow had begun to fall in thick flakes that were quickly covering the ground. Supposedly, according to the local newspeople, a storm was going to drop several inches of snow over the Willamette Valley before moving east. But there was no cause for concern—maybe a slick road or two, but for the most part the broadcasters were downplaying the hazards of the storm and seemed happy to predict the first white Christmas to visit western Oregon in years.

Annie planned to fly to Atlanta to spend the holidays with Joel, Polly, and her nephews. She'd come a long way from her dark memories of the past year, managing to shove most of her pain aside and start a new life for herself. Even the news of David's marriage and the birth of his son hadn't affected her as adversely as she'd thought it would, though her own situation sometimes seemed bleak. She wondered if she'd ever become a mother when she couldn't begin to imagine becoming some man's wife.

Well, as Dr. James had told her after the last miscarriage, "There's always adoption."

Could she, as a single woman?

The scents of cinnamon and nutmeg filled the kitchen as she slipped her fingers through a hot mitt and pulled a tray of cookies from the oven. She glanced out the window and saw snow drifting in the corners of the glass. Ice crystals stung the panes and a chill seeped through the old windows. A gust of wind whipped the snow-laden boughs of the trees and rattled the panes. The newspeople were certainly right about the storm, Annie thought, feeling the first hint of worry. She turned on an exterior light and mentally calculated that there were two inches of white powder on the deck rail.

If this kept up, she'd have a devil of a time getting to the airport tomorrow. "It'll be all right," she told herself as she snapped off the oven.

Bam!

A noise like the backfiring of a car or the sharp report of a shotgun blast thundered through the house. Within seconds everything went dark.

"What in the world—?"

Riley was on his feet in an instant, barking wildly and dashing toward the door.

"It's all right, boy," Annie said, though she didn't believe a word of it. What had happened? Had a car run into a telephone pole and knocked down the electrical lines? Had a transformer blown?

It didn't matter. The result was that she was suddenly enveloped in total darkness and she didn't know when the electricity might be turned on again. Muttering under her breath, she reached into a drawer, her fingers fumbling over matches, a screwdriver, and a deck of cards until she found a flashlight. She flicked on the low beam and quickly lit several candles before peering outside into the total darkness of the hill. Though she was somewhat isolated, there were neighbors in the development down the hill, but no lights shone through the thick stands of fir and maple.

Alone. You're all alone.

"Big deal," she muttered as her eyes became accustomed to the darkness. She wasn't a scared, whimpering female. Shaking off a case of the jitters, she found her one hurricane lantern and lit the wick. "Okay, okay, now heat," she told herself as she opened the damper of the old river-rock fireplace, then touched one candle to the dry logs stacked in the grate. The kindling caught quickly and eager flames began to lick the chunks of mossy oak while Riley, not usually so nervous, paced near the front door. He growled, glanced at Annie, then scratched against the woodwork.

"That's not helping," Annie said. "Lie down."

Riley ignored her.

"Just like all males," she grumbled. "Stubborn, headstrong, and won't listen to sound advice." Bundling into boots, gloves, her ski jacket, and a scarf, she headed for the back porch where several cords of firewood had been stacked for the winter. She hauled a basket with her and after twenty minutes had enough lengths of oak and fir to see her through the night. The batteries on her transistor radio were shot, and the phone, when she tried to use it, bleeped at her. A woman's voice calmly informed her that all circuits were busy. "Perfect," she said grimly and slammed down the receiver.

I wanna wish you a Merry Christmas from the bottom of my heart . . . The lyrics tumbled over in her mind, though the music had long since faded. "Right. A Merry Christmas. Fat chance!"

As firelight played upon the walls and windows, she drew the curtains and dragged her blankets from the bedroom. She'd be warmer close to the fire and could handle a night on the hide-a-bed. In the morning she'd call a cab to drive her to the airport, but for now she needed to sleep. Riley took up his post at the door and refused to budge. He stared at the oak panels as if he could see through the hardwood and Annie decided her dog was a definite head case. "It's warmer over here," she said and was rewarded with a disquieting "woof," the kind of noise Riley made whenever he was confused.

"Okay, okay, so have it your way." Settling under her down comforter, she closed her eyes and started to drift off. She could still hear José Feliciano's voice in her mind, but there was something else, something different—a tiny, whimpering cry over the sound of Riley's whine. No, she was imagining things, only the shriek of the wind, tick of the clock, and . . . there it was again. A sharp cry.

Heart racing, she tossed off the covers and ran to the front door where Riley was whining and scratching. "What is it?" she asked, yanking open the door. A blast of ice-cold wind tore through the door. The fire burned bright from the added air. Riley bounded onto the front porch where a basket covered with a blanket was waiting. From beneath the pink coverlet came the distinctive wail of an infant.

"What in the name of Mary . . ." Leaning down, Annie lifted the blanket and found a red-faced baby, fists clenched near its face, tears streaming from its eyes, lying on a tiny mattress. "Dear God in heaven." Annie snatched the basket and, looking around the yard for any sign of whoever had left the child on her stoop, she drew baby, basket, and blankets into the house. "Who are you?" she asked as she placed the bundle on her table and lifted the tiny child from its nest.

With a shock of blond hair and eyes that appeared blue in the dim light, the baby screamed.

"Dear God, how did you get here?" Annie asked in awe. She immediately lost her heart to this tiny little person. "Hey, hey, it's all right. Shhh." *Who* would leave a baby on the porch in the middle of this storm? What kind of idiot would . . . Still clutching the baby, she ran to the window and peered outside, searching the powdery drifts for signs of footprints, or any other hint that someone had been nearby.

Riley leaped and barked, eyeing the baby jealously.

"Stop it!" Annie commanded, holding the child against her and swaying side to side as if she were listening to some quiet lullaby that played only in her head. She squinted into the night and felt a shiver of fear slide down her spine. Was the person who left the baby lurking in the woods, perhaps watching her as she peered through the curtains?

Swallowing back her fear, she stepped away from the window and closer to the warmth of the fire.

The baby, a girl if the pink snowsuit could be believed, quieted and her little eyes closed. Head nestled against Annie's breast, she made soft little whimpers and her tiny lips moved as if she were sucking in her dreams. Again Annie asked, "Who are you?" as she carried the basket closer to the fire to peer into the interior.

A wide red ribbon was wound through the wicker and several cans of dry formula were tucked in a corner with a small package of disposable diapers. Six cloth diapers, a bottle, two pacifiers, one change of clothes, and a card that simply read, "For you, Annie," were crammed into a small diaper bag hidden beneath a couple of receiving blankets and a heavier quilt. Everything a woman would need to start mothering.

Including a baby.

"I can't believe this," Annie whispered as again she walked to the window where she shoved aside the curtains and stared into an inky darkness broken only by the continuing fall of snowflakes. The moon and stars were covered by thick, snow-laden clouds, and all the electrical lights in the vicinity were out.

Annie picked up the phone again and heard the same message she'd heard earlier. "Great," she muttered.

As the wind raged and the snow fell in thick, heavy flakes, she realized that unless she wanted to brave the frigid weather and hike to the neighbor's house, she and this baby were alone. Completely cut off from civilization.

"I guess you're stuck with me," she said and worried about the baby's mother. Who was she? Had she left the child unattended on the stoop? What kind of mother was she? Or had the baby been kidnapped and dropped off? But by whom?

For you, Annie.

The questions chasing after each other in endless circles raced through her mind. She placed a soft kiss on the infant's downy blond curls and lay down on the couch, where she held the child in the warmth of her comforter. "I'll keep you safe tonight," she promised, bonding so quickly with the infant that she knew she was going to lose her heart. "Riley will keep watch."

The dog, hearing his name, woofed softly and positioned himself in front of the door, as if he truly were guarding them both. Annie closed her eyes and wondered when she woke up in the morning, if she'd be alone and discover that this was all just part of a wonderful dream.

Chapter Two

"Is this an emergency?" a disinterested voice asked on the other end of the line.

"Yes, no . . . I mean it's not life or death," Annie said, frustrated that after finally getting through to the sheriff's department she was stymied. "As I said, a baby was left on my porch last night and—"

"Who does the child belong to?"

"That's what I'm trying to find out." Annie glanced at the basket—and at Carol, the name she'd given the child upon awaking this morning and discovering last night's storm wasn't a nightmare, nor was the basket part of a dream.

"Are you injured?"

"No, but—"

"Is the baby healthy?"

"As far as I can tell, but her parents are probably sick with worry—"

"Look, lady, we've got elderly people without any heat, cars piling up on the freeways, and people stranded in their vehicles. Everyone here is pulling double shifts."

"I know, but I'm concerned that—"

"You can come down to the station and fill out a report or we can send an officer when one's available."

"Do that," Annie said as she rattled off her address. A part of her felt pure elation that she had more time alone with the infant and another part of her was filled with dread that she'd become too attached to someone else's baby.

"Deputy Kemp will stop by and I'll put calls into the local hospitals to see if a baby is missing. I'll also see that social services gets a copy of this message. A social worker or nurse will probably contact you in the next couple of days."

"Thank you."

"As I said, an officer will stop by as soon as he can, but I wouldn't hold my breath. It could be a day or two. We're shorthanded down here with all the accidents and power outages. He'll call you."

"Thanks."

Annie hung up and sighed loudly. The frigid northern Willamette Valley was paralyzed. Sanding trucks and snowplows couldn't keep up with the fifteen-inch accumulation and still the snow kept falling. Annie had no means of communication except for the phone and her driveway, steep on a normal day, was impassable. She was lucky in that she had plenty of food and a fire on which she could cook. She'd even managed to heat Carol's bottle in a pan of water she had warmed on the grate.

She'd been awakened in the middle of the night when the baby had stirred and fussed. It took a while, but she'd added water to the dry formula she'd mixed in the bottle, then waited as it heated. The baby had quieted instantly upon being fed and Annie had hummed Christmas carols to the child as she suckled hungrily. "You're so precious," she'd murmured and the baby had cooed. She couldn't imagine giving her up. But she would have to. Somewhere little Carol probably had a mother and father who were missing her.

She fingered the note again, turning it over and studying the single white page decorated with a stenciled sprig of holly. Who had sent her the baby and cryptic message? Obviously someone who knew her and knew where she lived. Someone who trusted her with this baby. But who?

Was the child unwanted? Kidnapped? Stolen from a hospital? Taken from her cradle as her parents slept? Part of a divorce dispute? Her head thundered with the questions that plagued her over and over again.

She'd called the airport and found that Portland International was closed, all flights grounded. She'd tried to reach her brother in

Atlanta, but all outside circuits had been busy and she figured Joel would eventually call her.

"So it looks like it's just going to be you and me," she told the infant as she changed her diaper and sprinkled her soft skin with baby powder. "You can have a bottle and I'll open a can of chili."

The child yawned and stretched, arching her little back and blinking those incredible crystal-blue eyes. "You're a cherub, that's what you are," Annie teased. She let her worries drift away and concentrated on keeping the fire stoked, the baby dry, clean, and fed, and allowing Riley outside where the snow reached his belly and clung to his whiskers.

Late in the afternoon while Carol was napping in her basket, Annie checked on the horses, then poured herself a cup of coffee and started writing notes to herself about the baby. The infant was less than a month old, Caucasian, with no identifying marks—no birthmarks or moles or scars—in good health. So who was she?

Though she tried to suppress it, an idea that the child might have been abandoned—legitimately abandoned—kept crossing her mind. Could it be possible? The note was addressed to her so . . . But why would someone who so obviously cared about the infant leave her in freezing weather? No, that didn't make sense—

"Stop it, McFarlane," she growled at herself as Riley lifted his head and stared at the door. He barked sharply, then jumped to his feet. "What is it?"

Bam! Bam! Bam!

Riley started barking like crazy as the person on the other side of the door pounded so hard that the old oak panels seemed to jump.

"Hush!" Annie hurried to the door. "Who is it?" she yelled through the panels, then smoothed away the condensation on the narrow window flanking the door so she could see outside.

She nearly gasped when she saw the man, a very big man—six feet two or three, unless she missed her guess. His face was flushed, his gaze intense, his long arms folded firmly across his chest.

Liam O'Shaughnessy. In the flesh.

"Oh, no—" she whispered and her stomach did a slow, sensual roll. Liam was the one man of all of Nola's suitors that Annie found sexy—too sexy.

And right now he was livid, his face red with fury—or the bite of the winter air. Blond hair, damp from melting snowflakes, was tousled in the wind. Wearing a suede jacket, jeans, and boots covered in snow, he was poised to pound on the door again when he caught sight of her in the window. His eyes, when they met hers, were as blue as an arctic sea and just as violent.

"Help me," she said under her breath.

Nervously, she licked her lips. Never in her life had she faced such a wrathful male. His jaw was square and set, his blond eyebrows drawn into a single unforgiving line. Power, rage, and determination radiated from him in cold, hard waves.

"Open the damned door or I'll break it down," he yelled as the wind keened around him and caused the snow-laden boughs of the fir trees near the porch to sway in a slow, macabre dance. "Annie McFarlane—do you hear me?"

Loud and clear, she thought, and swallowing against a mounting sensation of dread, she yanked on the door handle. Without waiting for a word of invitation, he stepped inside.

"Where is she?" he demanded, stomping snow from his boots.

"Who?"

"Your sister!"

"Nola?" Annie asked, remembering that he'd once been her sister's lover, but only for a little while, or so Nola had confided. Their brief affair had ended abruptly and badly. Nola had been heartbroken, but then she'd been heartbroken half a dozen times because she always fell for the wrong kind of guy.

"Nola isn't here."

He frowned, snow melting on the shoulders of his rawhide jacket as well as in his hair.

"What do you want with her? I thought you broke up—"

"There was nothing to break," he said swiftly. "But, it appears she and I have a lot to discuss."

"You do?" Why was he here, looking for her in the middle of this storm?

"So she isn't here, eh?" He seemed to doubt her and his restless gaze slid around the room, searching the shadowy nooks and crannies as if he expected to find Nola hiding nearby.

"No. I haven't seen her in months."

"Close relationship."

"It is—not that it's any of your business," she said, bristling at his condescending tone. "Now, was there something else you wanted?"

His eyes narrowed suspiciously. "Just to find your sister. She seems to have disappeared."

"No, she hasn't. She's just . . . well, she takes off for little mini-vacations every once in a while."

"Mini-vacations?" His laugh was hollow and the corners of his mouth didn't so much as lift. "I'm willing to bet there's more to it this time."

"I doubt it."

"Then where is she?" His nostrils flared slightly. "Where does she go on these—what did you call them?—mini-vacations. That's rich."

"Look, I don't have any idea. Nola sometimes just takes off, not that it's any business of yours."

He snorted. "It's my business, all right."

"Sometimes Nola goes to the beach or the mountains—"

"Or Timbuktu, if she's smart." He wiped a big hand over his face as if he were dead tired. "If you want to know the truth, I really don't give a damn about Nola."

"But you want to find her?"

"*Have to* is more like it." He raked the interior of the cabin with his predatory gaze once more. "Her beautiful carcass could rot in hell for all I care."

That did it. Annie didn't need to take insults from him, or any other man, for that matter. "I think you should leave."

"I will. Once I get some answers."

"I don't have any—"

Carol coughed softly and O'Shaughnessy's head snapped around. Without a word he crossed the living room, tracking snow and staring down at the baby as if he were seeing Jesus in the manger.

"Yours?" he asked, but the tone of his voice was skeptical.

She shook her head automatically. There was no reason to lie, though she felt a wave of maternal protectiveness come over her. "I—I found her."

"What?" He touched Carol's crown with one long finger. The

caress was so tender, his expression so awestruck, that Annie stupidly felt the heat of unshed tears behind her eyes. "Found her? Where?"

"On the front porch. Last night."

He looked up, pinning her with that intense, laser-blue gaze. "Someone left her?"

"Yes. I guess."

"Who?"

"I don't know."

"Nola." He scowled and picked up the basket. "Figures."

"You think my sister brought a baby here?" Annie laughed at the notion.

"Not just any baby," he said, his expression turning dark. "Her baby. And mine."

"What?" she gasped.

"You heard me."

"But . . . Oh, God." He couldn't be serious, but she'd never seen a man so determined in all her life. He glanced down at the beribboned basket. A muscle worked in his jaw and when he looked up again, the glare he shot Annie could have melted steel. "Listen, O'Shaughnessy, I don't know what you're talking about, what you're saying. I—you—we don't have any idea if Nola did this."

"Sure we do."

"Nola's never been pregnant."

"Give me a break."

"Really. I know my sister and I'm sure . . ." Her words faded away. What did she really know about Nola? When was the last time they'd talked besides a quick chat on the phone? The last time Annie had seen Nola had been months ago.

"You're sure of what?" he spat out.

"She would have told me about a baby." Or would she have? Nola knew how much Annie had wanted a child, how crushed and forlorn she'd been after each miscarriage . . . was it possible?

For you, Annie. Sweet Jesus, was the note in Nola's loopy handwriting? Her knees gave way and she propped herself against the back of the couch. As if he'd read her thoughts, he nodded grimly and reached for the basket.

No! "Wait a minute—" But he was already tucking the wicker holder under one strong arm.

She was frantic. He intended to take the baby away! Oh, God, he couldn't. Not now, not yet, not after Annie had already lost her heart to the little blond cherub.

"O'Shaughnessy, you can't do this."

"Sure I can." His face was a mask of sheer determination. "If you hear from Nola, tell her I'm looking for her, that we need to talk."

"No! You can't. I—I mean—" She threw herself across the room and placed her body squarely between him and the door. Fear and pain clawed at her soul at the thought of losing her precious little baby. "Don't leave yet."

"It's time. Give Nola the message."

"But the baby. You can't just take her away and—"

"I'm her father."

"But I don't know that. In fact, I don't know anything about you or the baby or—" Oh, God. In such a short time she'd come to think of the baby as her own even though the notion was impossible.

"Look, Annie, I won't hold you accountable as long as you don't give me any trouble, but tell Nola this isn't over. When I find her—"

"What? You'll what?" Her heart was racing, her head ached, and she knew she'd never let him take the child. She reached for the basket, brushing his sleeve with her hand. "You . . . you can't just barge in here and take the baby and leave."

"Can't I?"

"No!"

His face was etched in stone, his countenance without a grain of remorse. Without much effort he sidestepped her, brushed her body aside, and reached for the doorknob with his free hand. "Watch me."

Chapter Three

"You're not going anywhere with that baby, O'Shaughnessy."
Annie wasn't letting the baby out of her sight. Not without a fight.
She squeezed between him and the door again. Riley, the scruff of
his neck standing on end, growled a low, fierce agreement. "How
do I know she's yours?"

"She's mine, all right. Just ask your sister."

Annie glared up at him and felt the heat of his gaze, the raw
masculine intensity of this giant of a man, but she wasn't going to
back down. Not to him. Not to anyone. He seemed to think that
Nola was really Carol's mother. But it couldn't be . . . or could it?
Was it possible? Who else would know that she desperately wanted
a baby, that she would care for an infant as if it were her own,
that in her heart of hearts, she would love the child forever? "Now
why don't you back up a minute, okay? You're trying to convince
me that you and Nola—who, as I heard it, only dated you a short
while—that you had a baby together."

"Looks like it." Blond eyebrows slammed together and his jaw
was hard as granite. But Annie wasn't going to let him buffalo
her.

"Why didn't I hear anything about it?" she demanded.

"Why didn't I?"

"What?" She was having trouble keeping up with all the
twists and turns in the conversation.

"You know your sister. Figure it out. Just like her to try and
hide the kid here." He started to pull on the doorknob, but Annie

pressed her back against the hard panels and put all her weight into holding the door closed. "Get out of the way."

"No! You just stop right there. I don't know that this baby has any connection to Nola."

"Sure."

"I *am* sure," she said, her anger elevating with her voice. "This child"—she jabbed at the basket swinging from his right arm with her finger—"was left on my doorstep in the middle of a storm and then you . . . you—how did you get here?"

"It was tricky. I have four-wheel drive," he conceded. "And a lot of sheer grit."

That much was true. She didn't know much about him, but she believed that with his determination he could literally move mountains.

"Just listen for a second," he insisted, and she notched her chin up an inch. "I thought you knew all about her pregnancy."

"I haven't seen her in months. She was . . . busy with something, something she wouldn't talk about."

A trace of doubt darkened his gaze. A musky scent of aftershave mingled with the smoky odor of burning wood. God, he was close. "But you knew Nola was going to have a baby."

Shaking her head, Annie sighed and rammed fingers of frustration through her hair. "Nola never said a word. For all I know, you could be lying."

"I *don't* lie."

"No, you just storm into a person's house and take what you want."

A muscle jumped in his jaw and every muscle in his body seemed tense, ready to unleash. His words were measured. "I don't know why Nola left the kid here, but—"

"You don't even know *if* she left the baby here."

He hesitated, his lips pursing in vexation. His gaze, icy-blue and condemning, narrowed on her. Obviously he was trying to size her up, to determine how much she really knew.

Annie swallowed hard and tried to ignore the rapid beating of her heart. "Didn't . . . didn't you say you never *talked* to Nola?" she pressed. He was so close that the rawhide of his jacket brushed against her breast. "How do you know that this baby is hers—or yours, for that matter?"

"Who else's?"

"I don't know, but until I do, the baby stays."

His smile had all the warmth of the arctic sea and yet she had the fleeting thought that he was a hot-blooded man. Passionate. Bold. Fierce one second, tender the next. *"You're* going to stop me from taking her?" That particular thought seemed to amuse him.

"Damned straight."

"You're half my size."

"I—I don't think this is a matter of physical strength." She'd lose in a minute to a man who was hard and well-muscled, all sinew and bone. "But I won't give her up without a fight, O'Shaughnessy."

"It's a fight you're gonna lose."

"I don't think so." She tried to appear taller as she looked up at him and tossed her hair over her shoulders. "If I can't convince you, then I guess I'll just have to call the police. They already know about the baby, anyway. A deputy by the name of Kemp is supposed to come and take a statement from me after they check and find out if there are any missing infants in the area. He could be here any minute. So—why don't you and I just wait for him?" She folded her arms over her chest. "I'll even make the coffee."

"We don't need the police involved."

"They already are."

"Damn!" He shook his head. "That was a foolish move."

"It wasn't 'a move.' I just wanted to find out where she came from."

"Sure."

"I did."

"Doesn't matter. What's done is done." His muscles seemed to stiffen even more at the mention of the authorities and the lines of his face deepened. For some reason he didn't want the police involved and for the first time Annie felt a niggle of fear. Who was this man? What did she know about him other than he'd seen her sister a few times, dropped Nola when he'd gotten bored with her, then landed smack-dab in the middle of Annie's living room with some ridiculous story about Nola having a baby—*this* baby! None of it made any sense.

"Fine," he relented. Muttering something under his breath about headstrong women who didn't know when to back off, he crossed the short distance to the grouping of chairs and couch surrounding the fireplace and set the basket on the floor near a small table. Throughout it all, Carol slept peacefully.

Annie breathed a long sigh of relief. Now, at last, she was getting somewhere and, fool that she was, she felt that she didn't have anything to fear from Liam—well, other than the possibility that he might take the baby from her.

She settled onto one of the arms of the couch while he warmed the backs of his legs by the fire. "So, now, why don't you start over and tell me why you came here—you said something about looking for Nola."

His jaw slid to one side and Annie was struck again at how sexy he was when he was quiet and thoughtful. "That's right. I need to find your sister. I just found out a couple of days ago that she'd been pregnant and had a baby—presumably mine, considering the timing. Jake found birth records. No father was listed, but I'm sure that the kid's mine."

Her heart plummeted. Obviously he'd done his homework and she knew in an instant that her short-lived chance at motherhood was over. "Who—who is Jake?"

"A friend."

"Oh."

"He's also a private detective."

Great. She'd hoped his far-fetched story would prove wrong. "So you came here looking for Nola or information about her and just happened to stumble on the baby."

"Yep." He rubbed his jaw and avoided her gaze for a second, concentrating instead on the snow piling in the corners of the windowpanes. "There's another reason," he admitted.

"Which is?"

Leaning his hips against the side of the fireplace, he closed his eyes and pinched the bridge of his nose for a second as if he could ward off a headache. "Let's just say Nola and I have some unfinished business that doesn't involve the baby. I only found out about her"—he added as he cocked his head in the direction of the basket—"because Jake found out. I had no idea Nola was pregnant."

"She didn't tell you?" she asked, standing and walking to the basket to see that Carol was still sleeping.

"Nope."

"Why not?"

"Good question. One I can't wait to ask her, but let's just say that your sister and I aren't on the best of terms."

"Is that why you hired your friend?" What was Nola involved in? Normal, regular people didn't employ investigators—or even have their friends check up on old lovers. Or did they? Something was wrong here. Very, very wrong. He moved closer to her and she found herself so near this man she could barely breathe. The air in the little cottage seemed suddenly thick, the light through the windows way too dim.

"Nola lied. About a lot of things. Not just the baby."

"Such as?" Annie's heart was knocking, her breathing shallow as her gaze dropped from his to the contour of his lips, so bold and thin. Too much was happening, way too fast. She felt as if her life was spinning out of control.

"She set me up."

"For?"

He shrugged. "My guess is to get the blame off whoever she's protecting. She claimed she knew that before she left Belfry Construction, I was embezzling. One night, when she just happened to be driving by, she saw me go into the office. She concluded I'd gone to doctor the company books and was surprised by the security guard, so of course I killed him." He didn't elaborate, just stared at her with unforgiving eyes. "I didn't do it, Annie. I swear."

"But—but why would she lie?" Oh, God, what was he saying? Nola wouldn't . . . *couldn't* fabricate something so horrid. A man was dead. *Murdered* from the sound of it and Nola thought O'Shaughnessy was involved? "I—I think you'd better start from the beginning."

He did. In short, angry sentences he told her about his work, the projects he'd overseen, the discrepancy in the books, and Nola's suddenly recanted testimony that she'd known he was at the office that night. The problem was that he had been there, but when he'd left, Bill Arness was very much alive. Liam had thrown a wave to the old man as he'd stepped off the elevator and Bill had locked the door behind him. He finished there; he didn't tell her about being watched by the police, eventually hauled into jail, fingerprinted, and booked, only to have the charges dropped. Hell, what a nightmare.

Annie stared at him with disbelieving eyes. "On top of all this—which is damned incredible, let me tell you—you're sure that you're the baby's father and Nola's her mother?"

"I wouldn't put Nola in the same sentence with *mother*." O'Shaughnessy glanced down at the basket as Carol uttered a soft little coo. The hard line of his jaw softened slightly and a fleeting tenderness changed his expression, but only for a moment. In that instant Annie noticed the wet streaks in his hair where snow had melted and the stubble of a beard that turned his jaw to gold in the dim fireglow. As he unbuttoned his coat and rubbed kinks from the back of his neck, Annie was nearly undone.

She had to think, to buy some time and sort this all out. Since he was bound and determined to take the baby with him, she had to entice him to stay. At least for a while. "Would you like something? I've got a Thermos of instant coffee I made on the fire this afternoon. It's not gourmet by any means, but I can guarantee that it's hot."

"That would be great." He shrugged out of his jacket and tossed it over the back of the couch as Annie hurried to the kitchen, twisted the lid of the Thermos, and quickly poured two cups. Her hands were trembling slightly, not out of fear exactly, but because she was a bundle of nerves around this man.

"So tell me again about last night," he suggested as she handed him a steaming mug. His gaze kept wandering back to the basket where the baby slept.

Quickly, she repeated her story of finding the baby, the note, seeing no one, not even footprints leading away from the porch, nothing. As she spoke, he sipped from his cup and listened, not interrupting, just hearing her out. ". . . So this morning, once I could get through, I started making calls. Everyone from the sheriff's department to social services and the hospitals around here, but no one seems to know anything about her."

"I do."

"You think. You really don't know that Carol—"

"Carol?"

"I named her, okay? The point is that there's no way to be sure she's your daughter."

The baby, as if sensing the tension building in the small room, mewled a small, worried whimper.

"Oh, great. See what you've done?" Disregarding the fact that he was a good foot taller than she and, if he decided, could stop her from doing anything, Annie hurried to the basket, gently withdrew baby and blankets, and held the tiny body close to hers. "It's okay," she whispered into the baby's soft curls and realized that the blond hair and blue eyes of this little sprite were incredibly like those of the irate man standing before her.

The baby cried again and Annie all but forgot about Liam O'Shaughnessy with his outrageous stories and damned sexy gaze. "She's wet and hungry and doesn't need to deal with all this . . . this stress."

"She doesn't know what's going on."

"I think that makes three of us!" Annie felt him silently watching her as she changed Carol's diaper, then warmed her bottle in a pan of water that had been heated in the coals of the fire.

"Here we go," she said softly as she settled into the creaky bentwood rocker and, as she fed the baby, nudged the floor with her toe. For the first time since O'Shaughnessy had pounded against her door, there was peace. The wind raged outside, the panes of the windows rattled eerily and a branch thumped in an irregular tempo against the worn shingles of the roof, but inside the cottage was warm, dry, and cozy. Even O'Shaughnessy seemed to relax a little as he rested one huge shoulder against the mantel and, while finishing his coffee, surveyed his surroundings with suspicious eyes.

"Okay," Annie finally said once Carol had burped and fallen asleep against her shoulder. "Instead of arguing with each other, why don't we figure out what we're going to do?"

"You think you can trust me?" he asked, trying to read her expression.

"I don't have much choice, do I?"

That much was true. He was here and definitely in her face. She couldn't budge him if she tried. Annie McFarlane was a little thing, but what she lost in stature she made up for in spirit. He cradled his cup in his hands and tried not to feel like a heel for barging in on her, for destroying her peace of mind, for intending to take away the baby that already appeared to mean so much to her.

"Nope, you don't."

"Great. Just . . . great."

Firelight played in her red-brown hair. High cheekbones curved beneath eyes that shifted from green to gold. Arched eyebrows moved expressively as she spoke with as sexy a mouth as he'd ever seen. A sprinkling of light freckles spanned the bridge of her nose and her hazel eyes were always alive, quick to flare in anger or joy.

What he knew of her wasn't much. She was divorced, had moved from somewhere on the East Coast, saw her sister infrequently, and did some kind of secretarial or bookkeeping work.

"Come on, O'Shaughnessy," she prodded as she carefully placed Carol into the basket. "Why would Nola lie to you and about you? Did she just want to get you into trouble?"

"A good question." He wasn't quite ready to tell her that he'd spent several days in a jail cell because of Nola and her lies. If he confided in her now he was certain she'd be frightened or, worse yet, call the police. There was no telling what she might do. Maybe she'd accuse him of trespassing or kidnapping if he insisted upon taking Carol—*Carol?*—with him. Good God, he was already giving the baby the name she'd put on the kid.

She looked up to find him staring at her. "How'd you find me? Wait, let me guess. Your friend the detective, right?"

"Jake's pretty thorough."

"I don't like my privacy invaded."

"No one does," he admitted, "but then, I don't like being lied to about my kid." *Or lied about.* He finished his coffee and tossed the dregs into the fire. Sparks sputtered and the flames hissed in protest. "So why did Nola leave the baby here for you without so much as a word? It seems strange."

"I—I don't know."

She was lying. He could smell a lie a mile away.

"Sure you do."

"It's personal, okay?"

"So's my daughter."

She stopped cold, took in a long breath, and seemed to fight some inner battle as the baby began to snooze again. "I don't know what your relationship was with Nola," she said. "As close as my sister and I are, we don't share everything and she . . . she's been distant lately." Clearing her throat, she stepped over to the makeshift bassinet as if to reassure herself that the baby was still there. "I've been wrapped up in my own life, settling here, rebuilding, and I guess Nola and I kind of lost touch. The last time I called her apartment, a recording told me the number was disconnected. No one in the family—not even my brother or mother—has heard from her in a few weeks."

"Isn't that unusual?"

"For Nola?" A smile touched her lips and she shook her head, "Unfortunately, no."

God, this woman was gorgeous. Her eyes were round and bright, a gray-green that reminded him of a pine-scented forest hazy with soft morning fog.

"I've got to find her."

"Why? What good would it do?"

He considered that for a second. "First, I want sole custody of my child." He saw the disappointment in her features and felt suddenly like the scum of the earth. "And then there's the little matter of my innocence in Bill Arness's death. I want to talk to good old Nola and find out why she wanted to set me up. I've been cleared, sort of, though I think I'm still a—what do they call it when they don't want to say *suspect?*—a 'person of interest' in the case. I want to talk to Nola, find out why she lied about the break-in at Belfry and—" He jerked his head toward the basket.

"—The baby," she finished for him. "You know, O'Shaughnessy, you make it sound as if my sister's involved in some major criminal conspiracy."

As the fire hissed in the grate and the wind whistled through the trees outside, Liam leveled his disturbing blue eyes at her. "Your sister's in big trouble."

"With you."

"For starters. I think the D.A. might be interested as well."

"Well, if you think I can help you find her, you'd better think again. She's a free spirit who—"

"Is running for her life, if she's smart."

The baby let out a wail certain to wake up the dead in the next three counties.

"Oh, God." Annie jumped up as if she were catapulted by an invisible device, then carefully extracted the little girl from beneath her covers as if she were born to be this child's mother.

Liam couldn't hear what Annie was saying as she whispered softly and rocked gently, holding the child close to her breast. As if a fourteenth-century sorceress had cast a quieting spell, the infant instantly calmed.

It was damned amazing. Could he work this magic with the kid? Hell, no! Could Nola? At the thought of that particularly selfish woman, he frowned and plowed stiff, frustrated fingers through his hair. What was he going to do?

Carol—if that's what the kid's name was—sighed audibly and a smile tugged at the corners of Annie's mouth. For an instant Liam wondered what it would be like to kiss her, to press his mouth against those soft, pliant lips and . . . He gave himself a quick mental shake. What was he doing thinking of embracing her, believing her, wanting to trust her, for crying out loud?

He cleared his throat. "Look, Annie, the bottom line is this: You have my daughter. I want her. And I'll do anything—do you hear me?—*anything* to gain custody of her."

"Then you'll have to fight me," Annie said, her chin lifting defiantly and her back stiffening. "You don't have any proof that Carol is yours."

She tried to look so damned brave as she held the child and pinned him with those furious hazel eyes. For a second his heart turned over for her. She obviously cared about the baby very much. No matter what her true motives were, she had strong ties to the child, probably a helluva lot stronger than Nola's. Nonetheless he was the kid's father and as such he had rights, rights he intended to invoke.

"She's mine, all right."

"Then you won't be adverse to a paternity test."

"For the love of Mike. It's not like you could take a maternity test, right?"

"I've already talked to the powers that be. I'm not claiming to be the baby's mother."

"Fine. No problem. I'll take any damned test." He glanced out the window and scowled at the snow piling over his footsteps. Though he'd been inside less than an hour, the marks made by his boots were nearly obscured. In all truth, there was a problem, a big one. His four-wheel drive rig had barely made it to the end of the driveway because of the packed snow and ice on the roads. Without chains, his wheels had slipped and spun, nearly landing him in the ditch. Though sanding crews had been working around the clock, the accumulation of snow and freezing temperatures had reduced the snow pack to ice. As it was, driving any distance was out of the question, especially with an infant and no safety car seat.

Annie cast him irritated looks as she attended to the baby. Finally, when the child's eyelids had drooped again, Annie carefully placed Carol into the basket. She tucked a blanket gently around the baby and smiled when the infant moved her tiny lips in a sucking motion. "She's so adorable," Annie said. "If she is your child, Mr. O'Shaughnessy, she's darned near perfect, and you're one very lucky man."

He couldn't agree more as he stared at the tiny bit of flesh that sighed softly in a swaddle of pink blankets. An unaccustomed lump filled his throat. He'd never expected any kind of emotional attachment to the baby, not like this. Sure, he'd felt obligated to take care of the kid—duty-bound to see that his offspring was financially and emotionally supported. He planned on hiring a full-time nanny to start with and then, as the kid grew, employ the best tutors, coaches, and teachers that money could buy. If he had to, he had supposed, he could even get married and provide a mother of sorts. He glanced at Annie and felt a jab of guilt, though he didn't know why.

"However," Annie said, planting her hands on her hips, "if the blood tests prove that you're not her father, O'Shaughnessy, then you'll have a helluva lot of explaining to do. Not only to me, but to the police."

Chapter Four

The woman had him. No doubt about it. The last thing he wanted to do was get the police involved. She was smart, this sister of Nola's, and the firelight dancing in her angry green eyes made him think dangerous thoughts—of champagne, candlelight, and making love for hours.

"I've already told you I don't want to call the authorities. Not until I understand what's going on."

She lifted a finely sculpted eyebrow and desire, often his worst enemy, started swimming in his bloodstream. "And I've already told you," she said, poking a finger at his broad expanse of chest, "that I've talked to the police about the baby. I've got nothing to hide, so why don't you level with me?"

"I am."

Her hair shone red-gold in the dying embers of the fire. "I don't think so." Resolutely she crossed her arms under her chest, inadvertently lifting her breasts and causing Liam's mind to wander ever further into that dangerous and erotic territory. He couldn't seem to think straight when she was around; his purpose, once so honed and defined, became cloudy.

"I want you to help me find Nola."

"Why?"

"I need to talk to her and find out why she lied about the baby, why she lied about the break-in, why the hell she wanted to set me up for murder."

"If she did."

"She did, all right." Liam had no doubts. None whatsoever

when it came to Nola Prescott. Annie was another story altogether. Her forehead wrinkled in concentration, but she didn't budge and he figured he should back off, at least a little. "Think about it and I'll do something about the heat in here, okay?" He didn't bother waiting for an answer, but threw on his jacket and walked outside. Firewood was already cut and stacked on the back porch, so he hauled in several baskets of fir and oak, restocking the dwindling pile on the hearth and adding more chunks to the fire.

Annie busied herself with the baby, feeding her, changing her, burping her, rocking her, cooing to her, and looking for all the world as if she were born to be a mother. *Idiot,* he told himself. *Don't be fooled. She and that sister of hers share the same blood.*

The phone jangled and they both jumped. Annie froze and just stared at the instrument, but Liam was quick and snagged the receiver before the person on the other end had a chance to hang up. "Hello?"

"Hello? Who is this?" a male voice demanded. Whoever the hell he was, he didn't sound happy. "I'm calling Annie McFarlane."

"Just a sec—"

Liam handed the phone to Annie and, without a word, took the baby. It was incredible how natural it felt to hold the kid, even though his hands were larger than the baby's head. Little Carol gurgled, but didn't protest as Annie, eyes riveted on him, placed the receiver to her ear.

"Hello?"

"Annie?" It was Joel, her brother. "For crying out loud, who was that?"

"A—a friend." Why she thought she had to protect O'Shaughnessy she didn't know, but somehow she thought it best not to tell her brother about his wild story and her plight.

"A *friend?* I don't know whether to be relieved or worried. I'm glad you're not pining over David, but from what the news here says, you're in the middle of one helluva storm. I've been trying to get through for hours."

"Me, too," she said and since she didn't offer any further explanation about O'Shaughnessy, Joel didn't pry.

"So you're okay?"

"All things considered." She watched Liam with the baby and

her heart did a silly little leap. He was so big and the infant was so tiny, yet she sensed that this man who exuded such raw animal passion and fury would protect this child with his very life.

"Well, Merry Christmas."

"You, too."

"We all miss you."

"I know, but there's no way I can get to the airport." *Nor can I leave Carol.* At that particular thought her heart twisted painfully. How could she ever give up the baby?

"Yeah, I know." Joel sounded disappointed and they talked for a little while before she had the nerve to bring up their sister.

"You know, I haven't seen her since—geez, I can't remember when," Joel admitted, though there was some hesitation in his voice, a nervous edge that Annie hadn't heard earlier. "But then I didn't really expect to hear from her over the holidays. You know how it is with Nola—hit or miss. This year must be a miss."

"You don't have any idea where she is?"

"Nope. She did call, oh, maybe a month or so ago and said she was leaving Seattle, but that was it. No plans. No forwarding address. No damned idea where she'd end up. I can't imagine it, myself, but then I've got a wife and kids to consider." Annie could almost see her brother shaking his head at the folly that was his younger sister.

She noticed O'Shaughnessy studying her and turned her back, wrapping the telephone extension around herself and avoiding his probing gaze as she asked, "Do you know if she's been in any kind of trouble?"

"Nola? Always."

"No, no. I mean serious trouble."

There was a pause. "Such as?"

"Is it possible that she was pregnant?"

Another moment's hesitation and Annie knew the truth. "Joel?" Annie's heart was thundering, her head pounding, her hands suddenly ice-cold.

Her brother cleared his throat, then swore roundly. "I'm sorry, Annie, but Nola didn't want you to know." Annie closed her eyes and sagged against the kitchen counter. So it was true. At least part of O'Shaughnessy's story held up. Joel sighed. "Nola knew how badly you wanted a baby and with your miscarriages and the divorce and all, she thought—and for once I agreed with her—that you should be kept in the dark."

So the baby really was Nola's. "Did she say who the father was?" Annie's voice was barely a whisper.

"Nah. Some guy who was in and out of her life in a heartbeat. A real louse. She decided that the best thing to do was to . . . well, to terminate."

"No!"

"Annie, there's nothing you can do now. That was months ago. I tried to talk her into giving the kid up for adoption but she claimed she couldn't live with herself if she knew she had a baby out there somewhere with someone she didn't know raising it . . . I figured it was her decision."

"When was this?"

"Seven—maybe eight months ago. Yeah, in the spring. End of March or early April, I think. You'd just confirmed that David was about to be a father—the timing was all wrong."

"When . . . when was she due?"

"What does it matter?"

"When, damn it!"

"About now, I guess. No . . . wait. A few weeks ago, I suppose. I never asked her what happened. In fact, we never really talked again. I just assumed she did what she had to do and got on with her life."

"Did she say who the father was?"

"No."

"Just the louse."

She rotated out of the phone line coils in time to notice Liam wince.

"Right."

"Did she date anyone else?"

"I can't remember. There was the guy with the Irish name—the father, I think."

"O'Shaughnessy?"

"Right. That's the bastard."

"No one else?"

"What does it matter, for crying out loud."

"It matters, okay?"

"Well, let me think." He sighed audibly. "I can't think of anyone. Polly—" His voice trailed as he asked his wife the same question and there was some discussion. "Annie? Polly thinks there was another guy. Somebody named Tyson or Taylor or what?" Again his voice faded and Annie's heart nearly stopped beating. Liam was studying her so hard she could hardly breathe. "Yeah, that's right. Polly seems to think the guy's name was Talbott."

"Peter Talbott?" Annie said and Liam's expression became absolutely murderous.

"Yeah, that's the guy."

"Good, Joel. Thanks."

"Are you okay?"

"Right as rain," she lied. The room began to swim. Annie's throat was dry. She brought up his kids and, for the moment, Joel's interest was diverted. Liam, however, seemed about to explode. His hands balled into angry fists and his eyes were dark as the night.

"Look, I'll see you after the first of the year," Joel finally said before hanging up. "And if I hear from Nola, I'll tell her you need to speak to her."

"Do that." She unwound the cord from her body and let the receiver fall back into its cradle. "So," she said in a voice she didn't recognize as her own. "It looks like part of your story is true. Joel knew about the pregnancy."

Liam's jaw tightened perceptively. "All of my 'story,' as you call it, is true, Annie. You've just got to face it." Carol was sleeping in his arms and Annie's heartstrings pulled as she saw the baby move her lips. Golden eyelashes fluttered for a second, then drooped over crystal-blue eyes.

"Here—let me put her down."

She took Carol from his arms and in the transfer of the baby, they touched, fingers twining for a second, arms brushing. As she placed the baby in her basket, Liam rubbed the back of his neck nervously, then shoved the curtains aside to view the relentlessly falling snow. He had to get out of the cozy little cabin with its built-in family. Not only was there a baby who had already wormed her way into his heart, but the woman who wanted to be the kid's mother had managed to get under his skin as well. It was too close—too comfortable—too damned domestic.

"So Talbott's the guy."

"Polly, my sister-in-law, seems to think Nola was involved with him."

"Figures," he said, conjuring up Talbott's face. Short and wiry, with blond hair, tinted contacts, and freckles, Pete was as ambitious as he was dogged. But Joel hadn't thought him a crook. Well, live and learn. "When's this gonna end?" he growled, staring through the frozen windowpanes. Anxious for a breath of fresh air and a chance to clear his head, he snatched up his jacket and rammed his arms through the sleeves. Snagging the wood basket from the hearth, he was out the door in an instant. Outside, the wind keened through the trees. Snow and ice pelted his face and bare head. He shoved gloves over his hands and wished he'd never given up smoking. A cigarette would help. Confronting Nola and Talbott would be even better.

What the hell was he going to do about the situation here? When he'd first stepped inside the cabin he'd planned to interrogate Annie, find out everything he could about Nola, grab his kid, and leave. Then he'd come face-to-face with the woman and damn it, she'd found a way to blast past his defenses, to put him off guard, to make him challenge everything he'd so fervently believed.

"Hell, what a mess!" He piled wood in the basket and headed back inside. As he entered, a rush of icy wind ruffled the curtains and caused flames to roar in the grate. Annie didn't say a word and he dumped the wood, then stormed outside, needing the exercise, having to find a way to expend some restless energy, wanting to grab hold of his equilibrium again.

Annie heated water for coffee and more formula and tried not to watch the door, waiting for O'Shaughnessy. Somehow she had to get away from him, to think clearly. From the moment he'd barged into her life, she'd been out of control, not knowing what to do. She was certain that as soon as the storm lifted, he'd be gone. With Carol. Her heart broke at the thought, for though she told herself she was being foolish and only asking for trouble, she'd begun to think of the baby as hers. Hadn't the card said as much? *For you, Annie.* What a joke. Nobody gave a baby away. Not even Nola.

But the baby was here.

If Carol were truly Nola's child and if Nola had left the baby on Annie's doorstep—presumably to raise, at least for a while— then didn't she have some rights? At least as an aunt, and at most as the guardian of choice. *But what if the baby is really O'Shaughnessy's? What then? What kind of rights do you think you'll have if he's truly Carol's biological father? Face it, Annie, right now Liam O'Shaughnessy holds all the cards.*

He shouldered open the door, shut it behind him, and dropped a final basket of wood near the hearth. "That should get you through 'til morning."

"*Me* through? What about you?"

"I won't be staying."

Dear God, he hadn't changed his mind. He was leaving and taking Carol with him. Panic gripped her heart. "You don't have to go—"

"Don't worry, Annie," he said, his lips barely moving, his eyes dark with the night. "I won't rip her away from you. At least not tonight."

"Noble of you."

He snorted. "Nobility? Nah. I'm just looking out for my best interests. It's sub-zero outside and I don't think I could move the Jeep even if I tried. The kid's better off here, where it's warm."

So he did have a heart, after all. She should have been surprised, but wasn't. His gaze held hers for a breath-stopping second and she read sweet seduction in his eyes. Her blood thundered and she looked away, but not before the message was passed and she knew that he, too, wondered what it would feel like to kiss. Aside from the baby, they were alone. Cut off from civilization by the storm. One man. One woman. She swallowed hard.

"Carol will be safe here."

"I know." He dusted his gloved hands and reached for the door. "But I'll be right outside, so don't get any funny ideas about taking off."

"Outside?" She glanced at the windows and the icy glaze that covered the glass. "But it's freezing . . ."

"I don't think it would be a good idea if I slept in here, do you?"

The thought was horrifyingly seductive. "No—no—I, um . . . no, that wouldn't work," she admitted in a voice she didn't recognize. Sleeping in the same little house as O'Shaughnessy. Oh,

God. She swallowed even though her mouth was dry as sandpaper.

"Yeah. I didn't think so." He crouched at the fire, tossing in another couple of logs before prodding them with the poker that had been leaning against the warm stones. Annie tried not to stare at the way his faded jeans stretched across his buttocks, or at the dip in his waistband where the denim pulled away from the hem of his jacket. However, her gaze seemed to have a mind of its own when it came to this man. Annie licked her lips and dragged her gaze back to the baby.

He dusted his hands together. "That should do it for a while. If it dies down—"

"I can handle it," she snapped.

His smile was downright sexy. "I know. Otherwise I wouldn't leave. I'll see ya in the morning." For the first time she noticed the lines around his eyes. "Think about everything I've said."

"I will." She didn't know whether she was relieved or disappointed. Relieved—she should definitely be relieved.

His smile wasn't filled with warmth. "I won't be far."

"But the storm—"

"Don't worry about me, Annie," he said, one side of his mouth lifting cynically. "I learned a long time ago how to take care of myself." He was out the door and Annie watched at the window where, despite the freezing temperatures and falling snow, he settled into his Jeep.

"Just go away. Take your incredible story and wild accusations and leave us alone," she muttered under her breath. But she couldn't help worrying about him just a little.

Chapter Five

"Come on, come on." Liam pressed the numbers from memory on his cellular phone, but the damned thing wouldn't work. He was too close to the hills or the signals were clogged because of the storm and the holidays. Whatever the reason, he couldn't reach Jake. "Hell." He clapped the cell shut and stared through the windshield as he tugged the edge of his sleeping bag more tightly around him. Nothing in this iced-over county was working.

And he needed to talk to Cranston, to report that he'd had a run-in with Nola's sister, found his kid, and suspected Peter Talbott of being the culprit in Bill Arness's murder. But he didn't want to use Annie's phone—not while she was in earshot.

Nola was involved. Up to her eyeballs. There was a reason she'd fingered him for a crime he didn't commit and it wasn't just vengeance because he'd broken up with her and unwittingly left her pregnant. Nope, it had something to do with Pete Talbott.

Liam glowered through the windshield. Ice and snow had begun to build over the glass, but he was able to see the windows of Annie's cabin, patches of golden light in an otherwise bleak and frigid night. Every once in a while a shadow would pass by the panes and he'd squint to catch another glimpse of Annie. His jaw clenched as he realized he was hoping to see her—waiting for her image to sweep past the window. Nola's sister. No good. Trouble. A woman to stay away from at all costs.

But he couldn't. Not just yet. His thoughts wandered into perilous territory again and he wondered what it would feel like to kiss her, to press his lips to hers, to run the tip of his tongue along that precocious seam of her lips, to reach beneath her sweater, let his fingers scale her ribs to touch her breasts and . . .

"Fool!" His jaw clenched and he pushed all kind thoughts of Annie out of his mind. So what if she was a package of warm innocence wrapped in a ribbon of fiery temper? Who cared if the stubborn angle of her chin emphasized the spark of determination of her green eyes? What did it matter that the sweep of her eyelashes brushed the tops of cheeks that dimpled in a sensual smile?

She was Nola's sister. Big-time trouble. The last woman in the world he should think about making love to. Besides, he had other things with which to occupy his mind, the first being to clear his name completely. Then he'd claim his daughter and then . . . then he'd deal with Annie. Just at the thought of her his blood heated and his cock started to swell.

"Down, boy," he muttered to the image glaring back at him in the rearview mirror. "That's one female who's off limits—way off. Remember it." But the eyes reflecting back at him didn't seem to be the least little bit convinced.

Jake Cranston wasn't a man who gave up easily, but this time he was more than ready to throw in the towel. Nola Prescott seemed to have vanished off the face of the earth. How could a woman disappear so quickly?

He'd checked with her friends and relatives, called people he knew who owed him favors on the police force and at the DMV, even spoken to the Social Security Administration, with no luck.

"Think, Cranston, think," he muttered under his breath as he walked from one end of his twelve-by-fifteen office to the other. It was a small cubicle crammed with files, a desk, and a computer that, tonight, was of no help whatsoever.

Not that it mattered. He'd done his part. Now it was up to Liam. He didn't doubt that O'Shaughnessy would handle the Nola Prescott situation his own way. But still he was puzzled. Where the hell was she?

It wasn't often anyone eluded him, but then he hadn't given up yet. Not really. Deep in his gut he felt that Liam still needed his help and he owed the man his life. Years ago O'Shaughnessy had been the first man on the scene of the hit and run. It had been his grit and brute strength that had helped pull Jake from the mangled truck seconds before it exploded in a conflagration that had lit up the cold winter night and singed the branches of the surrounding trees. The driver of the other car had never been caught, but Jake had discovered a friend for life in O'Shaughnessy.

Now the tables were turned. It was time for Jake to pay back a very big favor and he wouldn't quit until he did. Getting Liam out of jail had been a start. The next step was hunting down Nola Prescott, no matter that she'd gone to ground. He grunted and reached into the bottom drawer for his shot glass and a half-full bottle of rye whiskey. His personal favorite. He poured himself three fingers, tossed them back, and felt the familiar warmth blaze its way down his throat to his stomach. Wiping the back of his hand across his mouth, he felt a little better. Finding Ms. Prescott was only a matter of time.

Liam awoke with a start, his heart pounding crazily, the dream as vivid as if he were still locked away. The sound of metal against metal, keys clicking in locks, chains rattling—all receded with the dawn. He was in the Jeep in the middle of a damned forest. Would it never end? Cramped and cold, he rotated his neck until he felt a release and heard a series of pops. Now all he needed was coffee and lots of it.

Sunlight penetrated the stands of birch and fir, splintering in brilliant shards that pierced his eyes and did nothing to warm the frozen landscape. He shoved open the door and, boots crunching through the drifting snow, made his way to the cabin to see the kid again. And Annie. That woman was playing with his mind, whether she knew it or not.

He lifted a fist to pound on the door when it flew open and she stood on the other side of the threshold. Before he could enter she stepped onto the porch, the dog at her heels, then closed the door softly behind her. "Carol's asleep."

"So?"

"I don't want her disturbed." Her gloved hands were planted firmly on her hips and she stood in the doorway as if she intended to stop him from entering. Her determination was almost funny— tiny thing that she was.

"She's my daughter."

Dark eyebrows elevated as the mutt romped through the drifts, clumps of snow clinging to his hair. "Your fatherhood has yet to be determined."

"You still want a paternity test?"

"For starters."

"Not a problem."

Her eyes, so fierce, were suddenly a darker shade of hazel, more green than gold and not quite so certain. "Good," she said with more bravado than he expected. "I'll arrange it. When the roads are clear."

"Fair enough." She was bluffing. And scared. Of what? Him? He didn't think so.

"But for right now, we're not going to wake her up—she had a bad night." Annie hitched her chin toward the barn. "I've got to feed the horses. You can help."

"Can I?" He couldn't help baiting her.

"Yep." She didn't waste a second, but stepped off the porch and started breaking a trail in the knee-deep powder. The dog galloped in senseless circles before bounding up the ramp that led to a wide door on rollers. With all of her strength, Annie pushed. The thing didn't budge. Liam placed his hands above hers on the edge of the door. His body covered her as he put his weight into moving a door that was frozen closed.

"Great," she muttered and was close enough that the coffee on her breath tickled his nose, the back of her jacket rubbed up against the buttons of his, and her rump pressed against his upper thighs. Through the denim of his jeans he felt her heat and his damned cock responded, stiffening beneath his fly.

"It'll give." He ignored the scent of her perfume and the way his body was reacting to the proximity of hers. Again he threw his weight into the task and the ice gave way, rusty rollers screaming in protest, ice shattering as the door sped on its track. Annie tumbled forward and Liam's arms surrounded her, catching her before she slipped on the icy ramp.

"Whoa, darlin'," he said, surprised that an endearment had leapt so naturally to his lips.

"I'm . . . I'm okay." She twisted in his arms and her face was only inches from his, so near that he could see the sunlight playing in her eyes. His gut tightened and his mind spun to a future that would never exist, a time when she would be lying naked in his arms, bedsheets twined through her legs, moonlight playing upon her bare breasts. At the thought, his mouth was suddenly dry as a desert wind and he cleared his throat. Slowly, making sure she had her footing, he released her. Her gaze shifted to his lips for a second before she stepped into the musty interior of the barn and he followed with an erection that pressed hard against his jeans. Silently he cursed himself. Hadn't he spent the night convincing himself that Annie McFarlane was off-limits?

A soft nicker floated on air that smelled of dry hay, leather, and horse dung.

"Think I forgot you?" she said as she popped off the lid of a barrel of oats and, using an old coffee can, scooped up the grain that she poured into the mangers of three horses. Liquid eyes appraised him and large nostrils blew into the air as the animals buried their muzzles into the feed.

Annie reached into the pocket of her coat and, walking to a stack of hay bales piled into the corner, pulled out a small jack-knife, opened the blade, and sliced the twine holding the first bale together. She glanced over to Liam. "You can make yourself useful by tossing down a few more of these from the hayloft." She went to work on the second bale and he climbed up a metal ladder.

Within minutes he'd dropped twelve bales and stacked them next to the dwindling pile near the stalls. Annie forked hay into the mangers and when he attempted to take the pitchfork from her hands to do the job, he was rewarded with a look that would melt steel. "I can handle this," she said.

"I just thought that—"

"That I was a female and since you were here you'd take over and give me a break. Thanks but no thanks. If you want to help out, grab a bucket and get them fresh water." She bit the edge of her lip. "You'll have to go back to the house, though, and use the faucets in the kitchen. I drained all the outside pipes just before the storm hit. Just be careful and don't wake—"

"—The baby. Yeah, I know." He grabbed a pail from a nail on the wall and trudged back to the cabin. He'd never met so prickly a woman and yet she was trusting him to be alone with his child.

He checked the makeshift bassinet as the bucket was filling and couldn't help but smile. The baby was indeed cutting a few z's. Barely moving, a blanket tucked all the way to her chin, Carol was lying there with such pure innocence that the little lump of flesh grabbed hold of Liam. How could something so perfect, so beautiful, have been conceived by an act of cold passion and grown in a womb devoid of love?

Despite Annie's warning, he pulled one of his gloves off with his teeth and touched a golden curl with the tip of his finger. The baby sighed quietly and in that barest meeting of callouses and perfect, baby-soft skin he felt a connection that wrapped around the darkest reaches of his heart and tied in a knot that could never be undone. Somehow, some way, no matter what, he would take care of this child.

With more effort than he would have imagined, he turned his thoughts to filling the pail over and over again until each animal had water enough for the day and the trail in the snow between the barn and the cabin was packed solidly.

Annie hung up the pitchfork and rubbed each velvet-soft nose as the animals ate, mashing their teeth together loudly and snorting.

"These belong to you?" he asked as she threw a winter blanket over the bay's back.

"No. I just care for them. They come with the house and grounds. This guy is Hoss, then there's Little Joe," she said, pointing to a dapple gray, "and Adam, there, the sorrel gelding." At the mention of his name, Adam's ears flattened. "All named after characters on *Bonanza*."

"I got the connection."

"Yeah, great guys, but they could use a little exercise." With a glance to the window, she frowned. "I usually walk them later in the day, but they'll have to wait for anything more substantial, at least for a few more days." Her eyes found Liam's. "Like we all have to."

"I might be able to get the Jeep out today."

She swallowed hard. "And what then?"

"I find Nola."

"Just like that?" she asked skeptically as she snapped her fingers.

"It might take a little time, but I'll catch up with her."

"You make it sound like she's running from you."

"She is. She just doesn't realize how futile it is." He said it with a determination that made her shudder, as if he were stating an obvious fact.

Nervously, Annie rubbed the blaze running down Little Joe's nose, then wiped her hands on the front of her jeans before leaving the stall. Liam shouldn't be here. He was too male, too intense, too close. Emotions, conflicting and worrisome, battled within her. She was attracted to him, there was no doubt about it, but he was here for one reason and one reason only—his child. "I—I'd better check on the baby."

"She's fine."

"I'll see for myself—"

He grabbed her arm so quickly she gasped. Even through the denim of her jacket and sweater beneath, she felt the iron grip of his fingers, the hard strength of the man. "Be careful," he said through lips that barely moved.

"Of what? You?"

"Of getting too attached to the baby."

"Too late." Tossing her hair over her shoulders, she glared up at him. "I'm already attached to that little girl and you may as well know that you can't bully her away from me."

"She's not yours—"

"Or yours." She tried to pull away, to keep her distance from him, but he drew her closer to his body, close enough that she noticed the pores of his skin and the red-blond glimmer that gilded a jaw set in silent fury. "She's mine, all right."

Oh, God, was that her heart beating so furiously? His gaze dropped to her throat and she sensed her pulse quicken. She licked her lips, tried to back away and was suddenly lost as his lips found hers. She was trapped, her breath caught somewhere in her lungs, her knees turning weak as his arms surrounded her. She tried to protest, to tell him to go to hell, to back away and slap him hard across the jaw but instead she opened her mouth willingly, invitingly.

It had been so long, so damned long since a man had held her, kissed her, caused her blood to race.

But this is wrong. And dangerous. This is O'Shaughnessy. He only wants you so he can get close to the baby.

She wouldn't listen to that awful, nagging voice. No, right now, she just wanted to be held. While the world was snowbound and frigid, she was warm here in Liam's arms. She felt his tongue touch the tip of hers. A hot shiver of desire, wanton and needy, skittered down her spine. With a moan she sagged against him and his kiss deepened, his tongue searching and exploring, causing the world to spin.

He's only doing this to get close to Carol, to find Nola, to further his own interests. Wake up, Annie. He doesn't care one iota about you. He's using you.

"No!" She dragged her head from his, ignoring the desire still singing through her veins. Breathing unevenly, she stepped back. "I mean, I can't . . . I won't . . . Oh, for the love of . . . just . . . just leave, would you?"

"That's what you want?" His lips tugged into a cynical, amused smile that sent her temper into the stratosphere.

"Yes. Just go!"

His teeth flashed white against his skin in a cynical I-don't-believe-you-for-a-second grin and it was all she could do not to slap him. "As I said, I—I'd better check on Carol." She tore out of the barn, gulped big lungfuls of crisp winter air, and hurried along the broken path to the cabin. Riley, barking madly at a startled winter bird, sprinted ahead of her.

She kicked off her boots on the porch and threw open the door. "How could you?" she muttered, berating herself as she saw her reflection in the iced-over windows. "I thought you were a smart woman." She pulled off her gloves, threw them on the back of her couch, ripped off her jacket, and closed her eyes. "Fool. Damned silly fool of a female!" What was she thinking, kissing O'Shaughnessy? No, *wanting* to kiss him, to touch him, to feel his body lying on top of hers . . . "Oh, for the love of Mike. Stop it!"

Thunk! The door banged open. A frozen blast of wind swept into the room, causing the fire to spark and the curtains to flutter as Liam stepped inside, his boots dripping on an old braided rug.

"You don't take a hint very well, do you?" she accused as he latched the door and they were again alone, away from the world, one man, one woman, and a sleeping infant. Her heart skipped a beat.

"You weren't serious." His eyes, blue as an August sky, held hers.

She cleared her throat and prayed her voice would remain steady. "About you leaving?" Why did she feel he could read her mind? "Believe me, O'Shaughnessy, I've never been more serious in my life." She turned toward a mirror mounted near the kitchen door and grabbed a rubber band from her pocket with one hand while scraping her hair away from her face with the other. With a flip of her wrist she snapped the ponytail into place. "I think it would be best for all of us if you just opened the door and took off."

"Liar." He was across the room in an instant, standing behind her, strong arms wrapping firmly around her torso, splayed fingers against the underside of her breasts. "You don't want me to leave."

"You arrogant, self-serving, son of a . . . oooh."

His lips brushed against her nape. Warm and seductive, his breath wafted across her skin.

A nest of butterflies, long dormant, exploded in her stomach as his tongue traced the curve of her neck. "Don't lie to me, Annie. You want me as much as I want you."

Oh, Lord, he knew. Her body trembled at his touch and she hated herself for the weakness. Slowly he turned her into his embrace and as she stared into his eyes, he kissed her, long and hard, and with a desperation that cried out for more. She shouldn't do this, shouldn't let her body rule her mind, and yet as he sighed into her open mouth, she wrapped her arms around his neck, closed her eyes, and didn't argue as his hands found the hem of her sweater and his fingers skimmed the skin of her abdomen with feather-light touches that caused her breasts to ache and her mind to play with images of making love all night long.

"I—I can't," she said as his fingers traced her nipple through the silky fabric of her bra.

"Can't what?" he said, kissing the side of her neck and bending farther down as his hands caressed her breast.

I can't love you! her mind screamed, but she swallowed back the ridiculous words. "Do—do this—oooh."

He unhooked her bra deftly and scooped both her breasts into his palms.

"Liam, please—" she whispered, but her protest went unheeded and she closed her eyes against the wave of desire that rippled through her. Without hurry he kissed the flat of her abdomen, then moved ever upward, his tongue and lips and teeth touching her so intimately she thought she might die. "Liam," she whispered as he found her breast and began to suckle. Wet and warm, his mouth seemed to envelop her and all thoughts of stopping him vanished. Together they fell upon the worn couch and he pulled her sweater over her head before tossing away her bra and kissing her again.

"Sweet, sweet Annie. God, you're beautiful." He stared at her breasts for a heartbeat, touched them lightly, watched in fascination as her nipples tightened, then resumed his ministrations.

Desire pulsed through her blood, throbbing deep in her center, creating a core of desire that played games with her mind. The fire crackled and cast the room in a golden glow that vied with the sunlight slanting through icy windows as Liam kissed her.

Annie trembled and held him close, her fingers running through the thick, coarse strands of his hair, her body aching for more of his touch. *This is wrong, Annie. So wrong. Remember, he's only using you.* That horrid voice—her reason—nagged at her. *And there's pregnancy—you can't risk it. Or disease. What do you know of this man? What, really?*

His fingers dipped below the waistband of her jeans and a series of pops followed as the snaps of her fly gave way easily. The lace of her panties was a thin barrier to the heat of his hands and as he traced the V of her legs with his fingers, she began to move to a gentle rhythm that controlled her body and mind.

He nudged her legs apart with deft fingers and pushed her panties to one side. Gently he touched her, slowly prodding and retracting, just grazing that sensitive bud that palpitated with need. She cried out as he plunged ever deeper and her thoughts spun wildly in a whirlpool of desperate need that swirled ever faster . . .

She clung to him as he kissed her. Sweat broke out across her forehead and along her spine. She wanted more—all of him, to feel his body joined to hers. But she could only take what he was giving, that special touch that made her feel she was drowning in a pool of pleasure, gasping and panting and unable to breathe, yet still fighting him, knowing in her heart that this was wrong.

"Come on, Annie," he whispered against her ear. "Let go."

"I—I can't. Oh . . . oh, God."

"Sure you can, baby. Trust me."

With all of her heart she wanted to. Tears sprang to her eyes and yet desire reigned as he traced the tracks of her tears with his tongue while never letting up, his fingers continuing to work their own special magic.

He kissed her breast again and something deep inside of her gave way.

"That's it, girl."

Hotter and hotter, faster and faster she moved. A small moan escaped her. His lips found hers. His tongue delved deep into her mouth. He touched that perfect spot and she convulsed. With a soul-jarring jolt, her resistance shattered. Her body jerked. Once. Twice. Three times.

She heard a throaty, desperate cry and realized it was her own voice.

"For the love of God," she said, staring into his enigmatic eyes. Never had she felt so sated. Never had she been so pleasured. And never had she been so embarrassed.

Who was this man? Why had she let him touch her, kiss her, feel her most intimate regions?

As swift as a bolt of lightning, the reality of what she'd done shot through her. "Oh, no." She pushed him away, scrambled into her clothes, and with her face blushing a hot denial of her own wanton deeds, she climbed to her feet. "Look, this was wrong. All wrong."

"You don't believe that."

"Yes, yes, I do. And I just can't have sex with you. What about . . . about condoms and—"

"I've been tested," he said, climbing to his feet.

"But, I could get pregnant and . . . listen, the reason Nola left the baby with me is that I can't have children, can't seem to carry them to term and—"

He folded her into his arms and she let the tears run from her eyes. All this emotion. What could she do about him? For God's sake, she was falling in love with him. She let out a broken sob and the strength of his arms seeped into her bones. Sniffing, she pushed him away. "You . . . you have to leave."

"Annie, don't—"

"I mean it." She yanked the band from her hair and swiped at her eyes. Chin thrust forward defiantly, she added, "I don't know what I was thinking."

"You weren't." He was standing near the window, sunlight casting his body in relief. Good Lord, he was big. And strong. And powerful. *And dangerous. Don't forget dangerous, Annie. He just wants Carol and information about Nola.*

"Listen, O'Shaughnessy, you've got to go, to leave me alone—"

"So we're back to calling me O'Shaughnessy."

"Yes. No. Oh, I don't know." She shook her head, trying to clear the passion-induced cobwebs from her mind. "I just know that you've got to leave. Go do what it is you have to do. Find Nola, figure out this . . . break-in at the company—burglary, embezzlement, or whatever it is and find out about Carol, if she really is yours."

"Is there any doubt?"

Annie glanced at the infant. Golden hair, crystal-blue eyes, arched eyebrows, cheeks as rosy as her father's. She swallowed hard. No, Liam was right. There wasn't a whole lot of question as to the baby's paternity.

"I'll take her in for a blood test as soon as I can get to the hospital. With DNA and all, it should be pretty easy to figure out."

"A snap." He reached for his jacket and shoved one arm down a sleeve. "I'll be back," he promised.

She didn't doubt it for a minute, but she had no idea what to do about it. She glanced at the phone. If she had any brains at all, she'd call the police. Biting her lower lip, she heard the sound of his Jeep's engine roar to life, then the crunch and slide of tires as the vehicle tried to find traction.

Carol let out a tiny whimper and Annie picked her up in an instant. Heart in her throat, she held the tiny body close and felt Carol's breath against her breast—a breast Liam had so recently kissed. Annie's stomach slowly rolled in anticipation at the thought of his touch. "This is such a mess," she admitted to the baby.

"Oh, Carol, I'm so sorry." She pressed her lips gently to the baby's soft, blond curls. "I love you so much."

And Liam—do you love him, too?

She snorted at the ridiculous thought. She didn't even know the man. And yet she was ready to make love to him. She should never, *never* have let him kiss her.

What could she do? What if Liam truly was Annie's father? What if he made good his promise and took the baby away from her? Tears stung her eyes as she thought about how long she'd wanted a child, how desperately she'd hoped that she could have one of her own and now this . . . this little one was in her arms and oh, so precious.

"I won't give you up," she whispered, though she knew deep in the blackest regions of her heart that her words were only a silly, hopeless promise without any meaning.

Carrying the child, she reached for the phone and while propping the receiver between her ear and shoulder she bit her lip and dialed the number of the sheriff.

Chapter Six

Nola drew on her cigarette, waited for the nicotine to do its trick, then flicked the butt into the toilet of the Roadster Cafe. She studied her reflection in the cracked mirror in the tiny bathroom of the truck stop where she'd taken a job just two weeks earlier.

Her face was beginning to show signs of strain. With a frown, she sighed and brushed her bangs from her eyes. Dark roots were showing in the blond streaks she'd added to her hair. This wasn't the way it was supposed to have turned out. Not by a long shot.

She still looked good, or so she tried to tell herself as she applied a new layer of lipstick. Hardly any lines around her eyes and mouth—well, nothing permanent. Though she was younger than her sister by nearly two years, most people thought she was the eldest.

"Hard livin'," she muttered under her breath as she dabbed at the corner of her mouth with a finger to swipe away a little raspberry-colored gloss that had smeared. "But things'll be better." They had to be. She couldn't stand too much of this. Life on the run wasn't all it was cracked up to be. She was forever looking over her shoulder or spying someone she was certain she'd known in that other life. Was that only months ago? How had she gotten herself into this predicament?

"Love." She spat the word as if it tasted foul. And it did. Would she ever learn? Probably not.

Determined not to follow the dark path down which her thoughts invariably wandered, she tightened her apron around her waist and felt a glimmer of cold satisfaction that her figure was returning to its normal svelte proportions. Still a little thick around the middle, she was otherwise slim and her breasts were no longer swollen. Back to 36C. Nearly perfect despite the pregnancy. "Hang in there," she told the woman in the reflection, then felt close to tears yet again. God, when would this emotional roller coaster end?

Probably never.

Sniffing loudly, she wiped away any trace of tears from beneath her mascara-laden lashes. In the end it would be worth it and she consoled herself with the simple fact that everything she'd done—be it right or wrong—she'd done for love.

She ducked through swinging doors that opened to the kitchen, where the fry cook—a greasy-faced kid with bad skin and dishwater-blond hair—gave her the once-over. For some reason he thought he could come on to her.

Like he had a chance.

But then the kid didn't know who she was, or that she'd worked in much better jobs than this, making a decent salary in an office in a big city. For a second she longed for her old life back. Then she caught herself. She'd made her decision and there was no turning back. Not ever.

"I could use a little help up here," the other waitress yelled through the open window between the counter and the kitchen.

"On my way, Sherrie." Checking her watch as she passed through another set of swinging doors, Nola frowned. The call she'd been expecting was half an hour late. Worse yet, there was a customer using the pay phone—that same man she'd seen in here three days running—going on and on about the weather on the interstate. Great. Ignoring the nervous sweat that beaded between her shoulder blades and under her arms, she gathered up knives, forks, and spoons from the baskets at the busing station and began to wrap the utensils in wine-colored napkins.

Surely the guy couldn't talk all night.

"Hey, baby, how 'bout a refill?" At the counter, one of the customers, a trucker from the looks of him, was leaning over a nearly empty cup of coffee. The wedge of pecan pie she'd placed in front of him fifteen minutes earlier had disappeared, leaving only traces of nuts in a pool of melted ice cream. God, this place was a dive.

She plastered a smile on her face, the smile guaranteed to garner the best tips from these cheapskates, and reached for the glass pot of coffee warming on the hot plate. "Sure," she said. "On the house."

He chuckled and pulled at the ends of a scraggly red moustache. "Thanks, doll."

"Anytime," she lied as she glanced at the pay phone again. The guy had hung up and taken a table in the corner. Good.

Now, for the love of Jesus, call!

"Order up!" the cook shouted and rang a bell to catch her attention. She nearly jumped out of her skin and sloshed coffee onto her apron.

"Geez, Lorna, you're a bundle of nerves," Sherrie observed with a shake of her head. Her teased, over-sprayed black hair barely moved. "That's the trouble with you big-city girls. Jumpy. You got to learn to relax."

"I'll try." Wonderful. Now she was getting advice from a woman who raised chihuahuas according to the phases of the moon and believed that space aliens had visited her on the anniversary of her second husband's death. Good-hearted to a fault, Sherrie Beckett was a woman who could never hope to get out of this tiny town in the southeastern corner of Idaho.

Nola, or Lorna, as she called herself in these parts, grabbed the platter and carried the special—a hot turkey sandwich with mashed potatoes and canned cranberry sauce on the side—to the booth in the corner where the man who'd been monopolizing the telephone had settled with a copy of *USA Today* and a cigarette. He barely glanced at her as she slid the plate in front of him, but she had a cold impression that she'd seen him somewhere before—somewhere other than this podunk little town.

"Anything else?"

"This'll do just fine." He flashed her a disarming grin, jabbed out his smoke, then turned to his meal.

Man, if she were paranoid she would believe that she'd met him somewhere. But that was impossible. No one knew where she was, not even any member of her family. She'd chosen this wide spot in the road to hide for a few weeks, just until things had cooled down; then, after she heard from her accomplice, she'd split. For Canada. From there the plan was to head to the Bahamas.

And you'll never see your baby again.

Again the stupid tears threatened to rain. Shit, she was a wimp. A goddamned Pollyanna in the throes of postpartum trauma or whatever the hell it was. She had to quit thinking about the baby. The little girl was safe. With Annie. No one in the world would take better care of her. So why the tears? It wasn't as if Nola had ever really wanted a kid.

But she couldn't stop thinking about that little red-faced bundle of energy that had grown inside her for nine long, nervous months.

Oh, hell, the guy hadn't even taken a bite of his food and he was back on the phone, tying up the lines. She glanced out the window at the bleak, dark night. A single strand of colored bulbs connected the diner with the trailer park. Inside, a twirling aluminum tree was placed in a corner near the old jukebox. Familiar Christmas carols whispered through the diner, barely heard over the rattle of flatware, the clink of glasses, and the buzz of conversation in this truck stop.

I'm dreaming of a white Christmas . . .

Nola sighed and poured coffee in the half-filled cups sitting before patrons at the counter. *Yeah, well, I'm dreaming of a tropical island, hot sun, and enough rum to soak my mind so I forget about all the mistakes I made. For love.*

"Hey, could we get some service over here?" an angry male voice broke into her reverie.

"On my way," she said with a brightness she didn't feel.

"Well, make it snappy, will ya?"

And Merry Christmas to you, too, you stupid s.o.b. "Sure." She handed the three twenty-odd-year-old macho yahoos their plastic-coated menus and prayed that he would call—and soon. Before she lost what was left of her mind.

"Looks like you were right about Talbott. I'll be sure soon." Jake Cranston's voice crackled and faded on the cellular phone.

"You talked to him?" Liam's hand tightened over the steering wheel and he squinted against the coming darkness. Heavy snowflakes fell from the slate-colored heavens so quickly that the Jeep's wipers were having trouble keeping the windshield clear.

"Not yet, but it won't be long."

"How long?"

"Well, I found our missing link."

"Nola?" Liam couldn't believe his ears.

"Bingo."

"Where?"

"Southeastern Idaho. A remote spot."

"But how?"

"Clever detective work." There was a chuckle, then his voice faded again. ". . . Got a break . . . speeding ticket . . . checked with the Idaho . . . police . . ."

"I can't hear you. Jake?" But it was useless. He couldn't hear a thing. "Call me at Annie's cabin. The phone there works." He rattled off the number that he'd memorized several days earlier. "Jake? Did you get that? Oh, hell!" The connection fizzled completely and he hung up. He'd spent the last three days doing some investigating on his own, if you could call it that. With his four-wheel drive rig and chains, he was able to travel around the hilly streets that had been sanded, plowed, and then snowed and iced over again and again. The entire northern Willamette Valley was caught in the grip of a series of storms that just kept rolling in off the coast and dropping nearly a foot of snow each time. Emergency crews were working around the clock and electrical service had been restored to some of the customers, only to be lost by others.

Liam had spent as much time as he could tracking down the people he'd worked with at the construction company and the rest of the time, he'd been at Annie's cabin, keeping his distance while trying to learn everything she knew about her bitch of a sister. The damned thing of it was he kept finding excuses to hang out there, to get closer to her. The baby was the primary reason, of course, and the most obvious, but, whether he wanted to admit it or not, his emotions ran deep for the woman who had decided to become the kid's new mom.

She'd been nervous around him although he hadn't touched her again and had resisted the compelling urge to crush her into his arms. He'd slept in the Jeep and dreamed about kissing her until dawn, making love to her until they couldn't breathe, holding her close until forever. He hadn't, because she was scared of him and the situation. Every time the phone had rung she'd jumped as if jolted by an electric shock. Twice he'd caught her looking out the window, staring down the drive as if she expected someone to appear.

Who?

Nola?

He'd begun to believe that she really didn't know if Nola was the mother of the baby, but something was keeping her worrying her lip and wringing her hands when she didn't think he was watching.

He turned into the drive and his headlights picked up fresh tracks in the snow. Someone had decided to visit Annie. Fear froze his heart. What if she'd decided to leave? To pack up the baby and take off? Had Nola sensed that Jake was on to her? He tromped on the gas past the main house and then, as he rounded the final corner to the cabin, he stood on the brakes. The Jeep shimmied and slid but stopped four feet from the back of a Sheriff's Department cruiser. Annie's Toyota truck was parked in front of the tiny garage, thirteen inches of snow undisturbed on the cab and bed.

What now? His hands, inside gloves, became clammy. For the first thirty-eight years of his life he'd respected the law and all officers thereof, but ever since his arrest and the days he'd spent in jail, detained on suspicion, his admiration had dwindled to be replaced by serious doubts. There were a dozen reasons the cops could be here—none of them good—but the worst would be if Annie or Carol were in some kind of trouble. Since there were no emergency vehicles screaming down the lane, Liam assumed that they were both all right.

No, this wasn't a medical emergency. The deputy was here because of him.

Bloody terrific.

He snapped off the engine, grabbed the two bags of groceries he'd bought in town, and stepped into the fresh snow. Whatever the problem was, he'd face it.

Annie heard the sound of the Jeep's engine and wished she could drop through the old floorboards. She'd called the Sheriff's

Department three days earlier, explained about her predicament, and been told by a patient but overworked voice that they'd send someone out when they could. Other life-threatening emergencies were deemed more important than being visited by a man who claimed to be the father of a child who had been abandoned but was being cared for. Social Services would call back. The Sheriff's Department would phone when they were able, but she was told to be patient.

She'd regretted the call since she'd placed it and now, seated on the edge of the sofa, feeding Carol a bottle, she felt foolish.

". . . It was a mistake," she said, not for the first time. "I shouldn't have bothered you."

"But the child's not yours." The deputy, fresh-faced and not more than in his mid-twenties, wasn't about to be put off. Determined to a fault, convinced that he was upholding every letter of the law, he scratched in his notepad and Annie gave herself a series of swift mental kicks for being so damned impulsive and calling the authorities.

Liam had returned and she'd never mentioned the call to him; instead she'd kept a distant and quiet peace with the man. He no longer frightened her and she nearly laughed when she remembered that she hadn't trusted him at first, that she feared for the baby's well-being. Since that first day she'd observed him with Carol and noticed the smile that tugged at his lips when he looked at his baby. His hands, so large and awkward while holding the infant, were kind and protective. No, as long as Liam O'Shaughnessy was around, the baby had nothing to fear.

"No, the baby isn't mine, but I have reason to believe that she is my sister's little girl. I've alerted the proper agencies and talked to Barbara Allen at C.S.D. She said they'd call when the storm passed."

"But this O'Shaughnessy was harassing you—"

"No."

"Trespassing?"

"No. He, um, just thinks the baby may be his. He's agreed to a paternity test and—"

Clunk! The door burst open and Liam filled the doorway. His eyes flashed blue fire as he set two full grocery bags on the table and kicked the door closed. "Is there a problem?"

"No." Annie was on her feet in an instant. Still carrying Carol, she stood next to Liam. "I was just explaining to Deputy Kemp how I found Carol—and about you."

"I'm her father."

The deputy scratched his chin. "So you came to claim her?"

"That's it."

"What about the mother?"

"Still looking for her. Annie's sister, Nola Prescott."

Deputy Kemp's eyebrows shot up to the brim of his hat and he started scratching out notes in his condemning little pad again. "The woman who accused you of breaking into the offices of the company where you worked, Belfry Construction, right? Where the night watchman ended up getting clobbered over the head and dying?"

"One and the same."

"You were hauled in for that one."

"Questioned and held. Charges were dropped." He saw Annie's eyes widen as she realized he'd spent time in jail.

"All because of Ms. Prescott's testimony—that she recanted."

Liam's nostrils flared slightly and he glared at Annie as if in so doing he could make her disappear. "Yep."

"Why would a woman you . . . well, you had a baby with want to send you to jail?"

"That's what I'd like to know." Every muscle in his body tensed and white lines around his lips indicated the extent of his ire. The stare he sent Annie would have melted nails. "When I locate Nola, believe me, I'll find out."

"The Seattle police don't seem to be very convinced that you weren't involved in the crime."

"They're wrong." Liam's lips were compressed into a razor-thin seam that barely moved when he spoke. "Was there anything else?"

"No." The deputy snapped his notebook closed and tipped his hat at Annie. "I'll be in touch."

"Thanks," she said weakly.

"And I'm sure C.S.D. will want to speak with you."

Liam followed him to the door and watched through the window as the cruiser skidded around his Jeep and slowly disappeared down the lane through the trees. Once satisfied that they were alone, he turned slowly, his irritation evident in the set of his jaw. "What was that all about?"

"I thought . . . I mean a few days ago when you came barging in here threatening to take Carol away and charging after Nola, I was scared and—"

"So you decided to turn me in?" he accused. "Damn it, woman, you're cut from the same cloth as that sister of yours!"

"No!"

"Both of you trying to set me up."

"Liam! No!"

Carol let out a whimper and Annie removed the nipple from her mouth and gently lifted her to her shoulder. Softly rubbing the baby's back, she sent Liam a look warning him not to raise his voice. He stalked to the window and stared outside while Annie, after burping and changing Carol, sat in the rocker and nudged the infant back to slumber.

Liam gave a soft whistle to the dog and stormed outside. Annie closed her eyes while rocking the baby. What a horrid predicament. With Carol smack-dab in the middle of it. As the rocker swayed she tried to sort out her life and came up with no answers. A few days ago, before the baby had been left on her doorstep, everything had been so clear, her days on a boring but regular track. Now she felt as if every aspect of her life was careening out of control. She loved Carol and was sure to lose her. She loved her sister, but was confused about Nola's intentions and she loved Liam . . . She stopped rocking. No way. She didn't love Liam O'Shaughnessy; she didn't even know the man, not really. What she felt for him was lust. Nothing more.

The baby let out a tiny puff of air and snuggled against her and Annie felt a tug on her heartstrings unlike any she'd ever felt before. *Precious, precious little girl, how am I ever going to bear to give you up?*

"I can't. I just can't," she whispered, her throat as thick as if she'd swallowed an orange. She thought to the future—first steps, learning to read, going off to school, soccer and T-ball, first kiss and high school prom. Oh, no, no, no! Annie couldn't not be a part of Carol's life. She blinked hard, realized she was close to tears, and finally, after Carol was asleep, placed the baby in her bassinet.

Sliding her arms through her jacket and wrapping a scarf around her neck, she walked outside where she donned her boots and gloves. She heard Liam before she saw him, the sound of an axe splitting wood cracking through the canyon. He was standing near the woodpile by the barn, the axe raised over his head. Gritting his teeth, he swung down and cleaved a thick length of fir into two parts, the split portions spinning to either side of the stump he used as a chopping block. Snowflakes clung to his blond hair and settled on the shoulders of his suede jacket. He reached down for another length of oak and set it in place.

"You want something?" he asked without turning. The axe was lifted skyward and came down with a thwack that split the wood easily as darkness fell.

"To explain."

"No need."

"But Liam—"

"So now it's 'Liam,' is it?" He slammed the axe down again, wedging the blade in the chopping block and turned to glare at her. "Just tell me one thing, Annie. What is it you expected to accomplish by drawing in the police?"

"I—I—just needed some peace of mind. You came in here like gangbusters, arguing and carrying on and threatening to take Carol away and I . . . I needed help."

He glanced at the sky and shook his head. "Did you get it? Peace of mind?"

"No." She shook her head.

"Me neither."

Swallowing back all of her pride, she lifted her head and stared him down. "Now it's your turn," she said. "You tell me just one thing."

"Shoot."

"What is it you want from me, Liam O'Shaughnessy?"

"Good question." His face softened slightly, the shadows of the night closing in. "I wish I knew."

She shivered, but not from the cold night air. No, her skin trembled from the intensity of his gaze and the way her body responded. She licked suddenly dry lips and willed her legs to move. "I . . . I'd better see about the horses."

"What is it you want from me?"

Like the icicles suspended from the eaves of the barn, his question seemed to hang in the air between them. *I want you to love me.* Oh, Lord, where did that wayward thought come from? She stopped short, her breath fogging in the frigid air. "I—I just want you to leave me alone."

His smile was as hard as the night. "I already told you what a lousy liar you are, so try again. What is it you want from me?"

"Nothing, Liam," she said and marched to the barn. She couldn't, wouldn't let him see how vulnerable he made her feel. Each day she'd snapped lead ropes to the horses' halters and walked them around the paddock for nearly an hour so that they trampled a path through the drifts, then returned them to their stalls with fresh water and feed and brushed the clumps of snow from their coats. They'd already been exercised for the day, but she walked into the barn and took in deep breaths of the musty air. From somewhere behind the oat bin, she heard the scurry of feet, a rat or mouse she'd startled.

She sensed rather than heard him enter. *Give me strength.*

"Annie."

Oh, God. She wrapped her arms around her middle, took a deep breath, and decided she had no choice but to meet him head-on. "Look, O'Shaughnessy—" Turning, she ran straight into him and his arms closed around her.

"No more lies," he said and she caught a glimpse of his eyes before his lips found hers in the darkness. She shouldn't do this, knew she was making an irrevocable mistake, but as his weight pulled her downward onto a mat of loose straw, she gave herself up to the silent cravings of her body. His lips were warm, his body strong, and she closed her mind to the doubts that nagged her, the worries that plagued her about this one enigmatic man.

She shivered as he opened her coat and slowly drew her scarf from around her neck, trembled in anticipation as he drew her sweater over her head and unhooked her bra, swallowed back any protest as he lowered his lips to her nipple and gently teased.

Warmth invaded that private space between her legs, and desire ran naked through her blood. Her fingers fumbled with the fastenings of his jacket and he shrugged out of the unwanted coat, tucking it beneath them, along with hers.

"I want you, Annie," he said as he threw off his sweater and her fingers traced the corded muscles of his chest and shoulders. His abdomen retracted as she kissed the mat of golden hair that covered his chest and he groaned in anticipation as she tickled his stomach with her breath.

"I want you, too," she admitted. "God forgive me, but I do."

His smile, crooked and jaded, slashed in the darkness. "It's not a sin, you know."

"I know," she agreed, but wasn't convinced. Only when his lips claimed hers again and his hands lovingly caressed her did she sigh and give up to the sorcery of his touch. His fingers tangled in her hair and he pressed urgent lips to her eyelids, the corner of her mouth, her throat, and lower still.

He skimmed her jeans over her hips and followed his hands with lips that breathed fire against her skin and through the sheer lace of her panties. She squirmed as he sculpted her buttocks, lifting her gently and kissing her with an intimacy that she felt in the back of her throat. Through the thin barrier he laved and teased until the barn with its smells of horses and grain disappeared into the shadows and she felt him pull away the final garment to reach deeper.

"Ooooh," she cried, wanting more, blind to anything but the lust that stoked deep in her soul. "Liam—"

"I'm here, love." In an instant he kicked off his jeans and was atop her, parting her knees with the firm muscles of his thighs, kissing her anxiously on the lips, breathing as if it would be his last.

She couldn't close her eyes, but watched in wonder as he made love to her, gasped and writhed, catching his tempo, following his lead, feeling as if her life would never be the same again.

"Annie," he cried as her mind grew foggy and she was swept on a current of sensations that brought heat to her loins and goose bumps to her flesh. "Oh, God, Annie." He threw back his head and squeezed his eyes shut. With a shudder, he poured himself into her and she convulsed, her body clamping around him, her mind lost somewhere in the clouds.

He collapsed against her and she willingly bore his weight. Dear God in heaven, how would she ever be able to give him up, to give this up? Her heart was pounding erratically, her breathing short and shallow.

You could get pregnant, Annie.

Would that be so bad? The thought of carrying Liam's child deep inside her was soothing rather than worrisome.

The doctor said you'd miscarry again, that you can't go to term.

But it was worth the risk.

Don't be a fool, Annie. Think!

Liam's arms tightened around her and he sighed into the curve of her neck, closing off all arguments with her rational mind. She knew he couldn't promise his undying love, realized that what she felt was not only one-sided but foolish as well, and yet she ached to hear the words that would bind him to her forever, inwardly cried to have him swear his undying love.

Slowly he lifted his head. Eyes still shining in afterglow, he pushed a stray strand of hair from her face. "There's something I want to tell you," he said, his voice still husky and deep.

Her heart did a silly little flip. "What's that, O'Shaughnessy?"

He winked at her and offered her that slightly off-center grin she found so endearing. "Merry Christmas, Annie McFarlane."

"To you, too, O'Shaughnessy."

"I think I've got a present for you," he added and his voice was rougher, more serious. She felt the first glimmer of despair.

"What's that?" she teased but saw that he was stone-cold sober.

He cleared his throat and plucked a strand of straw from her hair. Gazing into her eyes as if searching for a reaction, he said, "Jake found your sister."

"What?"

"That's right." He kissed her on the temple. "He's bringing Nola here sometime after the first of the year, after the storms have passed, and she's done dealing with the police and Peter Talbott."

Annie was stunned. The thought of seeing Liam with Nola and their baby, Carol, *her* baby, was overwhelming. "Good," she said without a trace of enthusiasm. It had to happen sooner or later.

"Once we talk to Nola, we'll figure everything out."

Annie's heart seemed to dissolve. She was going to lose them—both Liam and Carol. She knew it as well as she knew that tonight was Christmas Eve.

Chapter Seven

"Will you marry me?"

Annie stopped dead in her tracks. They'd been walking from the main house back to the cabin, through the mud and slush still lingering in the forest. Liam was carrying a front pack with Carol sleeping cozily against him.

"Marry you?" Her voice seemed to echo through the forest.

Liam took her gloved hands in his and as rain drizzled through the fir and oak trees, he smiled down at her. "Carol needs a mother—someone who loves her."

Annie's heart plummeted. For a second she'd expected him to say that he loved her. In the past two weeks of being together, never once had he uttered those three wonderful words. "I—I— well, I told myself I'd never marry again." This was happening too fast—way too fast.

"I thought you wanted to be with Carol."

She bit her lip as she saw Carol's blond curls peeking up through the top of the front pack. "I do, more than anything, but—"

His smile faded and he rubbed his jaw. "Look, Annie, I never thought I'd ever marry. I liked being a bachelor, but then I didn't realize that I was going to be a father, either. I'm glad about that. Ecstatic—and I want what's best for my daughter." He brushed a moist strand of hair from her eyes. "Carol couldn't have a better mother than you."

Her throat became swollen and he pressed a kiss to her temple. "Would it be so bad, married to me?"

No, she didn't think so. Though she'd barely known him for two weeks, she loved him. Foolishly and reverently. Maybe in time he would learn to love her and, if the truth be known, she couldn't imagine living her life without him. He'd proven himself, exonerating himself of the crime in Washington, refusing to prosecute Nola for her false claims against him, sticking by Annie through the holidays and helping her care for the main house, cabin, and livestock as the frozen countryside thawed, creating floods and mud slides. Also, more importantly, it was obvious that he was completely taken with his daughter.

They'd laughed together, fought a little, spent hours upon hours at each other's side only to make love long into the night. He'd helped clean the gutters, thaw the pipes, and repair the roof when icy branches had fallen on the old shingles. He'd exercised and fed the horses, shoveled the driveway, fixed her pickup that refused to start after being packed in snow for ten days, done the grocery shopping, and kept the fire stoked until the old furnace kicked in. He'd been a gentle lover, a concerned father, and, it seemed, a man determined to clear his name. He'd watched Carol as Annie had reconnected with her clients and worked on her word processor, but the bottom line was that he didn't love her. At least not yet.

"But . . . how? Where would we live? Wait a minute, this is all so fast." She held up a hand and he captured it in his larger one.

"We'll live here. I'm moving out of Washington anyway. I'll sell my house and start my own company, either in Portland or Vancouver. If it's money you're worried about—"

"No, no." She shook her head. Money was the last thing on her mind. In fact, she hadn't told him but she was three days late in her monthly cycle. Not a lot, but, considering that her periods came and went like clockwork, something to think about. Something very pleasant to consider.

"You can keep your job, or become a full-time mother. We'll buy a place of our own eventually, when the time is right."

"Are you sure?" Good Lord, she shouldn't even be contemplating anything so ludicrous.

Smiling, he used the finger of one gloved hand to smooth the worried furrow from her brow. "As sure as anything I've done lately. Come on, wouldn't you love to be Carol's mother?"

"You know I would," she admitted, wondering if she was about to make the mistake of her life. She'd suffered through one divorce and she wasn't about to go through another. If and when she married again, it would be for life. "What about Nola?" she asked, concern gnawing away at her optimism. "She'd be your sister-in-law."

Liam glanced to the gray sky and frowned. "As long as she doesn't live with us and doesn't interfere with Carol, it'll be okay."

"She accused you of murder."

His smile was cold as ice. "Don't worry about Nola, Annie. I can take care of your sister."

"I don't think anyone can take care of her." They hadn't seen Nola nor heard from her, though, according to Liam's friend Jake, she'd turned in her boyfriend, Peter Talbott, who had embezzled funds and killed Bill Arness when he was startled while doctoring the company books. Talbott had coached Nola into lying about Liam's participation in the crime, then skipped town, leaving Nola, who had been in love with him, alone to hold the bag. She'd gone to meet him somewhere in Idaho, but he'd never shown up and Jake had confronted her and convinced her to turn state's evidence against Talbott, who was already long gone, probably hiding out in Canada.

All that trouble seemed far away from their private spot here in the forest. Carol gurgled in the pack between them, a fine Oregon mist moistened their faces, and somewhere not too far off Riley was barking his fool head off at a rabbit or squirrel or some other creature hiding in the ferns and bracken.

She could be happy here with Liam and Carol, she thought, warmth invading her heart.

Hand in hand they walked back to the cabin where, despite the rumble of the furnace, a fire was burning and near her desk stacked with correspondence, the small Christmas tree still stood, draped in garlands and shimmering with tinsel. From the oven, the smell of pot roast and potatoes filled the air.

Liam carried Carol into the bedroom and placed her tiny body in the crib he'd purchased just two days earlier. The baby found her thumb and snuggled her little head against a gingham bumper as Annie adjusted her covers.

There was still so much to do. Social Services, upon learning that Liam was the father of the baby, had been lenient about Carol's situation. Marrying him would make the adoption all that much easier. And certainly Nola would comply. Though Annie hadn't spoken with her sister, she didn't doubt that Nola wanted her to care for the little girl. Liam had even gone through the formality of a paternity test, though the results wouldn't be confirmed for a few more days.

"Okay, Annie, what's it gonna be?" he asked and there was an edge to his voice she didn't recognize, a nervousness. He stood in the doorway of the bedroom, the firelight from the living room glowing behind him. "Will you marry me?"

"Yes." The word was out in an instant and Liam picked her up, twirling her in the small confines of the room. Startled, she gasped, then laughed. Carol let out a soft puff of a sigh. In the dim bedroom where only hours before they'd made love, she wrapped her arms around Liam's neck and kissed his cheek. "I'd love to marry you, Mr. O'Shaughnessy."

His smile was a slash of white as they tumbled onto the bed together. "We could fly to Reno tonight."

"Tonight?"

"Why wait?"

Yes, why? For years she'd wanted to become a mother. She thought of all the painful disappointments of her miscarriages, the guilt, the dull ache in her heart, the fear that she would never have a child. And now she had only to agree to marry the man she loved to become a mother. "All right," she finally agreed. "Tonight."

". . . Mr. and Mrs. Liam O'Shaughnessy." The justice of the peace, a robust man of about sixty, rained a smile down on Liam, Annie, and Carol while his wife, dressed in polka dots, sat at the piano and played the wedding march.

"That's all there is to it?" Annie asked as she and Liam walked out of the small, neon-lit chapel and another couple took their places. Outside, the traffic raced by and a wind cut through the dusty streets of Reno.

"It's legal and that's all that matters." Liam took her arm as she shielded Carol from the noise and cold night air. The city was ablaze in lights; the crowds, oblivious to the frigid temperatures, wandered in and out of the hotels and casinos lining the main drag.

Annie followed Liam back to the hotel where they'd booked a room for the night. She remembered her last wedding six years earlier—a church with stained-glass windows, a preacher in robes, three bridesmaids, Nola as the maid of honor, a flower girl, and a ring bearer. Ribbons and rose petals, David's sister singing a love song, candles and organ music, and all for what? Nothing. A marriage that had turned to ashes all too soon.

This time there were no false promises, no stiff ceremony, nothing borrowed, blue, old, or new. *And no love?* her ever-nagging mind reminded her.

They took the elevator to the fifth floor where a roll-in crib was waiting for Carol and a bottle of chilled champagne waited in a stand packed in ice.

While Annie changed Carol and fed her a final bottle, Liam uncorked the champagne. Once the baby was fed, burped, and put to sleep, he poured them each a glass and touched the rim of his fluted goblet to hers.

"Here's to happiness," he said with a grin.

And love, she thought, but added, "And more children."

"More?" Blond eyebrows raised.

She nodded. "Maybe sooner than you thought."

"You're pregnant?"

"I'm not sure, but . . . well, I could be."

His smile grew from one side of his face to the other. He sipped from his glass, took her into his arms, and as champagne spilled between them, carried her to the bed. "I'd say congratulations are in order, Mrs. O'Shaughnessy."

"That they are, Mr. O."

He kissed her and Annie closed her eyes, refusing to listen to the doubts, to the worries, to the damned negative thoughts that had plagued her ever since she'd agreed to become Liam's bride. Tonight, on her wedding night, she would give herself to him. Nothing else mattered.

"This is a big mistake." Nola scratched both her arms with her fingernails and wished she was anywhere else but in this damned car with Jake Cranston. Some sappy country ballad was battling with static on the radio.

"You've made worse."

She rolled her eyes, but didn't argue. How could she? Without his help, the police in Seattle would have held her as an accomplice or material witness or whatever the hell else they could come up with in the Belfry break-in and murder of Bill Arness. She still felt cold inside when she thought about Bill. Guilt pressed a ten-ton weight on her chest. She had nothing to do with his death, but she had known that Peter was behind it. Even though Bill had surprised him at the computer and Peter had only meant to knock him out, the old man had died.

Peter Talbott.

Embezzler. Killer. Jerk. And so much more.

Tears burned behind Nola's eyelids. Jesus, she was an idiot. But she was going to see Annie again. And the baby. Her heart lightened at the thought.

Jake turned off the freeway and onto a two-lane road that wound through the hills surrounding Lake Oswego and West Linn. Metropolis one minute, cow country the next. He grabbed a pack of Marlboros from the dash and tossed it to her. "Light one for me, too."

"Thanks." She punched in the lighter, slipped a filter-tip into her mouth, and then, once the lighter popped out, lit up. "Here," she said in a cloud of nerve-calming smoke. She handed him the first cigarette, then shook a second from the pack.

Jake took the smoke and punched another button on the radio. Country music faded and an old Bob Seeger tune met her ears.

Against the wind, I was runnin' against the wind . . .

Boy, and how, she thought, drawing hard on her cigarette and cracking the window. "He's gonna kill me."

"Who? Liam?" Jake snorted. "I doubt it. Not that he wouldn't have just cause."

"I know, I know. I was wrong, okay?"

"And lucky. Damned lucky that he's not got *you* up on charges."

"How could he? I'm his sister-in-law," she said, still hardly believing the news that Jake had given her only yesterday. According to Jake, Annie and Liam had gotten married over a week ago. "What a joke."

"It's no joke, believe me." Jake drove past a development, then turned onto a gravel road leading through a thicket of evergreens and scrub oak.

Nola's stomach clenched. What could she say to Annie? To Liam O'Shaughnessy? Oh, God. She took a long draw on her cigarette and noticed that her hands were cold as ice. This was no good—no damned good.

They passed a huge house with a peaked roof, turret, and dark windows, a gray Victorian that some people might think was quaint. Nola thought it looked like it had come right out of *Psycho*. "Annie lives here?" Nola asked, but Jake didn't stop and continued on the winding road to a much smaller house—a cottage of sorts—with a view of the lake and a barn nearby.

"She—well, they, I guess now, live here. Annie maintains the other house." He jabbed out his cigarette in the tray. "How close are you with your sister?"

"Sometimes closer than others," she said. "This hasn't been my best year."

"Amen." He cut the engine and reached across her to open her door. "Shall we?"

"If we must." She was already stepping out of the car and couldn't stop the drumming of her heart at the thought of seeing her baby again. How much had she grown? Did she smile? Would she recognize the woman in whose womb she'd grown for nine months? Heart in her throat, Nola took one last drag from her Marlboro, then cast the butt onto the lawn where it sizzled against wet leaves. "Okay. It's now or never." She walked up the two steps to the front porch and pushed on a bell.

In an instant Annie, flushed face, sparkling eyes, and easy smile, opened the door. In her arms was a blond baby with wide blue eyes—a baby Nola barely recognized as her own.

"Nola." Annie's voice broke.

"Oh, God, Annie, I—I—!" Tears sprang to her eyes and ran down her face. She threw her arms around her sister and smelled the scent of baby powder mingling with Annie's perfume. Happiness and worry collided in her heart. How had she ever given the baby away? But how could she possibly consider keeping her? Besides, she'd made a promise . . . Sniffing loudly, she hugged her sister and looked up to see Liam O'Shaughnessy in the small home, his presence seeming to loom in the interior. He was staring at her with harsh blue eyes that held no mercy, not a speck of forgiveness. Her blood congealed and she stepped away from her sister. "Liam."

"Nola." His voice was harsh.

"Look, I owe you a big apology."

"Save it." His jaw was set. Uncompromising.

"No, hear me out. I wish you and Annie the best."

He snorted. "Can it."

"Jake Cranston," the man with Nola said. He held out his hand and shook Annie's in a firm, sure-of-himself grasp.

"My wife, Annie," Liam said.

"I assumed."

Annie, her insides a knot, ushered Nola inside.

Jake grabbed a kitchen chair, twirled it around, and straddled it. "I think you should listen to what your sister-in-law has to say, O'Shaughnessy."

"Fair enough." Liam skewered Nola with his gaze. "Shoot."

"I know you hate me," Nola said and Liam didn't say a word, not a syllable of denial even when Annie shot him a pleading look, silently begging him to be forgiving. Nola had, after all, given them Carol. Nola cleared her throat and, cheeks burning, added, "But I did what I thought I had to because . . . well, because I loved Peter."

"Great guy," Liam muttered.

"I thought he was and"—she held up a hand when she saw the protest forming on Liam's lips—"I was wrong. I know that now. I'm sorry for all the trouble and pain I caused you. I am. But I can't undo what's already been done."

"She explained everything to the authorities," Jake said. "I've got copies of her statement to the police in my briefcase."

Nola blinked back tears. "I just hope in time, you'll forgive me."

"Of course he will," Annie answered, but Liam didn't respond. She didn't blame him. Nola had put him through a living hell, but it was painful to witness the hardening of his jaw again, the harsh intensity of his gaze. Ever since the wedding he'd been more relaxed and their lives here, with Carol, had been stress-free.

Until now.

Annie put a hand on Nola's shoulder and her sister turned. She spied the baby again and tears trickled from her eyes. "Can I hold her?"

"If you tell me what leaving her here was all about." Annie couldn't put off the inevitable talk another second. The baby was what her life was all about, the reason she got up in the morning, the impetus for Liam to have met her and married her. Even though there was probably another child growing within her, Carol would always be special. Carol yawned as Annie handed her to her natural mother and Nola bit her lower lip.

"She's beautiful."

"Yes." Annie's voice was low and hoarse with emotion. "But how did you leave her on the stoop?"

"That was Peter's idea," Nola admitted, avoiding her sister's gaze. "I knew I couldn't take care of a baby, couldn't raise her and give her the security and stability she needed. So Peter brought her here."

"And left her in the freezing temperatures on the porch," Liam said.

"Annie was home—"

"What if she hadn't heard the baby cry?"

"Peter heard the dog. He was careful to stay near the bushes and brush his tracks away with a branch from a fir tree. But he waited in the shadows until Annie answered the door."

"You didn't come with him?" Liam asked.

Nola shook her head and swallowed hard. "I—I couldn't. It was too hard."

"Did you ever think of calling me?" Liam asked.

"You?" Nola shook her head. "Why?"

"You know a father has some rights."

Nola's eyebrows slammed together. "That's why I went along with Peter's plan."

"What?"

"Since he didn't think it was time for us to settle down with a baby, I told him about Annie and we decided—"

"Wait a minute." Annie's head was spinning. She was missing something. Something important. "Why would Peter have any say about it?"

"Because he's, what did you name her—Carol? I like that. Well, because he's Carol's father."

"Father?" Liam asked, his voice low, like rolling thunder far in the distance.

"Yeah. He and I . . ." She let the words fade away. "Wait a minute. You didn't think that . . . oh, my God, Liam, did you really think the baby was yours?" She laughed for a second before she turned and looked at the horror shining in Annie's eyes. "The baby's Peter's."

"No!" Annie cried.

"Yes."

"You're certain?" Liam demanded.

"Of course. I would know—"

"But you would lie."

"Not about this and I know, Liam. You and I were over before I conceived this baby." She said it with such conviction Annie didn't doubt her for a minute.

"Oh, dear God . . ." Annie's stomach turned sour. Bile rose up her throat. How could they have made such a horrendous mistake? Why hadn't they waited for the paternity tests? She'd been so certain—so sure Carol was Liam's flesh and blood.

"Talbott's?" Liam's eyes flashed like blue lightning.

"Yes. But he didn't want her and—oh, sweet Jesus, you really thought you were her father, didn't you?"

"I am," Liam said, his jaw tight, the cords of his neck strident. "Make no mistake, Nola, I'm Carol's father. Now and forever."

"But—"

"That's the way it is." He looked past his sister-in-law and his eyes sought Annie's. "And you, Annie Prescott McFarlane O'Shaughnessy, are Carol's mother."

"As long as Peter or I don't interfere," Nola said, lifting her chin. "Now that Peter's gone and I have no one, I could . . . I mean, biologically and legally, Carol's my daughter."

Annie let out a little squeak of protest, but then bit her tongue. What did she expect? That her sister would hand over the precious baby, that Nola wouldn't have second thoughts, that Peter Talbott, whoever he was, wouldn't exert his rights as the baby's father?

"I'll fight you," Liam said, his voice deadly as he advanced upon Nola. "If you try and take Carol away from Annie, I swear, I'll hunt you down and make your life a living hell. And I'll tell the court what a swell mother and role model you'd make. Don't forget I know you, Nola. Inside and out. Your fears and weaknesses and the fact that you abandoned your daughter, left her in freezing temperatures in a basket on a porch because it wasn't convenient for you to keep her. Then there's the lying to the court. I've been told I could press charges." He crossed the room in three swift strides to glare down at Nola who, despite her bravest efforts, cowered under the power of his gaze. "You've had quite a list of lovers, you've been involved in an embezzling scheme, you've never held a job for more than two years, and you disappear for months at a time. I don't know about you, but I think the court might find you unfit."

Nola swallowed hard. "You wouldn't dare—"

"Think about it," he warned.

"No, no, no!" Annie was fighting tears and shaking her head. "I—we can't do this. Carol is . . ." *Sweet, sweet baby, how can I give you up?* ". . . She belongs to Nola. And Peter." The floorboards seemed to shift beneath Annie's feet and somewhere deep inside there was a rending.

"Oh, God, not Pete." Nola waved her hands frantically on either side of her head. "He's useless. A criminal. A killer, for Christ's sake."

Annie's head was swimming; she held onto the back of the couch for support. Her blood pounded in her ears. She was losing the baby . . . no, no, no.

"And you were not only his lover, but his accomplice." Liam turned to Annie and his expression was unrelenting. "We are Carol's parents," he said.

"No." Her voice cracked and the absurdity of the situation struck her. He'd only married her so that she would be Carol's mother. Her marriage was nothing more than a sham. Hollow. Empty. A fool's paradise. "We aren't Carol's parents legally, not yet and apparently not ever." She fought tears, blinking rapidly as she removed the wedding band that she'd worn for so few days. "Liam, I'm sorry." An ache burned through her.

"So am I, Annie," he said without a trace of warmth. "So am I."

The first pang struck her dead center and she thought it was just stress. The second was more painful and she gasped.

"Annie?" Liam's voice was edged in concern. The world started to go black. "Annie?" Again the pain and this time she felt the first ooze of blood, the fledgling life starting to slide from her. "Annie, are you okay?" Liam was standing over her and as she let go of the couch and started to sway, he caught her.

"She's bleeding," Nola said from someplace far away.

"Annie?" Liam's voice was strident, filled with terror, but she couldn't see him. "Call an ambulance—" Her eyes fluttered closed and a beckoning blackness enveloped her. The last thing she heard was Liam calling her name and there was something wrong with his voice—it sounded muffled and cracked. "Annie, hang in there. Oh, sweet Jesus, Annie!"

"Mr. O'Shaughnessy, why don't you go down to the cafeteria and get a cup of coffee? There's nothing you can do for her."

In the blackness, Annie heard the woman's voice as if from a distance. She tried to open her eyes, failed, and licked her lips—so dry.

"I'm staying." Liam's voice was firm. "She's my wife."

"I know, but—"

"I said, I'm not leaving her side, woman, so you can quit harping at me."

"Fine, have it your way. Sheesh. Newlyweds." Footsteps retreated and Liam let out his breath. "Come on, Annie, you can do it," he said as if she were running a marathon instead of just sleeping. "Come on, girl, don't you know that I love you?"

Love? Liam loved her?

"Don't let me down now. Show me some of that fighting spirit. I need you. Carol needs you."

Carol? Oh, yes, the baby.

Annie struggled, her eyes moving behind closed lids.

"She's waking up." Liam sounded surprised. "Annie, oh, thank God."

With an effort she forced her eyes to open, then winced at the light. "Where—?"

"You're in the hospital," Liam said as she focused on him and saw tears shining in his eyes. "And you're fine."

"Fine?"

"Everything's going to be all right, darling," he said, taking her hands and holding them in his as he sat near the hospital bed. "Nola's signed the papers, Peter's agreed that you and I are to be Carol's parents. Nothing's going to stop us now."

She smiled as a nurse entered the room. "Well, look who finally decided to wake up. How're you feeling, honey?" She rounded the bed, blood-pressure cuff ready.

Annie managed to hold up a hand and move it side to side.

"So-so? Don't worry about that—you'll be dancing a jig in no time." The nurse, a round little woman of about forty, slipped the cuff up Annie's arm. She took Annie's blood pressure, pulse, and temperature, admonished her to drink as much water as possible, and promised that food would arrive shortly.

"See, the red carpet treatment," Liam said, smiling down at her. "You had me worried for a while there, you know."

"What happened?"

"You fainted," he said, stroking the side of her cheek.

"Is that all?"

"No." Sighing, he held her gaze with his. "You were pregnant, Annie. And you lost the baby."

"No!" she cried and tears filled her eyes. Another child lost. Liam's baby.

"The doctor says we can try again. But that's up to you." Liam cupped her face in his big hands. "We still have Carol, Annie. And each other. That's more than most people have." He swallowed hard and pressed a kiss to her lips. She felt him tremble. "I love you, Annie O'Shaughnessy," he vowed, "and you just gave me the scare of my life. Don't ever do it again."

His words were like gentle rain, erasing some of the pain. "I won't," she promised, "and I love you, Liam, more than you'll ever know."

Again he kissed her and for the first time she felt she really was his wife.

Epilogue

Nearly a year later

". . . I'm telling you why, Santa Claus is coming to town . . ."

Annie sang off-key as she hung the stocking on the mantel of her new home, the old Victorian house that overlooked the little cottage where she'd first discovered Carol on her stoop. Outside, the Oregon rain peppered the mullioned windows and inside Carol was taking her first few steps, grinning widely and walking like a drunken sailor from the table to the chair and back again.

The rooms were decorated haphazardly. Some of her furniture, a little of Liam's, and the rest having come with the house, but a tree stood in the parlor, strung with popcorn, cranberries, and twinkling lights, which Carol found absolutely fascinating.

The front door burst open and Liam, smelling of pine and leather, wiped the dampness from his face. "All done," he said and flipped a switch. Through the window Annie spied thousands of lights ablaze in the surrounding forest.

"Oooh!" Carol said, toddling to the window and staring outside.

"Daddy did a good job, didn't he?" Annie asked and Liam laughed, crossing the room and snagging Carol from the floor. With a squeal she landed on his shoulders and Annie laughed, her life complete. She still had her secretarial business, but she was working less and less with the demands of being a wife and mother.

Liam, on the other hand, was so busy with his consulting firm in Portland that he was thinking of taking on a partner.

"Where's Jake?" Liam asked as he bussed his wife's cheek. Carol, still atop his broad shoulders, giggled.

"Sleeping, as usual."

"Let's wake him up."

"Let's not," Annie said, shaking her head. "Liam O'Shaughnessy, if you so much as breathe on that baby, I'll—" But it was no use, Liam was already climbing the stairs to the nursery, a small room off the master bedroom. Annie followed him and watched as he stared down in wonder at his son.

As if the baby sensed he was the center of attention, he opened his eyes and cooed. "And your mother didn't want you to wake up," Liam said as Annie picked up her son and felt him snuggle against her breast. Jake Liam O'Shaughnessy had been born on December seventh and the only problem Annie had experienced during the nine months of her pregnancy was an incredible craving for cherry vanilla ice cream.

Nola was working in Detroit and was engaged to a lawyer, Joel and Polly had promised to visit after the new year, and Annie's mother and stepfather promised to fly to Oregon once they'd returned from a trip to Palm Springs.

Life had become routine and nearly perfect. Riley barked at the back door as the little family hurried down the stairs. The smell of cinnamon cookies and gingerbread hung heavy in the air.

In the kitchen, Annie opened the door and the dog bounded in. Liam placed Carol in her high chair and offered her a cookie.

"You spoil her," Annie admonished.

"And you don't?"

"No, I spoil her rotten."

Liam reached into the cupboard and withdrew a bottle of Pinot Noir. "I think it's time for a toast," he said, opening the bottle as Annie held her son and Jake blinked up at her.

"To?"

"Us." He poured two stemmed glasses, then handed her one. "To the family O'Shaughnessy. Long may it prosper."

"Hear, hear." She touched the rim of her glass to his.

"And to the most beautiful woman in the world. My wife."

Annie blushed. "Here's to you, Mr. O. The most unlikely husband in the world, and the best."

They drank, then kissed, then found a way to personally wish each other the merriest Christmas ever.

The 24 Days of Christmas

Linda Lael Miller

Chapter One

The snow, as much a Thanksgiving leftover as the cold turkey in the sandwich Frank Raynor had packed for lunch, lay in tattered, dirty patches on the frozen ground. Surveying the leaden sky through the window of the apartment over his garage, Frank sighed and wondered if he'd done the right thing, renting the place to Addie Hutton. She'd grown up in the big house, on the other side of the lawn. How would she feel about taking up residence in what, in her mind, probably amounted to the servants' quarters?

"Daddy?"

He turned to see his seven-year-old daughter, Lissie, framed in the doorway. She was wearing a golden halo of her own design, constructed from a coat hanger and an old tinsel garland filched from the boxes of Christmas decorations downstairs.

"Does this make me look like an angel?"

Frank felt a squeeze in his chest as he made a show of assessing the rest of the outfit—jeans, snow boots, and a pink T-shirt that said "Brat Princess" on the front. "Yeah, Lisser," he said. "You've got it going on."

Lissie was the picture of her late mother, with her short, dark and impossibly thick hair, bright hazel eyes, and all those pesky freckles. Frank loved those freckles, just as he'd loved Maggie's, though she'd hated them, and so did Lissie. "So you think I have a shot at the part, right?"

The kid had her heart set on playing an angel in the annual Christmas pageant at St. Mary's Episcopal School. Privately, Frank didn't hold out much hope, since he'd just given the school's drama teacher, Miss Pidgett, a speeding ticket two weeks before, and she was still steamed about it. She'd gone so far as to complain to the city council, claiming police harassment, but Frank had stood up and said she'd been doing fifty-five in a thirty, and the citation had stuck. The old biddy had barely spoken to him before that; now she was crossing the street to avoid saying hello.

He would have liked to think Almira Pidgett wasn't the type to take a grown-up grudge out on a seven-year-old, but, unfortunately, he knew from experience that she was. She'd been *his* teacher, when he first arrived in Pine Crossing, and she'd disliked him from day one.

"What's so bad about playing a shepherd?" he hedged, and took a sip from his favorite coffee mug. Maggie had made it for him, in the ceramics class she'd taken to keep her mind off the chemo, and he carried it most everywhere he went. Folks probably thought he had one hell of an addiction to caffeine; in truth, he kept the cup within reach because it was the last gift Maggie ever gave him. It was a talisman; he felt closer to her when he could touch it.

Lissie folded her arms and set her jaw, Maggie-style. "It's dumb for a girl to be a shepherd. Girls are supposed to be angels."

He hid a grin behind the rim of the mug. "Your mother would have said girls could herd sheep as well as boys," he replied. "And I've known more than one female who wouldn't qualify as an angel, no matter what kind of get-up she was wearing."

A wistful expression crossed Lissie's face. "I miss Mommy so much," she said, very softly. Maggie had been gone two years, come June, and Frank kept expecting to get used to it, but it hadn't happened, for him *or* for Lissie.

I want you to mourn me for a while, Maggie had told him, toward the end, *but when it's time to let go, I'll find a way to tell you.*

"I know," he said gruffly. "Me, too."

"Mommy's an angel now, isn't she?"

Frank couldn't speak. He managed a nod.

"Miss Pidgett says people don't turn into angels when they die. She says they're still just people."

"Miss Pidgett," Frank said, "is a—stickler for detail."

"A what?"

Frank looked pointedly at his watch. "You're going to be late for school if we don't get a move on," he said.

"Angels," Lissie said importantly, straightening her halo, "are always on time."

Frank grinned. "Did you feed Floyd?"

Floyd was the overweight beagle he and Lissie had rescued from the pound a month after Maggie died. In retrospect, it seemed to Frank that *Floyd* had been the one doing the rescuing—he'd made a man and a little girl laugh, when they'd both thought nothing would ever be funny again.

"Of course I did," Lissie said. "Angels always feed their dogs."

Frank chuckled, but that hollow place was still there, huddled in a corner of his ticker. "Get your coat," he said.

"It's in the car," Lissie replied, and her gaze strayed to the Advent calendar taped across the bottom of the cupboards. Fashioned of matchboxes, artfully painted and glued to a length of red velvet ribbon, now as scruffy as the snow outside, the thing was an institution in the Raynor family. Had been since Frank was seven himself. "How come you put that up here?" she asked, with good reason. Every Christmas of her short life, her great-aunt Eliza's calendar had hung in the living room of the main house, fixed to the mantelpiece. It was a family tradition to open one box each day and admire the small treasure glued inside.

Frank crossed the worn linoleum floor, intending to steer his quizzical daughter in the direction of the front door, but she didn't budge. She was like Maggie that way, too—stubborn as a mule up to its belly in molasses.

"I thought it might make Miss Hutton feel welcome," he said.

"The lady who lived in our house when she was a kid?"

Frank nodded. Addie, the daughter of a widowed judge, had been a lonely little girl. She'd made a point of being around every single morning, from the first of December to the twenty-fourth, for the opening of that day's matchbox. This old kitchen had been a warm, joyous place in those days—Aunt Eliza, the Huttons' housekeeper, had made sure of that. Putting up the Advent calendar was Frank's way of offering Addie a pleasant memory. "You don't mind, do you?"

Lissie considered the question. "I guess not," she said. "You think she'll let me stop by before school, so I can look inside, too?"

That Frank couldn't promise. He hadn't seen Addie in more than ten years, and he had no idea what kind of woman she'd turned into. She'd come back for Aunt Eliza's funeral, and sent a card when Maggie died, but she'd left Pine Crossing, Colorado, behind when she went off to college, and, as far as he knew, she'd never looked back.

He ruffled Lissie's curls, careful not to displace the halo. "Don't know, Beans," he said. The leather of his service belt creaked as he crouched to look into the child's small, earnest face, balancing the coffee mug deftly as he did so. "It's almost Christmas. The lady's had a rough time over the last little while. Maybe this will bring back some happy memories."

Lissie beamed. "Okay," she chimed. She was missing one of her front teeth, and her smile touched a bruised place in Frank, though it was a sweet ache. Not much scared him, but the depth and breadth of the love he bore this little girl cut a chasm in his very soul.

Frank straightened. "School," he said with mock sternness.

Lissie fairly skipped out of the apartment and down the stairs to the side of the garage. "I know what's in the first box anyway," she sang. "A teeny, tiny teddy bear."

"Yup," Frank agreed, following at a more sedate pace, lifting his collar against the cold. Thirty years ago, on his first night in town, he and his aunt Eliza had selected that bear from a shoebox full of dime-store geegaws she'd collected, and he'd personally glued it in place. That was when he'd begun to think his life might turn out all right after all.

Addie Hutton slowed her secondhand Buick as she turned onto Fifth Street. Her most important possessions, a computer and printer, four boxes of books, a few photo albums, and a couple of suitcases full of clothes, were in the backseat—and her heart was in her throat.

Her father's house loomed just ahead, a two-story saltbox, white with green shutters. The ornate mailbox, once labeled "Hutton," now read "Raynor," but the big maple tree was still in the front yard, and the tire swing, now old and weather-worn, dangled from the sturdiest branch.

She smiled, albeit a little sadly. Her father hadn't wanted that swing—said it would be an eyesore, more suited to the other side of the tracks than to their neighborhood—but Eliza, the house-keeper and the only mother Addie had ever really known, since her own had died when she was three, had stood firm on the matter. Finally defeated, the judge had sent his secretary's husband, Charlie, over to hang the tire.

She pulled into the driveway and looked up at the apartment over the garage. A month before, when the last pillar of her life had finally collapsed, she'd called Frank Raynor and asked if the place was rented. She'd known it was available, having maintained her subscription to the hometown newspaper and seen the ad in the classifieds, but the truth was, she hadn't been sure Frank would want her living in such close proximity. He'd seemed surprised by the inquiry, and, after some throat clearing, he'd said the last tenant had just given notice, and if she wanted it, she could move in any time.

She'd asked about the rent, since that little detail wasn't listed—for the first time in her life, money was an issue—and he'd said they could talk about that later.

Now she put the car into park and turned off the engine with a resolute motion of her right hand. She pushed open the door, jumped out, and marched toward the outside stairs. During their telephone conversation, Frank had offered to leave the key under the doormat, and Addie had asked if it was still safe to leave doors unlocked in Pine Crossing. He'd chuckled and said it was. All right, then, she'd said. It was decided. No need for a key.

A little breathless from dashing up the steps, Addie stopped on the familiar welcome mat and drew a deep breath, bracing herself for the flood of memories that were bound to wash over her the moment she stepped over that worn threshold.

A brisk winter wind bit through her lightweight winter coat, bought for southern California, and she turned the knob.

Eliza's furniture was still there, at least in the living room. Every stick of it.

Tears burned Addie's eyes as she took it all in—the old blue sofa, the secondhand coffee table, the ancient piano, always out of tune. She almost expected to hear Eliza call out the old familiar greeting. "Adelaide Hutton, is that you? You get yourself into this kitchen and have a glass of milk and a cookie or two."

Frank's high school graduation picture still occupied the place of honor on top of the piano, and next to it was Addie's own.

Addie crossed the room, touched Frank's square-jawed face, and smiled. He wasn't handsome, in the classic sense of the word—his features were too rough cut for that, his brown eyes too earnest, and too wary. She wondered if, at thirty-seven, he still had all that dark, unruly hair.

She turned her head, by force of will, to face her younger self. Brown hair, not as thick as she would have liked, blue eyes, good skin. Lord, she looked so innocent in that photograph, so painfully hopeful. By the time she graduated, two years after Frank, he was already working his way through college in Boulder, with a major in criminal justice. They were engaged, and he'd intended to come back to Pine Crossing, as soon as he'd completed his studies, and join the three-man police force. With Chief Potter about to retire, and Ben Mead ready to step into the top job, there would be a place waiting for Frank the day he got his degree.

Addie loved Frank, but she dreamed of going to a university and majoring in journalism; Frank, older, and with his career already mapped out, had wanted her to stay in Pine Crossing and study at the local junior college. He'd reluctantly agreed to delay the marriage, and she'd gone off to Denver to study. There had been no terrible crisis, no confrontation—they had simply grown apart.

Midway through her sophomore year, when he'd just pinned on his shiny new badge, she'd sent his ring back, by Federal Express, with a brief letter.

Though it was painful, Addie had kept up on Frank's life, through the pages of the Pine Crossing *Statesman*. In the intervening years, he'd married, fathered a child, and been tragically widowed. He'd worked his way up through the ranks, and now he was head man.

Addie tore herself away from the pictures and checked out the kitchen. Same ancient oak table, chairs with hand-sewn cushions, and avocado green appliances. Even Eliza's antique percolator was in its customary place on the counter. It was almost as if the apartment had been preserved as a sort of memorial, yet the effect was heartwarming.

Suspended above the counter was Eliza's matchbox Advent calendar, the fraying ends and middle of the supporting ribbon carefully taped into place.

A powerful yearning swept through Addie. She approached the calendar, ran her fingers lightly from one box to another. Her throat closed, and the tears she'd blinked away earlier came back with a vengeance.

"Oh, Eliza," she whispered, "I'd give anything to see you again."

Pulling on the tiny ribbon tab at the top, she tugged open the first box, labeled, like the others, with a brass numeral. The miniature teddy bear was still inside.

She'd been five the night Frank came to live with his aunt, a somber, quiet little boy, arriving on the four o'clock bus from Denver, clutching a threadbare panda in one hand and a beat-up suitcase in the other.

Needing a distraction, Addie opened the cupboard where Eliza had kept her coffee in a square glass jar with a red lid. Bless Frank, he'd replenished the supply.

Addie started a pot brewing, and while the percolator was chortling and chugging away, she went downstairs to bring in her things. By the time she'd lugged up the various computer components and the books, the coffee was ready.

She set the computer up in the smaller of the two bedrooms, the one that had been Frank's. Other memories awaited her there, but she managed to hold them at bay while she hooked everything up and plugged into the telephone line.

In her old life, she'd been a reporter. She had done a lot of her research online, and kept up with her various sources via e-mail. Now, the Internet was her primary way of staying in touch with her six-year-old stepson, Henry.

The system booted up and—bless Frank again—she heard the rhythmic blipping sound of a dial tone. Evidently, he hadn't had the phone service shut off after the last renter moved out.

She was into her e-mail within seconds, and her first reaction was disappointment. Nothing from Henry.

Perched on the chair at the secondhand desk where Frank had

worked so diligently at his homework, when they were both kids, she scrolled through the usual forwards and spam.

At the very end was a message with the subject line, THIS IS FROM TOBY.

Addie's fingers froze over the keyboard. Toby was her ex-husband. They'd been divorced for two years, but they'd stayed in contact because of Henry. She'd had no legal claim to the child—in the darkest hours of the night she still kicked herself for not adopting him while she and Toby were still married—but Toby had a busy social life, and she'd been a free baby-sitter. Until the debacle that brought her career down around her ears, that was. After that, Toby's live-in girlfriend, Elle, had decided Addie was a bad influence, and the visits had all but stopped.

Trembling slightly, she opened the e-mail.

MEET THE FOUR O'CLOCK BUS, Toby had written. That was all. No explanations, no smart remarks, no signature.

"Damn you, Toby," she muttered, and scrabbled in the depths of her purse for her cell phone. His number was on speed dial, from the old days, before she'd become a *persona non grata*.

His voice mail picked up. "This is Toby Springer," he said. "Elle and I are on our honeymoon. Be home around the end of January. Leave a message, and we'll get back to you then."

Addie jammed the disconnect button with her thumb, checked her watch.

Three-ten.

She fired back an e-mail, just in case Toby, true to form, was shallow enough to take a laptop on his honeymoon. He was irresponsible in just about every area of his life, but when it came to his loan brokering business, he kept up.

WHERE IS HENRY? Addie typed furiously, and hit send.

After that, she drank coffee and paced, watching the screen for an answer that never came.

At five minutes to four, she was waiting at the Texaco station, in the center of town. The bus rolled in right on time and stopped with a squeak of air brakes.

The hydraulic door whooshed open.

A middle-aged woman descended the steps, then an old man in corduroy pants, a plaid flannel shirt and a quilted vest, then a teenage girl with pink hair and a silver ring at the base of her right eyebrow.

Addie crammed her hands into the pockets of her coat and paced some more.

At last, she saw him. A bespectacled little boy, standing tentatively in the doorway of the bus, clutching a teddy bear under one arm.

Henry.

She'd been afraid to hope. Now, overjoyed, Addie ran past the gas pumps to gather him close.

Chapter Two

Henry sat at Eliza's table, huddled in his favorite pajamas, his brown hair rumpled, his horn-rimmed glasses slightly askew. "So anyway," he explained, sounding mildly congested, "Elle said I was incrudgible and Dad had better deal with me or she'd be out of there."

Addie seethed. She hadn't pressed for details the afternoon before, after his arrival, and Henry hadn't volunteered any. They'd stopped at the supermarket on the way home from the Texaco station, stocked up on fish sticks and French fries, and come back to the apartment for supper. After the meal, Henry had submitted sturdily to a bath, a dose of children's aspirin, and the smearing on of mentholated rub. Then, exhausted, he'd donned his pajamas and fallen asleep in Frank's childhood bed.

Addie had spent half the night trying to track Toby down, but he might as well have moved to Argentina and taken on a new identity. It seemed he'd dropped off the face of the earth.

Now, in the chilly glare of a winter morning, Henry was more forthcoming with details. "Dad and me flew to Denver together; then he put me on the bus and said he'd call you when he'd worked things out with Elle."

Addie gritted her teeth and turned her back, fiddling with the cord on the percolator. The Advent calendar dangled in front of her, a tattered, colorful reminder that there was joy in the world, and that it was often simple and homemade.

"Hey," she said brightly, turning around again, "it's the second of December. Want to see what's in the box?"

Henry adjusted his glasses and examined the length of ribbon, with its twenty-four colorful matchboxes. Before he could reply, a firm knock sounded at the front door.

"Come in!" Addie called, because you could do that in Pine Crossing, without fear of admitting an ax murderer.

A little girl dashed into the kitchen, wearing everyday clothes and a tinsel halo. Addie was struck dumb, momentarily at least. *Frank's child,* she thought, amazed to find herself shaken. *This is Frank's child.*

Addie had barely had time to recover from that realization when Frank himself loomed in the doorway. His badge twinkled on the front of his brown uniform jacket.

One of her questions was put to rest, at least. Frank still had all his hair.

He smiled that slow, sparing smile of his. "Hello, Addie," he said.

"Frank," she managed to croak, with a nod.

He put a hand on the girl's shoulder. "This is my daughter, Lissie," he said. "She's impersonating an angel."

The brief, strange tension was broken, and Addie laughed. Approaching Lissie, she put out a hand. "How do you do?" she said. "My name is Addie. I don't believe I've ever had the pleasure of meeting an angel before." She peered over Lissie's small shoulders, pretending to be puzzled. "Where are your wings?"

The child sighed, a little deflated. "You don't get those unless you're actually in the play," she said. "Shepherds aren't allowed to have wings."

Addie gave Frank a quizzical look. He responded with a half smile and a you've-got-me shake of his head.

"I made the halo myself," Lissie said, squaring her shoulders. She'd been sneaking looks at Henry the whole time; now she addressed him directly. "Who are you?"

"Henry," he replied solemnly, and pushed at the nosepiece of his glasses. "My dad got married, and his wife says I'm incrudgible."

"Oh," Lissie said with a knowing air.

Frank and Addie exchanged glances.

"Sorry to bother you," Frank said, nodding toward the

Advent calendar. A smile lit his eyes. "Lissie was hoping she could be around for the opening of Box Number 2."

Addie's throat tightened. Those memories again, all of them sweet. "You do the honors, Miss Lissie," she said with a grand gesture of one arm.

Lissie started toward the calendar, and once again Frank's hand came to rest on her small shoulder. Although they didn't look at each other, some silent message traveled between father and daughter.

"I think Henry should open the box," Lissie said. "Unless being incrudgible means he'll mess it up."

Henry hesitated, probably wondering if incrudgibility was, indeed, a factor in the enterprise. Then, very carefully, he dragged his chair over to the counter, climbed up on it, and pulled open the second box. Lissie looked on eagerly.

Henry turned his head, his nose wrinkled. "It's a ballerina," he said with little-boy disdain.

Addie had known what was inside, of course, knew what was tucked into all the boxes. She'd been through the ritual every Christmas of her childhood, from the time she was five. Eliza had let her choose that tiny doll from a shoebox full of small toys, the very first year, dab glue onto its back, and press it into place.

She looked at Frank, looked away again, quickly. She'd been so jealous of him, those first few weeks after his arrival, afraid he'd take her place in Eliza's affections. Instead, Eliza had made room in her heart for both children, each lost and unwanted in their own way, and let Addie take part in the tradition, right from the first.

"We'd better be on our way," Frank said, somewhat gruffly. "Lissie's got school."

Addie touched Henry's forehead reflexively, before helping him down from the chair. Despite the aspirin and other stock remedies, he still had a slight fever, and that worried her.

"Are you going to go to my school?" Lissie asked Henry. "Or are you just here for a vacation?"

"I don't know," Henry said, and he sounded so bereft that the insides of Addie's sinuses burned. Damn Toby, she thought bitterly. Damn him for being selfish and shallow enough to put a small boy on a bus and leave him to his fate. Did the man have so much as a clue how many things could have gone horribly wrong along the way?

Frank caught her eye. "Everything all right, Addie?" he asked quietly.

She bit her lower lip. Nodded. Frank didn't keep up with gossip; he never had. It followed, then, that he didn't know what she'd been accused of, that she'd staked her whole career on a big story, that she'd almost gone to jail for protecting her source, that that source, as it turned out, had been lying through his capped and gleaming teeth.

Frank looked good-naturedly skeptical of her answer. He shrugged and raised a coffee mug to his lips. It was white, chipped here and there, with an oversized handle and Frank's name emblazoned in gold letters across the front, inside a large red heart.

"Thanks," he said.

Addie had lost track of the conversation, and it must have shown in her face, because Frank grinned, inclined his head toward the Advent calendar, and said, "It means a lot to Lissie, to open those boxes."

"Maybe you should take it back to your place," she said. Henry and Lissie were in the living room by then; one of them was plunking out a single-finger version of "Jingle Bells" on Eliza's ancient piano. "After all, it's a family heirloom."

"It seems fitting to me, having it here," Frank reasoned, watching her intently, "but if you'd rather we didn't come stomping into your kitchen every morning, I'd understand. So would Lissie."

"It isn't that," Addie protested, laying a hand to her heart. "Honestly. It was so sweet of you to remember, but—" Her voice fell away, and she struggled to get hold of it again. "Frank, about the rent—you didn't say how much—"

"Let's not worry about that right now," Frank interrupted. "It's almost Christmas, and, besides, this is your home."

Addie opened her mouth, closed it again. Her father, the judge, had quietly waited out her ill-fated engagement to Frank, but he'd been unhappy with her decision to go into journalism instead of law. When she refused to change her major, he'd changed his will, leaving the main house and property to Eliza. A year later, he'd died of a heart attack.

Addie had never been close to her father, but she'd grieved all right. She hadn't needed the inheritance. She'd buckled down, gotten her degree, and landed a promising job with a California newspaper. She'd been the golden girl—until she'd trusted the wrong people, and written a story that nearly brought down an entire chain of newspapers.

Frank raised his free hand, as though he might touch the tip of her nose, the way he'd done when they were young, and thought they were in love. Then, apparently having second thoughts, he let it fall back to his side.

"See you tomorrow," he said.

Chapter Three

Addie awoke to silvery light and the sort of muffled sounds that always meant snow. She lay perfectly still, for a long time, hands cupped behind her head, grinning like a delighted fool. Snow. Oh, how she had missed the snow, in the land of palm trees and almost constant sunshine.

Henry was trying to make a phone call when she got to the kitchen. After a moment's pause, she started the coffee.

"I hate my dad," he said, hanging up the receiver with a slight slam. "I hate Elle, too."

Addie wanted to wrap the child in her arms and hold him close, but she sensed that he wouldn't welcome the gesture at this delicate point. He was barely keeping himself together as it was. "No, sweetie," she said softly. "You don't hate either of them. You're just angry, and that's understandable. And for the record, you're not incorrigible, either. You are a *very* good boy."

He stared at her in that owlish way of his. "I don't want to go back there. Not ever. I want to stay here, with you."

Addie's heart ached. *You have no rights,* she reminded herself. *Not where this child is concerned.* "You know I'd love to have you live with me for always," she said carefully, "but that might not be possible. Your dad—"

Suddenly, Henry hurled himself at her. She dropped to her knees and pulled him into her arms.

There was a rap at the front door.

"Addie?" Frank called.

Henry pulled back and rubbed furiously at his eyes, then straightened his glasses.

"Come in," Addie said.

Frank appeared in the doorway, carrying his coffee cup and a bakery box. He paused on the threshold, watching as Addie got to her feet.

"Do you sleep in that stupid halo?" Henry asked, gazing balefully at Lissie, who pressed past her father to bounce into the kitchen.

"Henry," Addie said in soft reprimand. He wasn't usually a difficult child, but under the present circumstances. . . .

"You're just jealous," Lissie said with cheerful confidence, striking a pose.

Frank set his coffee mug on the counter with an authoritative thump. "Lissandra," he said. "Be nice."

"Well, he is," Lissie countered.

"Am not," Henry insisted, digging in his heels and folding his arms. "And your hair is poofy."

"Somebody open the box," Frank put in.

"My turn," Lissie announced, and dragged over the same chair Henry had used the day before. With appropriate ceremony, she tugged at the little ribbon pull at the top of the matchbox and revealed the cotton-ball snowman inside. He still had his black top hat and bead eyes.

"We could build a snowman, after school," Lissie told Henry, inspired. "And my hair is not *either* poofy." She paused. "You *are* going to school, aren't you?"

Henry looked up at Addie. "Do I have to?"

She ruffled his hair, resisted an impulse to adjust his glasses. He hated it when she did that, and, anyway, it might call attention to the fact that he'd been crying. "I think you should," she said. She'd had him checked out at the Main Street Clinic the day before, and physically, he was fine. She had explained his situation to the doctor, and they'd agreed that the best thing to do was keep his life as normal as possible.

Henry sighed heavily. "Okay, I'll go. As long as I get to help build the snow-dude afterwards."

Frank refilled his coffee mug at the percolator and helped himself to a pastry. "Sounds like a fair deal to me," he said, munching. He looked at Addie over the top of Lissie's head. "You going to help? With the snowman, I mean?"

Addie flushed and rubbed her hands down the thighs of her jeans. "I really should look for a job."

"School doesn't get out until three," Lissie reasoned, climbing down from the chair. "That gives you plenty of time."

"I'll take a late lunch hour," Frank put in, offering Addie a bear claw. Her all-time favorite. Had he remembered that, or was it just coincidence? "I heard there was an opening over at the *Wooden Nickel*. Receptionist and classified ad sales."

Addie lowered the bear claw.

"Kind of a come-down from big-city journalism," Frank said. "But other than waitressing at the Lumberjack Diner, that's about all Pine Crossing has to offer in the way of employment."

She studied his face. So he did know, then—about what had happened in California. She wished she dared ask him how *much* he knew, but she didn't. Not with Lissie there, and Henry already so upset.

"I'll take the kids to school," Frank went on, raising Addie's hand, pastry and all, back to her mouth even as he turned to the kids. "Hey, Hank," he said. "How'd you like a ride in a squad car?"

The snow was still drifting down, in big, fat, pristine flakes, when Addie set out for the *Wooden Nickel*, armed with a truthful resumé and high hopes. The *Nickel* wasn't really a newspaper, just a supermarket giveaway, but that didn't mean the editor wouldn't have heard about her exploits in California. Even though the job probably didn't involve writing anything but copy for classified ads, she might be considered a bad risk.

The wheels of the Buick crunched in the mounting snow as she pulled up in front of the small storefront where the *Wooden Nickel* was published. Like most of the businesses in town, it faced the square, where a large, bare evergreen tree had been erected.

She smiled. The lighting of the tree was a big deal in Pine Crossing, right up there with the pageant at St. Mary's. Henry would probably enjoy it, and the festivities might even take his mind off his father's disinterest, if only for an evening.

Her smile faded. *Call him, Toby,* she pleaded silently. *Please call him.*

Mr. Renfrew was the editor of the *Wooden Nickel,* just as he had been when Addie was a child. He beamed as she stepped into the office, brushing snow from the sleeves of her coat.

"Addie Hutton!" he cried, looking like Santa, even in his flannel shirt and woolen trousers, as he came out from behind the counter. "It's wonderful to see you again!"

He hugged her, and she hugged him back. "Thanks," she said after swallowing.

"Frank was by a little while ago. Said you might be in the market for a job."

It was just like Frank to try and pave the way. Addie didn't know whether to be annoyed or appreciative, and decided she was both. "I brought a resumé," she said. She had only a few hundred dollars in her checking account, until the money from the sale of her furniture and other personal belongings came through from the auction house in California, and now there was Henry to think about.

She needed work.

"No need for anything like that," Mr. Renfrew said with a wave of his plump, age-spotted hand. "I've known you all your life, Addie. Knew your father for most of his." He paused, frowned. "I can't pay you much, though. You realize that, don't you?"

Addie smiled, nodded. Her eyes were burning again.

"Then it's settled. You can start tomorrow. Nine o'clock sharp."

"Thank you," Addie said, almost overcome. Her salary at the *Wooden Nickel* probably wouldn't have covered her gym membership back home, but she blessed every penny of it.

Mr. Renfrew gave her a tour of the small operation and showed her which of the three desks was hers.

When she stepped back out into the cold, Frank just happened to be loitering on the sidewalk, watching as members of the volunteer fire department strung lights on the community tree from various rungs of the truck ladder.

Addie poked him good-naturedly in the back. "You put in a good word for me, didn't you?" she accused. "With Mr. Renfrew, I mean."

Frank grinned down at her. "Maybe I did," he admitted. "Truth is, he didn't need much persuading. How about a cup of coffee over at the Lumberjack?"

She looked pointedly at the mug in his right hand. "Looks as if you carry your own," she teased.

Something changed in his face, something so subtle that she might have missed it if she hadn't been looking so closely, trying to read him. Then his grin broadened, and he upended the cup, dumping the dregs of his coffee into a snowbank. "I guess I need a refill," he said.

They walked to the diner, on the opposite side of the square, Frank exchanging gruff male greetings with the light-stringing firemen as they passed.

Inside the diner, they took seats in a booth, and the waitress filled Frank's mug automatically, before turning over the clean cup in front of Addie and pouring a serving for her.

"What happened in California?" Frank asked bluntly, when they were alone.

Addie looked out into the square, watching the firemen and the passersby, and her hand trembled a little as she raised the cup to her mouth. "I made a mistake," she said, after a long time, when she could meet his eyes again. "A really stupid one."

"You've never done anything stupid in your life," Frank said.

Except when I gave back your engagement ring, Addie thought, and immediately backed away from that memory. "That's debatable." She sighed. "I got a tip on a big scandal brewing in the city attorney's office," she said miserably. "I checked and rechecked the facts, but I should have *triple*-checked them. I wrote an article that shook the courthouse from top to bottom. I was nearly jailed when I wouldn't reveal my source—and then that source turned out to be a master liar. People's reputations and careers were damaged. My newspaper was sued, and I was fired."

Frank shook his head. "Must have been rough."

Addie bit her lower lip, then squared her shoulders. "It was," she admitted solemnly. "Thanks to you, I have a job and a place to live." She leaned forward. "We have to talk about rent, Frank."

He leaned forward, too. "That whole place should have been yours. I'm not going to charge you rent."

"It should have been Eliza's, and she left it to you," Addie insisted. "And I *am* going to pay rent. If you refuse, I'll move."

He grinned. "Good luck finding anything in Pine Crossing," he said.

She slumped back in her seat. "I'm paying. You need the money. You can't possibly be making very much."

He lifted his cup to his mouth, chuckled. "Still stubborn as hell, I see," he observed. "And it just so happens that I do all right, from a financial standpoint anyway." He set the mug down again, regarded her thoughtfully. "Tell me about the boy," he said.

She smiled at the mention of Henry. For all the problems, it was a blessing having him with her, a gift. She loved him desperately—he was the child she might never have. She was thirty-five, after all, and her life was a train wreck. "Henry is my stepson. His father and I were badly matched, and the marriage came crashing down under its own weight a couple of years ago. I fell out of love with Toby, but Henry is still my man."

"He seems troubled," Frank remarked. The diner's overhead lights shimmered in his dark hair and on the broad shoulders of his jacket. Danced along the upper half of his badge.

"My ex-husband isn't the most responsible father in the world. He remarried recently, and evidently, the new Mrs. Springer is not inclined to raise another woman's child. Toby brought him as far as Denver by plane, then put him on a bus, like so much freight. Henry came all that way alone. He must have been so scared."

Frank's jawline tightened, and a flush climbed his neck. "Tell your ex-husband," he muttered, "never to break the speed limit in my town."

While Floyd the beagle galloped around the snowman in everwidening circles, barking joyously at falling flakes, Henry and Lissie pressed small stones into Frosty's chest, and Addie added the finishing touch: one of Frank's old baseball caps.

The moment was so perfect that it worried Frank a little.

He was telling himself not to be a fool when Almira Pidgett's vintage Desoto ground up to the curb. She leaned across the seat, rolled down the passenger window, and glowered through the snowfall.

"Well," she called, raising her voice several decibels above shrill to be heard over the happy beagle, "it's nice to see our chief of police hard at work, making our community safe from crime."

Lissie and Henry went still, and some of the delight drained from Addie's face. Out of the corner of his eye, Frank saw Lissie straighten her halo.

You old bat, Frank thought, but he smiled as he strolled toward the Desoto, his hands in the pockets of his uniform jacket. "Hello, Miss Pidgett," he said affably, bending to look through the open window. "Care to help us finish our snowman?"

"Hmmph," she said. "Is that Addie Hutton over there? I must say, she doesn't look much the worse for wear, for someone who almost went to prison."

Frank's smile didn't waver, even though he would have liked to reach across that seat and close both hands around Almira's neck. "You ought to work up a little Christmas spirit, Miss Pidgett," he said. "If you don't, you might just be visited by three spirits one of these nights, like old Ebenezer Scrooge."

Chapter Four

"It's a Christmas tree," Henry announced importantly, the following morning, after opening the fourth box. Frank had lifted him onto the counter for the unveiling. "Are *we* going to get a Christmas tree, Addie?"

"Sure," Addie said, a little too quickly. Her smile felt wobbly on her face. There had still been no call from Toby, no response to her barrage of e-mails and phone messages. And every day that Henry stayed with her would make it that much more difficult, when the time came, to give him up.

"It's too early for a tree," Lissie said practically, watching as Henry scrambled down off the counter with no help from Frank. She looked especially festive that day, having replaced the snow-soaked gold tinsel in her halo with bright silver. "The needles will fall off."

"We had a fake one in California," Henry said. "It was made of the same stuff as that thing on your head, so the needles *never* fell off. We could have left it up till the Fourth of July."

"That's stupid," Lissie responded. "Who wants a Christmas tree on the Fourth of July?"

"Liss," Frank said. "Throwing the word 'stupid' around is conduct unbecoming to an angel."

The little girl sighed hugely. "It's useless trying to be an angel anyway," she said. "I guess I'm going to be a shepherd for the rest of my life."

Addie straightened Lissie's halo. "Nonsense," she said, suppressing a smile. "I think it's safe to say that you most certainly will not be a shepherd three weeks from now."

Outside, in the driveway, a horn bleated out one cheery little honk.

"Car pool," Frank explained when Addie lifted her eyebrows in question.

She hastened to zip Henry into his coat. He endured this fussing with characteristic stoicism, and when he and Lissie had gone, Frank lingered to refill his cup at the percolator.

"No word from Wonder Dad, huh?" he asked.

Addie shook her head. "How can he do this, Frank?" she muttered miserably. "How can he just *not call?* For all he knows, Henry never arrived, or I wasn't here when he did."

"He knows," Frank said easily. "You've been calling and e-mailing, haven't you?"

Addie nodded, pulling on her coat and reaching for her purse. She wanted to get to work early, show Mr. Renfrew she was dependable. "But he hasn't answered."

"And you think that means he didn't get the messages?"

Addie paused in the act of unplugging the coffeepot. Frank had a point. Toby was a master at avoiding confrontation, not to mention personal responsibility. He wouldn't call, or even respond to her e-mails, until he was sure she'd had time enough to cool off.

She sighed. "You're right," she said.

Frank gave her a crooked grin and spread his hands. "Are we still on for the tree-lighting ceremony tonight?" he asked.

Addie nodded, glanced at the Advent calendar, with its four open boxes. Twenty to go. "Have you noticed a pattern?" she asked. "I mean, maybe I'm being fanciful, here, but the first day, there was a teddy bear. Henry was carrying a bear when he got off the bus. Then—okay, the ballerina doesn't fit the theory—but yesterday was the snowman. We built one. And today, it's the Christmas tree, and the shindig at the square just happens to be tonight."

Frank put a hand to the small of her back and gently propelled her toward the doorway. "The bear," he said, "was pure coincidence. The snowman gave the kids the idea to build one. And the fire department always lights the tree three weeks before Christmas."

They'd crossed the living room, and Frank opened the front door to a gust of dry, biting wind. Addie pulled her coat more tightly around her. "All very practical," she said with a tentative smile, "but I heard you tell Miss Pidgett she might be visited by three spirits some night soon. If that's not fanciful, I don't know what is."

They descended the steps, and Frank didn't smile at her remark. He seemed distracted. "Lissie really wants that part," he fretted. "The one in the pageant at St. Mary's, I mean. And Almira isn't going to give it to her, not because the kid couldn't pull it off, but because she doesn't like me."

Addie thought of Lissie's tinsel halo and felt a pinch of sorrow in the deepest region of her heart. "Maybe if you talked to Miss Pidgett, explained—"

Frank stopped beside his squad car, which was parked in the driveway, beside Addie's station wagon. "I can't do that, Addie," he said quietly. "I'm the chief of police. I can't ask the woman to do my kid a favor."

She touched his arm. Started to say that *she* could speak to Miss Pidgett, and promptly closed her mouth. She knew how Frank would react to that suggestion; he'd say she was over the line, and he'd be right.

Frank surprised her. He leaned forward and kissed her lightly on the forehead. "Thanks, Addie," he said.

"For what?"

"For coming home."

Chapter Five

Addie stopped on the sidewalk outside the *Wooden Nickel,* at eight forty-five A.M. precisely, to admire the glowing tree in the center of the square. She hoped she would never forget the reflection of those colored lights shining on Henry and Lissie's upturned faces the night before. After the celebration, they'd all gone back to Frank's place for spaghetti and hot cocoa, and Addie had been amazed that she didn't so much as hesitate on the threshold.

When she and her father had lived there, the very walls had seemed to echo with loneliness, except when Eliza or Frank were around.

Now another father and daughter occupied the space. The furniture was different, of course, but so was the atmosphere. Sorrow had visited those rooms, leaving its mark, but despite that, the house seemed to exude warmth, stability—love.

A rush of cold wind brought Addie abruptly back to the present moment. She shivered and pushed open the front door of the *Wooden Nickel,* and very nearly sent Mr. Renfrew sprawling.

He was teetering on top of a foot ladder, affixing a silver bell above the door.

Addie gasped and reached out to steady her employer. "I'm sorry!" she cried.

Mr. Renfrew grinned down at her. "What do you think of the bell?" he asked proudly. "It belonged to my grandmother."

Addie put a hand to her heart. The bell was silver, with a loop of red ribbon attached to the top.

"What's the matter?" Mr. Renfrew asked, getting down from the ladder.

In her mind's eye, Addie was seeing the little bell in the Christmas box Lissie had opened that morning. Silver, with red thread.

She smiled. "Nothing at all," she said happily, unbuttoning her coat. "It looks wonderful."

"There's a phone message for you, Addie," put in Stella Dorrity, who worked part-time helping Mr. Renfrew with the ad layouts. "He left a number."

Addie felt her smile fade. "Thank you," she said, reaching out for the sticky note Stella offered.

Toby. Where on earth had he gotten her work number? She'd only been hired the day before.

Shakily, she hung up her coat and fished her cell phone out of her purse. "Do you mind if I return the call before I start work?" she asked Mr. Renfrew.

"You go right ahead," he said, still admiring his bell.

"You'd better move that ladder," Stella told him, arms folded, "before somebody breaks their neck."

Addie slipped into the cramped little room behind the reception desk, where the copy machine, lunch table, and a small refrigerator stood shoulder to shoulder.

She punched in the number Stella had taken down, not recognizing the area code.

Toby answered on the third ring. "Yo," he said.

"It's about time you bothered to check up on your son!" Addie whispered.

A sigh. "I knew you'd take care of him."

"He's scared to death," Addie sputtered. "When I saw him get off that bus, all alone—"

"You were there," Toby broke in. "That's what matters."

"What if I hadn't been, Toby? Did you ever think of that?"

"Listen to me, Addie. I know you're furious, and I guess you have a right to be. But I had to do something. The blended-family thing isn't working for Elle."

Addie closed her eyes, counted to ten, then to fifteen, for good measure. Even then, she wanted to take Toby's head off at the shoulders. "Isn't *that* a pity? Tell me, Tobe, did you think about any of this before you decided to tie the knot?"

"It's love, babe," Toby said lightly. "Will you keep him—just until Elle and I get settled in?"

"He's a little boy, not a goldfish!"

"I know, I know. He wants to be with you, anyway. Do this for me, Addie—please. I'm out of options, here. I'll straighten everything out with him when we get back from—when we get back."

"What am I supposed to tell Henry in the meantime? He needs to talk to you. Damn it, *you're his father.*"

"I'll send him a postcard."

"A postcard? Well, that's generous of you. It's almost Christmas, you've just shipped him almost two hundred miles on a Greyhound, all by himself, and you're going to *send a postcard?*"

Another sigh. Toby, the martyred saint. "Add, what do you want me to do?"

"I want you to call him. *Tonight,* Toby. Not when you get back from your stupid honeymoon. I want you to tell Henry you love him, and that everything will be all right."

"I do love him."

"Your idea of love differs significantly from mine," Addie snapped.

"Don't I know it," Toby replied. "All right. Let's have the number. I'll give the kid a ring around six, your time."

"You'd better, Toby."

She knew he wanted to ask what she would do about it if he didn't. She also knew he wouldn't dare.

"Six o'clock," he said, with resignation, and hung up in her ear.

"I think Lissie sleeps in that dumb halo," Henry observed that night as he sat coloring at the kitchen table. Addie was at the stove, whipping up a stir-fry, and even though she had one ear tuned to the phone, she was startled when it actually rang. She glanced at the clock on the opposite wall.

Six o'clock, straight up.

"Could you get that, please?" she asked.

Henry gave her a curious look and stalwartly complied. "Hello?"

Watching the boy out of the corner of her eye, Addie saw him stiffen.

"Hi, Dad."

Addie bit her lip and concentrated on the stir-fry, but she couldn't help listening to Henry's end of the conversation. Toby, she could tell, was making his stock excuses. Henry, playing his own customary role, made it easy.

"Sure," he finished. "I'll tell her. See you."

"Everything cool?" she asked carefully.

Henry adjusted his glasses. "I might get to stay till February. Maybe even until school lets out for the summer."

Addie dealt with a tangle of feelings—exhilaration, annoyance, dread and more annoyance—before assembling a smile and turning to face the little boy. "Is that okay with you?"

Henry grinned, nodded. "Yeah," he said. "Maybe he'll forget where he put me, and I'll get to stay forever."

Although she wanted to keep Henry for good, Addie felt a stab at his words. He was so young, and the concept that his own father might misplace him, like a set of keys or a store receipt, was already a part of his thought system.

She dished up two platefuls of stir-fry and set them on the table. "We have to take this one step at a time," she warned. Toby was a creature of moods, changeable and impulsive. If things went badly with Elle, or if the new wife was struck by a sudden maternal desire, Toby might swoop down at any moment and whisk Henry away, once and for all.

"Do you think she sleeps in it?" Henry asked, settling himself at the table.

Addie was a few beats behind. "What?"

"Lissie," Henry said patiently, reaching for his fork. "Do you think she sleeps in that halo?"

Chapter Six

Seated at her desk, the telephone receiver propped between her left shoulder and her ear, Addie doodled as she waited for her sales prospect, Jackie McCall, of McCall Real Estate, to come back on the line. A holly wreath, like the one in that morning's matchbox, took shape at the point of her pencil.

The bell over the front door jingled, and Almira Pidgett blew into the *Wooden Nickel,* red-cheeked and rushed. Her hat, with its fur earflaps, made her look as though she should have arrived in a motorcycle sidecar or a Model T—all she lacked was goggles.

Alone in the office, Addie put down her pencil, cupped a hand over the receiver and summoned up a smile. "Good morning," she said. "May I help you?"

"Where," demanded Miss Pidgett, "is Arthur?"

Addie held on to the smile with deliberation. "Mr. Renfrew had a Rotary meeting this morning. He's in the banquet room at the Lumberjack."

Miss Pidgett, plump and white-haired, had been an institution in Pine Crossing for as long as Addie could remember. She had been Addie's teacher, in both the first and second grades, but, unlike Lissie, and Frank, for that matter, Addie had always enjoyed the woman's favor. She'd played an angel three years in a row, at the Christmas pageant, and graduated to the starring role, that of Mary, before going on to high school.

Now Miss Pidgett sighed and tugged off her knit gloves. "I wish to place an advertisement," she announced.

Jackie McCall came back on the line. "Sorry to keep you waiting, Addie," she said. "It's crazy over here. Would you mind if I called you back?"

"That would be convenient," Addie replied.

Miss Pidgett waited, none too patiently, at the counter, while Addie and Jackie exchanged good-byes and hung up.

"I don't think it's proper for you to spend so much time with Frank Raynor," the older woman blurted out, her expression grim.

Addie took a deep breath. Smiled harder. "Frank is an old friend of mine," she said. "Now, about that advertisement—"

"He's an outsider," Miss Pidgett insisted.

"He's lived in Pine Crossing for thirty years," Addie pointed out.

"His mother was the town tramp," Miss Pidgett went on, lowering her voice to a stage whisper. "God knows who his father was. Anybody but Eliza Raynor would have refused to take him in, after all that happened."

Addie felt a flush climb her neck. She couldn't afford to tell Miss Pidgett off, but she wanted to. "I don't know what you're talking about," she said, approaching the counter. "Were you interested in a classified ad, or something larger?"

"Full page," Miss Pidgett said, almost as an aside. "Don't tell me you didn't know that Janet Raynor ran away with Eliza's husband. That's why they have the same last name."

"I *didn't* know," Addie said carefully, feeling bereft. "And I don't think—"

Miss Pidgett cut her off. "Your father hired Eliza out of the goodness of his heart. She was destitute, after her Jim and that trollop ran off to Mexico together. They got a quickie divorce, and Jim actually *married* the woman, if you can believe it. A few years later, he ditched her, and Janet had the nerve to send that boy to live with Eliza."

Addie's face warmed. Oh, well, she thought. She could always apply for a waitress job at the Lumberjack. "I didn't know any of those things," she reiterated quietly, "but it doesn't surprise me to learn that Eliza took in a lonely, frightened little boy and loved him like her own. After all, none of what happened was Frank's fault, was it?"

Miss Pidgett reddened. "Eliza was a fool."

"Eliza," Addie corrected, "was the kindest and most generous woman I have ever known. You, on the other hand, are an insufferable gossip." She paused, drew another deep breath. "If I were you, I'd keep a sharp eye out for the ghosts of Christmas past, present, and future!"

"Well!" Miss Pidgett cried, and turned on the heel of one snow boot to stomp out the door.

The bell over the door jangled frantically at her indignant departure.

Mr. Renfrew, just returning from his Rotary breakfast, nearly collided with Miss Pidgett on the sidewalk. Through the glass, Addie saw the old woman shake a finger under his nose, her breath coming in visible puffs as she ranted, then storm off.

"I'll be darned if I could make heads or tails of what *that* was all about," Mr. Renfrew observed when he came inside. He looked affably baffled, and his ears were crimson from the cold. "Something about taking her business to the *Statesman.*"

"I'm afraid I told her off," Addie confessed. "I'll understand if you fire me."

"The old bat," Frank said at six o'clock that evening as he hung a fragrant evergreen wreath on Addie's front door, after listening to her account of Miss Pidgett's visit to the *Wooden Nickel.* The children were in the yard below, running in wild, noisy, arm-waving circles around the snowman, joyously pursued by Floyd the beagle.

Addie hugged herself against the chill of a winter night and gazed up at Frank, perplexed. "No one ever told me," she said. "About your mother and Eliza's husband, I mean."

Frank gave her a sidelong glance. "Old news, kid," he said. "Not the kind of experience Aunt Eliza would have shared with her employer's little girl."

"There must have been so much gossip. How could I have missed hearing it?"

He touched the tip of her nose, and Addie felt a jolt of sensation, right down to her heels. "You were Judge Hutton's daughter. That shielded you from a lot."

Addie bit her lower lip. "I'm so sorry, Frank."

He frowned, taking an unlikely interest in the wreath. "About what?"

"About all you must have gone through. When you were little, I mean."

He turned to face her, spread his hands, and spared her a crooked grin. "Do I look traumatized?" he asked. "Believe me, after five years of sitting outside bars, waiting for my mother, the gossips of Pine Crossing were nothing. Aunt Eliza loved me. She made sure I had three square meals a day, sent me to school with decent clothes on my back, and taught me to believe in myself. I'd say I was pretty lucky."

Addie looked away, blinked, and looked back. "I was so jealous of you," she said.

He touched her again, laid his hand to the side of her face, and the same shock went through her. The wheels and gears of time itself seemed to grind to a halt, and he bent his head toward hers.

"Daddy!"

They froze.

"Damn," Frank said, his breath tingling against Addie's mouth.

She laughed, and they both looked down to see Lissie gazing up at them from the yard, hands on her hips, tinsel halo picking up the last glimmers of daylight. Henry was beside Lissie, the lenses of his glasses opaque with steam.

"You can't kiss unless there's mistletoe!" Lissie called.

"Says who?" Frank called back. Then, to everyone's surprise, he took Addie's face in his hands, tilted her head back, and kissed her soundly.

Afterward, she stared up at him, speechless.

Chapter Seven

"A shepherd," Henry said when the matchbox was opened the next morning. Lissie peered in, as if doubting his word. Frank had brought the child to Addie's door before dawn that morning, haloed, still in her pajamas and wrapped in a blanket. There had been an automobile accident out on the state highway, and he had to go.

"Hurry up, both of you," Addie replied with an anxious glance at the clock. "I don't want to be late for work." To her way of thinking, she was lucky she still had a job, after the scene with Miss Pidgett the day before.

An hour later, Frank showed up at the *Wooden Nickel,* looking tired and gaunt. He filled his coffee mug from the pot in the small break room. "Where is everybody?" he asked, scanning the office, which was empty except for him and Addie.

"Mr. Renfrew had a doctor's appointment, and Stella went to Denver with her sister to shop for Christmas presents," Addie said. The office, never spacious to begin with, seemed to shrink to the size of a broom closet, with Frank taking up more than his share of space.

Frank rubbed the back of his neck with one hand and sighed before taking a sip of his coffee. "Hope she's careful," he said. "The roads are covered with black ice."

Addie waited.

"The accident was bad," he told her grimly. "Four people airlifted to Denver. One of them died on the way."

"Oh, Frank." Addie wanted to round the counter and put her

arms around him, but she hesitated. Sure, he'd kissed her the evening before, but now he had the look of a man who didn't want to be touched. "Was it anyone you know?"

He shook his head. "Thanks for taking care of Lissie," he said after a long silence. He was staring into his coffee cup now, as though seeing an uncertain future take shape there.

"Anytime," Addie replied gently. "You okay?"

He made an attempt at a smile. "I will be," he said gruffly. "It just takes a while to get the images out of my head."

Addie nodded.

"Have supper with us tonight?" Frank asked. He sounded shy, the way he had when he asked her to his senior prom, all those eventful years ago. "Miss Pidgett is casting the play today. I figure Lissie is going to need some diversion."

Addie ached for the little girl, and for the good man who loved her so much. "My turn to cook," she said softly. "I'll stop by St. Mary's and pick up the kids on my way home." There was no day care center in Pine Crossing, so the children of working parents gathered in either the library or the gym until someone came to collect them.

"Thanks," Frank said. He was on the verge of saying something else when Mr. Renfrew came in.

The two men exchanged greetings, and the telephone rang. Addie took down an order for a classified ad, and when she looked up from her notes, Frank was gone.

"Nice guy, that Frank," Mr. Renfrew said, shrugging off his overcoat.

"Yes," Addie agreed, hoping she sounded more casual than she felt.

"Miss Pidgett been back to place her ad?"

Addie felt a rush of guilt. "No," she said. "Mr. Renfrew, I'm—"

He held up a hand to silence her. "Don't say you're sorry, Addie. It was about time somebody put that old grump in her place."

With that, the subject of Almira Pidgett was dropped.

Henry raced toward the car when Addie pulled up outside the elementary school that afternoon, waving what looked like a brown bathrobe over his head. Lissie followed at a slower pace, head down, scuffing her feet in the dried snow. Even her tinsel halo seemed to sag a little.

Addie's heart went out to the child. She pushed open the car door and stood in the road.

"I'm a shepherd!" Henry shouted jubilantly.

Addie ruffled his hair. "Good job," she said, pleased because he was so excited. She watched Lissie's slow approach.

"I'm the innkeeper's wife," the little girl said, looking wretched. "I don't even get to say anything. My *whole part* is to stand there and look mean and shake my head 'no' when Mary and Joseph ask for a room."

Addie crouched, took Lissie's cold little hands in hers. "I'm so sorry, sweetie. You would have made a perfect angel."

A tear slipped down Lissie's right cheek, quivered on the shoulder of her pink nylon jacket. It was all Addie could do, in that moment, not to storm into the school and give Miss Pidgett a piece of her mind.

"Tiffany Baker gets to be the most important angel," Lissie said. "She has a whole bunch of lines about good tidings and stuff, and her mother is making her wings out of *real* feathers."

Addie stood up, steered the children toward the car.

"That sucks," Henry said. "Tiffany Baker sucks."

"Henry," Addie said.

"Last year she got to go to Denver and be in a TV commercial," Lissie said as she and Henry got into the backseat and fastened their seat belts. In the rearview mirror, Addie saw Lissie's lower lip wobble.

"There are six other angels," the little girl whispered. "I wouldn't have minded being one of them."

Addie had to fight hard not to cry herself. The child had been wearing a tinsel halo for days. Didn't Almira Pidgett have a heart?

"Maybe we could rent some Christmas movies," she suggested in deliberately cheerful tones.

Lissie pulled off her halo, held it for a moment, then set it aside. "Okay," she said with a complete lack of spirit.

Chapter Eight

Frank shoved a hand through his hair. "It's been nine days," he whispered to Addie, that snowy Saturday morning, in her kitchen. "I thought Lissie would be over this play thing by now. Is it really such a bad thing to play the innkeeper's wife?"

Addie glanced sadly at the Advent calendar, still taped to the bottom of the cupboard. Lissie hadn't shown much interest in the daily ritual of opening a new matchbox since the angel disappointment, and that morning was no exception. The tiny sleigh glued inside looked oddly forlorn. "It is if you wanted to be an angel," she said.

"I haven't seen her like this since Maggie died."

Addie sank into a chair at the table. Frank, leaning one shoulder against the refrigerator and sipping coffee, sighed.

"I wish there was something I could do," Addie said.

"Join the club," Frank replied, glancing toward the living room. Henry and Lissie were there, with the ever-faithful Floyd, watching Saturday morning cartoons.

"Sit down, Frank," Addie urged quietly.

He didn't seem to hear her. He was staring out the window at the fat, drifting flakes of snow that had been falling since the night before. "This isn't about Lissie," he said. "That's what makes it so hard. It's about me, and all the times I've butted heads with Almira Pidgett over the years."

Addie's mouth tightened at the mention of the woman, and she consciously relaxed it. "It's not your fault, Frank," she said, and closed her hands around her own coffee cup, grown cold since the pancake breakfast the four of them had shared half an hour before. "Miss Pidgett is a Grinch, plain and simple."

Just then, Addie thought she heard sleigh bells, and she was just shaking her head when a whoop of delight sounded from the living room. Henry. Henry, who was wary of joy, already knowing, young as he was, how easily it could be taken away.

"There's a man down there, driving a sleigh!" Henry shouted, almost breathless with glee. "He's got horses pulling it, instead of reindeer, but he sure looks like Santa!"

"Who?" Frank asked, pleasantly bemused.

Addie was already on her way to investigate. Henry was bounding down the outside stairs, followed by Floyd, and, at a more sedate pace, Lissie. Frank brought up the rear.

Mr. Renfrew, bundled in a stocking cap, ski jacket, and quilted trousers, all the same shade of red, waved cheerfully from the seat of a horse-drawn sleigh.

"Merry Christmas!" he called. "Anybody want a ride?"

Henry was jumping up and down. "I do!" he shouted. "I do!"

"Can Floyd come, too?" Lissie asked cautiously.

Mr. Renfrew's eyes twinkled as he looked over the children's heads to Frank and Addie. "Of course," he answered. Then, in a booming voice, he added, "Don't just stand there! Go put on your cold-weather gear and jump in!"

Chapter Nine

There were two bench seats in the back of that old-fashioned sleigh, upholstered in patched leather and facing each other.

"Want to ride up here with me, boy?" Mr. Renfrew asked Henry, his eyes twinkling.

Henry needed no persuading. He scrambled onto the high seat, fairly quivering with excitement. "Can Lissie have a turn, too?" he asked, his breath forming a thin, shifting aura of white around his head.

A sweet, almost painful, warmth settled over Addie's heart. She glanced at Frank, who hoisted the overweight beagle into the sleigh to join Lissie, who was already seated, facing backward.

"Sure, Lissie can have a turn," Mr. Renfrew said, turning to smile down at the child.

Lissie, who had been subdued since putting away her tinsel halo, perked up a little, grinning back at him. Floyd, perched beside her, gave her an exuberant lick on the cheek.

Frank helped Addie up into the sleigh, then sat down beside her, stretching his arm out along the back of the seat, the way a shy teenage boy might do on a movie date. He wasn't quite touching her, but she felt the strength and substance and warmth of him just the same, a powerful tingle along her nape and the length of her shoulders. The energy danced down her spine and arched between her pelvic bones.

It was all she could do not to squirm.

Mr. Renfrew set the sleigh in motion, bells jingling. There was a jerk, but then they glided, as though the whole earth had suddenly turned smooth as a skating rink. Addie bit down on her lower lip and tried to focus on the ride, wincing a little as Lissie turned to kneel in the seat, her back to them, ready to climb up front when she got the nod.

"Addie." Frank's voice. Very close to her ear. Fat snowflakes drifted down, making silent music.

She made herself look at him, not in spite of her reluctance, but *because* of it. The decision was a ripple on the surface of something much deeper, churning far down in the whorls and currents of her mind.

"Relax," he said. "You think too much."

Some reckless sprite rose up out of that emotional sea to put words in Addie's mouth. "You might not say that if you knew what I was thinking *about.*"

Frank lowered his arm, let it rest lightly around her shoulders. "Who says I don't?" he countered, with a half grin and laughter in his eyes. But there was sadness there, too, and something that might have been caution. Perhaps, like Henry, Frank was a little afraid to trust in good things.

Addie blushed and looked away.

They rode over side streets and back roads, and finally left Pine Crossing behind, entering the open countryside. After getting permission from both Addie and Frank, Mr. Renfrew let Henry drive the team, then Lissie. The snow came down harder, and the wind grew colder, and Floyd alternately barked and howled in canine celebration.

Addie had a wonderful time. Something had changed between her and Frank, a subtle, indefinable shift that gave her an odd thrill, a feeling both festive and frightening. She decided to think about it later, when Frank and Lissie weren't around, and Henry had gone to bed.

After an hour or so, they returned to Pine Crossing, traveling down the middle of the main street, between parked cars. Frank sat up very straight, looking imperious and waving in the stiff-handed way of royalty as various friends called amused greetings from the sidewalks.

Lissie climbed back down into the seat beside Floyd as they passed the school, and Addie noticed the deflation in the child's mood. Her small shoulders sagged as she looked at the reader board in front of St. Mary's. PLAY REHEARSAL TONIGHT, 6 PM, MARY, JOSEPH AND ANGELS ONLY.

Addie bristled inwardly. The sign was obviously Almira's handiwork, and it might as well have said, *Innkeeper's wife will be turned away at the door.*

"No room at the inn," she murmured angrily.

Frank squeezed her hand, so she knew he'd heard, but he was watching Lissie, who sat with her head down, obviously fighting tears, while Floyd nibbled tentatively at the pom-pom on top of her pink knitted cap.

"Life is hard sometimes, Liss," Frank said quietly. "It's okay to feel bad for a while, but sooner or later, you've got to let go and move on."

Addie's throat tightened. She wanted to take the child in her arms, hold her, tell her everything would be all right, but it wasn't her place. Frank was Lissie's father. She, on the other hand, was little more than an acquaintance.

They passed Pine Crossing General Hospital, then the Sweet Haven Nursing Home. An idea rapped at the back door of Addie's brain; she let it in and looked it over.

She barely noticed when they pulled up in front of the house.

Frank got out of the sleigh first, helped Addie, Lissie, and the dog down, then reached up to claim Henry from the driver's seat. Everyone thanked Mr. Renfrew profusely, and Frank invited him in for coffee, but he declined, saying he had things to do at home. Almost Christmas, you know.

"Better get Floyd inside and give him some kibble," Frank told his daughter, laying a hand on her shoulder. "All those snowflakes he ate probably won't hold him long."

Lissie smiled a little, nodded, and grabbed Henry by the arm. "Come on and help me," she said. "I'll show you where we're going to put up the Christmas tree."

Addie thrust her hands into the pockets of her coat and waited until the children were out of earshot. "What if there were more than one way to be an angel?" she asked.

Frank pulled his jacket collar up a little higher, squinted at her. "Huh?"

"You kept so many of Eliza's things," Addie said, looking up at him. If they'd had any sense, they'd have gone in out of the cold. "Do you still have her sewing machine?"

"Maggie used it for mending," Frank answered, with a slight nod, and then looked as though he regretted mentioning his late wife's name. "Why?"

"I'd like to borrow it, please."

Frank looked at his watch. "Okay," he said. "What's this about?"

Having noted the time checking, Addie answered with a question. "Do you have to work tonight, Frank?"

"Town council meeting," he said. "That's why I didn't suggest dinner."

"I'll be happy to look after Lissie and Floyd until you get home," she told him, so he wouldn't have to ask. But she was already on her way to the steps leading up to her over-the-garage apartment.

Frank caught up with her, looking benignly curious. "Wait a second," he said. "There's something brewing, and I'd like to know what it is."

"Maybe you'll just have to be surprised," Addie responded, watching as snowflakes landed in Frank's dark hair and on his long eyelashes. "Right along with Miss Almira Pidgett."

Frank searched her face, looking cautiously amused. "Tell me you're not planning to whip up a trio of spirit costumes and pay her a midnight visit," he said. "Much as I love the idea, it would be trespassing, and breaking and entering, too. Not to mention harassment, stalking, and maybe even reckless endangerment."

Addie laughed, starting up the steps. "You have quite an imagination," she said. "Drop off the sewing machine before you leave for the meeting if you have time, okay?"

He spread his hands and then let them flop against his sides. "So much for my investigative skills," he said. "You're not going to tell me anything, are you?"

Addie paused, smiled, and batted her lashes. "No," she said. "I'm not."

Chapter Ten

"Why are we going to a thrift store?" Henry asked reasonably. He blinked, behind his glasses, in that owlish way he had. He and Lissie were buckled in, in the back of Addie's station wagon, with Floyd panting between them, delighted to be included in the outing. Lissie was still very quiet; in the rearview mirror, Addie saw her staring forlornly out the window.

She flipped on the windshield wipers and peered through the increasing snowfall. The storm had been picking up speed since they got home from the sleigh ride with Mr. Renfrew, and now that dusk had fallen, visibility wasn't the best. "I plan to do some sewing, and I need material," Addie answered belatedly, wondering if they shouldn't just stay home.

Lissie showed some interest, at last. "Mom used to make my Halloween costumes out of stuff from the Goodwill," she said.

"I was Harry Potter Halloween before last," Henry said sadly, as Addie drew a deep breath, offered a silent prayer, and pulled out onto the road. "This year, Dad and Elle went to a costume party, but I didn't get to dress up."

Addie felt a pang of guilt, bit her lower lip. She'd thought of calling, inviting Henry to come trick-or-treating in her apartment complex, but she'd overruled the urge. After all, Toby and Elle had made it pretty clear, following all the publicity, that they didn't want her around Henry.

"With those glasses," Lissie remarked, perking up, "you wouldn't even need a costume to look like Harry Potter."

"I had a cape, too," Henry told her in a lofty tone. "Didn't I, Addie?"

Addie gazed intently over the top of the steering wheel. "Yes," she answered. Toby had dropped him off at her apartment that Halloween afternoon, a few months after their divorce became final, without calling first, flustered over some emergency at work. She'd fashioned the cape from an old shower curtain and taken him around the neighborhood with high hopes and a paper sack. They'd both had a great time.

"I was a hobo once," Lissie said. "When Mom was still alive, I mean. She bought an old suit and sewed patches on it and stuff. I had a broom handle with a bundle tied to the end, and I won a prize."

"Big deal," Henry said.

Addie pulled up to a stop sign, intersecting the main street through town, and sighed with relief. The blacktop, though dusted with a thin coating of snow, had recently been plowed. She signaled and made a cautious left turn toward the center of Pine Crossing.

The lights of St. Mary's shimmered golden through the falling snow. Addie would have preferred not to pass the school, with the rehearsal going on and Lissie in the car, but it didn't make sense to risk the children's safety by taking unplowed side streets.

When they rolled up in front of the thrift store, at the opposite end of town, Lissie hooked a leash to Floyd's collar. She and Henry walked him in the parking lot while Addie hurried inside.

An artificial Christmas tree stood just inside the door, offering a cheerful if somewhat bedraggled welcome. Chipped ornaments hung from its crooked boughs, and a plastic star glowed with dim determination at its top.

I know just how you feel, Addie thought, as she passed the tree, scanning the store and zeroing in on the women's dresses.

She selected an old formal, a musty relic of some long-forgotten prom. The voluminous, floor-length underskirt was satin or taffeta, with the blue iridescence of a peacock feather.

"I don't think that will fit you," said a voice beside Addie, startling her a little. "It's a fourteen-sixteen, and you can't be bigger than an eight. But you can try it on if you want to."

Addie turned and smiled at the young girl standing beside her. Her name tag read, "Barbara," and she was chubby, with bad skin and stringy hair. "I just want the fabric," Addie said. "Is there anything here with pearl buttons? Or crystal beads?"

Barbara brightened a little. "Jessie Corcoran donated her wedding gown last week," she said. "It's real pretty. Her mom told my mom she ordered it special off the Internet." She paused, blushed. "I guess things didn't work out with that guy from Denver. For Jessie, I mean. Since she came back home to Pine Crossing one day and chucked the dress the next—"

"She might want it back," Addie mused.

Barbara shook her head, and her eyes widened behind the smudged lenses of her glasses. "She stuffed it right into the donation box, out there by the highway—my friend Becky saw her do it. Didn't even care if it got dirty, I guess. People dumped other stuff right in on top of it, too. A pair of old boots and a couple of puzzles with a lot of pieces missing."

"My goodness," Addie said.

Barbara produced the dress, ran a plump, reverent hand over the skirt. The bodice gleamed bravely with pearls and tiny glass beads. In its own way, the discarded wedding gown looked as forlorn as the Christmas tree at the front of the store.

"How much?" Addie asked.

Barbara didn't even have to look at the tag. "Twenty-five dollars," she said. "Are you getting married?"

Addie was taken aback, as much by the price as by the question. "Ordered special" or not, the dress was hardly haute couture.

Barbara smiled. "It's a small town," she said. "I guess you used to live in Frank Raynor's house. Now you're staying in the apartment over his garage and working at the *Wooden Nickel*. Down at the bowling alley—my mom plays on a league—they're saying Frank's been alone long enough. He needs a wife, and Lissie needs a mother."

Addie opened her mouth, closed it again. Shook her head. "No," she said.

"You don't want the dress?"

"No—I mean, yes. I *do* want the dress. I'll give you ten dollars for it. But there isn't going to be a wedding." She wanted to make sure this news got to the bowling league, from whence it would spread all over the county.

Barbara looked disappointed. "That's too bad," she said. "Everybody got their hopes up, for a while there. Fifteen dollars, and the dress is yours."

"I'm sorry," Addie said. She glanced toward the front windows, bedecked in wilting garland, and thought of Lissie's halo, now a castoff, like Jessie Corcoran's wedding gown and the peacock-blue prom dress. "Fifteen dollars it is," she told Barbara. "I'd better hurry—the roads are probably getting worse by the moment."

Five minutes later, she was out the door, her purchases carefully folded and wrapped in a salvaged dry cleaner's bag. Henry, Lissie and Floyd were already in the backseat of the station wagon.

"Buckle up," she told them, starting the engine.

"What did you buy in there?" Henry wanted to know.

"Secondhand dreams," Addie said. "With a little creativity, they can be good as new."

"How can dreams be secondhand?" Lissie asked, sounding both skeptical and intrigued.

Addie flipped on the headlights, watched the snowflakes dancing in the beams. "Sometimes people give up on them, because they don't fit anymore. Or they just leave them behind, for one reason or another. Then someone else comes along, finds them, and believes they might be worth something after all."

"That's really confusing," Henry said. "Can we stop for pizza?"

"No," Addie replied. "We've got beans and weenies at home."

"I wanted to be an angel," Lissie said, very softly. "That was my dream."

"I know," Addie answered.

It was after ten when Frank climbed the stairs to Addie's front door, listened for a moment to the faint whirring of his aunt's old sewing machine inside, and knocked lightly. Floyd let out a welcoming yelp, the machine stopped humming, and Frank heard

Addie shushing the dog good-naturedly as she crossed the living room and peered out at him through the side window.

Her smile, blurred by the steamy glass, tugged at his heart.

"Shhh," she said, putting a finger to her lips as she opened the door. He wasn't sure if she was addressing him or Floyd. "Lissie's asleep in my room."

Frank stepped over the threshold, settled the dog with a few pats on the head and some ear ruffling, and eyed the sewing setup in the middle of the living room. Bright blue cloth billowed over the top of an old card table like a trapped cloud, the light from Eliza's machine shimmering along its folds.

He set Maggie's coffee mug aside, on the plant stand next to the door, and stuffed his hands into the pockets of his jacket. "Are you going to tell me what you're making, or is it still a secret?"

"It's still a secret," Addie answered with a grin. Her gaze flicked to the cup, then back to his face. "Do you want some coffee? I just brewed a pot of decaf a few minutes ago."

He hesitated. "Sure," he said.

"How did the meeting go?" Addie started toward the mug, then stopped. Frank handed it to her.

"Fine," he said.

"You look tired." Carrying the mug, she headed for the kitchen. "Long night?"

He stood on the threshold between the living room and the kitchen, gripping the doorframe, watching her pour the coffee. For an instant, he flashed back to that afternoon's sleigh ride, and the way it felt to put his arm around her shoulders. He shook off the memory, reached for the cup as she approached, holding it out. "Yeah," he said.

Hot coffee sloshed over his hand, and the mug slipped, tumbling end over end, shattering on the floor. The whole thing was over in seconds, but Frank would always remember it in slow motion.

Addie gasped, put one hand over her mouth.

Frank stared at the shards of Maggie's last gift, disbelieving.

"I'm sorry," Addie said. She grabbed a roll of paper towels.

He was already crouching, gathering the pieces. "It wasn't your fault, Addie." He couldn't look at her.

She squatted, a wad of towels in her hand, blotting up the flow of coffee. He stopped her gently, took over the job. When he stole a glance at her face, there were tears standing in her eyes.

"Maggie's cup," she whispered. He didn't remember telling her his wife had made the mug; maybe Lissie had.

"Don't," he said.

She nodded.

Floyd tried to lick up some of the spilled coffee, and Frank nudged him away with a slight motion of his elbow. He put the pieces of the cup into his pocket, straightened, and disposed of the paper towels in the trash can under the sink.

"Shall I wake Lissie up?" Addie asked tentatively, from somewhere at the periphery of Frank's vision.

He shook his head. "I'll do it," he said.

Lissie didn't awaken when he lifted her off Addie's bed, or even when he eased her into her coat.

"Thanks for taking care of her," he told Addie as he carried his sleeping daughter across the living room, Floyd scampering at his heels.

Addie nodded and opened the door for him, and a rush of cold air struck his face. Lissie shifted, opened her eyes, and yawned, and the fragments of Maggie's cup tinkled faintly in his pocket, like the sound of faraway bells.

An hour later, with Lissie settled in her own bed and Floyd curled up at her feet, Frank went into the kitchen and laid the shards of broken china out on the counter, in a jagged row. There was no hope of gluing the cup back together, but most of the bright red heart was there, chipped and cracked.

"Maggie," he whispered.

There was no answer, of course. She was gone.

He took the wastebasket from the cupboard under the sink, held it to the edge of the counter, and slowly swept the pieces into it. A crazy urge possessed him, an unreasonable desire to fish the bits out of the garbage, try to reassemble them after all. He shook his head, put the bin away, and left the kitchen, turning out the lights as he passed the switch next to the door.

The house was dark as he climbed the stairs. For the first six months after Maggie died, he hadn't been able to sleep in their room, in their bed. He'd camped out in the den, downstairs, on the fold-out couch, until the night Lissie had a walking nightmare. Hearing his daughter's screams, he'd rushed upstairs to find her in the master bedroom, clawing at the covers, as if searching, wildly, desperately, for something she'd lost.

"I can't find my mommy!" she'd sobbed. "I can't find my daddy!"

"I'm here," he'd said, taking her into his arms, holding her tightly as she struggled awake. "Daddy's here."

Now Frank paused at the door of his and Maggie's room. *Daddy's here,* he thought, *but Mommy's gone. She's really, truly gone.*

He went inside, closed the door, stripped off his jacket, shoes and uniform, and stretched out on the bed, staring up at the ceiling. His throat felt tight, and his eyes burned.

Maggie's words came back to him, echoing in his mind. *I want you to mourn me for a while, but when it's time to let go, I'll find a way to tell you.*

A single tear slipped from the corner of his right eye and trickled over his temple. "It's time, isn't it?" he asked in a hoarse whisper.

Once again, he heard the cup smashing on Addie's kitchen floor.

It was answer enough.

Chapter Eleven

Addie didn't even try to go to sleep that night. She brewed another pot of coffee—no decaf this time—and sewed like a madwoman until the sun came up.

It was still snowing, and she was glad it was Sunday as she stared blearily out the front window at a white-blanketed, sound-muffled world.

"Can I open the calendar box," Henry asked from behind her, "or do we have to wait for Lissie?"

Addie took a moment to steel herself, then turned to smile at her stepson. Still in his pajamas, he wasn't wearing his glasses, and his dark hair was sleep-rumpled. Blinking at her, he rubbed his eyes with the backs of his hands.

"We'd better wait," she said. Lissie might show up for the ritual, but she wondered about Frank. The look on his face, when that cup tumbled to the floor and splintered into bits, was still all too fresh in her mind.

Of course it had been an accident. Addie understood that, and she knew Frank did, too. Just the same, she'd glimpsed the expression of startled sorrow in his eyes, seen the slow, almost reverent way he'd gathered up the pieces. . . .

Something a lot more important than a ceramic coffee mug had been broken.

"Couldn't I peek?" Henry persisted, still focused on the matchbox calendar. In a way, Addie was pleased; he was feeling more secure with the new living arrangement, letting down his guard a little. In another way, she was unsettled. For all his promises that

Henry could stay until February, or even until school was out for the summer, Toby might appear at any moment, filled with sudden fatherly concern, and whisk the child away.

"I guess," she said, just as a firm rap sounded at the front door.

"They're here!" Henry shouted, bounding across the linoleum kitchen floor and into the living room.

Frank stepped over the threshold, looking grimly pleasant, and Addie knew by the shadows in and beneath his eyes that he hadn't had much more sleep than she had, if any. There was no sign of Lissie.

"Where's Halo Woman?" Henry asked, taking his glasses from the pocket of his pajama top and jamming them onto his face.

Frank smiled at the new nickname. "Lissie's got a fever this morning," he said. "The doctor's been by. Said she needs to stay in bed, keep warm, and take plenty of fluids."

"And you have to work," Addie guessed aloud, folding her arms and leaning against the framework of the kitchen door because she wanted to cross the room and embrace Frank. She sensed that he wouldn't welcome a show of sympathy just then.

He nodded. "The roads are wicked, thanks to all this new snow. I've got every man I could call in out there patrolling, but we're still shorthanded."

"We could baby-sit her," Henry announced. He grinned. "And dog-sit Floyd."

Addie watched Frank's face closely. He didn't like asking for help, she could see that. "Mrs. Jarvis usually watches her when there's a crisis," he said, "but her sister just moved into the nursing home, and she's been spending a lot of time there, trying to help her adjust."

"What's easier, Frank?" Addie said gently. "For Henry and me to come down to your place, or for you to bring Lissie and Floyd up here?"

He thrust a hand through his snow-sprinkled hair, glanced at the sewing machine and billows of blue fabric. "You've got a project going here," he reflected. "And Lissie would probably enjoy a visit. I'll wrap her up in a quilt and bring her up." He was quiet for a long moment. "If it's really all right with you."

"Frank," Addie told him, feeling affectionately impatient, "of *course* it is."

"I better get dressed!" Henry decided, and dashed off to his room.

"About the cup," Frank began, looking miserable. He'd closed the door against the cold and the blowing snow, but he didn't move any closer. The gap between them, though only a matter of a dozen feet, felt unaccountably wide. "I guess I overreacted. I'm sorry, Addie."

She still wanted to touch him, still wouldn't let herself do it. "It meant a lot to you," she said gently.

He nodded. "Just the same," he reasoned in a gruff voice, "it was only a coffee mug."

Addie knew it was much more, but it wasn't her place to say so. "Go and get Lissie," she told him. "I'll bring out some pillows and a blanket, make up the couch." She paused, then went on, very carefully, "Have you eaten? I'm going to make breakfast in a few minutes."

"No time," he said with a shake of his head. "I'll hit the drive-through or something." He hesitated, as if he wanted to say something else, opened the door again, and went out.

Because she felt a need to move and be busy, exhausted as she was, Addie went into her room and grabbed the pillows off the bed. She was plumping them on one end of the couch when Frank returned, carrying Lissie. Floyd trailed after them, snowflakes melting on his floppy ears, wagging not just his tail, but his whole substantial hind end. Addie would have sworn that dog was grinning.

Henry, dressed and hastily groomed, waited impatiently until Lissie was settled. "What about the calendar box?" he blurted. "Can we look now?"

"I know what it is anyway," Lissie said with a congested sniff. She was still in her flannel nightgown and smelled pleasantly of mentholated rub.

Henry looked imploringly up at Addie.

"Go ahead." She smiled.

Frank wrote down his cell phone number, handed it to Addie, kissed his daughter on top of the head, and left the apartment. The place seemed to deflate a little when he was gone.

"It's a dog!" Henry announced, returning to the living room. He'd dragged a chair over to the cupboards to peer inside that day's matchbox. "Brown and white, like Floyd. But a lot littler."

"It's snowing really hard," Lissie fretted, turning to look out the front window. "Dad said the roads are slick. Do you think he'll be okay?"

Addie sat down on the edge of the couch, giving Lissie as much room as she could, and touched the child's forehead with the back of her hand. "Sure he will," she said quietly. "What would you like for breakfast? Scrambled eggs, or oatmeal?"

"Oatmeal," Lissie answered.

"Scrambled eggs," Henry chimed in at the same moment.

Addie laughed. "I'll make both," she said.

The kids ate in the living room, watching a holiday movie marathon on television, while Addie washed the dishes. The phone rang just as she was putting the last of the silverware away.

"Hello?" she said cheerfully, expecting the caller to be Frank, checking up on his daughter.

"I'm in Denver," Toby said.

Addie stretched the phone cord to its limits, hooked one foot around a chair leg, and dragged it close enough to collapse onto. "*What?*"

"I can't believe this snow."

Addie closed her eyes. Waited.

Toby spoke into the silence. "How's Henry? Can I talk to him?"

She couldn't very well refuse, but stalling was another matter. Her stomach felt like a clenched fist, and her heart skittered with dread. "What are you doing in Denver?"

"Put Henry on, will you?"

Addie turned to call the boy, and was startled to find him standing only a few feet away, watching. She held out the receiver. "It's your dad," she said.

Henry didn't move. She couldn't see his eyes, because of the way the light hit the lenses of his glasses, but his chin quivered a little, and his freckles seemed to stand out.

"I can't leave," he said. "I'm a shepherd."

Addie blinked back tears. "You've got to talk to him, buddy," she said, very gently.

He crossed to her, took the phone.

"I can't leave, Dad," he said. "I'm a shepherd."

Addie started to rise out of her chair, meaning to leave the room, but Henry laid a small hand on her arm and looked at her pleadingly.

"In the play at school," he went on, after listening to whatever Toby said in the interim. "Yeah, I like it here. I like it a lot."

Addie rubbed her temples with the fingertips of both hands.

"No, it didn't come yet." Henry put a hand over the receiver. "Dad sent a box," he said to Addie. "Christmas presents."

Addie's spirits rose a little. If Toby had mailed Henry's gifts, he probably intended to leave the boy with her at least through the holidays. On the other hand, Toby was nothing if not a creature of quicksilver moods. And he was in Denver, after all, which might mean he'd changed his mind. . . .

"I understand," Henry said. "You're stuck because of the snow. You shouldn't try to drive here. The roads are really bad—Lissie's dad says so, and he's the chief of police."

More verbiage from Toby's end. Addie didn't catch the words, but the tone was upbeat, thrumming with good cheer.

"Right." Henry nodded somberly. "Sure, Dad." He swallowed visibly, then thrust the phone at Addie. "He wants to talk to you again."

Addie bit her lower lip, nodded for no particular reason, and took the receiver.

"Addie?" Toby prompted, when she was silent too long. "Are you there?"

"Yes," she said, sitting up very straight on her chair, which seemed to be teetering on the edge of some invisible abyss. One false move and she'd never stop falling.

"Look, I was planning to rent a car, drive down there, and surprise Henry with a visit. But it looks like that won't be possible, because of the weather. I'll be lucky to get out of here between storm fronts, according to the airline people."

Addie let out her breath, but inaudibly. She didn't want Toby to guess how scared she'd been when she'd thought he was coming to take Henry away, or how relieved she was now that she knew he wasn't. "Okay," she said.

Toby chuckled uncomfortably. "You know, I remember you as being more communicative, Addie. Cat got your tongue?"

She glanced sideways, saw that Henry was still standing close by, listening intently. Floyd had joined him, leaning heavily against the boy's side as if to offer forlorn support. "I guess I'm just surprised. I thought you were on your honeymoon."

"Elle got bored with the tropics. She's in Manhattan, doing some Christmas shopping. Her folks live in Connecticut, so we're spending the holidays with them. I decided I wanted to see the kid, and picked up a standby seat out of LaGuardia—"

The trip was a whim, to Toby. *Henry* was a whim.

Don't say it, Addie told herself. *Don't make him angry, because then he'll come here, if he has to hitch a ride on a snow-plow, and when he leaves, Henry will go with him.* "I'm sorry it didn't work out," she said instead. It wasn't a complete lie. As much as Henry wanted to stay in Pine Crossing with her, he was a normal little boy. He loved his father and craved his attention. A visit would have delighted him.

"Tell Dad you'll take a picture of me being a shepherd," Henry prompted.

Addie dutifully repeated the information.

"A what?" Toby asked, sounding distracted. Maybe they were announcing his flight back to New York, and maybe he had simply lost interest.

"Henry's playing a shepherd in the Christmas play," Addie said moderately and, for her stepson's sake, with a note of perky enthusiasm. "I'll take some pictures."

"Oh, right," Toby answered. "Okay. Look, Addie—I appreciate this. My dad sent you a check." He lowered his voice. "You know, for the kid's expenses."

Henry and Floyd returned to the living room, summoned by Lissie, who called out that they were about to miss the part where Chevy Chase got tangled in the Christmas lights and fell off the roof.

"Your dad?" Addie asked, very carefully.

Toby thrust out a sigh. "Look, we're kind of living on Elle's money right now. The mortgage business isn't so great at this time of year. And since Henry isn't hers—"

Chevy Chase must have taken his header into the shrubbery, because Henry and Lissie hooted with delighted laughter.

"Henry can stay with me as long as necessary," Addie said, again with great care, framing it as a favor Toby was doing for her, and not the reverse. "Try not to worry, okay? I'll take very good care of him."

Toby was quiet for so long that Addie got nervous. "Thanks, Add," he said. "Listen, it's time to board."

"Where can I get in touch with you, Toby? In case there's an emergency, I mean?"

"Send me an e-mail," Toby said hurriedly. "I check every few days." With that, he rang off.

They were all asleep when Frank let himself into the apartment at six-fifteen that evening, even the dog. Lissie snoozed at one end of the couch, Henry at the other. Addie had curled up in the easy chair, her brown hair tumbling over her face.

Frank felt a bittersweet squeeze behind his heart as he switched on a lamp, turned off the TV, and put the pizza boxes he was carrying down on the coffee table.

Floyd woke up first, beagle nose in overdrive, and yelped happily at the prospect of pepperoni and cheese. The sound stirred Lissie and Henry awake, and, finally, Addie opened her eyes.

"Pizza!" Henry whooped.

Frank laughed, though his gaze seemed stuck on Addie. The situation was innocent, but there was something intimate about watching this particular woman wake up. Her tentative, sleepy smile made him ache, and if she asked how his day had gone, he didn't know what he'd do.

"How was your day?" she inquired, standing up and stretching both arms above her head. Making those perfect breasts rise.

"Good," he managed, figuring he sounded like a caveman, barely past the grunt stage. He averted his gaze to Lissie, who was off the couch and lifting one of the pizza box lids to peer inside. "Feeling better?" he asked.

Lissie nodded, somewhat reluctantly. "I'll probably have to go to school tomorrow and listen to Tiffany Baker bragging about being an angel in the Christmas play," she said, but with some spirit.

"Probably," Frank agreed.

Floyd put both paws up on the edge of the coffee table and all but stuck his nose into the pizza. Grinning, Frank took him gently by the collar and pulled him back.

"I'll get some plates," Addie said, heading for the kitchen.

"Bring one for Floyd," Henry suggested.

Addie laughed, and Frank unzipped his uniform jacket and shrugged it off, thinking how good it was to be home.

Chapter Twelve

Much to Lissie's annoyance, and Frank's relief, the child was well enough to go to school the next morning. The snow had stopped, and though the ground was covered in glittering white, there was a springlike energy in the air.

Addie was in a cheerful mood, humming along with the kitchen radio while she supervised the opening—with a suitable flourish on Lissie's part—of that day's calendar box. Inside was a miniature gift, wrapped in shiny paper and tied in a bow.

Henry scrunched up his face, intrigued. "Is there anything inside it?"

"No, silly," Lissie responded. "It's supposed to represent a Christmas present."

"I'm getting presents," Henry said. "From my dad. He sent a box."

"You need a Christmas tree if you're going to get presents," Lissie reasoned. "Dad's getting ours tonight, after work."

Henry looked questioningly at Addie. "Are we getting one, too?"

"Sure are," Frank put in, before Addie could answer.

"A real one?" Henry asked hopefully.

"The genuine article," Frank promised, hoping he wasn't stepping on Addie's toes in some way. Maybe she wanted buying the tree to be a family thing, just her and Henry. It took some nerve, but he made himself meet her eyes.

She looked uncertain.

"You two put on your coats and head for the car," Frank told the kids. "I'll drop you off at school on my way to work."

They dashed off.

"Everything okay, Addie?" Frank asked quietly, when the two of them were alone in the apartment kitchen. She was dressed for another day at the *Wooden Nickel*.

She hugged herself. "I wasn't really planning on Christmas," she said. "And I've been so busy since Henry got here, I haven't really thought about it."

He wanted to cross the room, maybe touch her hair, but things were still a little awkward between them. Had been since Maggie's mug had struck the floor. "I shouldn't have said anything about the tree."

"It's okay," she said. "I don't have ornaments, though, or lights."

"A lot of your father's stuff is still in the storeroom," he reminded her. "I'm pretty sure there are some decorations." He paused, shoved a hand through his hair. "Damn, Addie, I'm sorry. I wish I'd kept my mouth shut."

Her smile faltered a little. "I vaguely remember strings and strings of those old-fashioned bubble lights," she said wistfully. "And lots of shiny ornaments. They must have been packed away when Mom died—Dad didn't care much about Christmas. Said it was a lot of sentimental slop, and way too commercial. He used to give me money and tell me to buy what I wanted."

Frank's spirits plunged like an elevator after the cable broke. *Way to go, Raynor,* he thought. *First, you put Addie on the spot in front of the kids, and now you remind her that her childhood Christmases wouldn't exactly inspire nostalgia.*

He found his voice. "Look, you helped me out yesterday when I needed somebody to look after Lissie. I'll spring for an extra evergreen. We could make a night of it—hit the tree lot, then have supper at the Lumberjack, afterward. The kids would like that."

She grabbed her coat off the back of a chair and shrugged into it. "Sure," she said, but she sounded sad. "Thanks, Frank."

He spent the rest of the day kicking himself.

The box from Toby was waiting on the doorstep when Addie arrived home from work late that afternoon. She'd picked Henry and Lissie up at school, and Henry was beside himself with excitement.

"Can I open it?" he asked, peeling off his coat. Lissie had gone to let Floyd out, but she'd be joining them in a few minutes for hot cocoa.

Addie's mood, bordering on glum ever since morning, lifted a little. She smiled as she hung up her own coat. "Let me peek inside first," she suggested. "Just in case the stuff isn't wrapped."

"Okay," Henry said. The two of them had wrestled the large box over the threshold, and it was sitting on the living room floor, looking mysterious. "I didn't think he'd really send it," he confided. "Sometimes Dad says he's going to do stuff, and he forgets."

Addie ruffled his hair. "Well, he didn't forget this time," she said. She got a knife from the silverware drawer and advanced on the box. Henry was fairly jumping up and down while she carefully cut the packing tape.

"I know about Santa Claus," Henry announced, out of the blue. "So you don't have to worry about filling my stocking or anything like that."

Addie stiffened slightly and busied herself with the box. She didn't want Henry to see her face. She pulled back the flaps and looked inside, relieved to find packages wrapped in shiny, festive paper and tied with curling ribbon. "It's okay to look," she said.

Henry let out a whoop of glee and started hauling out the loot. He had the packages piled around the living room in an impressive circle when Lissie and Floyd came in. Lissie was carrying her tinsel halo in one hand.

"Whoa," she said, beaming. "You really cleaned up!"

Floyd made the rounds, sniffing every box.

"I wish today was Christmas," Henry said.

Lissie sagged a little. "Me, too," she confessed. "Then that stupid play would be over, and I wouldn't have to feel bad about not being an angel."

Addie brought out the cocoa she'd been brewing in the kitchen, the old-fashioned kind, like Eliza used to make for her and Frank on cold winter afternoons. "Feeling bad is a choice, Lissie," she said. She'd made a few calls that day, when things were slow at the *Wooden Nickel;* her plan was coming together. "You could just as easily choose to feel good."

Lissie frowned. "About what?"

"About the fact that there are other ways to be an angel," Addie said.

The kids zeroed in on the hot chocolate and looked up at her curiously, with brown foamy mustaches.

"What other way is there," Lissie inquired, "besides getting hit by a truck or something?"

"That would be a radical method," Addie allowed, eyeing the sewing machine and her thrift-store creation of peacock blue taffeta. "I spoke to someone at the hospital today. At the nursing home, too. There are some people there who would really like a visit from an angel, especially at Christmas."

Lissie's gaze strayed to the sewing project, and the light dawned in her eyes. "You made me an angel dress?"

Addie nodded. "It's pretty fancy, too, if I do say so myself."

Lissie crossed to the card table, where the sewing machine was set up, and laid a tentative hand on the small, shimmering gown. Except for the hem, a few nips and tucks to make it fit perfectly, and some beads and sequins, rescued from the scorned wedding dress, it was complete.

"Would I have to sing?" Lissie asked in a voice small with wonder.

Addie laughed. "No," she said. "Not if you didn't want to."

"There aren't any wings," Henry pointed out, ever practical. "You can't be an angel without wings."

"I think I could rig something up," Addie said. The wings wouldn't be as fancy as Tiffany Baker's feathered flying apparatus, but the skirt of Jessie's wedding dress would serve if she bent some coat hangers into the proper shape.

"Do they need a shepherd, too?" Henry asked hopefully.

"A shepherd would be the perfect touch," Addie decided.

Lissie was standing on the coffee table, halo askew but on, looking resplendent in her blue angel duds, when Frank rapped at the door, let himself in, and whistled in exclamation. Addie, with a mouthful of pins, offered a careful smile.

"I get to be an angel after all," Lissie told her father.

Frank looked confused. "Don't tell me. Tiffany Baker has been abducted by space aliens. Shall I put out an all-points bulletin?"

Lissie giggled, though whether it was Frank's expression or the concept of her rival being carried off to another planet that amused her was anybody's guess. "I'm going to visit people in the hospital, and the nursing home. Addie's making my wings out of coat hangers."

Frank smiled. "Great idea," he said, looking at Addie. He took in the array of Christmas presents, lying all over the room. "Looks like Santa crashed his sleigh in here."

Addie, who had been kneeling to pin up Lissie's hem, finished the job and got to her feet. "Want some coffee?" she asked Frank, and then wished she hadn't. Now he'd be thinking about the broken mug again, missing Maggie. She blushed and looked away.

He made a show of consulting his watch, shook his head. "We'd better get to the tree lot," he said. "Everybody ready?"

Floyd yelped with excitement.

Addie's gaze flew to Frank's face. So did Henry's and Lissie's.

"Can Floyd go, too?" Lissie asked.

Frank sighed. "Sure," he said, after a few moments of deliberation. "He can sniff out the perfect tree and wait in the car while we're in the Lumberjack having supper. We'll bring him a doggy bag."

How many men would include a beagle on such an expedition? Unexpected tears burned in Addie's eyes. That was the moment she realized the awful, wonderful truth. She'd fallen in love with Frank Raynor—assuming that she'd ever fallen out in the first place. The downside was, he still cared deeply for his late wife. She'd seen his stricken expression when the cup was broken.

The children, naturally oblivious to the nuances, shouted with joy, and Floyd barked all the harder. Addie's hands trembled a little as she helped Lissie out of the gown.

"You're an amazing woman," Frank said quietly, standing very close to Addie, while the kids scrambled to get into their coats. "Thank you."

Addie didn't dare look at him. The revelation she'd just undergone was too fresh—she was afraid he'd see it in her eyes. "We'd better take my station wagon," she said. "It probably wouldn't be kosher to tie a couple of Christmas trees to the top of your squad car."

He didn't answer.

A light snow began as they drove to the lot, Frank at the wheel. From the backseat, the kids sang "Jingle Bells," with Floyd howling an accompaniment.

Within half an hour, they'd selected two lusciously fragrant evergreen trees, and Frank had secured them in the back of the station wagon. When they pulled up in front of the Lumberjack Diner, Floyd sighed with patient resignation, settled his bulk on the seat, and went to sleep.

"This feels almost like being a family," Frank said quietly, as the four of them trooped into the restaurant. "I like it."

The waitresses were all wearing felt reindeer antlers bedecked in tiny blinking lights. "Blue Christmas" wailed from the juke-box, and various customers called out cheerful greetings to the newcomers. There were a couple of low-key whistles, too, and when Addie stole a look at Frank, she was amazed to see that he was blushing.

"About time you hooked up with a woman, Chief," an old man said, patting Frank on the shoulder as he passed the booth where they were seated. "Good to see you back in Pine Crossing, Addie."

She felt warm inside, but it was a bruised and wary warmth. *Don't get your hopes up,* Addie warned herself in the silence of her mind. When she sneaked a look at Frank, unable to resist, she saw that he was blushing again. And grinning a little.

The meal was delicious, and when it was over, there were plenty of scraps for Floyd. He gobbled cheerfully while they drove home, the car full of merriment and the distinctive scents of fresh pine and leftover meat-loaf.

Frank sent Lissie and Floyd into the house when they arrived, and Henry plodded up the apartment stairs, worn out by a jolly evening. He didn't even protest when Addie called after him to start his bath.

She hesitated, watching as Frank unloaded the trees. The snow was falling faster, stinging her cheeks.

"It'll need to settle, and dry out a little," Frank said, setting the tree Addie had chosen upright on the sidewalk, stirring that lovely fragrance again.

Addie laid a hand on his arm. "Thank you, Frank," she said,

very softly. "For the tree, for the meal at the Lumberjack, and for caring about a dog's feelings."

He looked surprised. "I'm the one who should be doing the thanking around here," he said, and when she started to protest, he raised a hand to silence her. "Lissie's wearing her halo again. For one night, she gets to be an angel. I can't begin to tell you what that means to me, Addie."

Addie's throat tightened. If she stayed one moment longer, she'd tell Frank Raynor straight out that she loved him, and ruin everything. "I'd better make sure Henry doesn't get to looking at his presents, forget to turn off the tap, and flood the bathroom," she said, and hurried away.

She felt Frank watching her and would have given anything for the courage to look straight at him and see what was in his face, but she couldn't take the risk.

The stakes were suddenly too high.

Chapter Thirteen

"It's an angel," Lissie said dismally, before Henry got that day's matchbox open. The day of the pageant had come, and while the little girl was ready to play the innkeeper's wife to the best of her ability, Addie knew it wouldn't be any fun for her.

She glanced at Frank, then laid a hand on Lissie's shoulder. "We're booked at the hospital and the Sweet Haven Nursing Home," she reminded the child. She'd found an old white boa, on a second trip to the Goodwill, and planned to glue the feathers onto the clothes-hanger wings on her breaks and during her lunch hour. Lissie's wings wouldn't be as glorious as Tiffany's, but they would be pretty and, Addie hoped, a nice surprise. "Tomorrow night, six o'clock. The patients are looking forward to it."

Lissie nodded.

Frank took the kids to school that morning. Addie had an extra cup of coffee, then set out for work in the station wagon.

At three-ten that afternoon, Lissie burst into the *Wooden Nickel*, setting the silver bell jingling above the door. Addie, taking her break at her desk, quickly shoved the half-feathered wing she'd been working on out of sight.

"Is everything all right?" she asked.

Lissie beamed. "Tiffany got another commercial," she blurted. "She had to be in Denver *today*, and there's no way she can get back in time for the pageant. Miss Pidgett got so upset, she had to go lie down in the principal's office, and Mr. Walker, the teacher's aide, said *I* could take Tiffany's place!"

Stella and Mr. Renfrew applauded, and Addie rounded the counter to hug Lissie. "It's a miracle," she said.

"How come your fingers are sticky?" Lissie wanted to know.

Addie ignored the question. "Do you know the angel's lines?"

" 'Be not afraid,' " Lissie spouted proudly, " 'for behold, I bring you tidings of great joy!' "

"Guess you've got it," Addie said, her arm around Lissie's shoulders. "Have you told your dad?"

Lissie shook her head. "He's on patrol," she replied, and suddenly, her brow furrowed with worry. "Tiffany took her costume with her. I've got my dress—the one you made—but the wings—"

"There will be wings," Addie promised, though she didn't know how she was going to pull that off. There were still two hours left in the workday, and the pageant was due to start at six-thirty.

"Great!" Lissie cried. "Henry's over at the library. Are you going to pick us up, or is Dad?"

"Whoever gets there first," Addie said, her mind going into overdrive.

Lissie nodded and went out, setting the bell over the door to ringing again.

"Another angel gets its wings," Stella said with a smile.

"We'd better get to gluing," Mr. Renfrew added, eyes sparkling.

"Do you suppose there's anything seriously wrong with Miss Pidgett?" Addie fretted, gratefully parceling out feathers stripped from the thrift-store boa and handing Arthur Renfrew the second wing, which was made from the skirt of Jessie Corcoran's wedding gown.

"She's run every pageant since 1962," Stella put in. "Maybe she's just worn out."

"More likely, it's a case of the 'means,' " Mr. Renfrew said, opening a pot of rubber cement and gingerly gluing a feather onto an angel's wing.

Frank arrived at St. Mary's at six-thirty sharp, fresh from the office, where he'd filled out a lengthy report on a no-injury accident out on the state highway, and scanned the crowd. Miss

Pidgett, sitting in a folding chair toward the front of the small auditorium, fanned herself with a program and favored him with a poisonous look.

He smiled and nodded, just as though they were on cordial terms, and she blushed and fanned harder.

A small hand tugged at his jacket sleeve, and he looked down to see Lissie standing beside him, resplendent in her peacock blue angel gown and a pair of feathered wings.

"I thought you were the innkeeper's wife," he said stupidly. The fact was, he couldn't quite believe his eyes, and he was afraid to hope she'd landed the coveted role of lead angel. He checked his watch, wondering if he'd somehow missed the pageant, and Lissie had already changed clothes to make an unscheduled visit to Sweet Haven.

"Tiffany's in a toilet paper commercial, up in Denver," Lissie said, glowing. "She took her wings with her, but Addie made me these, so I'm good to go."

Addie. Frank felt as though the breath had just been knocked out of his lungs. He crouched, so he could look straight into his daughter's eyes. "Honey, that's great," he said, and the words came out sounding husky.

"Did you bring a camera? Henry promised his dad some pictures."

Just then, Addie arrived, looking pretty angelic herself in a kelly green suit. Her hair was pinned up, with a sprig of mistletoe for pizzazz. "I've got one," she said, waving one of those yellow throwaway numbers. "Hi, Frank."

"I'd better go," Lissie told them. "Maybe angels are like brides. Maybe people aren't supposed to see them before it's time!"

"Maybe not," Addie told her.

Lissie put up her hand, and the two of them did a high five.

The audience, mostly consisting of parents, grandparents, aunts, uncles and siblings, shifted and murmured in their folding chairs, smiling holiday smiles.

Frank made a point of looking at Addie's back.

"What?" she asked, fumbling to see if her label was sticking out.

"I was looking for wings," Frank said. "It seems some angels don't have them."

Her eyes glistened, and the junior high school band struck up the first strains of "Silent Night." "We'd better sit down," she whispered, and they took chairs next to Mr. Renfrew and Stella.

The lights went down, and the volume of the music went up. The stage curtains creaked and shivered apart. A small door stood on stage right, with a stable opposite. A kid in a donkey suit brayed, raising a communal chuckle from the audience.

Mary and Joseph shuffled on stage, looking suitably weary. Joseph knocked at the door, and it nearly toppled over backward. Henry peered out of the opening, blinking behind his glasses, and started shaking his head before Joseph could ask for a room. Addie took a picture with the throwaway, and the flash almost blinded Frank.

Henry, taking the innkeeper thing to heart, shook his head again. "No!" he shouted. "I said *no!*"

"Oh, dear," Addie whispered. "He's ad-libbing."

Frank laughed, which earned him a glower from Miss Pidgett, who turned in her seat and homed in on him like a heat-seeking missile.

"You can have the barn!" Henry went on. He was a born actor.

Joseph and Mary drooped and consigned themselves to the stable. Henry slammed the door so hard that the whole thing teetered. Addie gripped Frank's arm, and they both held their breaths, but the efforts of the eighth-grade shop class held.

The donkey brayed again, but he'd already been upstaged by the innkeeper.

Shepherds meandered onto the stage, in brown robes, each with a staff in hand. One carried a stuffed lamb under one arm. They all searched the sky, looking baffled. Henry, bringing up the rear, shoved at the middle of his glasses and wrote himself another line.

"What are all those things in the sky? Angels?"

The other shepherds gave him quelling looks, but Henry was undaunted.

"It's not every night you see a bunch of angels hanging around," he said.

In what he hoped was a subtle move, Frank took Addie's hand.

Miss Pidgett rose out of her seat, then sat down again.

There was a cranking sound, and Lissie descended from the rigging on a rope, wings spread almost as wide as her grin. Less splendid angels inched in from either side of the stage, gazing up at her in bemusement.

"Now *there's* an angel!" Henry boomed, looking up, too.

A ripple of laughter moved through the crowd, and Addie covered her face with her free hand, but only for a moment. She was smiling.

Lissie shouted out her lines, and the unseen stagehands cranked her down. Somebody made a sound like a baby crying, and attention shifted to Mary and Joseph. Darned if there hadn't been a blessed event.

After the pageant, refreshments were served in the cafeteria, and Addie took at least twenty pictures of Henry and Lissie. Practically everybody in town, with the noticeable exception of Miss Pidgett, stopped to compliment both kids on their innovative performances.

They glowed with pride, but the angel and the shepherd were soon yawning, like the rest of the cast.

"I'll take them home in the station wagon," Addie said.

"Meet you there in a couple of minutes," Frank replied, feeling oddly tender. "I just want to say hello to the mayor."

Addie nodded, gathered up the kids and their gear, and left.

Frank completed his social obligation and was just turning to go when there was a scuffle in a far corner of the room. Instinctively, he headed in that direction.

Miss Almira Pidgett lay unconscious on the floor.

Chapter Fourteen

It was after ten when Addie saw the lights of Frank's squad car sweep into the driveway. Lissie was asleep on the couch, still wearing her costume and covered in a quilt, and Henry had long since fallen into bed. Neither of them had wanted to leave the twinkling Christmas tree, standing fragrant in front of the window.

Addie pulled on her coat and went out onto the stairs. Frank had called her from the hospital earlier, where Almira Pidgett was admitted for observation, and she'd been waiting for news ever since. It had been difficult, pretending nothing was wrong while Lissie and Henry celebrated their theatrical debuts, but she hadn't wanted to ruin their evening, so she'd kept the old woman's illness to herself.

Frank appeared at the bottom of the stairs, paused, rested one hand on the railing, and looked up.

"Is she all right?" Addie asked.

Frank's shoulders moved in a weary sigh, but he nodded. "Looks like Miss Pidgett will be in the hospital for a few days. The doctor said it was diabetic shock. Good thing she wasn't home alone."

Addie sagged with relief. She might not have been Miss Pidgett's greatest fan, but she'd been desperately worried, just the same.

"Come upstairs and have some coffee," she said.

Frank grinned, started the climb. "You looked pretty good in that green outfit tonight," he told her.

She'd exchanged her good suit for jeans, sneakers, and a flannel shirt. "Lissie stole the whole show," she said with a laugh. The wind was cold, and it was snowing a little, but the closer Frank got, the warmer she felt. Go figure, she thought.

He ushered her inside, paused to admire the Christmas tree. They'd decorated it together, and it had been a sentimental journey for Addie. She'd been surprised to realize how many memories those old ornaments stirred in her. They hadn't been able to use the bubble lights—they were ancient, and the wires were frayed—but Frank had anted up some spares, and the whole thing looked spectacular, especially with Henry's much-handled presents wedged underneath.

Floyd, lying in the kitchen doorway, got up to waddle across the linoleum and greet his master. Frank closed the door, ruffled the dog's ears, and then went to stand next to the couch, looking down at his sleeping daughter.

"They were something, weren't they?" he asked quietly.

Addie smiled. "Oh, yeah," she said. "What a pair of hams."

They went into the kitchen, and Addie put on the coffee. Frank sat down at the table and rubbed his face with both hands. It was a weary gesture that made Addie want to stand behind him and squeeze his shoulders, maybe even let her chin rest on top of his head for a moment or two, but she refrained.

"The last thing I need," Frank muttered, "is a shot of caffeine."

"I've got decaf," Addie said.

"Perish the thought," Frank replied.

She laughed. "You're a hard man to please, Frank Raynor." She moved toward cupboards next to the stove, meaning to get out a bag of cookies, but Frank caught her hand as she passed.

"No, actually," he said, "I'm not." And he pulled her onto his lap.

She should have resisted him, but she didn't. Her heart shimmied up into her throat.

For a moment, it seemed he might kiss her, but he frowned, and touched the tip of her nose instead. "How come you gave back my engagement ring, Addie Hutton?" he asked, very quietly.

Tears burned behind her eyes. "I was young and stupid."

He moved his finger and planted a kiss where it had been.

"Young, yes. Stupid, never. I should have waited for you, Addie. I should have known you needed an education of your own."

She touched his mouth, very lightly. "You wouldn't have met Maggie," she reminded him. "And you wouldn't have had Lissie."

He sighed. "You're right," he said. "But you wouldn't have met Bozo the Mortgage Broker, either. And you wouldn't have gotten into all that trouble in California."

She couldn't speak.

"What are you going to do now?" Frank asked, his arms still tight around her. "You can't work at the *Wooden Nickel* for the rest of your life, selling classified ads. You're a journalist. You'll go crazy."

"I've been thinking about writing a book," Addie admitted.

Frank's eyes lit up. "Well, now," he said. "Fiction or nonfiction?"

"A romance novel," Addie said, and blushed.

He raised one eyebrow, still grinning. "Is that so?"

Just then, the phone rang.

Because it was late, which might mean the call was important, and maybe because the atmosphere was getting intense in that kitchen, Addie jumped off Frank's lap and rushed to answer it with a breathless, "Hello?"

"Addie," Toby said. "I hope you weren't in bed."

Addie blushed again. "No—no, I was up. Is everything okay? Where are you?"

"Connecticut," Toby answered. "Addie, I have news. Really big news."

Addie closed her eyes, tried to brace herself. He was coming to get Henry. She'd known it was going to happen. "What?" she croaked.

"Elle and I are going to have a baby," Toby blurted. "Isn't that great?"

Addie's eyes flew open. Frank was setting the cups on the counter.

"Great," she said.

"I guess you're wondering why I'd call you to make the announcement," Toby said, sounding more circumspect.

Actually, she hadn't gotten that far. She was still trying to work out what this meant to Henry, and to her. "Right," she said.

Frank raised his eyebrows, thrumming the fingers of one hand on the countertop while he waited for the coffee to finish brewing.

"The pregnancy will be stressful," Toby went on. "For Elle, I mean. That's why I was wondering—"

Addie held her breath.

"That's why *we* were wondering if you'd keep Henry for a while longer."

Addie straightened. "You'll have to grant me temporary custody, Toby," she said. "I won't have you jerking Henry back and forth across the country every time it strikes your fancy."

"Is that what you think of me? That I'd do something like that?"

What *was* the man's home planet? "Yes," she said. "That's what I think."

Toby got defensive. "I could send Henry to stay with my dad and stepmother, you know."

"But you won't," Addie said. She'd received a check from Toby's father in that day's mail. It would pay some bills, and provide a Christmas for Henry, and she was very grateful. According to the enclosed note, Mr. Springer and his third trophy wife were spending what remained of the winter in Tahiti.

"All right," Toby admitted. "I won't."

"Ground rules, Toby," Addie said, as Frank gave her a chipper salute. "I want legal custody, signed, sealed and delivered. And you will call this child once a week, without fail."

"You got it," Toby agreed with a sigh.

"One more thing," Addie said.

"What?" Toby asked sheepishly.

"Congratulations," Addie told him.

Frank poured the coffee, carried the cups to the table. He'd taken off his uniform jacket, hung it over the back of a chair. His shoulders strained at the fabric of his crisply pressed shirt.

"Thanks," Toby said, and the conversation was over.

"I take it a celebration is in order?" Frank asked.

Addie jumped, kicked her heels together, and punched one fist in the air.

"Not much gets past a Sherlock Holmes like me," Frank said.

Chapter Fifteen

Frank's tree glittered, and a Christmas Eve fire flickered merrily on the hearth. Three stockings hung from the mantelpiece—Lissie's, Henry's, and Floyd's. Nat King Cole crooned about merry little Christmases.

"They're asleep," Frank said from the stairway. "I guess that second gig at the hospital and the nursing home did them in. Who'd have thought Almira Pidgett would turn out to be a fan of the angel-and-shepherd road show?"

Addie smiled, cup of eggnog in hand, and turned to watch him approach. Miss Pidgett had warmed to Lissie and Henry's impromptu performance when they shyly entered her hospital room the night after the pageant, and tonight, she'd welcomed them with a twinkly smile. "Christmas is a time for miracles," she said.

Frank took the cup out of her hand, set it aside, and pulled her close. "You think it's too soon?" he asked.

"Too soon for what?" she countered, but she knew. A smile quirked at the corner of her mouth.

"You and me to take up where we left off, back in the day," Frank prompted, kissing her lightly. "I love you, Addie."

She traced the outline of his lips. "And I love you, Frank Raynor."

"But you still haven't answered my question."

She smiled. "I don't think it's too soon," she said. "I think it's *about time*."

"Do I get to be in your romance novel?"

"You already are."

He gave a wicked chuckle. "Maybe we'd better do a little research," he teased, and tasted her mouth again. Then, suddenly, he straightened, squinted at the Christmas tree behind her. "But wait. What's that?"

Addie turned to look, confused.

Eliza's Advent calendar was draped, garland-style, across the front of the tree.

"Why, it's Aunt Eliza's Advent calendar!" Frank said, and twiddled at a nonexistent mustache.

"You might make it in a romance novel," Addie said, "but if you're thinking of going into acting, don't give up your day job."

"We forgot to check the twenty-fourth box," Frank said, recovering quickly from the loss of a career behind the footlights.

"We did not forget," Addie said. "It was a little crèche. The kids looked this morning, before breakfast."

"I think we should look again," Frank insisted. "Specifically, I think *you* should look again."

She moved slowly toward the tree, confused. They'd agreed not to give each other gifts this year, though she'd bought a present for Lissie, and he'd gotten one for Henry.

The twenty-fourth box, unlike the other twenty-three, was closed. Addie slid it open slowly, and gasped.

"My engagement ring," she said. The modest diamond was wedged in between the crèche and the side of the matchbox. "You kept it?"

Frank stood beside her, slipped an arm around her waist. "Eliza kept it," he said. "Will you marry me, Addie?"

She turned to look up into his eyes. "Oh, Frank."

"I'll get you a better ring, if you want one."

She shook her head. "No," she said. "I want this one."

"Then, you will? Marry me, I mean?"

"Yes."

He pulled her into his arms, kissed her. "When?" he breathed when it was over.

Addie was breathless. "Next summer?"

"Good enough." He laughed, then kissed her again. "In the meantime, we can work on that research."

Christmas Eve

Virginia Henley

Chapter One

Eve Barlow was naked.

Her towel had slid to the floor with a whisper and here they stood, finally alone together, staring at each other. She posed provocatively, lifting her long blond hair and letting it waterfall to her shoulders.

"Am I beautiful?" she asked. "Am I sexy?"

The questions proved she was vulnerable, which was the very last thing she wanted to be.

Was that a critical look she detected? Silence filled the bedroom. If the answer to her questions took this long, perhaps the answer was *no!*

She looked straight into the green eyes, saw the humor lurking there, and her exuberant self-confidence came flooding back.

"Yes, you're beautiful; yes, you're sexy! You are also intelligent, successful, and independent," came the answer. The green eyes assessed the full, ripe breasts and watched as the nipples turned to spikes.

"You forgot *crazy,*" she told her reflection as her body shivered with gooseflesh. "Anyone who would stand naked before a mirror when it's below zero outside has got to be crazy!"

Eve knew Trevor Bennett's Christmas present would be a diamond ring. As she drew on her pantyhose, she asked herself if she was ready to be engaged. The answer came back *yes.* She was twenty-six years old—the perfect age for marriage. Everything else in her life was just about perfect, too.

Her career was in high gear, her finances were rock-solid, and her fiancé had all the qualities that would make him a perfect husband: sensitivity, kindness, and understanding. Trevor was an English professor at Western Michigan University and often quoted poetry to her.

Eve chose a red wool suit, then pulled on black, high-heeled boots. Even with a power suit she always wore heels. There were no rules that said a career woman couldn't have sexy-looking legs. The minute she picked up her briefcase, the telephone rang.

"Eve? You didn't give me a definite answer about coming home for Christmas, dear."

"Hi, Mom. I sent you an answer on e-mail last night."

"Oh honey, you know I don't understand that computer stuff. Daddy's tried to explain it to me, but I feel so much more comfortable on the phone."

"Of course Trevor and I are coming for Christmas dinner. It's my turn and I would love to take everyone out to The Plaza—I hate to see you cooking all day. But since you insist on a traditional, home-cooked turkey, I capitulate."

"You know it's fun for me. I just love doing all the things that make Christmas special."

"I know you do, Mom. That's why we all love you so much. I have to run—I have the keys to the office and have to open up today. See you Christmas morning."

"Drive carefully, dear."

Eve sighed. There was absolutely no point in trying to change Susan this late in life. Her mother was a perfectly contented housewife, an angel of domesticity who'd been kept in her place by the men in her life. She had no idea there were worlds to conquer out there.

Susie, as Eve's father insisted on calling her, had made a happy home for her air force family, no matter where they'd been stationed. It hadn't mattered much to Susie where she was; Ted was the center of her life and her two children orbited closely around him.

Ted was the macho major who wisecracked about everything, but ruled his family with an iron hand. She had gotten her name from one of her father's wisecracks. He had wanted a brother for his firstborn, Steven, but when Susie had a girl, he grinned good-naturedly and said, "Now it's Eve 'n' Steven!"

Her brother had followed in his father's footsteps, joining the military and becoming a macho ace before he was twenty. But Eve was determined not to become a clone of her mother. She avoided dominant, controlling men who thought a woman's place was in the kitchen, *unless she was in the bedroom.*

Eve pulled her Mercedes into the parking space that had her name on it, then unlocked the front door of Caldwell Baker Real Estate. Within six months she hoped to be a full partner in the privately owned company.

Before she read all the faxes, the other agents started to arrive. Bob and George arrived together because Bob had cracked up his Caddy on an icy road and it was in the shop awaiting parts. When Eve started working at the agency, they had joked about her aggressive salesmanship, calling her a ball-breaker, but now that her sales topped theirs, they gave her the respect she had earned.

"I'm sorry about your accident, Bob. It must be milder today— the ice was melting when I drove in."

"Warm enough to snow," predicted George, who tended to look on the dark side.

"Congratulations on breaking into the President's Circle, Eve," Bob said.

She had been in the Multimillion-Dollar Club for the last two years, but now that she was selling commercial as well as residential properties, she had reached new production levels. "I haven't quite made it yet, Bob, but thanks."

"Oh hell, it's only December twenty-third. Still nine days left before the year ends," he said, winking at George.

The sons-of-bitches hope I don't make it, Eve suddenly realized.

Other agents began arriving and the first thing they did was glance toward the coffee urn beside the bank of filing cabinets. When they saw there was nothing brewing, the second thing they did was glance at Eve. Well, they could wait until their Grecian Formula wore off before she would make coffee, she decided, going into her office to go over the listings. She was two hundred thousand dollars short, and determined to reach her goal if it was humanly possible.

When the secretary arrived, the men heaved a collective sigh of relief. They fell over each other helping her off with her coat and boots, then followed her en masse to the coffee urn. *Bo Peep has suddenly found her sheep,* Eve thought sarcastically.

Someone came through the front door. Since all the agents were at the back of the premises, Eve came out of her office to attend to the prospective customer. He was tall with jet black hair, wearing a heavy blue shirt and a leather vest with decorative bullet-holder loops above and below the pockets. This guy apparently didn't know they were decorative; they held real bullets.

"I'm Eve Barlow. May I help you?"

The man's deep blue eyes stared at her mouth, lingered on her breasts, went down to her legs, then climbed back up her body to her blond hair and, finally, to her eyes.

Why don't you take a bloody picture? It'll last longer, she thought silently.

"I don't think so. I'm looking for Maxwell Robin."

He had the deepest voice Eve had ever heard.

"Maxwell has an early appointment; he won't be here until ten. Are you sure I can't be of some service?"

"I can think of a dozen, none of them appropriate for a real estate office." He gave her a lopsided grin.

Eve did not smile back. She turned on her heel and walked back toward her office.

"You could get me a cup of coffee while I'm waiting for Max."

Eve stopped dead in her tracks and turned to give him a look that would wither a more sensitive male. She bit back the cutting retort that sprang to mind and said coolly, "Feel free to help yourself."

"Don't tempt me." He winked at her.

The sexist son-of-a-bitch actually winked at her! Eve went into her office and slammed the door. She turned on her computer, saw that she had e-mail and accessed it. The message was from Trevor, who stayed many weeknights at the university in Kalamazoo. *No classes Friday, so I'll see you tomorrow night. Would you like to go to Cygnus and dance under the stars?*

Eve answered in the affirmative.

Trevor, I would love to go to Cygnus for dinner, on condition we don't stay too late. I'm probably working Friday.

Within half an hour, Trevor replied. *I understand. It's a date!*

Eve smiled at the words on her computer screen. Trevor Bennett was the most understanding man in the world. He had no problem with her assertiveness, her career, or the fact that she made more money than he. She wondered briefly if she would keep her own name when they married. Eve Barlow Bennett . . . it sounded good to her and Trevor would never object. So why not?

Maxwell's voice came over the intercom, cutting her reverie short.

"Eve, are you free to come into my office?"

As she opened her door, she heard the deep voice say, "I don't want a female agent. I want you, Max."

"The property you're interested in is Eve Barlow's listing. It's exclusive."

She gritted her teeth and walked into the owner's office.

"Ms. Barlow, this is Mr. Kelly. He's interested in the lakefront property you have listed up past Ludington. I've just been explaining that's your exclusive."

Eve shook hands with Action Man, as she had already dubbed him, making sure her grip was firm. She knew Max was being generous. The listing *was* hers, given to her by a friend in Detroit who had been left the property by her late parents. However, there was no reason why Maxwell couldn't have sold it—except, of course, he wanted her to qualify for the President's Circle this year.

"I'd like to take a look at it." Kelly turned from Eve to address Maxwell. "Can you go with me?"

"I told you, it's Ms. Barlow's listing. I have appointments all day."

"I'll take you to see it, Mr. Kelly. Are you free to leave now?"

The rugged-looking man drew dark brows together in a frown. "It's a hundred miles."

Eve failed to see his point. "Slightly more. It's a two-hour drive, two-and-a-half in bad weather. Perhaps you don't have time today."

"I have all the time in the world."

"Well, that's terrific, Mr. Kelly. Just let me get my briefcase."

In spite of the fact that he resented dealing with a female agent, Kelly helped her on with her camel-hair coat and held the door open for her.

The condescending gestures were politically incorrect in this day and age. Any woman breathing could put on her own coat and open her own doors. Kelly had either been living under a stone, or was being deliberately annoying. She suspected it was the latter.

Eve walked toward her Mercedes, but he did not follow her.

"We'll use my vehicle," he stated.

"It's part of my job to provide the transportation, Mr. Kelly."

"We'll use my vehicle," he repeated.

Eve glanced at the Dodge Ram four-wheel-drive truck and repressed a shudder. They were already in a tug-of-war. "The Mercedes will be more comfortable," she asserted.

"This is a rough terrain vehicle," he pointed out.

"You don't trust my driving?"

"I have nothing against women drivers, but I wouldn't let a woman drive me unless I had two broken arms."

That could be arranged, you sexist swine!

He gave her a meaningful look. "Whatever happened to the idea that the customer is always right?"

Eve decided if she wanted this sale, she had better do things his way. She walked toward the Dodge Ram. It had flames painted across the doors, as if they were coming from the engine.

The first thing she saw when she climbed in was a gun rack holding a rifle. Action Man was obviously a hunter. She liked him less and less. He drove aggressively. He didn't race, but nothing passed him. Before they got out of the city, it began to snow-flurry.

"So, talk to me, tell me about yourself," he invited. He sounded patronizing.

I'm a feminazi who loathes macho men, she thought, then remembered her six percent commission. "My name is Eve Barlow. I was an air force brat. Lived in Germany, then the Orient. When my dad retired, we moved back to Detroit where he was born, but the crime rate spurred my parents to move to a more wholesome city. They chose Grand Rapids."

"I moved here from Detroit, too, a few years ago. My dad and brothers were police officers, so I know all about the crime rate."

Kelly. Irish cops. Tough as boiled owl, she thought. *Born with too much testosterone!*

"How did you get into real estate?"

"I chose it very deliberately. It's a field where women can excel. I didn't want to spend years at university, living at home. I wanted to be independent. I'm on my way to breaking the glass ceiling."

"Glass ceiling?" he puzzled.

He's got to be kidding; the man's a Neanderthal!

"Is that some sort of feminist term?"

"Yes. It's a ceiling erected by the men who run the corporate world, to keep women from high earnings and from achieving their potential."

"Bull! If a woman doesn't reach her full potential, she has only herself to blame."

Eve tended to believe that, yet she had an overwhelming urge to oppose him. He had a dark, dangerous quality about him, as if he could erupt. She turned away to look out the window. It was snowing harder now. It seemed to Eve that the harder it snowed, the faster he drove.

"Where's the fire?" she asked.

He began to laugh. His teeth were annoyingly white.

"Let me in on the joke."

"I'm a fire captain."

"You're kidding me! You're a firefighter?"

He nodded. "I'm a captain, studying for my chief's exams."

"The flames!" she said, suddenly comprehending.

"My attempt at humor."

Until this moment, Eve had had no idea one had to sit exams to fight fires. The property he was interested in was listed at a quarter of a million dollars. Did Action Man have this kind of money, or was she on a wild-goose chase? Eve cleared her throat. "How do you know Maxwell?" she probed.

"I teach scuba. He's in my diving class."

"Really?" Eve was a city girl. Scuba diving was out of her

depth of comprehension. It was too physical, too dangerous, too unnatural somehow. Encasing yourself in rubber, sticking a breathing tube in your mouth, then isolating yourself fathoms deep in murky water was not her idea of fun.

"That's one of the reasons I'm interested in the lakefront property. Michigan offers nine underwater preserves. There are miles of bottomland for exploring shipwrecks."

"I see. Wouldn't a summer cottage do just as well? This is a year-round log home." She was trying to hint at the price.

"I need something year-round for ice diving."

"Ice diving?" She said it with abhorrence as if he had said grave-robbing.

"You cut a hole in the ice with an auger. Of course, you tie yourselves together with a safety rope."

"You do this for pleasure, or as some sort of penance?"

"If that's a jab at my being Catholic, I believe you're being politically incorrect, *Miz* Barlow."

Eve stiffened.

"I'm astounded you even know what political correctness is, Mr. Kelly. You make sexist remarks every time you open your mouth!"

His eyes were like blue ice. His glance lingered on her hair and mouth, dropped to her breasts, then lifted to her eyes. "What a waste; you obviously hate men."

"Your father, the cop, must have shot you in the arse . . . you obviously have brain damage!"

"There you go again. He was a police officer, not a cop."

She saw the amusement in his eyes.

"You have a wicked tongue. I could teach you sweeter things to do with it than cutting up men, *Miz* Barlow."

"Don't call me that," she snapped.

"All right. I'll call you Eve. My name's Clint. Clint Kelly."

"Clint? My God, I don't believe it. You've made that up."

His bark of laughter told her that her barbs didn't penetrate his thick hide.

The visibility was deteriorating rapidly. "The weather's closing in. Would you like to turn back?" he asked.

His tone of voice was challenging, almost an insult.

She replied, "If I couldn't handle snow, I wouldn't live in Michigan."

He shrugged. "The decision's yours."

"Good. I like making decisions. And I don't have much use for macho males."

"That's all right, Eve. I don't have any at all for feminists."

Chapter Two

Eve lit up a cigarette. She was trying to stop smoking, but tended to reach for one when she was annoyed.

Clint frowned. "That's a dangerous habit."

"That's all right—if I set myself on fire, you're obviously qualified to put it out."

He refused to lecture her.

By twelve-thirty they reached Ludington, a thriving tourist port in the summertime but quiet in winter. Two hours was terrific time in adverse weather conditions.

Clint stopped at a service station for gas; Eve used the ladles' room.

"How about some lunch before we leave civilization?" he asked.

The town had two good restaurants, but both were closed for Christmas week. "I don't usually eat lunch," Eve said, relieved that she didn't have to sit across a table from Clint Kelly. All she wanted to do was show him the property and get back to Grand Rapids.

There was a fast-food place open as they pulled out of town. Clint stopped the truck. "Can I get you a burger? You should eat something."

"No, thanks. That stuff is incredibly bad for you."

Clint laughed. "And cigarettes aren't?"

She almost asked him to bring her a coffee, but remembered that she had not brought him one earlier.

Clint came back with two hamburgers and a milkshake. He

raised his eyebrow, offering her one. When she shook her head, he devoured them both.

Highway 31 turned into an undivided road and Eve recalled that they would have to turn off in just a few miles. She remembered Big Sable River, but couldn't recall if they had to turn off before or after they crossed it.

Clint turned on the radio, but not many stations came in clearly. He found one that was playing country music. "You like country music?"

"Actually, I loathe it." The moment the words were out of her mouth, she suspected she had made an admission she would regret. He made no effort to change the station; in fact, he turned up the volume.

Eve put up with the torture for five minutes, then reached out decisively to shut it off. She cut the announcer off in mid-sentence as he said, "I have an updated weather—" Then she had to do an about-face and turn it back on.

"—Snow, and lots of it. Blizzard conditions will prevail. Travelers are advised to stay off the roads unless it's an emergency."

"Where is that station?" she asked the air.

"Don't panic. It could be across the lake in Wisconsin, or it could even be Canada."

"I'm not the type to panic," she said coolly.

He gave her a fathomless look. "What type are you, Eve?"

"What type do you think I am, Kelly?"

"You're difficult to read. I can't decide if you're an ice queen or simply unawakened."

"You're not difficult to read. You're an arrogant, sexist swine!"

He grinned. "You sure have a short fuse; I was teasing."

"For your information, I'm engaged to be married."

His eyes looked pointedly at her hands.

"I'm getting my ring for Christmas," she explained, then wondered why in hellfire she found it necessary to explain herself to this insufferable devil.

"I take it he's the sensitive type."

"He's an English professor." Why did that sound so wimpy? "An intellectual," she added. "Trevor is the opposite of you. Yes, he's sensitive—and understanding."

"He's passive and I'm aggressive . . . he's a sheep and I'm a wolf."

Eve narrowed her eyes. "He doesn't drive a truck with flames on it."

"I bet he doesn't drive a Mercedes, either."

His arrow hit its target. "He isn't threatened by the fact that I earn more than he does."

"Then he should be. You intend to wear the pants in the family?"

"No, I intend to be an equal partner. But I admit I'm not domesticated. I don't cook, I don't sew, and I don't cower."

"I bet you even carry your own condoms."

Eve blushed. She had a couple in her shoulder bag. The fact that he could make her blush threw her off balance. "Oh, I think we should have turned off back there."

"You *think?*" He found a place where he could turn around, and showed no impatience. They drove down the snowy road for a couple of miles, but Eve saw nothing that looked familiar. She gave directions, but they were tentative. Finally, she admitted she was hopelessly lost, but only to herself.

"You don't know where this place is, do you?"

"We should be there. You must have passed it."

"Have you actually been to this property?" he asked.

"Of course I have, but it was in the fall. Everything looks different covered with snow. Go back across the river and—"

He held up a commanding hand. "Don't help. I'll find it myself."

By using logic and old-fashioned common sense, he wound his way down a couple of unplowed side roads until he came to the lake. Then he drove slowly along the lakeshore road until Eve finally recognized the private driveway. It was almost two-thirty. They were no longer making good time.

Eve took the keys from her briefcase and followed Clint Kelly from the truck. The winter winds from Lake Michigan had piled up a huge snowdrift across the front entrance to the house. Clint walked back to his truck, opened the hard box on the back, and pulled out a shovel. "Looks like we'll have to dig our way in," he said without rancor.

"If you had two shovels, I could help."

"Shifting light snow won't exactly prostrate me," he explained.

No, I'd have to hit you over the head with the shovel to do that, she thought.

By the time they got inside the house, it was three o'clock. Eve stamped the snow off her boots and shook it from her shoulders, but she didn't take off her coat because the log house was freezing. She walked straight to the telephone to call her boss to tell him they were running late.

"Damn, the phone's been put on holiday service; no calls can go in or out." She gave him a scathing look. "I have a car phone in my Mercedes."

"That isn't going to help you one bit."

"Exactly!" She threw up her hands.

"Can't you survive without a telephone?"

Eve didn't have to call the offfice. She lived alone; no one was expecting her. Trevor was in Kalamazoo. "If you don't need to call anyone, I certainly don't."

"If you mean, am I married, the answer is no. Both my brothers are divorced, so I'm wary of women."

"I meant no such thing! I'm not the least bit interested in your personal life."

"Curiosity's written all over your face. You're wondering if I can afford this place."

Damn you, Clint Kelly, you're too smart for your own damn good.

"You turn on the water and I'll check the electrical panel. It'll be dark before we know it."

Eve went downstairs to the basement in search of the water valve. She couldn't find it. She found laundry tubs, a washer and dryer, a water heater that was turned to *off*. She went into the basement washroom. It had a shower, a sink, and a toilet; it even had a shut-off valve, but only for the toilet it was connected to. Without lights, the basement was very dim. She looked under the stairs and finally admitted defeat.

"I couldn't find it," she said lamely.

He gave her a pitying glance.

"If you'd turned on the electricity, I might have been able to see down there!"

"The electricity's been cut off," he said shortly. "You start a fire; I'll find the water valve."

Eve stared at the small stack of logs beside the massive stone fireplace. There were no matches. She opened her purse, took out her lighter, and looked about for an old newspaper. Nothing! Paper, where could she get paper? She opened her briefcase and crumpled up some Offer to Purchase forms. Kindling, now she needed kindling. She couldn't start a fire with only paper and logs. Eve spied a basket of pinecones used for decoration and felt quite smug as she carried them to the fireplace. She piled up a pyramid atop the crumpled paper and set her lighter to it. It blazed up merrily, but gradually smoke billowed out at her and she began to cough.

A powerful hand pulled her out of the way, reached up the chimney and pushed an iron lever. "You have to open the damper," he explained.

"Did you locate the water valve?" she challenged.

"Of course."

He had the ability to make her feel useless. He soon had the logs in the fireplace blazing and crackling. "As soon as you get warm, you can give me the tour."

The log house was truly beautiful. It was a full two stories. Four bedrooms and two baths opened onto a balcony that looked down on the spacious open-concept living room and kitchen. The bedrooms also opened onto an outside balcony that ran around the entire perimeter of the house.

The views over the lake and forest were breath-stopping. Clint lifted his head and breathed deeply, drawing in the smell of the lake and the woods. She watched, fascinated, as his eyelashes caught the snowflakes.

"Last night was a full moon. It had a ring around it; that always predicts a change in the weather."

"Been reading the *Farmers' Almanac,* have we?"

"I suppose yuppies find folklore exceedingly quaint, but I've learned not to scoff at it."

They went back inside to explore the rooms downstairs. A cobalt blue hot tub had been built into a glass-enclosed room along with a sauna.

How romantic, Eve thought.

"Decadence," Clint said, grinning.

Eve quickly switched her thoughts to the business at hand. "As you know, the asking price is a quarter of a million, but that's furnished. A lot of this furniture is handcrafted. Isn't it lovely?"

"It is. I make furniture like this. In fact, that sleigh bed upstairs is one of my pieces. Sorry, I digress."

Why was she surprised? The man was an entity unto himself. She began to believe Clint Kelly could very well afford the property.

"I want to look over the acreage before the light goes."

Eve groaned inwardly; it was a blizzard out there.

"Do you have a survey of the property in that briefcase of yours, or is it just for show?"

Eve snapped open the case and rifled through the papers. She pulled out the survey and thrust it at him. "I didn't think you'd be able to read anything so technical," she said sweetly.

Clint ignored the barb. "We'd better hurry. If much more of this comes down, we might not get out of here tonight. I can look around by myself, if the elements are too fierce for you," he goaded.

"Is that more Clint claptrap? You don't have to keep proving what a physical man you are."

"If I intended to prove how physical I can be, I'd have you down to your teddy by now."

Why did her mouth go dry at his provocative words?

Outside, he opened his truck, pulled out a down-filled jacket, and shrugged into it. Then he took a big steel tape from his toolbox. As they set off through the trees, she thought, *Surely he's not going to take measurements in the snow? Please don't let him expect me to hold the other end of the tape. From now on, I'll stick to my own turf: good old city property.*

As if he could read her thoughts, he said, "This is the reason I would have preferred Maxwell to come with me. This isn't a woman's job."

Eve ground her teeth. "There are no such things as *men's* jobs and *women's* jobs."

"Bull! The world has gone nuts. They're even telling us women can be firefighters!"

"You sound like my father: air force women shouldn't fly combat jets."

"Your father is right. Women are perfectly capable of flying jets, but they shouldn't allow them into combat zones."

Eve had walked out on an argument with her father and brother on this subject, and she was close to walking out on Clint Kelly. *That would be gutless,* she decided. *I'll make this sale if it kills me!*

The barn loomed before them. Clint used his booted feet to kick the drift of snow from the entrance, then they went inside to look around. The first thing Eve noticed was the smell. The scent of hay and straw mingled with the lingering miasma of horses, who had occupied the stalls once upon a time. How was it barns and hay always conjured fantasies of lovemaking, Eve wondered? She'd certainly never had a romantic encounter in a barn . . . yet.

"This place has amazing possibilities."

She turned away quickly so he wouldn't see her blush. She knew perfectly well that his thoughts did not mirror hers; it was simply because of his overt masculinity, and their close proximity in the romantic setting.

All too soon, Clint was again ready for the great outdoors. After they tramped what felt like miles through the deep snow, he selected a spot beside a wire fence and began to dig with his hands.

He had big, strong, capable hands that were well calloused. Eve reluctantly admitted to herself that she found them strangely attractive.

Clint found what he was looking for—a one-inch-square iron surveyor's bar. He didn't ask her to hold one end of the tape, as she expected; instead he began to follow the fenceline, counting his strides.

Eve pulled up her collar and jammed her hands into her pockets. She was freezing. Clint, hatless, didn't even seem to notice the cold.

"An abundance of wildlife here . . . raccoon, weasel, fox, deer, even elk."

Eve hadn't noticed the animal tracks until he pointed them

out. He didn't miss much, she decided. *I bet women fall all over him.* Where the devil had that thought come from? It certainly didn't matter to her what effect he had on women! He had a decidedly abrasive effect on her, yet she didn't think the abrasiveness would affect the sale. He seemed to enjoy sparring with her.

Suddenly, as they came upon a bushy undergrowth, a covey of pheasants flew up into the trees. One bird huddled on the ground.

"It's caught in a snare," Clint said. "Its leg's broken." He immediately wrung the pheasant's neck, then ripped the snare apart in anger and flung it away. "Goddamn snares are as bad as leghold traps."

Eve stared at him in horror. "You cruel bastard! Why did you do that?"

"I'm not cruel, nature is. The bird's leg was broken. As soon as it's full dark, a fox would have eaten it."

"We could have taken it with us and nursed it back to health."

"The cold's getting to your brain."

"And you're suffering from necrosis of the cranium! Too bad you didn't have your gun—you could have shot them all." She turned away furiously and hurried in the direction of the house.

"Eve, get back here." It was an order.

Eve kept on going.

"Don't you dare go off on your own." This time it was more than an order, it was a command. She took great satisfaction in defying it.

Darkness was descending rapidly, but because of the white snow he could see her figure disappearing through the trees. Her black coat soon blended in with her surroundings, however, so that he could no longer see her.

"Bloody women! Can't live with 'em, can't shoot 'em." He tucked the bird inside his jacket and set off after her.

Eve had a soft spot for animals, especially injured ones. She and her mother had once nursed their cat back to health after it had been poisoned. They'd stayed up with it night after night, soothing it, trying one food after another, until they found something its stomach would not reject. The only thing that worked was honey, a dab at a time on its paw. The cat licked it off, again and again, and was able to stay alive.

Looking after injured animals took a great deal of patience

and time. Patience she had in abundance—much more for animals than humans—but these days, time was in short supply.

Eve was totally preoccupied with her thoughts and as a consequence, she paid little attention to where she walked. She was going in the general direction of the house and when she saw a clearing where the trees thinned out, she crossed it. Suddenly, a crack like a rifle shot rent the air and Eve felt the ground give way beneath her.

She cried out in alarm, not knowing what was happening. Then ice-cold water closed over her head. Dear God, she had walked out onto the pond and gone through the ice!

Chapter Three

"Help! Help me!" Eve screamed, then the icy water covered her mouth, effectively cutting off her cries. She knew the water was deep. Her feet touched bottom once before she struggled to the surface and grabbed hold of the ice at the edge of the hole she had made. Eve could swim, but her soaked coat and boots felt ten times heavier.

There was no time to pray, no time even to think coherently; sheer panic took control. The more she struggled to grab hold of something, the more ice broke from the edges, until the hole gaped wide. Eve had never experienced cold like this in her entire life. It penetrated her skin, seeped into her blood, froze her very bones to the marrow.

Clint heard her screams—a sound with which he was on intimate terms. He ran through the dusk on the path she had taken, knowing not to run across the open clearing. He saw nothing until she surfaced and cried out again. His eyes went swiftly to the hole in mid-pond—he was alarmed to see Eve was submerged to her neck.

"I see you!" he shouted. "Try not to panic."

"Clint," she wailed. Her voice a mixture of relief and hope.

"Can you stand up?" Clint demanded.

"No!" came the urgent reply.

"Can you swim?" His deep voice carried well.

"My coat is too heavy!"

"Remove it!" he ordered sternly.

Clint's mind flashed about like mercury. He knew if the ice

wouldn't support her, it would never hold him. He remembered seeing a long wooden ladder in the garage. He had rope in his truck; he never traveled without it. The danger was twofold: she could drown or she could die from hypothermia.

He would try to rescue her with rope and ladder. If that failed, he would have to go in after her. Clint preferred to keep his clothing dry. He knew he would need to keep himself warm during the long night that loomed ahead.

He focused all his attention on Eve. "Take off your coat!" he ordered a second time.

Eve's fingers were numb. She fumbled with the buttons. "I can't!" The water closed over her again as she struggled.

"Keep your head up. Concentrate on those buttons. Rip it off!" If she did not get the coat off, she could die, but he hesitated to tell her.

Finally, miraculously, the waterlogged coat came off and immediately sank from its own weight. Eve felt even colder without the blanket-like coat, but she could move her arms and legs easier.

"I have to get a rope from the truck. Stay afloat, no matter what. Try not to flounder about and break any more ice!"

Clint lunged off toward the house. Inside the garage, he removed his down jacket and threw the dead pheasant on the floor. Then he took the wooden ladder that lay against the wall and carried it outside. He got the long rope from his truck, tied it to the ladder, then raced back to the pond.

When he was halfway there, he began shouting encouragement for her to hang on. His heart started hammering when he got no reply. It was full dark now as he peered across the snow-covered pond to the gaping black hole. He saw nothing!

"Eve! Eve!" he bellowed. Then he heard a whimper and knew she was still alive.

"Hold on, sweetheart, I'm coming. You're so damn brave. I'll have you out in a minute." His voice exuded total confidence, though Clint felt no such thing. It was something he had learned to do over the years. Confidence begot confidence!

Eve could no longer speak. She could only gasp and make small animal sounds every once in awhile. She could no longer feel her arms and legs, and the rest of her body was also slowly becoming numb. She was on the brink of total exhaustion—the icy-cold water had numbed her thought processes as well. She kept her mouth above water by sheer instinct alone, but was dangerously close to the edge of unconsciousness.

Clint Kelly carefully laid the ladder across the ice of the pond, making sure the end of it stopped well back from the black hole. He took the rope firmly in both hands and lay down flat on top of the ladder.

Slowly, inch by inch, he moved his body toward the hole. He was totally focused—there was no room in his mind for failure. He intended to get her out, one way or another. The tricky part was to get her out before it was too late.

When he was halfway along the ladder, he heard a faint cracking noise, but resolutely ignored it and inched forward. He braced himself for the big crack that would sound like a rifle shot. Clint held his breath in dreaded anticipation and forced himself to breathe normally.

The crack did not come while his full weight was distributed on the ladder. It came when he slithered his torso across the bare ice, keeping his feet and knees hooked onto the rungs. Clint did not hesitate; he was too close to back off now. With a superhuman effort he lifted her enough to loop the rope around her body, beneath her arms. Only then did he back off, slithering as swiftly as a serpent.

When his whole weight was back on the ladder, he wound the rope around his body, then hauled as he slowly crawled backward. Sounds of splintering ice filled the darkness, but it didn't matter now. She was anchored firmly to him.

When Clint threw off the rope, then lifted her high against his chest, he saw that Eve was unconscious. He refused to panic, telling himself that this was only to be expected. The falling snow looked like big white goose feathers, blanketing everything it touched. Their tracks were filled in, but by now Clint could have found the house if he'd been blindfolded.

He laid Eve facedown on the floor before the dying embers of the fire. Then he straddled her, splayed his large hands across her rib cage, and pressed and released in a rhythm that simulated natural breathing. In less than a minute, Eve coughed up water, gagged up more, then groaned. She opened her eyes briefly, then closed them again, but Clint was satisfied that she was breathing normally.

They needed heat and they needed it now. He immediately piled the remaining wood on the fire and poked it up into a blaze. He gathered half a dozen towels from the linen closet and three large blankets from the bedroom and brought them to the fire. Before Clint went out to his truck, he glanced at Eve to make sure the bluish color was leaving her face.

Clint brought in his tackle box, his rifle and ammunition, and a forty-ounce bottle of whisky he had picked up for a raffle at the fire hall. He spread out the towels and began undressing her. He removed her boots first and set them on the hearth. While she was still facedown, he pulled off her suit skirt, then peeled off her pantyhose.

Clint rolled her onto the towels so that she lay faceup. His sure fingers unbuttoned the red jacket, deftly removed it, and tossed the icy wet object beside the fire. A curse dropped from his lips as he noted the logs were already half burned away. He glanced at the girl who lay helplessly before him in a short red slip and bra.

Eve's face and hair had a delicate, unearthly fairness about them that stirred a deep protectiveness within him. Clint tried to crush down the personal feelings she aroused, trying to be detached and totally professional. When he peeled off her wet undergarments, he tried not to stare at her nakedness. He covered her with a towel and began to rub her limbs briskly.

After a couple of minutes, he had her completely dry, but he did not succeed in warming her body. The glowing logs were giving off their last heat, so he knew the fire would be of little use in raising her body temperature. He thanked providence for providing the whisky and for teaching him emergency techniques. He opened the bottle, poured the amber liquid into his cupped palm, and applied it to her neck and shoulders.

With long, firm strokes he massaged her with the whisky. He had once seen an older firefighter revive a newborn baby with this technique even after oxygen had failed. Clint pulled the towel completely away from her upper body, palmed more whisky and stroked down firmly over her breasts, then between them, across her heart.

Eve opened her eyes and threw him a frightened look. "Don't!"

"Eve, I have to. This is no time for false modesty. I *must* raise your body temperature. You have no food inside you for fuel, you have exhausted all your energy, and we have no wood left."

Eve stiffened.

"No, no, don't be afraid. Relax! Trust me, Eve, trust me. If you can feel what I'm doing to you, that's good. Relax . . . give yourself up to me . . . feel it, feel it."

He poured some of the amber liquid onto her belly, then swept his hands in firm circles, rubbing, massaging, kneading it into her flesh, so that her circulation would improve.

When Clint lifted her thigh and began to stroke it firmly, the word *silken* jumped into his mind. He tried valiantly not to become aroused, but failed miserably! Resolutely, he lifted her other thigh and repeated the ministrations. Clint had never done anything like this before, but it was suddenly brought home to him how pleasurably erotic a body massage could be. If you substituted warm oil, or perhaps champagne, for whisky, you could have one helluva sensual celebration!

He censured himself for his wicked thoughts and gently turned her over. On Eve's back, his strokes became longer, reaching all the way from her shoulders to her buttocks. He bent over her with tender solicitude. "Eve, are you any warmer?"

"Colder." Her voice was a whisper.

As he massaged the backs of her legs he said, "That's because your skin is getting warmer and the alcohol feels cold as it evaporates. It's a good sign that you can feel the surface of your skin."

He sat her up. "I want you to drink some of this. It will warm up your insides."

Eve nodded. She had no energy to protest, no will to object; all she wanted to do was obey him.

There was no time to search for a glass. Etiquette went the way of her modesty as he held the bottle to her lips and she took a great gulp. It snatched her breath away and she began to cough.

"Easy, easy does it." His powerful arm about her shoulders supported her until she could breathe again. Then he gently tipped the bottle against her lips so she could take a tiny mouthful.

By the third or fourth sip she felt a great red rose bloom in her chest; by the eighth, she felt a fireglow inside her belly. Clint moved her from the damp towels onto a blanket and starting again at her neck and shoulders, gave her a second whisky rubdown.

As Eve lay stretched before him, she gradually became euphoric. She thought Clint Kelly's hands were magnificent, and she wanted him to go on stroking her forever. As she watched him beneath lowered lids, a nimbus of light seemed to surround his dark head. She pondered dreamily about what it could be. Was it magic? Was it his aura? Did he emanate goodness and light? Then suddenly it came to her, and the answer was so simple. It was energy! This man exuded pure energy.

When Clint had anointed every inch of her with the warm, tingling whisky, he wrapped her up in the blanket and lifted her to the couch. "Eve, listen to me. I have to leave you for a while. I imagine we're snowed in here for a couple of days and there are things I need to do."

Eve was far too languorous to speak. Instead she smiled at him, giving him permission to do anything he had to. The smile made her face radiant. Clint knew she was intoxicated and would be asleep in minutes.

He retrieved his jacket from the garage and cut a length of green garden hose that was stored inside for the winter. Then he hiked to the barn to get a milk pail he had seen. He carried both to his Dodge Ram and proceeded to siphon the gasoline from the truck. Clint hated the taste of petroleum in his mouth, but he knew of no other way to siphon gas. He spat half a dozen times, then took a handful of fresh snow to his mouth.

He carried the pail of gasoline very carefully to the generator that stood inside a cupboard in the kitchen. Fortunately it had a funnel beside it. *Winter storms in this area must make a generator a necessity,* he concluded.

Clint opened his tackle box and removed a stringer with several large hooks and lures on it, then slipped the box of ammunition into his pocket and picked up his rifle. He shut the front door quietly and went in the direction of the lake. The snow was coming down heavier than ever and the visibility was zero. He stepped cautiously when he sensed he was on the edge of Lake

Michigan. He knew it would be frozen, but if the ice on the pond hadn't held Eve, the ice on the great lake couldn't be very thick.

Noting the formation of the trees, he kicked a hole through the ice and set the stringer, then fastened the other end to the closest tree. He turned up the collar of his jacket and set off toward the bush at the back of the property where he had seen a wild apple tree. In the heavy snow, it took him quite some time to locate it, but when he did, he loaded his rifle and hunkered down with his back against a tree trunk to wait.

Eve slept deeply for two hours, then she drifted up through a layer of sleep and began to dream. She was in her parents' house where the air was filled with delicious smells and the atmosphere was warm and inviting. Her mother was cooking, while her father decorated the Christmas tree.

"Susie, can you help me with this?"

When Susan came into the living room wearing oven mitts, Ted grabbed her and held her beneath the mistletoe.

"You devil, Ted Barlow. This is just one of your tricks; you don't need help at all!"

"I couldn't resist, sweetheart; you're so easy to fool."

Eve saw her mother's secret smile and realized she knew all about the mistletoe. Susan went into her husband's arms with joy. The kiss lasted a full two minutes. She looked up at him. "Do you remember our first Christmas?"

"I love you even more than I did then," he whispered huskily, feathering kisses into Susie's hair.

"We had no money, no home; I was pregnant with Steven, and you'd just been posted overseas."

"What the hell did you see in me?" Ted asked, amusement brimming in his deep blue eyes.

"I was so much in love with you, I couldn't think straight, fly boy."

Ted's hands slipped down her back until his hands came to rest on her bottom cheeks. "But why did you love me?" he pressed.

"It was your strength. You were my rock; you made me feel safe. Even though we had almost nothing, I wasn't afraid to go halfway around the world with you."

He kissed her again. "That's the nicest thing anyone ever said to me."

"It's true, Ted. You inspire confidence. Now, it's true confession time for you. What did you see in me?"

"Besides great legs? You were willing to give up everything for me. I made the right choice. We're still lovers, aren't we?"

"Passionate lovers," she agreed.

"Do you think Eve is serious about Trevor Bennett?"

"I think so."

"You don't think she'll marry him, do you?" he asked, untangling a string of lights.

"Don't you like him?"

"Oh sure, I like him well enough, but I don't think he's right for Eve."

"Why not?" Eve demanded, but they couldn't hear her. Eve realized she was invisible. Her parents had no idea she was in the room with them.

"He's one of these sensitive, modern types, always politically correct. He even teaches courses where men get in touch with their feminine side."

Susan laughed at her husband. "And you don't believe you have a feminine side?"

"Christ, if I did, I'd leave it in the closet where it belongs!"

"You worry too much about Eve. She isn't your little girl anymore."

"Oh, I know she does a terrific impression of being able to take care of herself, but she has a vulnerable side."

Am I that transparent? Eve asked.

"And don't kid yourself . . . she'll be my little girl until I give her away—hopefully to a real man."

"What I meant was, don't worry about her making the wrong choice. Eve knows exactly what she needs. And remember, it's her choice, not yours, fly boy!"

Ted grinned at her. "I just want her to have skyrockets, like we do."

Eve was no longer at home. She was somewhere dark and cold, in deep water, and she was desperately searching for a rock.

Chapter Four

Clint Kelly held his breath as he saw a shadow move. He had waited two hours because he knew they would come. Deer loved apples. The shadow separated into three when it reached the trees. He selected his target, a young buck, then lifted his rifle and squeezed the trigger. The two does flew past him, sending down an avalanche of snow from the overhanging branches; the buck dropped.

When Clint stood up from his cramped position, he stretched up to fill his pockets with apples; he could hardly feel his feet. He stomped about for a few minutes to restore his circulation before he hoisted both rifle and carcass to his shoulders. Their food worries were over—now he could concentrate on providing fuel.

For the last two hours, thoughts of Eve had filled his head. He knew she would recover from her ordeal, but worried about the pond water she had ingested. Bacteria from the murky water could make her very sick. If luck was with them, however, the germs may have been killed off by the cold.

Clint's thoughts had then drifted along more personal lines. He couldn't lie to himself; he found Eve Barlow extremely attractive in spite of their differences. Perhaps it was even *because* of their differences. She was a new experience for Clint; independent, assertive, competitive, even combative. A far cry from the clinging types he had dated recently.

Eve was an exciting challenge. Beneath the polished veneer, he might find a real flesh-and-blood, honest-to-God woman! All his thoughts were sexual now. In retrospect, giving Eve the whisky

massage had been a very erotic experience. When he had his
hands on her body, he had tried to be detached. Now, however,
he relived every stroke, every slide of skin on skin. She was ice, he
was fire—a combustible combination!

Hers was probably the loveliest female form he had ever seen
or touched. She had everything to tempt a man: long blond hair,
silky skin, nipples like pink rosebuds, and a high pubic bone covered by pale curls. And long, beautiful legs.

Back in the garage, with axe and hunting knife, Clint skinned
the carcass, then dressed and hung the venison. He was considerably warmer by the time he finished. He glanced ruefully along
the wall where the woodpile was customarily stacked. All that remained were wood chips, evidence that split logs were usually
stored in abundance.

He saw a wooden pallet marked "Evergreen Sod Farm" and
speculated that there must be a lawn buried deep beneath the
snow. The wood from the pallet wouldn't last an hour, but perhaps he could put it to better use than burning. The beams and
column supports in the barn were fashioned from whole trees. If
he used the pallet as a sled, perhaps he could drag a tree trunk up
here to the garage where he could axe it into logs, then split the
logs into firewood. He looked about for his rope, then remembered it was still at the pond with the ladder. *Necrosis of the cranium*—wasn't that what Eve had flung at him? Perhaps she was
right, he thought wryly.

Eve stirred in her sleep, then awoke with a start. She felt dis-
oriented for a moment. She knew she had been dreaming, but as
she tried to call back the dream, it danced out of her reach. Then
she remembered where she was.

The room was silent, dark and very cold. For a moment, panic
assailed her. Had he gone off and left her here? Had he abandoned her? Then she laughed at her own foolishness. Clint Kelly
wasn't the kind who would desert a damsel in distress. He had
rescued her from a watery grave and was probably out gathering
wood. He would relish the challenge of being snowbound.

Eve's belly rolled. Lord, she was hungry. She struggled to sit
up and realized she had no strength. Her head dropped back to

the couch cushion as she drew the blanket closer and closed her eyes. Clint would take care of everything.

The task of dislodging one of the upright tree trunks was more difficult than Clint had anticipated. None of them budged even a fraction, in spite of the stout shoulder he pressed upon them. He selected the one closest to the barn door, wedged the ladder against a beam, then chopped with his axe until he felled it.

He knew the hardwood would have made a fine piece of furniture and under any other circumstances it would be sacrilege to burn it. But it was exactly what they needed. Hardwood burned longer and gave off a fiercer heat than other timber, and even more to the point, it was dry.

Try as he might, Clint could not lift the tree trunk. He decided that expending his energy was foolish. After studying the problem for a moment, once more he put the rope to good use. He tied it to the tree trunk, threw the other end over a barn beam and used it as a pulley to lift the huge log onto the pallet.

With the rope around his chest, he pulled the makeshift sledge through the snow. Fancifully, he realized he was doing what men had done in past centuries: bringing home the Yule Log. The only difference was that he had to do it alone.

Clint needed a rest to catch his breath before he started cutting wood. He slipped quietly into the living room to check on Eve. Though he didn't feel it after his strenuous exertion, he knew the room was far too chilly for someone who needed to keep her body temperature from falling again.

He bent over her with concern. He heard her even breathing and saw the crescent shadows of her lashes as they lay upon her cheeks. Two fingers to her forehead told him that she wasn't fevered. A proprietary feeling stole over him as he stood close to her. Who the devil was this Trevor guy who wanted to marry her? He sure as hell wouldn't be able to give her an engagement ring for Christmas. It was way past midnight, already Christmas Eve.

Clint flexed weary muscles as he thought of all the wood that needed to be chopped, but strangely, he knew he would rather be here tonight than anywhere else on earth.

* * *

Clint spent the next three hours alternately sawing the tree into huge rounds and splitting them into logs that would fit in the fireplace. He only stopped working once, and that was to build a roaring fire in the living room.

By the time he was finished, he vowed the first thing he would buy for the new house was a chain saw, and the second, a log splitter. He lifted the long axe handle behind his head to stretch the kinks out of his shoulder muscles and yawned loudly. Food! His body needed refuelling. Clint carved some thin slices of venison and went in search of a frying pan. He set it on the flames, cut up an apple amongst the meat and sat down on the hearth.

"Mmm, that smells heavenly."

He turned to the couch in time to see Eve stretch and open her eyes. "How do you feel?" he asked, hiding all trace of anxiety.

"Hungry," she replied, eyeing the contents of the pan. "Thanks for cooking my breakfast," she teased, "but what are you going to have?"

He laughed, but warned, "You're going to have to take it easy. If you eat too much or too fast, your stomach will reject it." He searched her face; it didn't look flushed.

"Don't stare! I know I must look a damned fright."

Clint was so relieved she wasn't fevered, he was perfectly happy to let her have the food and cook more for himself. He found her a plate and took the empty pan into the garage with him. When he returned, she said, "This is absolutely wonderful. What is it?"

"Meat," he said evasively, knowing her aversion to guns.

"What kind of meat?"

"Venison."

She went all quiet, but kept on chewing. *He went hunting last night when I fell asleep.* It wasn't a question, it was a deduction. Her gaze moved from Clint to the fireplace. *I woke up about two o'clock. The fire was almost out. He chopped wood after he bagged the deer. He hasn't slept all night!*

Eve was deeply impressed by what he had done for her. From the moment she had gotten herself into such dire peril, all her ideas about this man had been turned upside down. She experienced an overwhelming gratitude. He had saved her life. He had warmed her and sheltered her and fed her. She hadn't had to lift a finger.

Eve felt more than gratitude; she felt respect and admiration. As she searched her emotions, it suddenly hit her like a bolt of lightning. What she felt was desire!

She put her fork down. Damnation, she mustn't let him see how she felt about him.

"Something wrong with the food?"

"It needs salt . . . and you could use a shave," she said.

"Thankless little bitch," he murmured. He wasn't smiling, but Eve saw that he couldn't hide the amusement in his eyes.

"Why are you always laughing at me?"

"Because you're an impostor."

"What the devil do you mean?"

"You want the world to think you're the competent, self-sufficient, woman-of-the-year type, but it's just a facade. Scratch the surface and you're a little girl who needs someone to take care of her. A little girl from hell perhaps, but nevertheless—"

"You're wrong!" Eve interjected.

"Am I? Even your clothes give you away."

"My clothes?" She became conscious of the fact that she wasn't wearing any beneath the blanket.

"The briefcase and the power suit present a false image. Once I stripped them away, what did I expose? The most feminine lingerie I've ever seen. It's not just Victoria's Secret, it's also Eve's Secret."

"You're crazy!"

Clint rubbed his backside. "Brain damage from when my father—"

"Shot you," she finished. Suddenly, she began to laugh. Clint joined in.

"I like to see you laugh," he told her. "It really suits you. You should let your hair down and have fun more often."

"*Fun*—what a concept. I haven't had any in so long, I've forgotten how."

"I could teach you."

She lowered her lashes. He was too damned tempting. "Having my eye on advancement and my nose to the grindstone is very demanding."

262 / Virginia Henley

"It's also a helluva funny position to go through life in. I could teach you other positions."

Her lashes swept up; green eyes met blue.

"I just bet you could, Action Man."

Clint had to call on all his willpower not to kiss her. His need to taste her was so overpowering at that moment, he had to physically remove himself from her space. He could not make love to her right now—it would be taking advantage of her vulnerability. When he made love to Eve, and he fully intended to, he wanted her to be able to give as good as she got. He wanted her energy to be high voltage.

"I need something to wear." She looked at the red heap on the hearth that had once been an Alfred Sung suit. Oh well, perhaps her underwear could be salvaged.

"I'll see what I can find in the bedrooms," Clint offered.

The moment he disappeared upstairs, she struggled into her bra and short satin slip, shoved the mangled pantyhose and briefs beneath the red heap and pulled the blanket back around her.

"Lean pickings, I'm afraid." Clint presented her with his findings, a pair of red long johns and some ski socks. "Here, take my shirt—it'll cover the long johns."

He stripped off vest and shirt before she could protest. Eve's eyes slid across the wide expanse of muscled chest, covered by a thick mat of black hair. He put the leather vest back on, leaving his hard biceps exposed.

She simply couldn't help staring at him. "What do you do to keep in shape?" she asked in wonder.

"Nothing. My job and my hobbies do it for me."

There was absolutely no point in her asking him if he would be warm enough. A man like this couldn't possibly feel the cold. He looked like the Marlboro Man!

"I'll bring in more wood while you get dressed," he said tactfully. "There's water, but it's cold. Don't stand under a cold shower long, Eve," he cautioned.

She was devoutly thankful that she had left her shoulder bag with her briefcase when they went out to look over the property yesterday. In the bathroom, she took the shortest shower on record and pulled the long johns over her satin slip. When she turned to the mirror she was dismayed to see that she looked like a hillbilly from an old *Hee-Haw* rerun.

Eve quickly covered the red long johns with Clint's blue wool shirt. His male scent enveloped her. She closed her eyes, trying to define its essence. It was a combination of apples and wood smoke mixed with honest-to-God sweat. It was like an aphrodisiac!

She pulled on the thick socks and ran her comb through her hair. Miraculously, the pond water hadn't done much damage. If anything, her hair was curlier than usual. The only makeup she had with her was a lipstick. She had chosen it to match the Alfred Sung; now it matched the long johns.

When she came out of the bathroom, he was waiting for her. She said quickly, "Let's go on a scavenger hunt and see if we can turn up anything at all that will be useful."

He grinned at her. "Brilliant as well as beautiful."

When they entered the kitchen, Clint opened a cupboard and showed her its hidden treasure. "This is a generator. I siphoned the gasoline from the truck so we can have electricity. We should ration it, though. Tonight, when it gets dark, we can have lights, use the stove to cook something, and maybe listen to the weather reports on the radio."

Eve grinned at him. "Brilliant as well as handsome."

Inside the numerous kitchen cupboards they found every pot and pan known to man. There was china, silverware, glasses and mugs, but almost nothing edible. There was a rack that contained fifteen different herbs and spices, a box of candles, some tinfoil, a package of napkins from Valentine's Day, and a lone package of Kool Aid that lay forgotten in an empty drawer.

The last cupboard produced a half-jar of instant coffee. To Eve and Clint it was like finding a gold nugget in an abandoned mine.

"Coffee!" they chorused with joy. Clint filled the kettle and set it on the fire. Eve measured a spoonful of the magic brown powder in each of two mugs, then they sat by the fire with bated breath, waiting for the water to boil.

"They say anticipation is the best part," she teased.

"Don't you believe it." His voice was so deep, his double entendre so blatantly clear, a frisson of pleasure ran down her spine.

When he poured the boiling water into her mug, Eve closed her eyes and breathed in its aroma. To Clint, it was a sensual gesture, revealing her passion for everything in life. When he added a drop of whisky to his coffee, Eve held out her mug. When she tasted it, she rolled her eyes. "Now that is decadent!" She took two big gulps. "My God, it's better than sex."

Clint laughed. "If that's true, you've had very inadequate lovers, Eve Barlow."

She wondered if that were true. Until yesterday she would have vehemently denied that, but after spending twenty-four hours with Clint Kelly, her perceptions about a lot of things were changing. She looked him straight in the eye. "I think it's time for your cold shower."

Clint knew it would take more than a cold shower to cure his condition. It would take an ice dive, at least. Then he remembered his fishing line. He picked up his coat.

"Where are you going?"

"To check on my stringer."

When she was alone, she wondered what the devil a stringer was. She also wondered why she had brought up the subject of sex. She must be out of her mind. Then she recalled she had read somewhere that female captives always became enamored of their abductors. It was some sort of syndrome.

Suddenly, Eve began to laugh. Clint Kelly had not abducted her. The captor/captive scenario was a fantasy. *Quit kidding yourself! He's the most desirable man you've ever met in your life, and the attraction is definitely mutual.*

Chapter Five

Clint took his axe with him to the lake because the temperature had plummeted and he knew the ice would be thicker now. The snow was still coming down, but it had changed to fine stuff that never seemed to melt.

He followed the line from the tree, taking great care not to walk out onto the lake. When he chopped open the hole, he was gratified to see that he had hooked two walleyes. He carefully removed the lures and set the stringer back in the lake.

Eve's eyes widened when she saw the fish. "You *are* a magic man!"

He held them up by the mouth. "Hocus pocus, fish bones choke us."

She followed him to the kitchen and watched, fascinated, as he skinned and filleted the walleyes. When he was finished, he said, "Now I need that shower."

When Clint came downstairs, she noticed how his black hair curled when it was wet. He hadn't been able to shave and the blue-black shadow on his jaw added to his overt masculinity. With effort, Eve forced herself to stop staring at him.

She busied herself spreading tinfoil to wrap the fish. They selected the herbs together. It seemed a great luxury to have so many choices in the spice rack. They finally decided to sprinkle the fillets with chervil, basil, and dried parsley. Then he sealed the tinfoil and set it amid the smouldering logs.

When the tantalizing aroma of the herbs began to permeate the air, both of them realized how hungry they were.

"I'm drooling," Eve breathed.

Clint's glance flicked over her mouth. "Me, too," he confessed.

The amused look she threw him told him she understood exactly what he meant. She waited most patiently for the fish to cook and then she thought she smelled it burning. They both reached out at the same time. Eve pulled the tinfoil from the fire, but it burned her fingers. With a yelp, she hastily dropped it into Clint's calloused palms.

He set it on the hearth and reached for her hands. His face exuded tenderness as he examined her fingers.

"It's all right, I didn't get burned," she assured him. *Not yet, at least,* she added silently, as she felt heat leap from him into her hands and run up her arms. He gave her back her hands, but not her heart.

When she tasted the walleye, she knew it had been worth waiting for. The delicate flavor was ambrosia to the palate.

"I ate a whole fish, all by myself!"

"Your body needed the nourishment. I'm going to make a spit and roast us a haunch of venison for dinner."

"I'm profoundly grateful to you, Clint Kelly."

"Why do I get the feeling you're going to add a *but* to the end of your sentence?"

"You're a perceptive man. It's time we got down to business."

For one split second his mind went blank. She had the power to make him forget there was anything beyond this moment. Then he realized she wasn't talking about them, she was talking about the house.

"Are you sure you're up to this?"

"I'm positive," she assured him.

"Okay, I make an offer of one hundred and fifty thousand."

"Please be serious, Mr. Kelly."

"I'm deadly serious, Ms. Barlow. My offer is one-fifty."

"You're wasting my time."

That's a moot point, he thought, but kept a wise silence.

"The asking price is *two* hundred and fifty thousand."

"You surely don't expect me to offer the asking price?"

"Well no, but one-fifty is simply unacceptable."

"To whom? You? You aren't the owner, Ms. Barlow. You merely present the offer."

"I won't present an offer of one-fifty on a property that's worth two-fifty!"

"Just a moment. No one said anything about how much this property is worth. We're discussing the asking price. It isn't worth anywhere near two-fifty."

Eve had heard those words before, from her longtime friend who owned the property. She could hear Judy's voice now. *"It can't be worth more than about one hundred and eighty thousand, Eve. Let's list it for two hundred."*

Eve had replied, *"No way. They aren't making any more lakefront property, you know. If you aren't in a hurry for the money, I'd like to list it at two-fifty and see what happens."*

Actually, nothing had happened. The property had been for sale for nine months without a single offer. Eve knew what she could get for a city property within a few dollars, but country places were not her bailiwick.

"In your exalted opinion, Mr. Kelly, what do you think it is worth?"

He didn't beat about the bush. "It's worth a hundred and eighty thousand."

With all she had learned about him, why had she underestimated his business acumen? "You're wrong, Mr. Kelly. It's worth two hundred and twenty-five. Lakefront property is at a premium and this place is furnished."

"What was the last offer you received, Ms. Barlow?"

"That's privileged information, Mr. Kelly."

Clint grinned. "You've had no offers on this place!"

Eve could have kicked herself for being so transparent.

"How long has it been on the market?" he demanded. "I bet it's been over a year."

"Only nine months!" There was a pregnant pause. "Damn you, Clint Kelly." Eve's resolve hardened. She needed another two hundred thousand to make the President's Circle and she'd get that much if it killed her!

"Write up an offer for one-fifty and I'll sign it."

"No. The asking price is two-fifty and I've already admitted it's only worth two-twenty-five. I've come down, but you haven't budged!"

"I don't have to budge until the seller rejects my offer."

"Mr. Kelly—"

"Clint," he amended.

"Clint, let me explain about real estate. There's a leeway of about five percent. It's like an unwritten law."

"Thanks for the economics lesson. Now let me teach you poker."

"You're laughing at me again."

"Eve, you're required by law to make out an Offer to Purchase. I *have* bought real estate before, you know."

"A cemetery plot?"

"Sarcasm is the lowest form of wit. As a matter of fact, when my dad retired from the force, we became partners in a sports bar."

Eve stared at him. "Not Kelly's?"

"Afraid so," he said, grinning. "Business is my long suit."

"Then you can bloody well afford two hundred."

"I can, but I won't."

"*Why* won't you make me a counteroffer?"

Clint's grin widened. "I don't have to; you keep dropping the price."

She covered her ears and screamed in frustration.

"I was afraid you weren't up to this," he said softly.

"Of course I'm up to it . . . well, maybe I'm not." Eve decided to throw herself on his mercy. "Clint, let me be honest with you. If I make a sale of two hundred thousand my earnings for the year will get me into the President's Circle, a very prestigious achievement."

"Now, let me get this straight," he said, trying not to show his amusement. "You want me to up my offer from one-fifty to two hundred because you need the sales figures? Your logic escapes me. We have an impasse. I suggest we take a time-out."

"Do you have to talk to me in sports terms? I know nothing about football."

"We must have something in common. How about hockey?"

"I loathe it!"

* * *

Clint brought in firewood and stacked it by the hearth. The fire had to be kept at a constant temperature to roast the venison. The pile of wood that had seemed so large was half gone. Timber on the property was mostly pine that burned too fast, but it was better than nothing. He decided to cut some and bring it into the garage so it could dry a little.

Clint cut a haunch from the deer, found a meat spit in the barbecue, and wedged it in the fireplace, over the glowing logs. "You decide what flavor you'd like."

Eve studied the bottles in the spice rack and came back with fennel and garlic powder. Almost as soon as they were sprinkled on the meat, the air became redolent with a piquant aroma that awoke their taste buds.

"Call me if the fire burns low."

Eve was restless. She was in a tug-of-war with herself, wanting Clint Kelly to come close, yet keep his distance at the same time. She felt extremely guilty—when Trevor arrived to take her dancing, she wouldn't be there.

To stop her outrageous thoughts about Kelly, Eve went in search of something to read. She was delighted to find a book; when she discovered it was a collection of O. Henry stories, she took the precious volume back to the fire and lost herself in its pages.

Throughout the afternoon, Clint came in and out. He tended the fire and turned the spit, then returned to his woodcutting. The atmosphere between them was cozy and companionable. Eve was palpably aware that they were forging a bond. Strangely, she didn't feel guilty that he was working so hard. He was a man, she a woman; it felt right.

She saved *The Gift of the Magi* for last. It was a Christmas story, a love story so poignant that it evoked tears. When she came to it, however, she found that she could not read it. It was simply too sentimental, too emotional.

Clint removed his jacket and turned the venison, which had crisped to a delicious deep brown. He immediately sensed Eve's melancholy and set about banishing it. He put a couple of apples to roast, then went into the kitchen and flipped the electrical switch to "generator." Light flooded the living room, dispelling all real and imaginary shadows.

Clint brought a carving board to the hearth. When he cut into the venison, succulent juices ran from the pink slices. Eve brought plates, cutlery, and napkins, and filled crystal goblets with water.

As they sat before the fire to dine, Clint lifted his goblet. "Happy Christmas, Eve."

She touched her glass to his. "Happy Christmas, Clint."

They ate in companionable silence, paying tribute to the food. When they were almost done, Clint set about amusing her. "We must have something in common, let's find out what it is." He deliberately suggested something he knew she would hate. "How about camping?"

She grimaced. "How about shopping?"

He shuddered. "Darts?"

She shook her head. "Chess."

"Read the comics?"

"Poetry," she said softly.

"Phil Collins?" he suggested.

"Barbra Streisand," she countered.

Clint chuckled and turned on the radio. Between Christmas carols, the only topic of conversation was the weather. They described how many inches had fallen and how many more were expected. They warned drivers to stay off the roads and told of flight cancellations. They reported power failures, downed lines, and overloaded telephone circuits. They asked everyone to exercise patience. They announced that the snowplows would be working all night.

Clint tried every station. The reports were identical. He switched it off just as Nat King Cole's beautiful voice sang, *Unforgettable, that's what you are.* He and Eve looked at each other, knowing they were exactly where they wanted to be.

"Coconut cream pie?" he suggested.

She shook her head. "Lemon."

"Baseball?"

Eve got to her feet. "Yes!"

"Detroit Tigers!" Clint shouted.

"Yes! Yes!" Eve's face was radiant. "Blame it on my father— it's in my genes."

"Cecil Fielder," he said with reverence.

"Mickey Tettleton," she enthused.

Clint took hold of her hands. "One hundred and seventy-five thousand."

"You devil, you know I need two hundred!"

"I know what you need," he said huskily, drawing her into his arms and covering her mouth with his.

The way he kissed made her weak at the knees. There was nothing tentative about it. He kissed the same way he did everything else; he simply took charge. His mouth was firm and demanding and possessive. His mouth was . . . perfect. He kissed her the way a man should kiss a woman, but seldom did.

Clint did not try to part her lips with his tongue. He was in no hurry. Even kissing had its foreplay. Her mouth was soft and yielding and told him without words that she loved what he was doing.

Clearly, he enjoyed kissing; probably because he was so good at it. His hands cupped her face and he lifted it for another kiss. He did it reverently as if he held something delicate and priceless. Clint's hands were just as sensual as his mouth. They were calloused, capable, and downright carnal as they caressed her skin. His fingertips explored her features, and the backs of his fingers stroked across her cheekbones.

"Sweet, sweet," he murmured, seeing how her lashes were tipped with gold, seeing the fine down upon her brow, seeing her cheeks tint shell-pink, seeing everything.

Her breath came out on a sigh. How beautiful he made her feel, how utterly lovely. He conveyed with a look, with a touch, how special he found her. He kissed her eyelids and the corners of her mouth, delighting when they turned up with pure pleasure. And then his whole focus centered on her mouth, and she opened to him as a flower being worshipped by the sun.

He outlined her lips with the tip of his tongue. When the tip of her tongue touched his, a tremor of need made her throat and breasts quiver. His fingers slid into her hair, holding her, then his tongue mastered hers. This was only the first part of his body to enter hers, but she moaned low with the deeply erotic sensations it evoked.

Her hands moved from his leather vest to grip his bare arms where his biceps bulged so boldly. She clung to him, relishing his strength, loving his hardness, both above and below. She longed for more. It was her first experience with raw lust. She was already love-drunk, and all he had done was kiss her!

His lips were against her throat. "Evie," he murmured. How the diminutive pleased her; she never wanted to be called Eve again. How feminine it made her feel. He was teaching her the nuances of domination and submission, the sheer bliss that transforms a female who yields all to the male.

She stood obediently while his powerful hands removed the shirt and stripped the long red undergarment from her slim body and long legs. She was impatient for him to remove his own clothes, but she didn't paw at him; she waited, knowing it would be worthwhile.

With the lights blazing, they stood and looked at each other. Really looked. His body tapered down to slim hips. His flanks were long and hard. The dark pelt on his chest narrowed to a line of black hair that ran down his flat belly, then bloomed like a blackthorn bush. His manroot stood up, thick and powerful—a testament to her breath-stopping beauty.

Clint's eyes licked over her like a candle flame. "Have you any idea how lovely you are?"

Truly, she could not answer his question. He took hold of her hand and traced her own fingertips from her temple to her lips. "Your eyes are Irish green, your mouth tastes like honeyed wine." He drew her fingertips slowly down the curve of her throat, then down to her breast, where a golden tress lay curled. "Your hair is the color of moonlight."

His voice, so low, so deep and masculine, did glorious things to her. He drew her fingers across the swell of her breast to the nipple. He drew her fingers down her body. "Your body is like silk." He touched one fingertip to her navel. "It has hidden depths."

Eve caught her breath. Surely he wouldn't make her touch herself? But he did. He held their hands so that their fingers threaded through the curls of her mons. Then he traced one of her fingertips along the folds of her pink cleft, then slipped it inside to touch the center of her womanhood. "A rosebud drenched with dew." He brought her fingers to his mouth and tasted them.

Eve was adrift on a sea of sensuality. His powerful hands cupped her shoulders to steady her. "I'm going to turn out the lights now to conserve our fuel. Don't move; I want to see you by fireglow. Then I'm going to pull down the couch. It has a bed inside."

Nothing escapes him, she thought dreamily. She knew she didn't have to worry about protection; Clint was the kind of man who took care of everything.

Chapter Six

Clint set lighted candles on the hearth before he came back to her. After he kissed her, he placed her in front of him so that she faced the fire. She leaned back, revelling in the solid feel of him. His hands were free to seek out all her secret places. He warmed her at the fire before he lifted her to their bed.

But Eve was already on fire. His arousal made her feel as if she were smouldering, longing for the moment she would burst into white hot flame. When the firestorm came, and she knew it would, it might consume her. But she was ready, nay eager, to go up in smoke.

He never left her mouth for long. In the first hour, they shared what seemed like ten thousand kisses. One powerful arm enfolded her as his calloused palms cupped her breasts, and then he began to focus all his attention upon her nipples.

Clint knew that when he licked, some sensation would be lost as it moved back and forth under his tongue. To prevent this, he placed his fingers on either side of her nipple and pressed down, not hard, but firmly. Then he spread his fingers apart, holding it totally immobile, and lowered his lips to her.

Her nipple swelled up into his mouth like a ripe fruit. When he began to slowly lick her, Eve went wild! She covered his breastbone with tiny love bites, then took his other hand to her mouth, drew one of his fingers inside, and began to suck, hard. His loveplay made her drown in need. She writhed against him. The friction of sleek skin on skin made her flesh feel like hot silk.

He knew she needed immediate release. Then he would be able to start again, building her passion slowly, so they could make love for hours. He moved her up in the bed until his cheek lay against her silken thigh. Then she felt a wet slide of tongue, followed by a deep thrust. His tongue curled about her bud exactly as it had her nipple, and she was undone. She cried out into the flickering shadows that hid their secret rites, and arched herself into his masterful mouth.

Clint moved up in the bed so that he could catch her last soft cry with his mouth. Eve tasted herself on his lips and felt delicious as original sin. Most of the sensations she experienced were new to her, and Clint's earlier words drifted through her consciousness: "I can't decide if you're an ice queen or if you're simply unawakened." *Obviously, I was both!*

She couldn't believe how highly aroused he had made her or how she had peaked so beautifully, and they hadn't even completed coitus. That adventure still lay ahead. She wanted to scream from excitement.

Now he began to whisper love words, each phrase more erotic than the last. She would never have guessed he could be poetic. But had she not underestimated everything about him?

Clint expected her second arousal to be slow, but it was not. She became wildly inquisitive about his body—the feel of it, the man-scent of it, the salt taste of it. The masculine roughness of his beard sent thrills spiralling through her consciousness, driving her to touch his male center, to stroke, squeeze, play and tease. His testes were big and heavy, more than a handful for her. How she loved the feel of this big, hard man.

Clint slipped a finger into her sugared sheath. This was the second part of his body he'd put inside her, and it was every bit as exciting as the first. He withdrew it slowly, and she gasped as he slid two fingers into her. Her sheath pulsated and clung to him tightly. When she became slippery, he knew she was ready.

He positioned the swollen head of his shaft at the opening of her cleft, then pushed up gently, inch by inch, until he was fully seated. Then all semblance of gentleness fell away. His lovemaking became fierce and savage. She adored every rough, elemental stroke as he anchored deep in her scalding body, then pulled all the way out so he could repeat the deep penetration over and over until her nails raked him. He took her to the edge of sanity. She became aware of every pulse point on her body.

The moans in his throat were raw and it came as a blinding revelation that he was receiving as much pleasure as he gave. Then suddenly the night exploded for both of them. They keened and arched as they spent, and she mourned that she could not fully feel his white-hot seed spurt up inside her.

Eve thrashed her head from side to side with the intensity of her release, and Clint's hand came up to cup her cheek and hold her still. Then his mouth joined hers in a deep kiss.

When he rolled from her, he brought her against his side possessively. Eve had never felt more alive in her life. Her eyes sought his, but they were closed and she realized he was asleep. Her face softened as she gazed at him. He hadn't slept in over forty hours.

Eve lay entranced for a long time, savouring the feel of her body, watching the play of firelight make strange shadows on the ceiling. Their lovemaking had been a ballet of domination and submission, yet the strange thing was, they had each given and taken in equal measure. Male and female were only halves of one magnificent whole. *Equal* halves! She had not been diminished in any way; she had been exalted.

Inevitably, reality stole into her consciousness. She pushed away all thought of Trevor. She would deal with it later. In this isolated haven, where the pristine snow lay all about them, she wanted no footprints of others to mar the beauty that enfolded them. At least for tonight, the world must be held at bay.

Eve, a million miles from sleep, brought book and candle back to the bed. She propped herself up quietly and turned to *The Gift of the Magi*. She was transported back in time to another Christmas Eve. The couple in the story were so real, she was in the room with them.

O. Henry's words brought her deep pleasure. When she finished the story, her eyes were liquid with unshed tears. The young man had pawned his watch to buy combs for his wife's beautiful hair; she had sold her hair to buy him a watch chain. The objects in the story were symbols. What they had really given each other were gifts of love.

More than anything, she wanted to give Clint Kelly a gift of love, and she knew exactly what it would be. She slipped from the bed, opened her briefcase, and removed an Offer to Purchase form. Then she made out the offer in the amount of one hundred and seventy-five thousand dollars. She knew Judy would accept it and the knowledge filled her with joy. He belonged here; this house and property were already a part of him.

That she would not qualify for the President's Circle seemed unimportant when she compared it to making him happy. She blew out the candles and curled up beside him. This Christmas Eve had been pure magic.

The first sound Eve heard on Christmas morning was a groan. She sat up quickly and looked down at Clint stretched beside her. He looked flushed. "Are you all right?"

"I'm fine," he croaked.

His beautiful, deep voice had been replaced by a rasp. "You're not fine at all! You have laryngitis at the very least." She touched his brow. "You're warm; you have a fever."

"I never get sick," Clint protested in a hoarse whisper.

"You mean, you never admit you get sick."

"Same thing." He gave her a lopsided grin and threw back the covers.

"Oh, no, you don't," Eve said, pushing him back down and covering him with the blankets. "You're sick because you over-taxed yourself, hunting and cutting wood and going without sleep."

He laughed at her. His throat sounded like he'd been gargling with gravel. "It was child's play compared to a twelve-hour night shift, fighting a fire in below-zero temperatures."

Eve glared at him, daring him to make a move from the warm bed. "Wasn't it another Clint who said, A *man should know his limitations?* It's my turn to take care of you."

She took a one-minute cold shower, pulled on her satin slip, then stepped into the red long johns and blue wool shirt. She felt Clint's amused eyes on her as she built up the fire. In the kitchen she turned on the generator just long enough to boil the kettle for coffee. She mixed up the orange Kool-Aid, sliced some cold veni-son from the haunch, and carried a tray to the bed.

His dark eyebrow lifted at the glass of Kool-Aid.

"It's pretend orange juice. Didn't you ever play pretend?"

"I played house, too," he croaked.

She made sure he ate everything, then poured the last of the whisky into his coffee. "I want you to go back to sleep."

"It's Christmas Day—there's stuff that needs doing," he protested.

"And I'm the one who's going to do it," she said flatly.

As Clint sipped his coffee, he took delight in looking at her. He didn't know what had brought about this transformation to domesticity. Perhaps his slight ailment brought out a need to nurture him. It felt strange to be pampered. He handed her his empty mug, pulled up the covers, and turned over.

By the time she finished her breakfast, she heard his even breathing and knew he was asleep. Eve's mind overflowed with plans for their Christmas Day. She pulled on her boots, ignoring the fact that the insides had hardened as they had dried by the fire. She slipped into Clint's down jacket and went to the garage for his axe.

When she went outside, she saw that it had stopped snowing and the sun was turning the landscape into a glittering fairyland. She didn't have to venture far to find a small pine tree. The one she selected was literally buried beneath the snow, with only its growing point sticking up. It took her quite a while to scoop away the snow so that she could reach its trunk with the axe. Her hands were freezing by the time she chopped it free and dragged it up to the house.

Eve warmed her hands at the fire, glancing at Clint's unmoving form in the bed. When he awoke, he would be surprised. It was fun trying to make their Christmas special. Eve needed something that would act as a tree stand. She went into the garage and looked about carefully, knowing she had to use her ingenuity. There was a cement block, probably used as a door prop, and she decided that would do the trick.

When her eyes fell on the pheasant, she felt a pang of regret that the poor creature had been caught in a snare. That thought drifted away as she realized, here was their Christmas bird! Eve had not lived years in the Orient without learning how to pluck and clean fowl.

She hummed to herself as she boiled the water and performed the odorous chore. A flash of remembrance came to her. Hadn't she seen a few onions hanging in the basement when she'd been searching for the water valve? She went downstairs to retrieve them, wondering how she'd overlooked such a treasure.

Eve sprinkled the bird with sage and thyme, set it in a shallow roasting pan with a square of tinfoil over it, and put the pan on the logs. Then she carried in the cement block and stuck the tree upright in it. She certainly didn't have much in the way of decorations, but again she used her ingenuity. She took the red Valentine napkins and fashioned paper flowers of a sort.

She had seen some old dried corncobs in the barn. She wondered if she could pop the kernels and string some popcorn. It wouldn't be edible, but it would be okay for decorating the tree. Nothing seemed too much trouble. Once more she slipped on the boots and coat and plodded off to the barn.

Stable smells assailed her as she entered, and it was suddenly brought home to her that this day was celebrated because of the Christ Child born in a manger. She thought of Mary giving birth in such a place, and then she thought of her own mother. How worried Susan must be because Eve hadn't shown up this morning. They would be searching for her, and it would very likely ruin their Christmas.

She felt guilty. She loved them very much and regretted causing them worry. It was so frustrating when she could do nothing about it, but Eve had learned to accept things that couldn't be altered.

Back in the kitchen, she cut the kernels from the old corncobs and turned on the generator long enough to pop the corn on the stove. She carried the big bowl to the living room and opened Clint's tackle box, thinking to thread the popcorn on fishing line. Some of his lures were so colorful that she hung them on the tree.

Before she sat down to thread the popcorn, she basted the pheasant, leaving the tinfoil off so it would brown. The onions in the roasting pan gave off a tantalizing aroma. Eve offered up a prayer of thanks.

In Grand Rapids, Susan Barlow was also praying. She had called her daughter to wish her a happy Christmas, but there had been no answer. She assumed Eve was already on her way, but when half an hour elapsed and she didn't arrive, a vague uneasiness touched her. After a whole hour, she voiced her worry to her husband, who had just finished shoveling the driveway.

"Ted, I called Eve over an hour ago. When she didn't answer, I assumed she was on her way, but she should be here by now."

"The main streets are all plowed, so she shouldn't have had any trouble. Maybe she and Trevor are stopping somewhere before they come here."

Susan pulled back the sheers. "Oh, here's Trevor's car now. Thank heavens!"

Still wearing his boots, Ted went outside to greet them. Trevor was alone. "Where's Eve?"

"I couldn't get her on the phone and when I got to her apartment, the Mercedes was gone. I assumed she was here."

"No," Ted said, shaking his head. "We're worried about her."

"Oh, I wouldn't worry too much, Mr. Barlow. Eve can take care of herself."

Ted frowned at Trevor, but bit back a retort. When they went inside, Ted got on the computer. *Eve, if you're there, please answer. If you're sick, let us know. If you can't start your car and are waiting for the Motor League, send a message.*

Susan brought them coffee and hot muffins with homemade jam. Trevor had just taken his first bite when Ted said, "I'm going over there. Come on." He touched his wife's cheek to reassure her. "Don't worry, sweetheart, we'll find her."

When Ted saw that Trevor was right and his daughter's Mercedes was not in the parking lot of her apartment building, he went upstairs and banged on her door. Then he banged on the superintendent's door and insisted he open up Eve's apartment. At first the man said he couldn't do that, but he hadn't reckoned with Ted Barlow. Reluctantly, he finally agreed to use his master key.

Trevor demurred. "I don't really think this is wise . . . you're violating Eve's privacy."

"Bullshit!" Ted replied shortly.

Inside the apartment, everything was in its place but her winter coat, her purse, and briefcase were missing. As they looked about, Trevor said, "See how efficient and organized she is? By the time we get back to your house, she'll be there."

Her father decided to drive to Eve's office; she was a voracious worker. A lone car sat in the parking lot. When he brushed off the foot of snow, he saw it was Eve's Mercedes. Ted was really worried now and even Trevor was beginning to feel uneasy. "There has to be a logical explanation for this," he assured her father.

Ted drove back home and got on the phone to Maxwell Robin. "Max, Eve's missing! Her car is parked at the office. Do you know where she is? Have you spoken with her?"

"No, Ted. The last time I saw her was the day before yesterday. She drove a client up to that country property she has listed for that friend of hers. Well, actually, now that I think of it, the client did the driving."

"Damn, they must have got caught in the storm. It's been a real blizzard north of here. Who is the client? Do you know anything about him?"

"Yes, I know him personally. Name's Clint Kelly. He's a diving instructor and also a fire captain. In an emergency situation she couldn't be in better hands."

"Thank God for that. Where exactly is the property?"

"I don't know off the top of my head, but it has to be in the files at the office. I'll meet you there."

"I'll call her friend Judy and get it from the horse's mouth. Your kids probably haven't opened their presents yet," Ted said.

"You've got to be kidding; they were up at six o'clock! Listen, Ted, call me if you need me."

Ted Barlow telephoned Eve's friend in Detroit and got directions to the log house, while Susan silently prayed that her daughter was safe. When Ted got off the phone he announced, "I'm on my way!"

"I think we should call the police," Trevor advised.

"The police won't even file a missing person's report until after seventy-two hours."

"The state troopers then. They'll search the highways. They'll have any accident reports and can check out the hospitals."

"That's a great idea, but I'm still going," Ted insisted.

"Leave it to the professionals. It's too risky in blizzard conditions. You could get stuck or lost and that would just compound the problem."

Susan looked at Trevor bleakly. He might as well save his breath to cool his soup. If Eve needed rescuing, Ted Barlow would be in the vanguard!

Chapter Seven

When Clint awoke, he felt miraculously restored. He threw off the blanket and stretched. Before he could lower his arms, the mouthwatering aroma of roasting game assaulted his senses. He sat up and blinked his eyes. Where the devil had the Christmas tree come from, or its decorations?

"Evie," he bellowed. His throat was much improved, sounding only slightly husky.

She had been waiting for him to awake, anticipating his reaction to her surprise. She pulled off his blue shirt and stood in front of the bathroom mirror in the red long johns. She stuffed the cushion down the front and fastened the buttons over the bulge. She had taped her blond curls across her face as a makeshift beard and mustache, and knew she looked ridiculous. But Eve didn't care; inside, her silly juices were bubbling.

She took a deep breath and bounded into the living room. "Ho! Ho! Ho! Merry Christmas!"

Clint began to laugh. If he hadn't, Eve would have been devastated. She joined in the laughter, holding her cushion belly with both hands.

"I see you're feeling better."

His eyes glittered with amusement. "You were so much woman, you almost finished me off."

Eve's blush competed with her long johns, but she needed the acknowledgment that he remembered last night's glow—that she lingered in his consciousness, as he did in hers.

"You went out and cut a tree all by yourself, then thought up these ingenious decorations."

"I'm not just a hairy face," she beamed.

"And the pheasant! I thought you told me you couldn't cook."

"No, I told you I *didn't* cook, not that I couldn't. My mother was Susie Homemaker—I had to learn how to cook."

"Santa Claus, you're full of surprises."

She handed him an envelope.

Clint opened it and read the Offer to Purchase. "What's this?" he asked softly.

Eve smiled into his eyes. "I know the seller will accept a hundred and seventy-five."

"What about your President's Circle?"

"My gift to you means more than the President's Circle." She bent down to kiss him.

"Germs," he warned huskily.

"Santa is immune," she whispered.

He took her in his arms and brushed her curls away from her mouth. Then he claimed it, kissing her thoroughly.

In the same husky voice he had used last night, she repeated his words: "I know what you need."

"What?" he murmured, wanting her to say it.

"A sauna."

Clint groaned with anticipation.

"I've already stacked the wood into it. After we eat our pheasant, all we have to do is light that fire."

"All these gifts for me. What can I give you, Evie?"

She almost melted with desire. "I'll think of something, Action Man," she whispered.

"I was going to give you scuba lessons, but it pales in comparison to your generosity."

Suddenly, she began to laugh. Her pillow belly bobbed up and down. She pulled it from her long johns and threw it at him. "Only an insensitive male could offer diving lessons to a woman who almost drowned in murky pond water!"

He gave her a lopsided grin, his teeth showing white against his dark, unshaven jaw.

Eve realized that with Clint Kelly beside her, she wouldn't even be afraid of being submerged underwater. She set the table as elegantly as she could for their Christmas dinner, with crystal goblets of water and lighted candles.

Clint donned his leather vest and held out her chair with a flourish. The flesh of the pheasant, seasoned with the sage and thyme, tasted better than any turkey she could ever remember. The roasted onions were elevated from common vegetables to savory delicacies.

Clint was beguiled by Eve's transformation from career woman to chatelaine. The role suited her to perfection, in his eyes. He speculated on what had brought it about. Was it the Christmas season, being snowed in, or a direct result of what had happened between them last night? He had known from the moment he undressed her that she was a real flesh and blood woman.

Eve watched the man sitting across the table from her. What was it about him that brought out her domesticity? She believed his masculinity called out to her femininity. She had no desire to compete with him; she had only the desire to nurture him and make him happy.

Her thoughts drifted to her mother and father, and she realized that was the kind of relationship they had. Susan was fulfilled as a woman and her contentment and happiness was visible to everyone. It was a heady sensation to have the power to make a man completely happy. She was revelling in that new-found power at the moment. Their time together here would be so short.

When they finished dinner, Eve picked up an apple and held it out to him. The picture she made entranced him. In the Bible, Adam said, *The woman tempted me.* Well, if Adam's Eve was anything like his Eve, no wonder he had succumbed.

"We can have dessert in the sauna," he said, rising and taking her hand. She knew he had something more exotic than apples in mind. "I'll light the fire so the logs will have a chance to glow, while we undress."

Eve wrapped her nakedness in a towel; Clint was less modest. He opened the sauna door and peered into its dark interior. "We'll need a candle." There was no way he was going to make love to her without being able to see her.

When Eve stepped inside, the aromatic cedar wood of the walls and seats gave off a heady scent that filled her senses. It was already deliciously warm and inviting, like a cocoon that enveloped them in a small, private world. Along two of the walls, the bench seats were normal height, while the third wall had a very low one, so you could stretch out your legs across the floor. The remaining wall had just the opposite, a bench seat set high so it could be used as a ledge to set things on, or to perch upon for maximum heat.

Clint set the candle on the ledge and lifted off her towel. Eve had no objections. When Clint lifted her against him, she cried out with excitement; she wrapped her arms around his neck, clinging to him as he took total possession of her mouth.

"Wrap your legs around me," he demanded. Eve obeyed willingly, loving the feel of his big calloused hands beneath her bottom. When beads of moisture formed along his collarbone, she licked them off playfully at first, then sensually, as she became more highly aroused.

The feel of her rough pink tongue gave Clint desires of his own. He lifted her high until she was perched on the shelf, opened her thighs and stepped between. His mouth was on a level with her belly. He trailed kisses down it, taking the drops of moisture onto his tongue. Then with his fingers, he opened the delicate pink folds between her legs and gazed at her woman's center. He worshipped her with his eyes, then dipped his head and made love to her with his mouth. With his lips against her cleft, he murmured, "God, you're so hot inside."

She was hot because she was on fire. Eve knew it had very little to do with the sauna. She writhed and arched, threading her fingers into his black hair and holding him to her center, faint with the ravishing. He swung up to perch beside her, gathering her close to watch her green eyes glitter with passion.

Eve needed to vent that passion in an abandoned act of worship. She slid down from the high seat. Her head was on the level of his knees. She parted them and stepped close. Standing on tiptoe, she delicately licked the tiny opening at the tip of his phallus, then drew its swollen head into her hot mouth. She swirled her tongue, spiralling it around and beneath the ridge of his cock.

"Enough, Evie, or I'll spill." It was all new to her. She was receiving as much pleasure as she was giving. Clint slid from his high perch. "No, sweet, I don't want it that way."

Dimly, she realized that though Clint had loved what she was doing, he could not spend in such a passive manner.

He stood her on the low seat, pressed her against the wall and thrust up inside her. The savage force of his entrance lifted her, and he took her hips in powerful hands to anchor her in place for his plundering. Their bodies, drenched with moisture, slid against each other like wet silk, driving them wild. He slowed his thrusts deliberately to draw out the loving. Then he told her in that dangerous, deep voice all the things he was going to do to her that night, when they went to bed.

Ted Barlow decided to take his snowmobile with him on his drive north. Pulling a trailer would slow him down and even add to the hazard of driving, but he had a gut feeling it would come in very handy if the roads to the property had not been plowed out.

Trevor was on the telephone to his mother. He was about to tell her that Eve was missing, but he detected such a plaintive note in her voice, that he hesitated. "Are you all right?" he asked anxiously.

"Oh, I'll be all right, Trevor. Don't worry about me being here alone—I'm used to it. Just so long as you're enjoying your Christmas; that's all that matters to me, dear."

Trevor was covered with guilt. He was torn between conflicting duties, as usual. Being in the middle was so unfair. He had given up his date with Eve last night to stay at his mother's. Thank heavens her illness had turned out to be merely indigestion. In retrospect, things had worked out for the best, because Eve apparently wasn't here anyway.

She had a tendency to be willful and impulsive and as a result had gone dashing off to show a property a hundred miles away. She certainly wouldn't appreciate his rushing after her. Eve Barlow had a mind of her own. That's what attracted him, however. His mother was so clinging, he only sought out independent females.

Trevor glanced through the window and saw Ted Barlow hook up his trailer and snowmobile. God, the man was so gung-ho! He'd flown rescue missions during the Korean War and had obviously bought into the hero syndrome. Now he was off on a wild-goose chase that would physically exhaust a much younger man. Into the phone he said, "You sound like you need my company, Mother. I'll be there in about an hour."

Trevor went outside and stood beside Susan Barlow. "My mother's not very well."

"Oh, Trevor, I'm so sorry."

Ted rolled down the van window and said to Trevor, "Are you coming?"

Susan spoke up quickly. "His mother is ill. He has to go to Kalamazoo, honey."

"Oh, sorry. Susie, I'll call the minute I have news. Try not to worry, love."

She waved until he was out of sight. "I'll call you right away, if there's any news, Trevor."

He took her small hand in his. "Thanks, Mrs. Barlow. I'm so sorry about all the food you cooked."

"Don't give it a second thought. The people we love come first."

For the most part the highways had been plowed up as far as Ludington. It took Ted Barlow over three hours to cover the hundred miles. Everything was closed for Christmas Day, even the gas stations; it was a good thing he carried extra cans in the van.

The highway ended north of Ludington where the forests began. Ted located a state troopers' headquarters and explained the situation. They told him they had been in constant communication with the Department of Highways, who'd had their plows out since the blizzard began, as well as Michigan Power who had their linemen on overtime.

Ted Barlow showed them a sketch he'd made of Judy's property.

"Back on the twenty-third, traffic was still going in and out of that particular area until late afternoon. After that, anything that went in didn't come out."

They put in a call to the Department of Highways to see when the lakeshore road leading to this property would be plowed out, and then sipped coffee and waited for the information to be relayed to them.

It occurred to Ted Barlow that he should take advantage of a telephone while there was one available. He asked the clerk for a phone directory and began calling hospitals. None of them had admitted a young woman by the name of Eve Barlow. That was good, he told himself, that was very good news indeed.

The state troopers' office checked over all the accident reports filed in the area since the twenty-third of December. Ted cursed himself for not finding out what Clint Kelly was driving, but at least neither the name Kelly nor the name Barlow showed up in any of the reports. Ted was an optimist and honestly believed his daughter and her client were holed up at the property, safe and sound. They had simply been snowed in and knew they wouldn't get out until the roads were cleared. The alternative was unthinkable.

Finally a report came in from the Department of Highways. Though they would be working all night, they wouldn't get to isolated roads until morning. It was strictly a matter of priorities. Ted Barlow was faced with two choices. He could stay at the troopers' headquarters tonight and follow the first plow in the morning, or he could head out on his snowmobile.

It was one of the easiest decisions he'd ever made. He took an extra gas can from the van and put it under the seat of the snowmobile in the storage compartment. A state trooper tried to talk him out of it, but realized if his own daughter were missing, he'd do exactly the same thing.

Ted changed into his snowmobile suit, then put on his goggles and heavy leather gauntlets. The visibility was good, but his progress was slower than usual. A snowmobile was at its peak performance on fresh powder or when a crust of ice had formed on top of the snow. Today, the sun had produced a partial thaw and as a result, the snow was wet and heavy.

He kept his goal foremost in his mind, telling himself over and over that it was less than twenty miles. When his snowmobile hit a particularly slushy patch and bogged down, he got off the machine and dug it out with his hands.

He shook his head and chuckled at the irony. His son couldn't come home this Christmas. Steven was halfway around the world in a new posting at Camp Page in South Korea. Although there was no war, he flew jets very close to the border of the unpredictable North Koreans. Up until today, Ted's thoughts had been preoccupied with the danger his son might be in this Christmas season, so far away from his family and his country. Then, wouldn't you know it? It was Eve, who lived in little old Grand Rapids, a place renowned for its safety and security, who was missing!

Ted offered up a prayer for both of his children as he restarted the stalled machine and set off again with renewed determination.

Eve yawned as she sat before the fire. She was so relaxed after the sauna and Clint's lovemaking, she couldn't lift a finger, and what was more, she didn't wish to. *It should be against the law to feel this content,* she thought. Eve had never been cut off from the world before; it certainly had its advantages.

Although she hadn't been too keenly aware of it before, now she realized she'd been on edge lately. The stress of city living and constantly competing in a man's world had made her uptight. Now she felt at peace with herself; she felt happy.

Clint stood gazing out the window. He realized their idyll would soon be over. It hadn't snowed all day, and by tomorrow at the latest, the roads would likely be plowed out and they would be connected with civilization again.

His gaze traveled possessively over the landscape. He felt elated that it would soon be his. No matter the asking price, he had decided this property would belong to him. He had discovered something precious here—a peace and quiet that had a healing quality about it. He loved his job and would have no other, but it was said that the constant flow of adrenaline brought on by danger was addictive.

After fighting a great conflagration, when he had beaten it and knew his men were safe, he felt totally drained. This house, this land not only cleansed him, it renewed his vitality and filled him with strength and power. The woman in the room with him had a similar effect. She filled him with a glorious feeling of omnipotence.

Clint wondered why he was so pensive. He had just found his dream home—why wasn't he dancing an Irish jig? The answer was simple; his heart was sinking because there was a piece missing from his happy picture. At the moment everything was perfect, but once Eve departed and took up her life where it had left off, there would be a hole in his future existence.

He didn't want their time together to end.

He didn't want to let her go!

Clint turned from the window. His face softened as he watched her sitting curled up, dreaming and drowsing before the fire.

"I love this place . . . share it with me, Evie."

Chapter Eight

Eve's lashes flew up. The magic spell was broken. Their idyll was over. He'd said the words that rang the death knell to their intimate interlude. Reality suddenly raised its unwelcome head and rushed in upon her.

She leapt off the couch and took two steps toward him. By that time, Clint had reached her. She raised her fingers to his lips as if to stay his words, but of course it was too late. They had been uttered and could not be recalled.

Eve agonized over her reply. The last thing on earth she wanted to do was hurt this man who had saved her life, fed her, warmed her, and loved her. She had to find the right words. Guilt assailed her from all sides. Not guilt over what they had done—she would never feel even the smallest pang for that, nor one tiny shred of regret. But guilt because she had somehow conveyed the possibility that what they had shared could go beyond this time, beyond this place.

And terrible guilt toward Trevor. She had betrayed his trust and in doing so had discovered another man who eclipsed him in her eyes. What made it worse, unforgivable almost, was the undeniable fact that the things she found irresistible were Kelly's dominance, macho attitude, and strength. Poor Trevor with his gentleness, kindness, and understanding came off a poor second.

Clint watched the play of emotions cross her lovely features, one after another. He had known from the outset that this woman was committed to another, yet he had deliberately set out to seduce her. To him she had been fair game. He was a man, she was a woman; they were alone together. To a male predator, that was all that counted.

She had been a great challenge to him, with her feminist attitudes. Then providence had tipped the scales in his favor. By almost drowning, she had become completely vulnerable. Then he was able to shine at all the things he did best. But, underneath her polished veneer, he had found trust, generosity, and an innocence that captured his heart.

At first, he had thought, if he couldn't steal this female from a passive professor of English who spouted poetry, he wasn't worth his salt as a red-blooded American male. But the seduction had backfired. Once he stole her, he wanted to keep her.

Eve took a tremulous breath. "Clint . . . I can't," she said softly. His face seemed to harden.

"You have such formidable attributes, Clint. I'm attracted to everything about you. I'm racked with guilt, but I could never leave Trevor."

Clint's bright blue eyes took on the cold gray of Lake Michigan.

"Trevor is such a fine person, so completely understanding and sensitive. I can't just leave him and come to you. I couldn't be that cruel!"

"You don't think you're capable of cruelty?" he asked drily.

She tried desperately to make him understand. "We have an understanding, a commitment. God help me, Clint, I can't walk out on him. I have too much compassion for that."

Clint was acutely aware that she made no protestations of love.

Eve avoided speaking of love; did not dare even think of love. It would open a door she wished to keep firmly closed. Her gaze slipped from his hard mouth to his powerful shoulders, then down to his big, calloused hands. *He's so tough, I bet he's never cried in his life.*

"Clint, you do understand?" she agonized.

"No." Silence filled the room and stretched to the breaking point. "I've asked you once. I won't beg," he said quietly.

Their heads turned at the same time as they heard a noise.

"That's some sort of machine. Is it a plow?" she asked.

Clint went to look out the window. "I don't think so. The sound of the motor is too high-pitched." He went to the door and opened it. "It's a snowmobile," he said over his shoulder. "We have company."

Eve peeped out from behind Clint, not wanting anyone to get a clear view of her in the red long johns. "It's my father!" she cried.

Removing his boots and snowmobile suit, Ted Barlow began to joke. "Since you didn't show up for Christmas, the mountain decided to come to Mohammed."

"Oh, Dad!" She threw her arms around him, knowing how worried he must have been, and how he must have struggled for hours to get to her. His wisecracks camouflaged his enormous relief.

Still holding her hands in his, he held her away from him and looked askance at her red suit. "Did you mug Santa?"

"Dad, this is Clint Kelly, who intends to buy the house; Clint, this is Ted Barlow."

The men shook hands, assessing each other in the first thirty seconds. Both liked what they saw. Ted realized Clint had given the shirt off his back to his daughter and he wondered what had happened to her clothes.

"We wouldn't have been snowed in if it hadn't been for my stupidity. We were out on the property Thursday afternoon, just before it got dark, when I walked straight onto the pond and went through the ice."

"Is the pond deep?" Ted asked.

"About fifteen feet. I almost drowned, but Clint saved my life!"

Ted looked from one to the other. "How did you manage to rescue her?"

"With a rope and a ladder. I'm a firefighter; I know rescue techniques."

"Thank God you were with her."

"He didn't just rescue me from the pond. I was unconscious from the cold water. He revived me and spent the rest of the night chopping wood for the fire."

Ted's eyes showed his admiration. They all moved to the fireplace and sat down to recount the rest of what happened.

"Was there stuff here to eat?" Ted inquired.

"No. Clint hunted for food. I've dined like a queen on venison and pheasant—oh, and walleye . . . he fished, too!"

"Walleye? Lord, I haven't had a feed of walleye in a donkey's age. My mouth is watering."

"There's probably some out there on my stringer now. I'll go take a look." Clint knew father and daughter might want a private conversation. He put on his jacket and disappeared through the door.

When they were alone, Eve's father asked, "Are you okay, honey? You weren't afraid of this guy, were you?"

"No, I wasn't afraid of him. At first we rubbed each other the wrong way. He wanted Maxwell to show him the property, hated like hell having a woman agent. I didn't like him any better. He was so damn macho, I called him Action Man. But Dad, when I got into trouble, he really came through for me. I stopped laughing at his muscles when he used them to save us."

Ted observed her closely, wondering what had gone on between them. A man and woman isolated together for days was tempting, intimate, even romantic. He didn't ask; it was none of his business, and he wouldn't be upset if Eve did form a romantic attachment to someone like Clint Kelly.

"I'm sorry I couldn't call you. The telephone service has been temporarily discontinued. Even the electricity is off. Clint siphoned gas from his truck to run the generator, but we've had to ration it." She asked the question uppermost in her mind. "Did I really upset Mom?"

"She was worried, but she hides it real well. She's had a lot of practice with some of my hare-brained adventures, and Steven's."

"How did you find me?"

"Well, Trevor arrived without you this morning, so we drove back to your place and when your car wasn't there, I went to your office. Then I called Max and told him your Mercedes was still at work. He told me the last time he saw you, you were driving up here to show this guy the property. I phoned Judy to get directions, and here I am!"

"I ruined your Christmas."

"Like hell you did! Instead of sitting around eating my head off and being a couch potato in front of the television set, I had a great snowmobile adventure! And the best part is it had a happy ending . . . I found you safe and sound."

Eve grinned at her father. "Actually, it was a great adventure for me, too. Don't breathe it to a soul, especially Trevor, but I wouldn't have missed it for the world. I learned so many survival techniques." Eve blushed because of the other techniques she'd learned.

"Trevor didn't come because his mother was ill. But he was reluctant anyway. Some bull about you not appreciating him running after you. Is he afraid of you, Eve?"

She smiled. "Aren't most men afraid of women when it comes right down to it?"

"Most," he acknowledged, "but not all." He winked at her. "Action Man doesn't look like he'd intimidate easily."

Clint returned with five beautiful walleyes. Ted couldn't believe their size.

"It won't take me long to clean them and we can cook them on the fire," Clint offered. "You probably haven't eaten since breakfast."

"That's too tempting to refuse," Ted admitted.

Eve wondered why everything her father said made her want to blush. "We had pheasant for our Christmas dinner, but I made such a pig of myself, there's none left."

Clint glanced at Ted. "She was entitled; she not only cooked it, she plucked and cleaned it first."

"You must have taken Trevor's course in how to get in touch with your feminine side," Ted wisecracked.

Clint was amused; Eve was not.

Her father relished the fresh-caught fish. Clint sat down with him and devoured a whole one himself. Eve was amazed at Clint's hearty appetite. She wouldn't be able to manage another mouthful of food until tomorrow.

"How close did you get with your car?" Clint asked.

"Less than twenty miles. Only took me about an hour. I stopped at the state troopers' headquarters and they checked on all the accident reports for this area and the Department of Highways to see what had been cleared out. The plows won't be on this road until tomorrow. There aren't many residents at the lake this time of year, so it's a matter of priorities."

"The first thing I'd better get is a plow blade for the front of my truck," Clint decided.

"Well, I hate to eat and run, but we'd better get started. It'll take us an hour to get to the van and three hours from Ludington to Grand Rapids."

"I have no clothes! My winter coat is at the bottom of the pond, and my wool suit is shrunk beyond recognition."

"Take my jacket; I'm not going anywhere until tomorrow. I have no gasoline anyway."

"I have an idea. We'll leave your jacket at the troopers' office. I'll even give you enough gas to get there in the morning," Ted offered.

A worried frown creased Clint's brow as he handed Eve his coat. "On a snowmobile your legs will freeze!"

"I'll wrap towels around them and I'll take one of the blankets, too," Eve decided.

Ted donned his snowmobile suit and pulled on his boots.

"Don't forget my briefcase."

"Your case will fit in the storage under the seat, after I remove the extra gas tank. I'll just fill up, and you can have what's left, Clint." He held out his hand. "I don't know how to thank you for what you did. Everyone thinks Eve can take care of herself, but her old dad knows better."

Alone, she and Clint faced each other. Eve Barlow's sophistication had gone the way of the Alfred Sung suit. She gave him back his blue shirt in exchange for the down jacket. She looked a fright wrapped in the blanket and towels.

Clint reached for his belt. "Why don't you wear my jeans—"

She held up her hand. "Keep your pants on, Action Man." She tried not to let the sound of tears show in her voice.

"It's a bit late for that, Evie."

She burst into laughter. It kept the tears at bay. She wanted him to hold her. *If only things were different,* she thought. "I'll put in your offer first thing in the morning and be in touch as soon as I have something."

He nodded and watched her go out the door. Once she was a safe distance away, she turned to wave. "It was the best Christmas Eve I ever had," she called impulsively.

She watched him cup his hands around his mouth to call back, but the noise of the snowmobile drowned it out.

* * *

"Hang on tight—this is going to be a bumpy ride!"

Eve smiled as she put her arms around her dad. The old Bette Davis line dated him. She suddenly realized he must be close to fifty, yet his vigour belied his age. She pressed her cheek against his back. Not only did it shelter her from the cold wind, it made her realize how safe she felt with this man in control. She tried not to think of Clint Kelly. It was no good longing for what could not be. She had lived the fantasy, but now it was time to leave it behind.

Ted was making much better time on the trip back. The sun had disappeared early, as the afternoon advanced. Because the temperature had dropped, the snow was no longer mushy, and had a fine coat of ice on its surface.

In less than an hour they reached the state troopers' headquarters. Eve refused to go inside. "It's Christmas, not Halloween," she protested.

"Okay, I'll turn on the heater in the van. You can give me Clint's jacket and put on my snowmobile suit. It'll be too warm to keep it on while I'm driving. I'll call your mom. Are you sure you won't come in and talk to her? These guys probably haven't had a good laugh all Christmas!"

"Just tell her I love her, and ask her to call Trevor for me." Designer clothes were no longer quite as important to Eve, but she'd be damned if she'd let a bunch of macho officers see her in red long johns!

When she removed Clint's jacket, she experienced a sense of loss—not just the warmth, but a loss of security. And something else, harder to define: an invisible link that connected them. Eve was brought out of her pensive mood when Ted opened the van door and climbed in. "Your mom was so relieved about both of us. Imagine worrying about me!" But Eve could tell he was delighted with his wife's response.

"I promised her I'd drive slowly and told her not to expect us until after nine. She's going to call Trevor and tell him we'll celebrate our Christmas tomorrow."

On the drive home they sang carols and Eve was amazed that her father knew all the words to the parodies of Christmas songs that were currently popular. They were also extremely irreverent, but men get a kick out of being irreverent in these times of political correctness.

When they finally turned down their street, Susan had all the Christmas lights blazing. "Poor Mom—she's had such a lonely day."

Ted looked up at the lights as he turned off the engine. "She's always been my beacon."

Eve's memory stirred faintly as she remembered them kissing beneath the mistletoe. It was a shining strand, a thread, ephemeral as a dream. "You're still in love, after all these years."

"Passionately," Ted said, watching his beautiful wife fling open the front door and run down the steps to welcome them home.

The first thing Eve did was telephone Trevor. "Hi! I'm so sorry about all this. I guess my mother explained I was snowed in at a country property I was trying to sell."

"Eve, you know there's no need to apologize to me. These things happen. I understand, just as you would have understood when I couldn't take you dancing the other night."

When Eve realized he hadn't shown up either, she suddenly felt a little less guilty. But only a little!

"I knew there was a logical explanation for your absence, and I knew you would be perfectly all right."

But I wasn't all right, Eve thought. *Aren't you even going to ask me about the man I spent the last three days with?*

"Things usually have a way of working themselves out for the best. My mother needed company over the holiday. It's lonely being a widow. We'll celebrate our Christmas tomorrow."

"That'll be lovely, Trevor. I hope we don't get any more snow. Drive carefully from Kalamazoo. I'll see you around noon."

"Good night Eve. I can't wait until you open your present!"

After she hung up, she stood with her hand on the phone. Surely he was the most understanding man in the whole world. Apparently she wasn't going to get the third degree. Trevor would never display childish jealousy. He was a mature adult.

Susan made them turkey sandwiches and hot chocolate. Eve nibbled on homemade shortbread and Christmas cake soaked in rum while she told her mother about the incredible things that had happened over the last three days. "Can I stay here tonight?"

"As if you need to ask! It'll be fun to have you sleep over," her mother said, delighted to have her baby under her roof again.

"I need a warm bath, and I really need to wash my hair."

"Didn't you have water to bathe?"

"We had water, but it wasn't warm. We had to take cold showers."

"I'll get you a warm robe and some slippers," Susan said, running upstairs. Eve followed her, but she was too tired to run.

When Susan came downstairs, she put her arms around Ted. "Thanks for going all that way and bringing her home."

"You should have seen this Clint Kelly she spent the last three days with. Muscles, shoulders, a real lady-killer. She calls him Action Man. Well, you heard what she said."

"What?" Susan asked.

"They had to take cold showers!"

"Oh, you!" Susan gave him a punch.

Chapter Nine

Eve slipped down in the warm water and sighed with pure pleasure. How good the simple things of life feel when you've been deprived of them!

She tried not to analyze the conversation she'd had with Trevor, or her reaction to his attitude. They had been dating steadily for over a year and she had spent a lot of that time asserting her independence, so that they didn't live in each other's pocket. Now, she felt neglected. What a perverse creature she was!

It would be simply awful if the man she was about to become engaged to flew into a jealous rage and demanded she tell him everything. And the truth was, he had lots to be jealous about! Eve blushed, and slid further down in the warm, scented water.

Though she was tired, her body felt good. A bath was a sensual experience when you relaxed. Her thoughts drifted inexorably toward Clint Kelly. Fancifully, she decided a bathroom was the most private place in a house. You always locked the door so that no one could intrude, then you removed your clothes and were free to indulge in your most intimate thoughts.

Eve leaned her head back, closed her eyes, and allowed herself to relive every moment she'd spent with Kelly. Every look, every word, every smile, every touch, every kiss, every act . . . every climax!

As the water grew cold, thoughts of Trevor intruded. His last words repeated themselves in her mind: *I can't wait until you open your present!* Resolutely, she pushed those words away and climbed from the tub. She'd feel differently tomorrow. A new chapter of her life would begin. She would close the door on her past and open up another to the future. She knew she should count her blessings.

Sunday dawned dull and overcast. The temperature rose, and by the time the Barlows finished breakfast, all the white snow had turned to gray slush.

Still in robe and slippers, Eve opened her briefcase and took out the Offer to Purchase, then she telephoned Judy.

"Hello, Eve? How dare you get yourself into a scrape without me!"

"You don't know the half of it. I'll fill you in on the details someday when you have a few hours to kill."

"How in the world did you manage up there without food, heat, electricity, or telephone? I suppose getting snowed in put an end to any hope of selling the white elephant?"

"Judy, it's not a white elephant. It's a valuable piece of real estate. I'd buy it myself, if I could afford it."

"Come on, Eve, you're a city girl, like me. Watching trees grow can't be your idea of fun."

Judy was in the marketing department at one of Detroit's largest automakers, and Eve knew she hadn't visited her late parents' property in about two years.

"Judy, I have an offer for you."

"You're kidding! What the hell did you have to do to get it?"

Eve blushed. "Mr. Kelly is offering a hundred and seventy-five thousand. I'll fax it to you in about an hour." A slight pause on the other end of the phone prompted Eve to be scrupulously honest. "Kelly is a stubborn negotiator, but I really believe he'll go to two hundred thousand if you turn down this offer."

"Turn it down? Eve, bite your tongue. I accept the offer. Fax it to me right away so I can sign it before he changes his mind."

"He won't change his mind, Judy. He genuinely loves the place, and the house and property seem to have accepted him. He's a real outdoorsman; scuba dives and all that."

"He sounds like a hunk."

"He is, but he's also a male chauvinist."

Judy sighed. "In my experience you can't have it both ways. If they're hunks, they're chauvinistic; if they accept you as an equal, they're either wimps or they're gay!"

"Fax me a closing date. I have a check here for you. If it's a done deal and the weather cooperates, I could drive to Detroit Tuesday or Wednesday."

"Why don't I meet you halfway and we could have lunch together?"

"Wonderful idea. There's this terrific restaurant I know in Lansing. Mountain Jacks-Okemos on Grand River Avenue; they specialize in seafood or prime rib. I remember that used to be your favorite."

"Still is, to which my hips will grandly attest!"

"Well, this is great. I can't wait to see you. I'll call and let you know which day."

"Okay. Thanks a million, Eve. I appreciate it."

"Hey, it's my job, for which I am well paid."

Eve went into the kitchen where her mother was already working on their Christmas feast. "Mom, will you lend me a pair of slacks? I have to drive to my place to pick up your Christmas presents and put on something glamorous for Trevor."

Ted took out his keys. "Do you want to take the van, or do you just want me to drive you to your car?"

"If you don't mind going out, I'd rather you took me to my car. Leaving a Mercedes just sitting there is asking for it to be stolen."

Eve faxed Judy the Offer to Purchase before she changed her clothes. Back in her own bedroom, she found herself before the mirror exactly as she had been the last time she was in this room. "Not exactly," she said to her reflection. She no longer needed to ask if she was beautiful or sexy. She knew she was both. Clint Kelly had convinced her of that.

She went to her closet and moved aside a red dress. After the red suit, followed by the red long johns, she was ready for a change. She looked at the lavender; her favorite color, both because it enhanced her pale hair and because she thought it lucky. However, it wasn't exactly a Christmas color, so she decided on the avocado green silk with matching suede belt and shoes.

Eve unlocked the top drawer of her desk and took out the envelope that held her Christmas gift to her mother and father. Trevor's gift wouldn't be so easy to carry. She got out her luggage carrier and loaded the carton onto it. It wasn't really all that large, just heavy.

Eve heard her fax machine and was surprised at the speed Judy had returned the signed Offer to Purchase. The closing date she suggested was thirty days, or sooner, if it suited the client. Eve knew Clint Kelly would be thrilled. How she would love to hand him the acceptance and watch the grin spread across his face. But that was out of the question. She mustn't see him again, if it was at all possible. They had made a clean break, and that's the way she had to keep it.

She would send all the papers by courier, then his lawyer could collect the check and the signed documents. She glanced at her watch. Kelly couldn't possibly be back yet. This was a good time to call and leave a message. She dialed the number. Her stomach lurched as she heard his deep voice.

"You've got my machine, so talk at it."

"It's Eve Barlow, calling Sunday the twenty-sixth. Your offer has been accepted with a thirty-day closing date, or sooner, if you can arrange the money. I'll send the documents over by courier. Congratulations!"

When she hung up, her hands were shaking and her mouth had gone dry. What the devil was the matter with her? She was behaving like an adolescent with her first crush. She admonished herself sternly to pull herself together. Today would probably be one of the significant days of her life. It was a special day for Trevor as well, and she had to be very careful not to spoil it in any way. Trevor was a sensitive man who could pick up on her vibrations, so she had to make sure they were happy ones.

Eve threw on her coat, picked up her briefcase, and pulling the luggage carrier behind her, took the apartment elevator to the ground floor. She was relieved that she arrived back at her parents' house before Trevor got there. Her mother warned her, "Don't go in the family room. Your dad's setting up your Christmas present."

Eve was mystified about what it could be.

"That's a beautiful dress, dear."

"Thank you," Eve said, rubbing her hands over her hips. "I love the way it feels."

The doorbell chimed.

"Oh Lord, he's here," Eve murmured. "Don't tell me it's already noon."

Trevor came in bearing gifts. He gave Susan a huge poinsettia and when Ted slipped in from the family room to greet him, Trevor handed him a bottle of imported sake.

"Thanks! I haven't tasted this stuff in years."

Eve smiled at Trevor. He'd put a lot of thought in the bottle he'd selected for her dad. "How's your mother?" she asked, taking his coat.

"Much better. She'll be just fine."

"Shoo," Susan said. "If everyone stays out of the kitchen, I'll have dinner ready in an hour."

Eve and Trevor moved toward the living room and Ted began to follow them.

"Not you, dear," Susan called after him. "I need your help."

Trevor caught Eve's hand and pulled her beneath the mistletoe. He kissed her gently and, after a brief hesitation, she kissed him back. "You look lovely," he told her. "Would you look at this tree—it must have cost a fortune." He sounded as if he didn't quite approve of spending so much money on something that was simply for decoration. When they sat down on the couch, he asked, "How did you make out up north?"

For a moment, Eve stared at him, not knowing exactly what he was asking. She colored slightly, before the penny dropped into the slot. "Oh, I sold it."

"Good for you," he said, patting her knee with his smooth white hand. "You have to forgive your dad. He's from a generation that doesn't realize a woman can do anything a man can do."

But a woman can't do all the things a man can do, Eve protested, silently. She had been prepared to tell him about the frightening pond episode, but suddenly decided against it. If she admitted to fear and helplessness, it would negate her equality, and she would seem diminished in his eyes. At least she suspected she would. It was all very well to claim equality on an intellectual level, she thought, but the reality was that on a physical level, comparing strength and endurance, a man was superior to a woman, or he should be.

Eve changed the subject so that the conversation focused on Trevor. A few months back he had been passed over at the university for head of department. It had been a bitter pill, but with Eve's support, he had gotten over the disappointment.

He told her there were rumors flying all over the campus that the professor who had been promoted over him was proving unsatisfactory. Everyone in the English department was grumbling over one thing or another.

Eve gave him all her attention and sympathy, but she couldn't help wondering if this was what the rest of her life would be like—politely listening while Trevor catalogued his grievances. *Stop being a bitch!* she told herself. Trevor had been devastated when he was passed over. He was a sensitive man who craved approval and affirmation, and up until now she had been happy to oblige.

Eve was relieved when dinner was ready and they joined her parents for the festive meal. The table was a work of art. Her mother was an accomplished hostess and a gourmet cook. There was turkey with chestnut dressing and giblet gravy, as well as a whole glazed ham patterned with cherries and cloves. The vegetable dishes were culinary delights. Mushrooms with almonds and shallots sat beside cinnamon yams, tender steamed leeks, and balsamic-glazed pearl onions. Baby brussels sprouts sat on a bed of wild rice, and a whole squash had been stuffed with gingered pork.

Susan's homemade pickles included walnuts, olives, and dills, and she had combined cranberries with orange peel for a sauce that was piquant in taste and aroma. Ted opened both red and white wine so they could have their choice. They drank to Steven's health, toasting him across the world.

When the dinner was over, none of them had room for dessert, so they decided to have it later, after they had opened their gifts. They moved into the family room and Eve saw her Christmas present immediately.

"Oh my gosh!" she exclaimed with genuine surprise. "When I mentioned I needed a treadmill to keep in shape, I never expected you would actually buy me one! Thank you both, so much."

Ted showed her the different speeds and how to preset a program with the multi-window electronics. He also demonstrated it, then Eve tried it out and so did Trevor, who seemed as pleased with the useful gift as she was.

Eve opened her purse and handed her mother the envelope. Susan opened it and cried out with delight. "Oh, honey, you shouldn't have. Ted, it's cruise tickets! We fly to Tampa, then sail ten days in the Caribbean. We visit Martinique, Barbados, Antigua, St. Maarten, St. Thomas, and San Juan. I can't believe it!"

"Well, I'm ready for a second honeymoon; when can we leave?" Ted teased.

Eve was filled with so much warmth, her heart overflowed. Her parents usually went to Florida or Arizona for a month in the wintertime, but they'd never been on a cruise.

Susan made Ted dig out the atlas so they could see the route the cruise ship would take. Trevor presented each of them with an identically wrapped gift and sat back to watch as they were opened. He hadn't really approved of Eve spending so much money on her parents, but what could he say? She earned the money and was free to spend it any way she chose. He had not protested because he avoided confrontations at all costs.

Susan and Ted unwrapped them at the same time. They were monogrammed passport holders. "Thank you so much, Trevor. I guess you knew about the cruise tickets."

Ted handed Trevor the present Susan had picked out for him, with their daughter's advice. Trevor was delighted with the pair of brass bookends, declaring they were exactly what he needed. When he opened Eve's gift, a great lump came into his throat. It was a leather-bound collection of the complete works of Shakespeare. He'd coveted books like this since he was a boy.

Eve watched Trevor's hand caress the volumes with reverence. She preferred Dickens, but Trevor lusted for Shakespeare, and when she saw how he treasured the books, she was glad she had ordered them all those months ago.

The afternoon light was gone from the sky; it looked as if they were in for another snowstorm. Ted turned on all the lights in keeping with the cheery holiday atmosphere. "Let's have that dessert now, Susie," Ted suggested.

Trevor was just as happy to wait a little while longer before he gave Eve her present. A little suspense was good before a dramatic moment. Rather like a play, he thought fancifully. Trevor winked at Eve and whispered, "They say anticipation is the best part."

Don't you believe it. Clint Kelly's words slipped into her mind with amazing facility. Eve forced her memories away from Kelly to focus on her mother's delicious desserts—rum pecan pie, lemon cheesecake, and traditional mince pie.

As Eve forked the last mouthful of lemon cheesecake, she sighed, "I'm surely going to need that treadmill after today."

Trevor helped himself to another piece of mince pie. "These are even better than my mother's."

Ted could not resist trying everything Susan had baked. "The woman is a temptress."

"Well, the way to your heart is certainly through your stomach. Help me load these in the dishwasher. Trevor would probably like to give Eve her gift in private."

Ted's eyes met Eve's. She wanted to cry, *Don't leave me!* Ted looked mutinous, as if he didn't want to leave his daughter with this man, but he rose reluctantly and carried out the plates.

As Eve watched Trevor take a small wrapped gift from his pocket, his movements seemed to distort into slow motion. Eve experienced a moment of sheer panic. She jumped up quickly and babbled, "I'll be right back. I have to go to the powder room. I don't want to spoil this moment for you."

Eve locked the bathroom door and leaned back against it. She had had to get out of the room; she had felt it closing in on her. She was so tense, her stomach muscles were in knots. *Dear Lord in heaven, what am I going to do?*

The answer came back clearly, *Pull yourself together and get back out there. You cannot spoil this man's precious moment for him.* She did not dare look at herself in the mirror. She turned on the tap and let cold water run over her wrists, then she splashed her flushed cheeks until they felt cooler. She had let this thing go too far to draw back now. She straightened her shoulders. She would not allow a brief infatuation ruin her future plans. She took a deep breath and unlocked the bathroom door.

As Trevor handed her the gift, she gave him a tremulous smile. She removed the silver ribbon and wrapping paper with steady hands, but when they held the velvet jeweler's box, they began to tremble. With an iron resolve she pushed away a feeling of dread. She opened the box and stared down at a pair of diamond earrings!

Chapter Ten

Eve looked up at Trevor in disbelief, then her gaze dropped to the small velvet box to make sure her imagination wasn't playing a trick on her.

"You look so stunned, Eve. I thought you guessed I was buying you diamonds."

"Diamonds did cross my mind," she admitted in a faraway voice. A small ripple of relief began inside her that spread through her veins. By the time it reached her brain, it was a tidal wave! Trevor was not giving her an engagement ring. This man was not asking her to marry him!

"Trevor, I don't think I can accept these."

He looked a little sheepish. "They are sort of a bribe, or I suppose a more correct word might be *incentive*. I think it's time we started living together, Eve. If we can do that successfully, then I would have no hesitation about getting married down the road."

"Down the road?" she repeated vaguely.

"Perhaps next Christmas. It's time we started thinking about a permanent commitment."

"Next Christmas?" She felt like a parrot.

"It's economically unwise for us to pay rent on two apartments when we could share one. The only thing is, I've been considering living in Kalamazoo, where I work, and where my mother lives. Of course, I understand this will be a big decision for you, and want to give you plenty of time to think about it."

Eve's eyes made direct contact with Trevor's. She took a deep breath. "You're right. This is a big decision. I don't know if I can accept what you're offering me, Trevor, though it's an honor to be asked." She smiled feebly. *At least you believe you're honoring me, you poor deluded man,* she added silently.

Ted Barlow walked in on them. "Sorry to intrude, but there's a weather advisory on TV. We're in for a severe ice storm. Perhaps you'd better get cracking, unless you're going to stay put for the night."

"Oh, no, I have to get home—I have work to do," Eve said quickly. "I'll leave my car, though; Trevor will drive me." She showed her parents the diamond earrings, which they admired thoroughly. At the same time Ted and Susan exchanged glances and raised their eyebrows. Both of them had expected Trevor to present Eve with an engagement ring. Ted was relieved; Susan only wanted what Eve wanted.

They all said their goodbyes and thanked each other again for the Christmas gifts and Susan's marvelous dinner.

"Mom, I want all your recipes. Do you have one for coconut cream pie?"

"You're going to start cooking?" her father asked with a frown. Perhaps these two were going to move in together after all.

"A New Year's resolution," Eve replied.

On the drive to her apartment, Eve was strangely silent. The rain, which was rapidly turning to ice, was coming down pretty heavily and Trevor had to keep his mind on his driving. She knew when they got to her place, he would take it for granted that he could spend the night. Eve knew she had to speak up before he parked and turned off the engine.

She turned to look at him. "Trevor, I don't want you to spend the night at my place." It was brutally blunt. She softened it a little. "You've given me a lot to think about and I have some decisions to make. I need to be alone."

Trevor's mouth turned sulky, but after a minute he said, "I understand. Take all the time you need."

"Thank you. Good night, Trevor." The kiss she gave him was a generous one. It was probably the last kiss they would ever share.

"I'll call you tomorrow," he said.

"I'm going to the office, so call me tomorrow night."

* * *

Once Eve was safely inside her own apartment, she pushed the dead bolt on the door and let the second wave of relief wash over her. She felt free, like a bird escaped from its cage. Perhaps the cage had been safe and sensible, but it had come to her in a flash that she hated safe and sensible!

She threw off her coat and shoes and danced about the room. She had no plans for the future, but she was very sure of one thing: that future did not include Trevor Bennett. She sat down at her desk and began preparing the papers that Clint Kelly would need to sign, about a dozen in all. There would be more later, on closing. She then prepared a list of costs and adjustments regarding paid-up taxes, settlement and transfer charges, and brokerage fees.

Eve then called the courier service and was surprised when they arrived for the pickup within thirty minutes. She gave the young man a generous tip because it was Boxing Day, because the weather was appalling, and because she felt benevolent toward everyone on earth tonight!

As she climbed into bed, she realized it had been an emotional day—emotionally exhausting, then emotionally exhilarating. Her mind flitted about like a butterfly, momentarily touching one thing, then off to another. But always, it came back to Clint Kelly. Thoughts of him clung to her; he was completely unforgettable.

As she drifted off to sleep she heard a far-off fire siren and she knew she would never hear that sound for the rest of her life without thinking of him.

The following morning, Eve took a cab to the office. The streets were extremely icy, but the sky looked clear. Only a couple of agents showed up and it was quiet enough that she got caught up on all her paperwork. Eve felt restless, so at lunchtime, she took a cab to her parents' place so she could pick up her car.

Her mother insisted she stay for lunch, and her dad turned off the one o'clock news on television so he could join them in the kitchen. "Fire last night," he informed them.

"I heard the siren. What was it?" Eve asked.

"Industrial warehouse across the city."

"Eve, your dad and I were convinced Trevor was going to give you a ring for Christmas."

Eve shook out a napkin and sat down at the counter. "To be honest, so did I. When I opened that velvet box and saw diamond earrings instead of a diamond ring, I couldn't believe my eyes!"

"Were you terribly disappointed, dear?" her mother asked gently.

"No! It sounds awful, but I was relieved. Trevor isn't right for me, and what's more, I'm not right for him either. I feel wretched that it took me this long to realize it."

"I've always known he wasn't right for you," Ted insisted.

Eve gave her dad a curious look. "You never said anything."

"Your mother wouldn't let me!"

Eve gave him a skeptical look. "Right. As if that would stop you."

"It's true. She insisted I trust you to make the right decision."

"Why, thank you . . . both of you. I had no idea you didn't like Trevor."

"Honey, we have nothing against him. He's a fine man, but we want you to have skyrockets!"

Eve looked from one to the other. "You have skyrockets, don't you? It's funny, but I've only realized that lately."

"Did you end it last night?" her mother probed.

"No. It took me by surprise. I was all psyched up to get engaged and resign myself to being a professor's wife—I couldn't think on my feet when he threw me a curve."

"When will you tell him?" Susan asked.

"Tonight. I'll tell him tonight. The last thing in the world I want to do is hurt him, but a quick, clean break is best for everyone."

Her parents didn't pursue the subject any further. Ted suspected her weekend with Clint Kelly had put an end to Trevor Bennett's hopes. But he knew Eve would confide in them in her own good time.

"If you're going home now, why don't I bring over your treadmill and set it up for you?"

Eve almost told him he was too old to be carrying heavy stuff like that. She bit her tongue. He was only fifty, and he was the best judge of his ability. She had to trust him to make his own decisions, as he had trusted her.

As he was adjusting the digital settings on her treadmill, her father talked about the International Fly-In that Oshkosh, Wisconsin, held every summer. Because of his experience with planes, he'd been invited to be a judge of the "home-built" flying machines entered in the weeklong event.

As Eve listened to him, she finally understood why her mother was still in love. He took a vital interest in everything and he kept himself in great shape. Eve had always known that her father was a man's man; now she saw that he was also a woman's man.

"Thanks, Dad. I could never have figured it all out on my own." It was only a slight exaggeration; she couldn't have learned how to set it half so quickly.

When she was alone, she began walking on the new treadmill. She decided it was a wonderful invention. It gave the body a workout, while allowing the mind total freedom. She spent the next couple of hours rehearsing what she would say to Trevor when he called. When the phone rang at exactly five o'clock, she said to herself, *God, he's so regimented!*

The moment Trevor spoke, she could hear the vulnerability in his voice. He was expecting her to reject his offer and she was going to fulfill his expectations. Eve felt like a monster. She knew the kindest thing to do was get straight to the heart of the matter. She would not indulge in a cat and mouse game. It was at this point that she became absolutely convinced she was doing the right thing. When she was cast in the role of cat and he was reduced to a mouse, it was all over.

"Trevor, I've thought about us all day and it isn't going to work. We're wrong for each other. You need someone I'll never be. I take the blame for the failure of our relationship. You've been gentle, kind, and understanding from the beginning and none of this is your fault."

"Eve, please don't be so hasty. Give us another chance. I won't pressure you into living together; I'll forget about marriage."

"It's best to make a clean break, Trevor. I don't want to give you pain, but I think we should end it."

There was a long silence, then in a resigned voice, he said the thing he always said: "I understand."

Eve sat down to write him a kind letter. He understood and appreciated the written word. She used a philosophical tone, implying "What will be, will be." She knew he read Omar Khayyam. She told him she had been enriched by their relationship, and that with all her heart she wished him well. Then Eve wrapped up the diamond earrings and called the courier.

It was the same young man she had generously tipped the night before. He returned the package of papers addressed to Clint Kelly.

"I'm sorry, Ms. Barlow, there was no one home at this address. I tried to deliver it last night and again today."

"Hang on a minute—I'll telephone him." Eve dialed Kelly's number and heard his deep voice, but only on the answering machine. "It's Eve Barlow, six o'clock, Monday the twenty-seventh. Would you give me a call as soon as you can?"

She told the courier, "Leave the package and take this one instead." She gave him another generous tip.

Eve made herself dinner, then hesitated to go down to the laundry room in case she missed Kelly's call. She rinsed out a few things in the bathroom sink. She was in such a reflective mood, feeling guilty over Trevor, justifying ending their relationship. Eve desperately needed an escape from her introspection. She felt like running five miles or climbing a mountain, but the weather was so foul, she couldn't even go for a drive.

She almost turned on the television set, then she happened to remember she had bought a Christina Skye novel just before Christmas and hadn't had a chance to read it. Eve curled up on the couch and began to read *Hour of the Rose*. Skye was a superb writer. From the first haunting sentence, Eve was swept away to another time and place.

It was after midnight when she glanced at her watch. She was torn between reading 'til dawn and putting the book down so she could savor it and make it last longer. She decided on the latter; she just might be spending a lot of her evenings alone for awhile.

When she got to the office the next day, Eve was inundated with people who were looking for new office space. It seemed as if every lease in Grand Rapids expired in January. She tried phoning Kelly a couple of times, and when she was unsuccessful, called Judy to tell her their lunch would have to be postponed.

"Do you think there might be a problem?" Judy asked.

"No, no," Eve assured her. "Mr. Kelly is a fire chief who

works shifts. It's just taking a while to get together with his lawyer. It will probably be after New Year's before I have everything for you."

"That would be better for me too, Eve. By the way, I had the phone taken off holiday service and also had the power put back on. I don't want anyone else getting into difficulties up there."

"That was a good idea. I'll put the costs in the adjustments," Eve assured her.

She worked late at the office, then on impulse on the way home, took a detour to Clint Kelly's apartment. There was no answer to her knock. She pulled out a business card, wrote on it, "Call me!" and shoved it under his door.

She waited for his call all evening. When it didn't come, she convinced herself that he had taken such offense over her rejection that he was deliberately avoiding her. *To bloody hellfire with all men!* Eve picked up *Hour of the Rose* and took it to bed with her.

When dawn arrived, Eve found herself lying awake, reflecting on all that had happened over the holidays. She recalled reading somewhere that more romantic relationships ended at this time of the year than any other. It was like the adage said—if it wasn't rock solid, it wouldn't survive Christmas!

Men seemed to fall into two categories. They were either mothers' boys or macho chauvinists. Where were all the men in between? Where were the men who could be strong and take control when it was necessary, yet show ineffable tenderness or be moved to tears at life's poignant, touching moments?

Eve laughed at herself and threw back the covers. The ideal man was a myth. And if there was such a paragon, he was seeking the ideal woman!

When she opened her closet, she knew she needed to choose something that would lift her spirits. She decided to wear her lucky color. Eve pulled on a pair of lavender slacks and a lambswool sweater to match. They were the antithesis of a power suit, making her look soft and feminine. She even put on her amethyst earrings that were strictly evening wear deciding she would never be regimented again.

Eve's car seemed to have a mind of its own this morning, heading in the direction of Kelly's apartment building rather than her office. Upstairs, she knocked politely on his door and waited. Perhaps he was sleeping. If he'd worked all night he could be dead to the world by now. Eve lifted her fists and pounded. Absolute silence met her ears. She should have saved herself the trouble by phoning!

Eve was annoyed. This was no way to conduct business. She was his broker, representing his purchase of a house. He should at least have the common courtesy to touch base with her. She drove to the office, fuming all the way. When Maxwell arrived, she followed him into his office.

"Did you have a scuba lesson last night?"

"No. There was no lesson scheduled for the week between Christmas and New Year's. We pick up again after the holidays. Thinking of joining the class?" he asked casually.

"No," she said sweetly, "I'm thinking of drowning someone."

By noon, her patience snapped. She decided to track Action Man down. Eve was hungry and knew exactly where she was going to eat lunch.

Kelly's Sports Bar and Grill was crowded. She searched the room looking for a six-footer with black hair and dark blue eyes. She ordered a corned beef sandwich and a draft beer. The dill pickle was so good it made her taste buds stand at attention. It must have been pickled in a barrel.

At one o'clock the crowd thinned out dramatically, and Eve carried her empty mug to the bar. The resemblance was so marked she had no difficulty realizing this was Kelly's father. The retired policeman was heavier, of course, and his handsome face lay in ruins, but he was hard-edged and cocksure; still master of his domain.

"Hello, Mr. Kelly. I'm Eve Barlow and I'm looking for your son, Clint."

"Call me Clancy," he said, giving her an appreciative look that swept from breasts to thighs.

Clancy? I don't believe it. He's more Irish than Paddy's Pig!

"You're not a reporter, are you?" he demanded.

"No. I'm his real estate agent."

Clancy whistled with disbelief. "Well, I'll be damned. He sure knows how to pick 'em!"

"Mr. Kelly—"

"Clancy."

"Clancy. Do you know where I can find your son?"

"Nope."

"You have no idea where he might be reached?"

"Nope."

"It's imperative I get in touch with him. Doesn't he come here to the bar?"

Clancy rubbed his nose thoughtfully, then seemed to come to a decision. He reached beneath the bar and pulled out a newspaper. It was two days old.

Eve's eyes ran down the page, then stared hard at the picture. It portrayed a firefighter carrying a child in his arms. His helmet was decorated by a row of icicles. His face was grim, his eyes stark. Quickly she read the headline, then the article.

Two boys had been playing with matches on the third floor of a furniture warehouse. The ten-year-old had been rescued and taken to a hospital. The nine-year-old had not survived.

"Fire Chief Kelly said the floor collapsed before he could reach the second boy. He performed cardiopulmonary resuscitation for over an hour, but it was hopeless. Kelly's crew fought the fire for twelve hours in below-zero temperatures."

Eve looked up from the newspaper to find Clancy's eyes on her.

"When something like this happens, we don't see him for a few days. He likes to be alone."

Eve nodded. She looked at the eyes in the picture again, and felt his pain. She handed back the paper. "Thank you," she whispered.

Eve Barlow threw jeans, sweaters, and underclothes into an overnight bag, then grabbed makeup and shampoo. Her instincts had taken over and she had a gut feeling about where she would find Clint Kelly.

On the drive north to the property she made one stop at a store to purchase a present and put it in the trunk with her overnight bag. Eve drove carefully, but as fast as road conditions allowed.

She could not get the picture of Kelly holding the dead child out of her mind. Why in the name of heaven had she thought Clint incapable of tears? His job did not merely deal with danger, it encompassed anguish, fear, and tragedy. It involved the loss of life, as well as property. On a daily basis Clint Kelly was expected to perform heroically, and to deal with death when heroics weren't enough. No wonder he had taken over so completely when her life was in danger. He had been trained to cope with emergencies and disasters. Treating hypothermia was probably second nature to him; he and his team must have experienced it firsthand fighting fires, soaked to the skin, in below-zero temperatures.

Clint was a born leader; a take-charge kind of man who made instant decisions and issued orders, expecting them to be obeyed. The time she spent with him had taught her so much about him, certainly enough to make her fall head-over-heels in love! But she now realized she had barely scratched the surface. There were still volumes to learn, depths to plumb.

Clint saw her Mercedes as it pulled into the long drive. He started running. He reached the car in time to open the door for her.

She watched him run toward her. He was carrying something black in his hand. She smiled when she saw it was a camera.

"Eve!"

"Hello, Clint. I've been trying to get hold of you for days. I didn't know about the fire until I went to your dad's bar."

"He didn't know where I was."

"No, but I did," she said quietly, getting out of the car and standing close, looking up at him. *Thank God the pain has left his eyes. This place is good for him!* She would be good for him, too. She'd start by making him laugh. "Remember that engagement ring I was getting for Christmas? It turned out to be diamond earrings."

He didn't laugh; his eyes burned into hers. "Marry me, Eve!"

It wasn't a question, it was more like a command. His arms went around her. "Evie, if that's what it takes to win you, I'll even quote poetry."

She laughed into his eyes and called his bluff. "Let's hear you."

Clint's dark brows drew together for a minute. Then he said:

* * *

"I'm only a man,
We'll get along fine,
Just so long as you remember
I'm not yours; YOU'RE MINE!"

Eve melted into his arms and lifted her lips for his kiss, knowing that was an effective way to stop his dreadful doggerel.

"I take it your answer is yes?"

"Clint Kelly, it's no such thing! You're going way too fast for me."

"When I see what I want, I walk a direct path to it."

"We have nothing in common. You would turn my life upside down."

"We can work things out. Come inside and we'll negotiate. If we talk, we can find common ground."

"We have so little in common, it would be a disaster."

"You think I can't handle disaster?" He raised one black eyebrow.

"I know you can," she said softly. She knew if he began to touch her, her objections would dissolve along with her bones.

In front of a blazing fire, with Clint Kelly sitting across from her, Eve's resistance began to thaw. He was such a persuasive man—she knew she had to negotiate while she still had her wits about her.

"I want a fifty-fifty partnership. I don't want a marriage where the man is the boss and the woman is the little housewife."

Clint grabbed a piece of paper and began making a contract. "Agreed; fifty-fifty," he promised.

"I intend to work, whether you like it or not. I won't stay home baking coconut cream pies."

"Agreed," he said, scribbling furiously. She was independent, assertive, competitive, and combative, but every once in a while he knew she would lean on him.

"And I don't want to have to break your arms every time I want to drive."

His face was sober, but his eyes danced with amusement. "You missed your calling. You should have been a comedian."

"This isn't meant to be funny—I'm serious! These are definitely not jokes."

"Then why am I laughing?"

"Because you're a sexist swine, of course."

"Evie, I'm so much in love with you, I'll agree to anything."

Eve stopped talking and looked at him. This man was everything she'd ever wanted. It was time to face the truth. She tore the paper into small pieces and threw it into the air. It came down like confetti. "Clint, I wouldn't want you any other way!"

He threw back his head and yowled like a wolf. It was a cry of victory. "Now that we've got business out of the way, can we indulge in a little pleasure?"

She took his hand. "Come with me. I have a present for you." Eve unlocked the trunk and handed him her overnight bag. Then she gave him his present. When Clint opened the brown bag and saw the bottle of whisky, a wicked grin spread across his face.

"I'll let you be the judge of that, Action Man. You're going to have to reel out more hose, or get closer to the fire. Just don't rub me the wrong way!"

"After experiencing Christmas Eve," he said, making a word-play of her name, "I can't wait for New Year's Eve!"

A MISTY HARBOR
CHRISTMAS

Marcia Evanick

Chapter One

Olivia Hamilton took the kettle off the stove as soon as it started to whistle, and poured the boiling water into the waiting teacup. Her grandmother always told her that there was no problem in the world that a good cup of tea couldn't solve. Her grandmother had been wrong.

There was no way a cup of herbal tea would bring her grandmother back to life. This particular cup of tea wouldn't even stop the tears she could feel once again pooling within her eyes. For the past week, all she had been doing was crying. It had to stop. Her grandmother would have never approved.

Olivia blinked back the tears and carefully carried her cup over to the solid oak table and the windows that overlooked the backyard. The same table Olivia had sat at as a little girl helping her grandmom roll out pie dough or dropping heaping teaspoons of cookie dough onto baking sheets. Every summer since she had turned two, she had visited her grandmother in the small Maine town of Misty Harbor for months on end. The visits had stopped about the time Olivia had turned sixteen and her summers back in California became busy with working, boys, and school activities. Between high school, college, and then a career, Olivia hadn't stepped foot in Misty Harbor in ten years. Over those years, her grandmother had been the one to fly out to California, at least twice a year, to stay with her son and daughter-in-law. Olivia, being her only grandchild, had seen her at her parents' home, but those visits had never been the same as the ones from her youth.

She had always meant to come back to Misty Harbor for a

nice long stay with her grandmother. She just never had the time. Now it was too late. She was once again in her grandmother's house, but it wasn't the same.

Olivia's fingers trembled as they traced a bright red poinsettia on the tablecloth her grandmother must have put on the table before coming to California for her semiannual family visit. There were a few other touches of the holiday spirit throughout the house. A wreath hung on the front door, two baskets overflowed with silk poinsettias in the front parlor, and a beautiful red and green centerpiece graced the formal dining room table. It was as if her grandmother would be walking in the front door at any moment.

Maybe that was the reason her grandmother's death hit her so hard. It had been so sudden. So unexpected. Her grandmother, Amelia Hamilton, had never been sick a day in her life. At seventy-five years old, she had been the picture of both mental and physical health. One day she had flown out to California for a four-week visit, and the next she had suffered a massive heart attack while shopping for Christmas presents at Macy's.

Olivia had never even gotten to say goodbye. The trip to bring her grandmother home to Misty Harbor had been an emotional drain on both her and her parents. The services, which were held yesterday morning at the local Methodist church and then again at the cemetery, had gone by in a blur. People, names, and faces had all tangled together as she had stared, huddled in her winter coat for warmth, at the bronze-colored casket under the weak December sun. Winter on the coast of Maine wasn't conducive to outdoor activities.

The only one who had stood out in her memory was her grandmother's best friend, Millicent Wyndham. Olivia hadn't seen Millicent in ten years, but the town's matriarch hadn't seemed to age one bit. Millicent and the Women's Guild from the church had organized what they called a "small luncheon" for after the funeral. The "small" get-together had well over a hundred people in attendance. Her grandmother had been loved and admired both in town and the surrounding community. Amelia's son, her father, had been greatly comforted by the support, but she had been in such a daze that nothing really registered but the simple fact her grandmother was gone.

After the luncheon, she and her parents had driven to Sullivan, a nearby town. They had an appointment with Amelia's lawyer, a Mr. Francis Haskel. Mr. Haskel turned out to be eighty-five years old, if a day, and tended to fall asleep during the lulls in the conversation. Amelia's will had been simple, and surprising.

Her grandmother had left her church a very generous gift. To her only son she had left all of her stocks and investments. The surprise had been that her grandmother had left the balance of her estate, including the house and all its furnishings, to her only grandchild, Olivia.

Olivia slowly sipped the hot tea as she glanced around the large kitchen. Her large kitchen. What in the world was she going to do with a large house on the coast of Maine, when she lived in sunny southern California? As a weekend retreat it was a bust.

The chiming of the doorbell interrupted her thoughts. Hopefully it wasn't another neighbor with more food. Thanks to Millicent and the Women's Guild, the refrigerator and freezer were already jam-packed with more food than she could eat in a month. She made her way to the front door, turning on some lights as she went. The dreary and wet afternoon had made the rooms look gloomy and depressing. The only good news was, it wasn't snowing. Yet. They were predicting snow by tomorrow night.

Olivia opened the front door without checking to see who it was first. She was in Misty Harbor now, not southern California. A bone-chilling wind whipped across the porch as she stared at the man before her. She didn't feel the wind or the chill. What she felt was a heated vibration in the pit of her stomach.

Her gaze traveled up from expensive loafers, over perfectly creased brown pants, to a buttery soft golden sweater. A well-worn brown leather Bomber jacket completed the relaxed yet stylish look. It was the man's face that captured and held her attention. A face she hadn't seen in ten years.

A stubborn chin, with just a hint of a five o'clock shadow, was exactly as she remembered it. He had worn his golden brown hair longer back then, but his nose still had the same cute little bump at the bridge of it from when he had fallen off his bicycle. His mouth looked as tempting as it had been all those summers ago. At sixteen, she had no idea what had been so tempting about it. Now, at twenty-six, she knew. His light brown eyes were different. Older, wiser, and they didn't hold the amusement or the annoyance they had had back then. Now they held a spark of interest. Male interest.

She softly smiled at the distant childhood memories of summers past. The gorgeous college boy had turned into one very sexy-looking man. "Ethan Wycliffe."

It might have been her imagination, but Ethan's gaze seemed to linger on her mouth a moment before he slowly smiled. "Ah, Summer Breeze, you remembered me."

She chuckled in delight when Ethan used the nickname he had given her when she had been about twelve. For the first time in days she felt like laughing. Her heart felt lighter. "Who would ever forget you, Ethan?" She refused to think about the fool she had made of herself all those years ago when she had ceaselessly followed him around town. Ethan had the distinct honor of being her first adolescent crush. "Come on in out of the cold." She moved aside and opened the door wider.

The enticing scent of his aftershave teased her senses as he walked past her and entered the house. She closed the door against the elements and asked, "Would you care for a cup of tea? The water's already hot."

"No, thank you. I don't want to impose." Ethan glanced around the house. "Where are your parents?"

She glanced at the grandfather's clock softly ticking away in the hallway. "I'd say somewhere over Utah about now. I drove them to the airport this morning."

"They left you alone here?" Ethan kept glancing down the hallway toward the kitchen as if he expected someone to join them any moment.

"I'm all grown up, in case you haven't noticed." Ethan sounded like he wanted to call child welfare and report her parents for abandoning a child to the wilds of Maine. "I've been living on my own for four years now. Ever since I graduated from college."

She tried not to laugh at the flush sweeping up his cheeks, but she knew her voice held amusement. Ten years was a long time to finally turn the tables on someone. "Heck, out there in California they even let me drive, drink beer if I want to, and vote."

Ethan's gaze drifted to the front of her old UCLA sweatshirt. "I noticed."

"Noticed what?" There were a lot of things she wouldn't mind Ethan noticing. Her baggy sweatshirt and ratty jeans weren't two of them. Leave it to her to change into her oldest clothes right before the sexiest boy, *no, make that the sexiest man,* in Misty Harbor paid her a visit. So much for first impressions.

"That you went to UCLA." Ethan leaned against the newel post of the formal staircase leading to the second floor. "Amelia told me you got your degree in 'those darn fancy machines.' I figure you know something about computers, or you're a Maytag repairman."

"My grandmom hated computers." She rapidly blinked away a fresh wave of tears. "She was missing some pieces to her good china set that she had gotten for a wedding present. While she was out in California, I was going to show her how to go on eBay and see if we could find her pattern and then bid on some of those missing pieces."

Ethan took a step closer. "I'm sorry, Olivia." His fingers grabbed ahold of her hand and gave it a gentle squeeze. "I came over to offer my condolences and to see if there was anything I could do. I didn't mean to make you cry."

"I'm not crying." She wiped the sleeve of her sweatshirt across her eyes. "My grandmother thought tears were a waste of precious time, and didn't solve a thing. A cup of tea was her remedy for whatever ailed you."

"If that offer for a cup of tea is still open, I think I would like one." Ethan looked at her with concern in his eyes.

"Of course you can have one." She led the way back toward the kitchen. "Take your coat off and stay awhile." She could use the company. The house was beginning to feel too big and lonely for one person. How did her grandmother stand it for all those years?

Ethan hung his jacket on the back of one of the chairs. "Do I get a splash of Amelia's secret ingredient?"

"What secret ingredient?" She had no idea what Ethan was talking about. As far as she knew, a cup of tea was a cup of tea.

"Sit." Ethan flashed her a smile and waved his hand at the chair she had been sitting in earlier. "I'll make you a fresh cup using Amelia's secret recipe."

Olivia sat and watched as Ethan bustled around the kitchen.

330 / Marcia Evanick

He seemed quite at home in her grandmother's kitchen. "I take it you've done this before?"

"I've watched Amelia make tea countless times over the years, but she never let me help." Ethan flashed her a sexy grin. "My specialty was lemonade." The grin slowly faded. "Amelia loved my lemonade."

Her grandmother used to mention Ethan once in a while over the years, but she had never known they were that close. "I take it you saw my grandmother a lot?"

"Nearly every day during the summer. Amelia was always puttering around in her garden." Ethan leaned against the counter. "Not as much in the colder months."

She knew Ethan's parents owned the house directly behind her grandmother's. There was even a wide wooden gate between the two properties. A gate that was never locked, and hardly ever closed. "You still live with your parents?" Ethan was thirty years old, and didn't seem the type to be living with mom and pop.

Ethan gave her an indignant glare before reaching for the whistling teakettle. "My parents live in Naples, Florida. They retired and moved there about six years ago. I bought their house."

"Now that you mention it, my grandmother did say something about your parents living in Florida." She had completely forgotten that piece of news. She watched as Ethan reached up into the cabinet above the refrigerator and pulled down a bottle of blackberry brandy. A half-filled bottle at that. "My grandmother drank?"

Ethan chuckled as he splashed a drop or two into the two cups of tea he had steeping. "Of course not. Amelia only touched the stuff during the winter months. She claimed it warmed her old bones."

"Hmmm, my father claims it puts hair on your chest."

Ethan glanced between the cups and her baggy sweatshirt. "Lord, I hope not."

She chuckled and relaxed into the chair. "So how are your parents? Your father still like to play golf?" From what she could remember, all Stan Wycliffe had ever talked about was playing golf. The Wycliffes even had a miniature putting green in their backyard which no one was allowed to walk on.

"He finally dragged my mother into the insanity." Ethan placed both cups of tea on the table and sat down. "They play golf nearly every day. My mom's parents are still living down there, so they are close by to keep an eye on them." Ethan took a sip of his tea. "I was just down there visiting for a few days. Got home too late last night to stop over, and this morning I had to check in at the gallery to make sure I still had a business. I'm sorry I missed the services yesterday."

That was why she didn't see Ethan at the church service or at the cemetery. Daze or no daze, she would have remembered seeing him there. "That explains it."

"Explains what?" Ethan's golden brown gaze never left her face.

"Your tan." She flashed him a big smile. "I've been trying to figure out how you got one, because I can't picture you lying in some tanning booth toasting your buns." Lying on some sandy beach with a bikini-clad woman, definitely. Artificial lighting, never. She glanced at his strong, neatly manicured fingers holding his cup of tea. Not a ring in sight. Which didn't mean a thing nowadays.

She was pretty sure her grandmother would have mentioned it if Ethan had gotten married.

Ethan flashed her a sexy grin that looked incredibly white in his deeply tanned face. "I can't recall ever toasting my buns, in or out of a tanning booth." He took another sip of tea. "My parents' condo not only has its own golf course, it has a dozen tennis courts, an indoor gym, and the biggest pool I have ever seen. The seniors have activities scheduled from early morning to late at night. Visiting them is like a trip to a spa." His grin grew wider and just a tad wicked. "My buns never saw the light of day at their poolside."

"That's a shame."

Ethan raised a brow at her comment.

"From what I remember of your buns, the sight of them would have given more than one senior citizen the thrill of her lifetime." She could still remember the sight of Ethan and about three of his friends skinny-dipping down at Sunset Cove one hot summer day. She had to have been around ten at the time and hadn't seen anything more than a quick flash of pale skin. The boys hadn't known that. All they had known was that they had been spied on by a bunch of giggling girls hiding in the bushes. Ethan hadn't looked her in the eye for the rest of that summer. He also had barred her from using his tree house.

"I was only fourteen at the time." A brilliant flush swept up Ethan's cheeks, turning his tan darker. "I was doubled-dared by Paul Burton. What was I supposed to do? Go through life being called a yellow-bellied sissy?"

"Absolutely not." Her smile was so wide her cheeks actually ached. "You did the right thing, and I thank you for the experience."

Ethan slowly lowered his cup. "I don't remember you being such a smart-ass."

Olivia's only response was a wide smile.

What he did remember of Olivia Hamilton hadn't been anything to write home about. Olivia had been all skinny arms and legs, a mouth full of metal braces, and a tangled mess of black curls she had called hair. Oh, and at sixteen, she had been totally flat-chested.

Ten years had turned the summer pest into one gorgeous woman. As much as the baggy sweatshirt tried to hide the fact, it couldn't conceal generously rounded breasts and a trim waist. Faded denim caressed every inch of her long shapely legs and hugged her curved bottom like a pair of desperate hands. Olivia was all grown up and he had nearly tripped over his own tongue when she had answered her grandmother's door moments before.

The college graduation picture, which Amelia had framed and was sitting on the mantel in the front parlor, didn't do Olivia justice. The black robe and black cap, with Olivia's black hair and pale face, all just washed one another out.

He hadn't even realized Olivia's eyes were blue. Let alone the same exact shade of the pale, light blue of the morning sky in July. The tangled mass of black knots that Amelia, on more than one occasion, had sworn bats had nested in, were now soft shoulder-length silken curls that made his fingers itch to touch one.

Ten years ago Olivia had followed him around town as if she were some loyal puppy and he had been the master. It had been embarrassing and he had suffered more than one teasing about his shadow. Truth be told, he hadn't minded too much. In a way he'd felt sorry for Olivia. He couldn't imagine what it must be like to travel halfway across the country to stay with one's grandmother every summer. Away from your parents. Away from all your friends.

Every summer Olivia blew into town with her California tan, the latest fashions, and the strangest vocabulary. Half the kids in town picked on her. The other half were envious. He hadn't been either. What he had been was protective of the young girl who had seemed to shadow his every move. Everyone in town knew whoever messed with Olivia would answer to him. Thankfully, he hadn't had to step in and act the "older brother" too often. There had been only one incident that he could remember with certainty. It had taken place out at Sunset Cove about a week before Olivia had returned to California the last summer she had visited.

He watched Olivia sip her tea and stare out the window. In the fading light of a weak December sun, Amelia's gardens looked depressing. He couldn't remember if Olivia had ever visited her grandmother during the winter. If she hadn't, the sight of the now-dormant gardens must be unsettling. During the summer months, Amelia's gardens were a riot of color and a thing of beauty.

"How come your parents went back to California, and you didn't?" He was curious as to why she had stayed.

"Dad and Mom both had to get back to work, and there really wasn't anything for them to do here." Olivia lowered her empty cup back to the saucer.

"You don't have to get back to work?"

Olivia gave a weak laugh. "I'm currently in between jobs. The computer industry has been hit hard, first by the bottom dropping out of the dot com business, and now with the recession. California in particular was hit hard."

"I heard." He had never been laid off himself, but he understood about struggling in a business. It had taken him two years before his art gallery could support him. Now, after five years, good years, he was ready to expand. "Anything look promising out there?"

"I was at an interview the morning my grandmother had her

heart attack." Olivia shrugged and blinked back a fresh wave of tears. "They told me I was overqualified for the job, so they weren't even going to offer it to me."

"Why not? You would think they'd snap you up in a hurry."

"They were smarter than that." Olivia gave him a crooked smile. "They knew that as soon as a better-paying job came along, one that I was qualified to do, I'd take it."

"So in the meanwhile you are unemployed?"

"True."

"So how long are you planning on staying in Maine?"

"I have no idea." Olivia glanced around the kitchen as if the answer would be written on the wall. "I guess as long as it takes."

He didn't like the sadness that was in Olivia's eyes or the fact that she was alone in this great big house. "How about I take you out to dinner? There's a great restaurant in town, Catch of the Day." He didn't add that it had been one of Amelia's favorite places to eat. He had been back in Misty Harbor only a day, and already he was missing the old gal.

"Thanks, but I have a better idea." Olivia stood up and walked over to the refrigerator. She swung open the door and said, "How about you stay here for dinner and help me eat some of this food?"

He stared in awe at the jam-packed shelves. He had never seen so much Tupperware, casserole dishes, and plastic wrap-covered bowls in his life. The Women's Guild had struck again.

Chapter Two

Olivia tugged her new hat down lower over her ears, and then grinned at her reflection in the plate-glass window of Krup's General Store. She looked twelve years old in her new fluffy purple knitted hat and the matching mittens. Krup's selection of outerwear had been dismal and uninspiring, so she had gone with warmth. The short stroll from her grandmother's house to the Main Street shopping district had all but frozen her ears off.

The cup of hot chocolate she had had at Krup's soda fountain counter had warmed her insides and brought back some wonderful memories. Many a summer afternoon she had sat at that same counter with her friend Carol Ann drinking cherry Cokes and discussing boys, fashion, makeup, and gorgeous movie stars.

Carol Ann Black had been one of those girls who at sixteen had more than filled out the bikini top her parents hadn't known she owned. Carol Ann had also smoked cigarettes, knew how to drive her boyfriend's stick-shift pickup truck, and had known all about French kissing and what everyone did up at "Lookout Point." If there was something going on in town, Carol Ann knew the who, what, and where of things.

Carol Ann had been a whole eleven months older than Olivia, and her idol, ten years ago. Next time she saw Ethan, she was going to ask if he knew whatever became of Carol Ann. If her friend was still in the area, she would like to get together to relive some old times and hear any current gossip going around. Especially if it concerned a certain art gallery owner.

Olivia swung her bag holding more recent purchases from

Krup's General Store as she window-shopped her way down Main Street. There wasn't much to see. The one thing that caught her eye was the mannequin in the window of Claire's Boutique. The plastic woman with the mop of blond curls was wearing the most wonderful black evening dress and shawl. It was the beaded and fringed black shawl that caught and held her attention. It would make a wonderful birthday gift for her mother, whose birthday was next week.

Twenty minutes later the brightly wrapped present was added to her bag as she left the shop. It had been a little more than what she had been planning on spending, considering her unemployed state. But once she was in the boutique, she couldn't pass it up. It was perfect for her mother.

Directly across the street was the store she had been looking for and the main reason she had braved the cold walk from her grandmother's house up on White Pine Street to Main Street. Ethan's Wycliffe Gallery looked just like she had pictured it last night when he had told her about it. She still couldn't get over the fact that Ethan owned his own gallery. An art gallery at that.

Ethan's gallery was one half of the single-story building. Bailey's Ice Cream Parlor and Emporium had the other half. Bailey's was closed for the season. Its pink and white striped awning, which shaded the couple of tables and chairs placed out on the sidewalk during the height of the tourist season, was neatly rolled away. The plate-glass window, with its fancy white-painted border and neatly printed words proclaiming for all the world to see that this was Bailey's, was dark and deserted looking. The bubble gum-pink front door with its oval glass was closed tightly against the winter wind and could definitely use a fresh coat of paint come spring.

Bailey's looked sad and neglected, while Ethan's gallery looked expensive and exclusive. She couldn't remember seeing such a mismatched pair of shops side by side.

She looked in both directions before crossing the street and headed for the gallery. She told herself that the slight hitch in her heart rate was due to the excitement of exploring the shop, not because she was going to see Ethan again. What woman didn't like to shop.

Ethan's half of the building was painted a brilliant white with deep burgundy trim. Glittering brass on the doorknob, the kick plate, and a reproduction of an antique lantern hanging by the door reflected the afternoon light. An iron bench, painted the same shade of burgundy, sat beneath the display window, encouraging tourists to sit a spell.

Olivia wasn't interested in sitting outside on a day like today, but she did stand in front of the window to check out what kind of merchandise Ethan sold. The gallery's window was smaller than Bailey's and bordered in elegant gold swirls. Dark green velvet material covered the display area, but there were only a few pieces of jewelry and some carelessly tossed gold ribbon lying on the velvet. It looked like Ethan was in the middle of rearranging the items and adding some holiday trimmings.

All of the stores on Main Street were already decked out for Christmas. Even the antique lantern-style streetlights had garlands wrapped around the posts and huge red and gold bows atop each light. Ethan was behind schedule, yet he had made time in his busy day yesterday to stop by and pay his respects. Ethan had also stayed for dinner and had helped dry the dishes. He had even insisted on walking through the house to make sure everything looked all right before leaving her alone in the big house.

Ethan was not only gorgeous, he was sweet and nice. Thirty years old, single and never married, owned his own home and business, and wasn't in a steady relationship. The way he had been checking out her body last night, there was no way he was gay. So what was Ethan's flaw? The man had to have one, and it must be a humdinger. Why else wasn't he married with at least a baby or two drooling on his broad shoulders and a minivan in the driveway?

She entered the shop and slowly looked around the gallery and then at the chaos surrounding Ethan. By the frazzled and dazed look upon his face, she was afraid she knew his flaw. Ethan Wycliffe was either a perfectionist, and the mess in the shop was getting to him, or he was one of the most disorganized persons she'd ever met.

Her money was on him being a perfectionist.

"Hi," she said as she made sure the door was securely closed against the blustering December wind. "Did I catch you at a bad time?"

"No, but you did catch me in a UPS nightmare." Ethan stood with his hands on his hips glaring at about three dozen boxes. The cartons were blocking just about everything in the store. "I can't believe that orders from six different suppliers arrived on the same day."

"When it rains, it pours." She stepped around a few boxes to study a stunning watercolor hanging on the far wall. The artist had done a wonderful job depicting Misty Harbor in full summer glory. The discrete price tag made her flinch. She could pay two months' rent on her apartment back in California for the asking price. "I see you are in the middle of decorating for Christmas."

An eight-foot tree took up a good portion of space toward the back of the front room. Through a wide opening she caught glimpses of a second display room. The pine tree was bare except for a halfway-strung string of white lights.

"Trying to decorate would be more accurate." Ethan piled two boxes on top of each other. "By the time I'm ready for Christmas, it will be January."

"I thought you said you had an assistant." She didn't see anyone else in the shop, and there weren't that many places a person could hide. The shop had two other doors. One, she could see, led out back. The other was behind the cash register area and was closed. It probably led to an office, a storage area, and a small powder room. The shop wasn't big enough for anything else. Ethan had been right last night. He definitely needed more room.

"I gave Karen a couple days off, so she can get her own home ready for the holidays. She did an outstanding job filling in for me while I was in Florida visiting my parents and grandparents. She has three school-age children, and hasn't even started her own Christmas shopping yet."

Ethan piled more boxes on top of each other so there was more room to walk around. "Who would have thought everything would come in on the same day?"

She lowered her bag to the floor and helped Ethan stack the boxes and move them off to the side. "How about if I help you unpack these or at least decorate your tree for you?"

"I can't ask you to do that."

"I'm not asking for a job or a paycheck, Ethan." She gently placed two smaller boxes, marked FRAGILE, on the counter so that they wouldn't get stepped on. "Since I'm not putting up a tree at my grandmother's place, I would like to help you with yours here. It will help me take my mind off of cleaning out my grandmother's things." Which was the main reason for the walk into town. She couldn't face packing up all of her grandmother's clothes for charity just yet. Heck, she couldn't even bring herself to borrow a pair of gloves or a scarf from the hall closet. Her fingers had lovingly smoothed out a wrinkle in the bright red scarf hanging on the back of her grandmother's closet door. But she couldn't bring herself to put it on.

Packing up her grandmother's belongings was going to be the hardest thing she had ever done. What was one more day? There wasn't any hurry.

Olivia dropped her newly purchased mittens and hat into her shopping bag and started to unbutton her coat. "Since you already have up half the lights, and they are the hardest part of decorating a tree, the rest should be easy. You just tell me what you want on it, and I'll try to do it."

"Are you sure?" Ethan glanced between her and the bare tree. "Karen usually does all the fancy decorating. She has a more 'feminine touch' than me. But Kevin didn't drop the tree off until yesterday afternoon. I set it up before coming over to Amelia's yesterday so the branches had a chance to fall."

"I'm not Martha Stewart, but I can hang a few balls and bows." She draped her coat over the doorknob to the office and rubbed her hands together in glee. "Just show me what goes on it, and what kind of look you are going for here."

Ethan reached over the cash register, and grabbed a torn-out page of a magazine. "I can do better than that. I'll show you." Ethan handed her the picture. "This is the look we are going for this year."

She glanced down at the picture and nearly choked. The twenty-five-foot full and bushy Scottish pine looked like it belonged in the White House. The gold room of the White House. There was no way that a normal dad, mom, and little Tiny Tim had decorated that tree. It would take a team of professional decorators a month, working seven days a week, twenty-hour days, to complete such a masterpiece. Ethan wanted her to do this to the Charlie Brown–looking twig in the corner?

She handed him back the picture. "No way could I do that, Ethan. The most I could guarantee you is that I would try not to put two of the same-colored balls next to each other."

Ethan chuckled and pushed the page back into her hand. "You already offered, and I accepted." He headed for the tree. "Come on, it won't be that hard. Karen has already purchased everything we need, and she made the bows. The rest of the stuff that goes on the tree is merchandise. Karen has already priced it. All you have to do is hang the stuff to its best advantage, and to make sure people can see the price tags without knocking anything off the branches."

She noticed boxes filled with handblown glass ornaments, hand-painted balls depicting everything from the harbor to Santa Claus, and intricate white lacy angels trimmed in what looked like real pearls. Another box held gold ribbon, gold beads, and several dozen gold bows. A gold satin tree skirt and a stack of brightly wrapped presents were nearby. Everything one would possibly need to do up a Christmas tree right.

"Okay, I'll try this, but I'm not promising anything spectacular." She picked up the string of lights and waved Ethan away. "Go do whatever you have to do with all those boxes. If I need your help, I'll holler."

An hour later Ethan had all of the boxes either stacked in the office, or in the tiny space behind the register. Four boxes had been unpacked and their contents inventoried, priced, and now displayed throughout the shop. He should have had twice as much done, but he had been too busy watching Olivia.

He enjoyed watching Olivia.

The woman was never still or quiet. Olivia sang off-key to the soft Christmas carols he had playing on the gallery's stereo system. She talked, whispered, and sometimes argued with the decorations and the tree. She bounced up and down the stepladder like the Energizer Bunny. He had even learned a new creative use for a common verb when it came slipping out of Olivia's mouth while she was untangling a massive knot in the string of gold beads.

All in all, it was one of the most pleasant afternoons he had ever spent in the shop. The tree wasn't looking too bad either.

He placed a green pottery bowl, with hand-painted holly leaves and berries, on the display shelf between two carved reindeer. There were another dozen or so pieces of the same design throughout the shop. Last year he had sold every piece of it and customers were already looking for it again this season. If he had a bigger place, he could keep it in stock throughout the year. As it was, the summer design of blue pottery with hand-painted blueberries on it had been taken off the shelves to make room for the winter holly design.

It had been after the Christmas season last year that he had decided he needed a bigger place. Finding just the right place was the problem. Marv Bailey wasn't interested in getting out of the ice cream business, so he couldn't expand the gallery. He needed a place either on Main Street or close enough that the tourists would find the gallery during the peak selling season. So far nothing suitable had come onto the market.

He stepped behind Olivia and smiled at the way she worried her lower lip with her teeth every time she placed a ball onto the tree. "Relax, Summer Breeze, it looks great. You're doing a fantastic job."

Olivia worried her lip more. "You think so? I only put up half the balls and glass ornaments and six angels. I didn't want to crowd the tree, or people won't be able to see the details. Plus I figured you need the spares to replace what people bought. Right?"

"Right." He pulled his gaze away from Olivia's tempting mouth. If anybody was going to be nibbling on that luscious lower lip, he wanted to be the one. "I've got some fancy boxes in the stockroom. We can fill them with colorful tissue paper and place some of the ornaments in there to display them." He headed for the office.

Two minutes later he stood in the middle of his shop and watched the enticing sway of Olivia's jean-clad bottom as she shimmied her way under the tree and tried to straighten out the satin tree skirt around the stand. He finally figured out what he wanted for Christmas. He wanted Olivia under his tree, and in roughly the same position. Now that was one present he would love to unwrap come Christmas morning.

"Ethan?"

"Yeah?" He wondered if she was stuck. He hoped so.

"Do you remember Carol Ann Black? She was about three years younger than you." Olivia wormed her way out from under the tree and started to arrange the brightly wrapped presents on the skirt.

"Sure I know Carol Ann. What about her?" Ethan handed her two more presents. Both boxes were empty, but Karen had done a superb job of wrapping them to make them look like a million bucks.

"Is she still in the area? I haven't seen her in ten years and I thought it would be nice to get together with her since I'm in town."

"She married Tom Burton right out of high school if I remember right."

"She's married?"

"And a mother."

"Carol Ann has a baby?"

"Last I saw her, she had three kids. The oldest boy must be around six. There's a girl a little younger than that, and a baby around a year or so." He remembered seeing Carol Ann pushing a stroller with a screaming baby inside down Main Street with a kid on either side of her. The little girl had her fingers jammed in her ears. He also remembered praying they wouldn't be coming into his shop. He liked children. Just not in his gallery.

Olivia sat on the floor and stared up at him. "She has three kids?"

"At least." By the look on Olivia's face, one might think he'd just told her that Carol Ann had delivered humpback whales instead of babies.

"I told her that French kissing would get her in trouble." Olivia chuckled as she shook her head, placed the last present just so, and stood up.

He tried to hide his smile. "I don't think it was the kissing, French or otherwise, that got her pregnant."

"No, but that's how it starts." Olivia shook her head. "Who did you say she married?"

"Tom Burton, Paul's younger brother."

"The skinny-dipping, double-daring Paul Burton?"

He refused to blush again at something that had happened

half a lifetime ago. So what if Olivia had seen him in the buff. A lady wouldn't have looked. "One and the same."

The sound of the front door opening interrupted whatever Olivia was about to say. By the sparkling gleam in her eye, he had a feeling it would have been some smart-ass comment.

"Go see to the customer, while I straighten up some more." Olivia carefully folded the stepladder and carried it back to the office.

He went to handle the customer.

By closing time he had unpacked another dozen or so boxes, and sold a painting, two pieces of pottery, and an amber and silver necklace. Olivia had finished the tree, placed all the spare ornaments out in the fancy boxes, and arranged the display window with mostly Christmas merchandise. He might have chosen to place one or two of the more expensive items in the window, but he would never have thought to hang a few of the ornaments from gold ribbon in the window.

Ethan made sure that the office light was off and that the back door was locked before joining Olivia near the front door. "I think I owe you dinner tonight for a job well done."

Olivia tugged on her new hat and mittens and picked up her shopping bag. "Nonsense, I enjoyed myself too much. I owe *you* dinner, and I still have a full refrigerator. Want to come over for more leftovers?"

If this were a normal night, he would go home, eat a solitary meal, and then come back to the shop to finish unpacking the shipment that had arrived today. Tonight wasn't normal, and he had just been invited to dinner by a very beautiful woman. He wasn't stupid. "I would love to join you for dinner." He ushered Olivia out front and locked the door. "Did you drive?"

"No, did you?" Olivia tugged her hat lower over her ears against the cold.

"Afraid not." He took the bag from Olivia, tucked her arm under his own, and hurried down the street. "I think we'll need a cup of tea with Amelia's secret recipe once we make it home."

Olivia used his body to block the wind. "Heck with the tea, just pour me a shot or two of the brandy."

He tried to pick up his pace, but he didn't want to leave Olivia behind. He shook her bag. "What did you buy today?"

"I found my mom a birthday present at Claire's." Olivia's breath was clouds of white fluff. "I also picked up this hat and mittens from Krup's, along with warmer pajamas and some socks."

"I like the hat and mittens." He thought she looked adorable in them. "What kind of pajamas?" They turned off Main Street and onto White Pine. He was trying to keep Olivia talking and her mind off the fact that her teeth were chattering so badly he was afraid she was going to damage the enamel. Thinking about Olivia's pajamas kept him warm.

"Warm ones." Olivia was taking two steps to his every one. "Long-sleeve, thick flannel ones."

He tripped over his own feet. "You sleep in flannel pajamas?" So much for his fantasies. He was picturing flowing gowns of gossamer silk or at least a very enticing oversized T-shirt and panties.

"I do when in Maine." Olivia moved closer to him as a snowflake landed on her nose. "In case you haven't realized it, it's darn cold up here."

He chuckled as he hurried her up her grandmother's walk and onto the porch. "This is nothing, Summer Breeze. You should be here during a nor'easter." He took her keys out of her mitten-covered hand, found the right one, and got her into the house before she hopped the next plane back to sunny southern California. "Maybe you don't have the heater set high enough."

"The radiators banged and clanged all night long. At one time I thought it was the ghost of Jacob Marley coming to visit." Olivia flipped on some lights.

He closed the door and peeked into the shopping bag. Amused, he pulled out a plastic-wrapped pair of red flannel pajamas with white polar bears and igloos printed all over them. A six-pack of men's thick over-the-calf white cotton socks was still in the bag. Eskimos slept in less. "You couldn't have been that cold."

"Make a bet?" Olivia glanced out the front parlor window to the streetlight beyond. "It's starting to snow. Maybe I should have bought two pairs of jammies and that thick robe. The navy blue one that was down to my ankles, made out of some bed-spread, and zipped up the front."

He glanced at the flakes and chuckled. "Those are only flurries. We aren't expecting more than an inch or two."

"Two inches of snow in southern Cal would cause major accidents and the freeways would be backed up for miles."

"This isn't southern Cal, Olivia. You're in Maine now. We don't even break out the snow shovels until at least half a foot has fallen."

"Oh, great," groaned Olivia. "I knew I should have bought that electric blanket back at Krup's. I'll never be warm again."

Chapter Three

"I think I see the problem already," said Ethan as he stepped into her bedroom. "Your bed is right up against the window. These old windows are pretty drafty and totally energy inefficient."

Olivia glanced at the twin bed with its pink billowy bedspread and half a dozen pillows. All the furniture in the room was white French provincial and a good twenty years old. Her grandmother had bought her the entire set when she was about five years old. At five, Olivia had felt like a princess anytime she came to visit. By sixteen she had hated it, but didn't have the heart to tell her grandmother.

Amelia had kept the room dusted and clean, but hadn't changed a thing in it for the past ten years. When she had first opened the door, it had been like entering a time warp to her past.

The pink rosebud wallpaper and pink lace curtains didn't help the decor. The room reminded Olivia of the time she gorged herself on sugary sweet pink cotton candy at a local fair, and the Pepto-Bismol she had consumed afterward. Not the best memories to be sleeping with every night.

"I guess I can move the bed to another wall." She glanced at the writing desk and chair. Her laptop and a stack of papers were spread out across the desk.

"Grab one end of the desk, and we'll do it now." Ethan moved the chair out of the way and picked up his end of the desk.

She unplugged the laptop and helped maneuver the desk away from the wall to make room for the bed. The bed was harder to move. The frilly bedspread kept getting caught in the wheels, and while the headboard was bolted to the frame, it was anything but sturdy. Ethan's chin got wacked twice in the process.

After the desk was in position under the window, Ethan rubbed his chin and asked, "Explain to me again why you are sleeping in this Disney nightmare instead of some other room. I happen to know there are three other perfectly good bedrooms in this house, and that doesn't include the attic."

She frowned at a few dust bunnies that skidded along the edges of the wooden floors. "I always slept in this room. This is my room. When I was five, my grandmom asked me what my favorite color was." She tossed one of the pillows, which had fallen during the move, back onto the bed. "I told her pink."

"Amelia probably did some psychological damage to you by making you sleep in this mess. It reminds me of Bailey's Ice Cream Parlor." Ethan pushed aside the curtain and glanced out into the night. "Didn't you have nightmares sleeping in that bed?"

"Nope. In the summer I used to open the curtains and the window wide and stare up at the stars. The Big Dipper was always above your house." Her bedroom window was directly across from Ethan's. The last couple of summers she had spent more time staring at his window than at the stars.

Ethan allowed the curtain to fall back into place. "Nice view."

"I liked it." She grinned. She knew Ethan had noticed the youthful crush she had had on him way back then. Only a complete idiot wouldn't have noticed the totally flat-chested girl with the mouth full of metal following him wherever he went.

She'd be heading back to California as soon as she figured out what to do with the house and her grandmother's things. A real estate agent was stopping by tomorrow morning to work up an appraisal. It seemed contemptible to sell her grandmother's house, but what else was she supposed to do with it? Her father didn't want it, and legally it was now hers to do with as she pleased.

What would really please her was to move the whole house to some southern California harbor town overlooking the Pacific Ocean instead of the Atlantic. But that wasn't going to happen. Three thousand miles was one hell of a commute.

The cash inheritance that came along with the house would be enough to pay for upkeep for a couple of years at the most. Then what? The simple truth was, she couldn't afford to keep it.

The house had to go.

But in the meanwhile, Ethan was still her neighbor, and while she couldn't say she still had a crush on him, she did think he was incredibly sexy. How many women got a chance to relive a ten-year-old crush?

"Olivia? Are you listening?" Ethan was kneeling next to the radiator on the far wall and looking at her strangely.

"What? I'm sorry, my mind must have been drifting. What did you say?" She had a sick feeling her cheeks matched the decor perfectly.

"I asked if your father turned the radiators up in all the rooms? Amelia probably didn't keep them all operating at full steam when there was no one staying here but her." Ethan felt the nickel-plated radiator with the palm of his hand. "It's warm, but not as hot as it should be."

"It's working." She touched the metal and was surprised it wasn't nearly as hot as the ones downstairs. "I heard it banging and clanging all night long."

Ethan turned the nozzle at the base of the radiator. "The valve was only opened a little bit. Enough for some warmth to come through, but not enough for actual heat." Ethan gave the nozzle another turn before standing up. "That should do it. You might want to think twice before wearing your hat and mittens to bed tonight."

She felt the radiator, and the warmth from only moments before was now decidedly more intense. "You did it." She gave Ethan what she hoped was a sexy grin. "How can I ever thank you?" It was a loaded question to ask a man whom you were alone with in a house, and in your bedroom. She knew what most men would say, but she was curious as to how Ethan would respond.

"You already fed me tonight, so that's thanks enough." Ethan headed for the doorway as if suddenly realizing how alone they were. "Plus you spent hours at the gallery helping me this afternoon. How would I ever sleep tonight knowing you were freezing in your bed and shaking the poor polar bears right off your pajamas?" Ethan stepped out into the hallway and headed for the stairs. "Did you want me to check the radiators in the other bedrooms?"

"No thanks. I'll turn them up when I start going through them to pack away my grandmother's stuff." She didn't even want to think about how long that was going to take, or what she was going to do with it all. Every room in the house was filled with antiques and sentimental items. She followed Ethan down the stairs and into the living room. The front parlor was for entertaining guests and more formal occasions. The living room was for relaxing, watching television, and enjoying a blazing fire on a cold winter's night.

Tonight it was cold, and Ethan had started a fire while she had warmed up dinner.

"Do you know what your father is planning to do with the house?" Ethan added another log to the burning pile. "Are he and your mother going to keep it as a vacation home? Maybe they will retire here."

"My grandmother didn't leave my father the house." Olivia curled up at one end of the sofa and watched the muscles bunch and release in Ethan's thigh as he stood. Tonight Ethan wore another pair of Dockers. This pair was charcoal gray, and the burgundy sweater he wore contrasted perfectly with them. She wondered if Ethan knew that he matched his gallery.

"She didn't?" Ethan seemed surprised. "I thought your father was an only child."

"He is." She hugged a needlepoint pillow against her chest. In a small town news would travel fast, and it wasn't as if it was some secret. Amelia Hamilton's last wishes would be known all over town in a matter of days anyway. "My grandmother left him all her stocks and investments. She left me the house and all its contents."

Ethan stared at her for a long moment before softly asking, "What are you planning on doing with it?" Ethan's gaze caressed her face. "Any chance that you'll be moving to Maine and keeping Krup's profit margin up by buying every pair of flannel pajamas in stock?"

For one insane minute she wanted to tell him yes, she would be staying and was thinking about a career change. How does lobster fisherman sound? Sanity prevailed as she remembered the résumé upstairs she had been trying to enhance and improve upon last night after Ethan had left. She was a California girl, born and bred. Her family was out there, and so was her career, once she found it again. Misty Harbor, Maine, needed a computer systems specialist like Palm Springs needed a lobster fisherman.

She gave Ethan a small forced smile as she shook her head. "I've got a real estate agent coming tomorrow morning to appraise the house and get it on the market."

"You're selling the house?"

"I can't take it back to California with me, Ethan." She could feel the tears once again pool in her eyes as she glared across the room at him. Didn't he realize how hard this was on her? "What do you want me to do with it? Let it sit here empty and abandoned?"

"I'm sorry, Olivia." Ethan sat on the other end of the couch and gave her a small smile. "It's your right to sell it. What else can you do?"

"Nothing." She turned her head and stared into the fireplace at the dancing orange and yellow flames. "Absolutely nothing."

Ethan stood in what was his old boyhood bedroom, but now was his office, and stared out into the night. Two inches of freshly fallen snow blanketed the ground and tree branches. Next door, Selma Moore had left her back porch light on again, and she was lighting the neighborhood. He had a perfect view of Olivia's dark bedroom window.

She had gone to bed about an hour ago.

He tried to ignore the heat and desire pumping through his veins. It was impossible. Even when he pictured Olivia in those oversized flannel pajamas with goofy-looking polar bears all over them, thick white socks, and an afghan wrapped around her shoulders, she was still the most desirable woman he had ever seen. How could ten years change a person so much?

A sixteen-year-old Olivia had been a royal pain in the ass.

Every summer, since he turned sixteen, he had taken a job down at the docks or worked for one of the local fishermen. He knew by the time he was seventeen that making his living on the sea wasn't the life for him. Today, the smell of ripe bait could still make him gag. His father had called it character building. He had called it torture. Looking back on those summers, he really hadn't had it that bad. Most of the fishermen worked hard, but they also knew how to play hard.

For his twenty-first birthday, a group of the older fishermen had taken him out to The One-Eyed Squid and had gotten him stinking drunk. His mother still hadn't forgiven Abraham Martin or his cronies for, as she liked to put it, corrupting her boy. His father hadn't said too much about it, but he had been the one to wake his son's sorry butt up at the crack of dawn the next morning, and send him off to work. He could still remember the gleam of laughter in his father's eyes that morning.

Nearly every day Olivia, usually with Carol Ann in tow, had shown up at the docks. Carol Ann had been one of those girls who just naturally flirted with every boy. Olivia had been shy and barely said a word to anyone. He had known why Olivia had been there. Anyone with eyes in their head could see the girl had a severe case of puppy love. It had been painful to watch, but he hadn't once encouraged her.

Ten years later, and he was afraid he'd be the one who started following her all around town.

For all the good it would do him. Olivia was going back to California just as soon as she handled her grandmother's estate. She had been very clear about that fact. There could be no future between them. She was bikinis and palm trees, and he was blazing fires and thick cable-knit sweaters.

He studied the shadowy outline of what was now Olivia's house. In the light of day he knew the large, spacious house had clapboard siding that was painted yellow with white trim. The shutters, the front door, and the decking of the porch were all painted a soft green. From the second-floor balcony, off the master bedroom, there was an unobstructed view of the harbor. A white picket fence and large gardens surrounded the entire property.

It was a wonderful house, and if his memory served him right, it had been built by one of Olivia's distant ancestors. It was a real shame that it was now going to be sold out of the family. But Olivia was right. What else could she do? Seeing the graceful old lady fall into disrepair as it sat neglected year after year with only the occasional visit would be heartbreaking.

Who would tend Amelia's wonderful gardens? Who would

give Ethan beautiful bouquets of freshly cut flowers in exchange for tall glasses of his famous lemonade? Whom was he going to sip tea laced with blackberry brandy with on those long cold winter nights? Amelia was gone, and soon Olivia would head back to sunny California.

But the house would remain. Amelia's wonderful house that was only a short distance away from Main Street and what constituted Misty Harbor's shopping district. Tourists would surely find it easily. It was as close to perfect as he was likely to find.

Amelia's house was bigger than what he had been looking for, but with all the woodwork and character of the home he wouldn't want to overcrowd the rooms. He could even carry a few antique pieces of furniture and still have plenty of room left over for his usual stock. Karl James, a local artist who worked mainly in wood, wanted him to carry some of his larger pieces. At the current gallery it would be impossible. Some of Karl's work was massive. Amelia's yard and wide porches would make perfect display areas for work not only by Karl but by other artists as well.

It would be the perfect solution to his gallery problem. Now if only he could figure out what to do about Olivia and the attraction he felt growing between them.

"So, how was your day?" Ethan asked as he set a match to the kindling in Olivia's fireplace. He had been held up at the gallery for longer than he had expected. Twice during the day he had tried to reach Olivia by phone. She hadn't answered either time. Now, it was way past the dinner hour and he wasn't even sure if she had eaten yet. He had stopped by her house on his way home from work just to check on her. Olivia looked depressed as all hell.

"Horrible." Olivia cradled a cup of steaming coffee in her hands as she sat curled up on the couch.

"Didn't the real estate agent show up?"

"He was here about ten o'clock." Olivia took a sip of the coffee. "He practically drooled all over everything in the house and handed me two different business cards of antique dealers. He also told me the house wouldn't be on the market long, considering its location and condition."

"That's good news, right? So what's the problem?" He

brushed off his hands and joined her on the sofa. "I thought that would make you happy."

"After he left, I took a drive into Bangor." Olivia set the cup on the table next to her. "I figured if I could commute to Bangor, where I just might be able to get a job in my field, I could stay here and keep the house."

Last night he had lain in his lonely bed and thought of ways to turn the house into a gallery and what was the top amount he could afford to spend on the transformation. He also had spent a ridiculous amount of time thinking about Olivia and the attraction he felt for her. Right at this moment he would give up the possibility of buying the house if Olivia would stay in Misty Harbor. He wanted to spend time getting to know her better. There was something there between them, he just knew it. Every time he looked into Olivia's eyes, he saw his future. Strange, he had never once believed in love at first sight or any such nonsense. Besides, he had known Olivia since she was two and his parents made him share his sandbox with Amelia's granddaughter.

"What happened?" Downtown Bangor was over an hour away on clear roads, sunny days, and with perfect traffic conditions. He would hate to know how long it had taken Olivia to drive into the city on a miserable day like today.

"I can't drive in snow." Olivia's sky blue eyes filled with tears. "It's not in my genes or something." With a couple of rapid blinks, the tears were gone. "I did pretty well until around Ellsworth. They got a lot more snow than we did, and it got worse the closer I got to Bangor. I slipped and slid all over the place. The front end of the car went one way, the back another, and the steering wheel another. The slower I went, the more people blew their horns." Olivia gave him a watery smile. "Some old man, who had to be around ninety, yelled at me and asked me if I got my license in a Cracker Jack box."

He tried not to laugh. He really did. It was impossible. "You never drove in snow before?" Instead of questioning Olivia, he should be counting his blessings that she hadn't been in an accident.

"Never even tried until today. The few times I've been skiing, either my father or friends had been behind the wheel." Olivia rubbed her hands together as if remembering how hard she had gripped the steering wheel. "An hour commute out in California isn't unreasonable. Out there you have to put up with rain, smog, and twenty miles of bumper to bumper traffic. Today I had drifting snow, ice patches the size of Iowa, and fifty-mile-an-hour wind gusts blowing me all over the road. I didn't need my grandmother's Chrysler, I needed a Hummer or a tank."

"Commuting to Bangor every day isn't for the faint of heart, Olivia. I wouldn't even do it."

"Because from November to April the weather sucks, and blizzards have been known to swallow whole anything smaller than a Mack truck?"

"It's not quite that bad, but the winter months are hard. The summer months, with the rubber-necking tourists clogging every coast road, aren't much better."

"Forget it. It was just some lamebrain idea I had." Olivia pressed her cheek against the back of the couch and stared at him.

She looked so sad that he wanted to pull her into his arms and give her a big hug. "Did the real estate guy give you a fair market value?"

Olivia gave him the price.

He ran some quick calculations through his mind. If he nixed any major improvements for a year or so, it was doable. The decision had been made late last night so it was senseless to run any more figures. "I'll take it."

"Take what?"

"The house." He glanced around the living room and grinned at the confused look upon her face. "I'll buy Amelia's house for the fair market value."

"You want to live in my grandmother's house?"

"No, but this house would make a perfect gallery." Ethan stood up and paced around the couch. He could see into the foyer, the front parlor, and the formal dining room. "I told you I've been looking for a bigger place. This is as close to perfect as I can get." He glanced up the stairs and visualized framed artwork going the whole way up. "What do you say?"

"You'll pay the asking price? No haggling?"

"I wouldn't dream of haggling." He hadn't been expecting any discounts for being Amelia's neighbor.

Olivia shrugged her shoulders. "Okay, it's yours."

"Really?"

"Really." Olivia gave him a small smile. "It saves me the aggravation of cleaning it and showing it constantly until it does sell."

"Good." He stopped in front of her and pulled her up into his arms. "Now that that is settled, I can do what I've been dying to do for the past two days." He lowered his mouth and kissed her.

Olivia melted into the warmth of Ethan's arms and the tenderness of his kiss. Her arms encircled his neck and she pressed herself closer. Ethan kissed like she always knew he would. Ethan kissed like a dream. A hot erotic dream.

One of them moaned. She was pretty sure it had been Ethan, but it could have been her. Ethan's hands pulled her closer as he deepened the kiss. Her teeth nibbled on his lower lip. His tongue outlined her upper lip before slipping past it to explore her mouth.

For the first time in hours she wasn't cold. The harrowing drive home from Bangor was forgotten. She felt safe, warm and incredibly sexy. She was coming apart in Ethan Wycliffe's arms. The sixteen-year-old girl inside her cheered. The woman she was today wanted more.

More than she had the right to want. She didn't make love with a man just because he was handsome and willing. The bulge in Ethan's pants pressing against her hip told her how willing he was. There had to be more, way more.

It didn't matter how much she wanted to take their relationship to the next step, it wasn't going to happen. She'd be heading back to California soon enough. With Ethan buying the house, it would be sooner, rather than later.

With a slow lingering caress of her mouth, she broke the kiss. She couldn't tell which one of them was breathing the hardest. Ethan's golden eyes were dark and hungry as they searched her face. She was afraid if she looked into a mirror the same desire would be reflected back at her.

She stepped out of his arms and tried to appear confident and sophisticated. It was impossible to achieve, considering Ethan had just rocked her world. "I don't do casual sex, Ethan." Her fingers trembled as they brushed a wayward curl out of her eye. "I'll be leaving Misty Harbor soon. Maybe it would be a good idea if you went home now." It wasn't that she didn't trust Ethan. She didn't trust herself.

The pad of Ethan's thumb traced her lower lip. "I'll leave now, because you asked." He brushed a quick kiss across her mouth. "Lock up tight after I'm gone." Ethan picked up his jacket, which he'd tossed over the newel post half an hour ago. "And, Olivia?"

"Yes?"

"When we make love, there will be nothing casual about it."

She listened to the front door softly close behind Ethan. Heat still pooled low in her gut and her breasts still ached for his touch. Ethan hadn't said "if we make love"; he had said "when." The man had seemed quite confident and sure of himself and of her.

Considering the way she had kissed him, she didn't blame him one bit.

There had been nothing casual in their first kiss.

Chapter Four

"Tell me again why I'm doing this." Olivia looked at Ethan, who was busy setting the table in the large kitchen. Ethan was setting places for seven.

"Because you wanted to see Carol Ann again, and were curious about her husband and kids." Ethan aligned the forks perfectly with the knives. "When she invited you to dinner, you decided it would be easier if you, not Carol Ann, cooked for everyone."

Olivia glanced in the oven at the meat loaf baking away. The potatoes were ready for mashing, two different vegetables were in the microwave, and the rolls were ready to slip into the oven. Carol Ann and her family were due to arrive at any minute. "You didn't hear the baby screaming in the background. There was no way I could have let her cook me dinner." She still shuddered remembering that constant screaming and yelling. Carol Ann probably hadn't had a good home-cooked meal in months. She frowned at the bowl of freshly made salad. Ethan had been the one to cut up the tomatoes and cucumbers. "Do you think they will like meat loaf?"

"What did Carol Ann say about it?"

She chuckled. "She said the 'monsters' would eat anything, and that Tom would probably bow down and kiss my feet if I served him a meal that hadn't come from a box."

"I think meat loaf will be fine, Olivia. Stop worrying. I don't think Carol Ann has changed that much over the years."

"She's married with three kids! How could she not change?"

She had been so worried that when Carol Ann and her family showed up tonight, she would have nothing in common with them. Or that she and Carol Ann would pick up just where they had left off ten years ago, and then Tom would be left out of the conversation. She had gone grocery shopping, and then stopped at Ethan's gallery to invite him to her first, and probably her last, dinner party in Misty Harbor. "Tell me again about Tom Burton. Which one was he?" She remembered different boys from back then, but she couldn't place Tom.

"Tom's a diesel mechanic, and a darn good one from what I hear." Ethan leaned his hip against the counter and smiled. "He was always down at the docks, usually showing off for Carol Ann. He was the one with dark brown hair and he never had his shirt on."

"What's with those Burton boys? Paul couldn't keep his pants on, and Tom had problems with his shirts." She picked up the masher and started to pound on the potatoes. "I remember him now. He always had a tan and real white teeth. His shorts hung so low on his hips that Carol Ann and I used to bet cherry Cokes about when they would fall down." She laughed at the memory. "Carol Ann bought me a lot of cherry Cokes that summer."

"Which way were you betting?" Ethan didn't look amused by the story.

She was saved from answering as the doorbell rang. All of a sudden she was nervous. "They're here." She looked down at the half-mashed potatoes. "I'm not ready yet."

Ethan gently took the masher out of her hands. "Go answer the door, while I finish pulverizing these."

"Really?"

Ethan's mouth tenderly brushed her lips in a kiss so soft and quick that she might have imagined it if she hadn't felt the heat.

"Go." Ethan gently pushed her toward the hall. "Let the party begin."

Two and a half hours later Olivia glanced over at Carol Ann and cracked up laughing. She couldn't tell if the laughter was because she was so darn happy to see Carol Ann again, or because she had drunk a little more wine than she was used to. It didn't matter—she was sitting in the living room with her best friend from her childhood, reliving the past.

A good past, filled with marvelous memories of great people and a wonderful town. Memories filled with her grandmother's love. She hadn't realized how much she had missed Maine until now.

"What's so funny?" Carol Ann sipped her wine and sank deeper into the couch.

"You. I can't believe you have gotten married, have three adorable children, and you are still the same Carol Ann I remember." She took another sip of wine and put her feet up on the coffee table. She wasn't driving anywhere. Neither was Carol Ann. Tom had taken the kids home about half an hour ago, giving his wife time to catch up with her friend. Ethan had left shortly thereafter. "What I want to know is how Tom puts up with you."

"Tom puts up with me? Shouldn't that be the other way around? The man is constantly in a great mood. The blasted man wakes up happy, even when I make him get up with Devin in the middle of the night. Nothing fazes Tom. You should have seen his face when I told him I was pregnant with Elizabeth. Samuel wasn't even a year old and we had decided to wait a few years before having our second child. I was ready to slice my throat because Samuel was a colicky baby, and there's Tom grinning like a fool and calling everyone he knew."

Olivia smiled at the thought of having a husband one day that would be that devoted. "Tom's so sweet." She raised her glass and toasted Carol Ann. "You caught a good one there." She took another sip and mentally reminded herself to congratulate Ethan on choosing such a great wine. "Most men would never have taken the kids home to get them ready for bed, and left you here."

"Most of the time I swear Tom handles the kids better than I do." Carol Ann finished off her glass of wine. "With Sam in school all day and Elizabeth Claire in kindergarten, I have to admit, life is getting more manageable. But Devin is a handful. He's what his doctor calls a 'verbal' baby. Devin loves to hear himself talk, scream, babble, and sometimes just cry. When he was first born, I was in the doctor's office every week swearing there must be something wrong with him. Turns out he's physically fine. Tom says he'll probably end up being the lead singer in some heavy metal band."

"And this doesn't bother you?" She silently laughed at the image of Carol Ann and Tom in some mosh pit at age fifty cheering on their son.

"As long as he doesn't practice in our garage, I wouldn't care." Carol Ann gave her a look that said she was about to get serious. "I might have stayed the same, but you've changed." Carol Ann's mouth turned up into a teasing smile. "For the better."

"Hey, what was wrong with the way I was?" There had been a lot wrong with her ten years ago, but she didn't think Carol Ann had cared if her friend had been flat-chested and had more metal in her mouth than most refrigerators.

"Nothing was wrong, you're just different now." Carol Ann picked up the wine bottle they had brought into the living room with them, and divided the rest of the wine between their two glasses.

"How?" Olivia wasn't sure, but she thought that might have been the third bottle of wine they had polished off. Of course, the guys had helped during dinner.

"You're not as shy as you were." Carol Ann toyed with her glass. "You're more self-confident. You grew into your beauty."

"You mean I finally grew boobs." She glanced down at the sweater she was wearing and grinned at her chest.

"Oh, Ethan definitely noticed them, and Tom noticed too. Of course, he would never admit it, because he knows I would have to hurt him then." Carol Ann's stockinged feet were resting on the coffee table, and she was staring into the dying fire. "Ethan's fire is going down."

Olivia gave a misty smile at the slowly dying embers. "He always makes one for me. Isn't that sweet?"

"Yeah, sweet." Carol Ann glanced at the glass in Olivia's hand. "So, what's the story with you and our local art gallery owner?"

"No story."

"You still got a crush on him, or are you just toying with his affections?"

"I'm not toying with his anything." She waved her hand in the air and chuckled when she realized how wrong that had sounded. "He's buying the house from me."

"So I heard over dinner. Something about turning it into a gallery and enlarging his business." Carol Ann gave her an amused look. "I couldn't help but notice the lip lock he put on you before he headed home for the night." The wine in her glass sloshed around as she set the glass back on the table. "It's awfully convenient him living directly behind you. He could come and go at all hours of the night, and no one in town would even know it."

Olivia snorted. "Selma Moore would. That woman is up all hours of the night. Her back porch light is always lit, but I never see her dog."

"Selma doesn't have a dog, Olivia. The woman is eighty-seven and goes to bed by eight every night." Carol Ann shook her head. "She probably just forgets to turn the light off, that's all."

"Her electric bill must be outrageous." She shook her head and wondered how the dear sweet woman could afford it. "Someone should tell her."

"Tom's mother knows her daughter. I'll tell her tomorrow, and maybe they can either take the lightbulb out of the porch light, or put the switch on a timer." Carol Ann brushed her hair away from her face. "So you still haven't told me what's going on between you and Ethan."

"Nothing, nada, zip."

"Why not?"

"I live in California, and will be heading there as soon as the lawyers and the real estate people get their heads out of their butts and figure out how and when Ethan can close on this place."

"So there is a boyfriend back in sunny California waiting for you."

"No boyfriend, no fiancé, no husband." She stared at her glass and wondered if perhaps she hadn't had enough. She was starting to depress herself. "There's no one there but my parents and some real good friends."

"You've got friends here." Carol Ann opened her arms and said, "What am I, chopped liver?"

She laughed at the absurdity of it. Carol Ann was chopped

liver the day Olivia Hamilton became a glamour queen. "Lord, I have missed you."

"Ditto. We should have stayed in touch. Once in a while when I ran into your grandmother, I asked about you and what you were up to."

"You did?" She remembered Ethan saying about the same thing. "Ethan asked too."

"So what are you going to do about Mister Gorgeous Gallery Owner?" Carol Ann stood up and stretched. "I might be an old married woman, but I know there was more than just meat loaf cooking in that kitchen, Olivia."

"I'm not into casual sex." She stood up and swayed for a moment before catching her balance. "Ethan says there will be nothing casual about it."

Carol Ann started to choke or laugh; it was hard to tell which. "And you let him walk out of this house after a comment like that?"

"What was I supposed to do? Invite him upstairs?"

"Hell yes." Carol Ann shook her head. "Aren't you curious to see where all those sparks you two shot off each other can lead to? You're a grown woman. He's a grown man. There's no one back in California waiting for you. And I'm pretty sure he's not seeing anyone from around here. So what's stopping you?"

At one time Carol Ann had known all of her secrets. They had shared everything, from their fears to their desires. Even though they were as different as night and day in some ways, deep down inside they had been the same. There had been nothing but truth between them. In a rush of fear, Olivia blurted out the truth. "I don't want to be hurt."

Carol Ann gave her a big hug. "You can do nothing, go back to California and not be hurt, but you would never know the 'might-have-beens.' Or you could take what time you have left here and explore a couple of those possibilities. I'm not saying to jump his bones the next time he comes over"—Carol Ann wiggled her eyebrows—"even though I can think of worse ways to spend an evening together."

Olivia walked Carol Ann out into the foyer. "They are such nice bones too."

Carol Ann chuckled as she stepped into her shoes and pulled on her coat. "I'm not blind. I noticed."

Olivia stepped into her shoes and started to lace them up. "I'll tell Tom on you."

"He won't believe you because I'll be too busy jumping his bones." Carol Ann frowned at her. "Where do you think you're going?" She pulled on her hat and gloves.

Olivia pulled on her own coat, buttoned it way up, and then tugged on her purple knit hat and mittens. "I'm not letting you walk home alone."

"It's only two streets over. I think I can find my own house."

"Never doubted that you couldn't." She picked up the key to the front door and stepped out on the porch. "We always walked each other halfway home. Why stop now?"

"Because you're half drunk." Carol Ann chuckled as she stepped off the porch.

"Fresh air will cure that, and I'm not that drunk that I wouldn't be able to find my way home again." They started to walk down the middle of the street. For only being nine-thirty at night, the streets were empty of traffic. The residents of Misty Harbor were all tucked in their warm little houses. The cold night air felt crisp and fresh. "There's no smog in Maine."

"Can't say that there is." Carol Ann turned right onto Main Street. "Did I thank you for a wonderful dinner? You didn't have to go through all that trouble of baking cupcakes for the kids. But they were so cute, with those snowmen faces on them."

"It was only meat loaf, and I enjoyed decorating the cupcakes." She had packed up the remaining treats and sent them home with Tom and the kids earlier. The alcohol haze in her brain was starting to clear. "And your kids aren't monsters. They were adorable and polite."

"I know, but in our house 'monster' is a term of endearment." Carol Ann stopped and glanced down Main Street. All the antique lantern lampposts were lit and decorated for Christmas. The display windows in all the shops were lit and cast a warm golden glow over the sidewalks. Snow blanketed roofs, lawns, and the occasional spot where the snowplows or shovels hadn't reached. "It's beautiful, isn't it?"

"I used to think it was as near to perfect during the summer months. Now, I'm not too sure. Winter here has its own charm."

Carol Ann turned up Ethan's street. "Come on, I know a shortcut."

Olivia followed her up the street and smiled at the houses all decorated for Christmas. Multicolored lights were strung everywhere. Lit icicles hung from eaves of houses. Plastic Santas, complete with sleigh and reindeer, were perched on rooftops. She loved the decorations, but she hadn't bothered to put any up at her grandmother's. The wreath her grandmother had hung on the front door before coming to California was the only exterior ornament. She wanted to cry at the thought of that lonely wreath.

"This is where I leave you, Liv." Carol Ann gave her another hug. "We need to get together again before you leave. Maybe do some Christmas shopping or stop in at Krup's for a cherry Coke or two."

"Definitely." It had been great seeing Carol Ann and her family. Her friend had made her laugh and cry and brought back all those wonderful memories.

Carol Ann pointed to Ethan's house, up the street. "Ethan won't mind if you cut through his yard. Then you'll be home safe and sound."

"Where are you going?"

"Through old man Thompkins's yard. I live right behind him, and he never minds when the kids use his yard as a soccer field. I just have to outrun his stupid dog, Salisbury, and I'll be home free."

"His dog?" She didn't like the sound of that. "What kind of dog?"

"A little one, don't worry." Carol Ann gave her another hug, hurried across old man Thompkins's front yard, and then disappeared around the side of the big dark house.

Olivia stood there in the middle of the street wondering what she should do now. Should she go check on Carol Ann or just head home? A vicious high-pitched barking emerged from the back of the house Carol Ann had just disappeared around. She heard her friend yell something that suspiciously sounded like, "Oh shit," and the barking grew more frenzied.

The little dog sounded like it was going to have a heart attack or at least bite Carol Ann's leg off. Lights in a few of the surrounding houses went on, and she could tell that a couple of back patio lights were flipped on as well. She hurried across the front yard and moved closer to the side yard that Carol Ann had disappeared around.

A moment later, while she was looking for a big stick, she heard Tom's voice yelling at Salisbury to be quiet before he woke the kids. Then Tom was yelling at a giggling Carol Ann. She could tell that Tom wasn't angry at his wife, and in the middle of his tirade his words stopped suddenly. A moment later she heard Tom curse and say, "Let's go inside before someone sees you and we'll get arrested for indecent exposure."

Carol Ann's laughter was probably waking up the kids and half the neighborhood. A moment later a door slammed somewhere and the barking stopped. Quiet filled the neighborhood once again.

Amused, yet encouraged that her friend had found what she had been looking for right in her own hometown, Olivia wondered if she should just head home the way they had come, or should she cut through Ethan's yard. Ethan didn't have a dog, but he had something much more dangerous.

She was afraid that Ethan had the power not only to turn her world upside down. Ethan held the power to hurt her like she had never been hurt before.

Chapter Five

Ethan jotted down another idea on the yellow legal pad in his lap. The ten o'clock evening news had just started, but he wasn't paying it any attention. He had more important things to concentrate on, like the expansion of his gallery. Watching Carol Ann's kids enjoy their snowmen cupcakes earlier tonight in Olivia's kitchen had given him another idea.

He could open up a tearoom in the large kitchen. The kitchen was big enough to hold a couple of small tables and chairs. Amelia's slate patio had room for quite a few more tables, possibly with umbrellas for shade. Customers could enjoy a tall glass of something cold to drink and fancy little cookies, or some other delicacy, while enjoying the gardens and some discretely tagged exterior merchandise. Winter months there would be plenty of coffee, hot chocolate, and cinnamon tea served in the toasty warm kitchen.

The more he thought about it, the more he liked the idea. Of course, that meant hiring some additional help, but he would be needing to do that anyway if he increased the size of the gallery. It would give potential customers another reason to step into his shop.

The ringing of the doorbell pulled him away from his latest brainstorming. Who could that be at this time of night? He wasn't expecting anyone. He put the pad and pen down and went to answer the door.

He opened the door and felt his heart rate kick up a beat or two. Olivia, bundled up against the cold, stood on his doorstep.

"Hi, is something wrong?" He stepped back and allowed her to enter his home. "Where's Carol Ann?"

"I just walked her halfway home." Olivia glanced around the foyer with interest. "I was going to cut through your yard, but I decided to stop in and say hello first." Olivia stepped into the living room. "Am I disturbing you?"

Under his breath he answered, "More than you would ever guess."

"What was that?" Olivia tugged off her hat and mittens and started to unbutton her coat.

He noticed that Olivia wasn't quite walking right. She was listing to the side. Olivia and Carol Ann had obviously celebrated their reunion in style. Adorably cute Summer Breeze was drunk. "I said no, you didn't disturb me. I was just writing down some ideas, that's all."

"And watching the news." Olivia frowned at the television screen, which was showing some perky weather girl pointing out the smiling-faced clouds blowing wind across the entire state of Maine. A few fancy snowflakes dotted the shoreline. She pointed at the screen and demanded, "Does that mean *more* snow?"

Considering that the grass was still peeking up through the snow on his front lawn, he didn't want to see how Olivia would act when a full-blown nor'easter hit. "That means flurries. Probably won't amount to much."

"What's your not much?"

"An inch or two." He wondered if she realized how cute she looked with her black curls all over the place and the flush of cold brightening her cheeks. Or the way her blue eyes sparkled like precious gems. Olivia was pure temptation. "Did you and Carol Ann open that last bottle of wine?" Maybe buying three bottles of wine hadn't been that good of an idea. The second bottle of wine had been half empty when he had left.

Olivia gave him a lopsided smile as she tossed her coat onto the recliner he had been sitting in earlier. "Did you know that you have excellent taste in wine?" Olivia sat down on the couch and flashed him a come-hither look that heated his blood.

"You finished that third bottle, didn't you." He couldn't tell how tipsy she was. Olivia wasn't falling-down drunk, but that didn't mean she was in her right mind.

"Carol Ann poured it about the same time she was advising me to explore the possibilities." Olivia glanced around the large living room and smiled. "I like your house. You changed it from when I was here last."

"My parents liked everything dark. Dark paneling, dark carpet, dark furniture. I prefer something lighter." During the six years he had owned the house, every room had gone through a total transformation, except for the guest bedroom. He kept that the way his parents liked it, because they were the ones who used it the most. He knew he shouldn't ask, but he was curious. "What possibilities were you and Carol Ann talking about?" *Was there a chance that Olivia was thinking about staying in Misty Harbor?*

"About all the possibilities life throws at us, and then how we choose which one to go for." Olivia nodded toward the fireplace, where a low-burning fire was glowing. "You have a thing for fires, don't you? Every time you come over to my place, you light one."

"I'm a winter-type guy. I like to relax in the evening in front of a fire, especially if snow is falling."

"I'm a summer person. I love lazy days swimming, sunning, and eating ice cream. I even like to putter around in a garden." Olivia gave him a strange sad look. "We're total opposites, aren't we?"

"That's one way to look at it." He had to wonder if it was true that opposites did attract. "Or we could have complementary personalities. You know, like on a color wheel, the complete opposite is a complementary color." He liked that theory better.

"I never thought of it that way." Olivia grinned. "It must be the artist in you."

"I'm no artist." He chuckled at the memory of all the art courses he had taken over the years. He had passed every one of them, but not because he had any talent. His grades had reflected his effort. He had tried like hell to be something he wasn't. He had tried his hand at painting, sculpturing, pottery, animation, and even a course in stained glass. He had been mediocre at best. The only hobby he enjoyed and still did was photography. He didn't possess the talent to make it in the art world, but he could take a decent picture. "You know the old saying, those who can't, teach? Well, in the art world there's a saying, those who have no talent, sell it."

"That's a little harsh."

"But true." He liked the fact that Olivia was trying to stick up for him. "I might not be able to draw or paint, but I know a great painting when I see one. I can spot talent a mile away. Most artists prefer to be left alone to do their craft. They know virtually nothing on how to sell it, price it, or even where to find the customers. Their only concern is to make enough money to barely get by and to buy more supplies so they can go on to their next project."

"That's where you come in, right?"

"Right." Olivia didn't seem so tipsy now, but there still was no way tonight would be ending the way he wanted it to end. With Olivia in his bed. He had never taken advantage of a woman in his life, and he wasn't about to start with Summer Breeze. "Come on, I'll walk you home."

"Now? Don't I get a tour of your home?"

"Yes, now." Olivia's soft fluffy sweater clung to her breasts, and considering how wonderfully tight her jeans were, they would be outlawed in three different states that he knew of. Just having her in his living room, all soft and inviting, was enough to test his resolve. There was no way he was getting Olivia within twenty feet of his bedroom. "You can have a tour tomorrow night if you still want one."

Olivia stood up and her slight wobble confirmed his resolve to take her home. He got on his shoes and coat and watched as she tugged on her winter gear. He checked his fireplace, to make sure it would be fine for the next couple of minutes, and then headed for the back door. "We'll go through the backyards. It's shorter than walking around the block." He opened the door and followed her out into the night. Selma had left her back porch light on again, and while the yards were cast in shadows, there was still plenty of light by which to see.

Olivia stopped under an old oak tree and looked up. "You got rid of the tree fort."

"About eight years ago. I was too old to play in it, and the lumber was starting to rot." He had many fine memories of his old tree house. If memory served him right, Olivia had been in the fort only twice. Both times had been at his parents' urging.

"That's a shame." Olivia shook her head and walked through the gate separating her backyard from his. "My grandmother never closed this gate, did she?"

"Not that I can remember. Once in a while I did, but never Amelia."

"To keep me out of your hair, right?" Olivia laughed. "I was a royal pain, wasn't I?"

"That's a double-edged question if I ever heard one. If I say yes, you'll be mad. If I say no, you'll know I'm lying."

Olivia laughed as she stepped onto the slate patio and nearly slid. He wrapped his arms around her before she went down. "Watch your step, it's icy." Her purple mittens clung to his arms. A fat black curl had escaped her hat and was tickling his nose. He could smell the fruity scent of her shampoo. Olivia smelled like apples and pears.

What was it with women and their fruity temptation? Wasn't it Eve who offered Adam a bite of the forbidden fruit?

He slowly released her and gently held her elbow as they walked the rest of the way across the slick patio to the kitchen door. "Got your key?"

"It's unlocked."

He turned the knob, and sure enough, it was unlocked. He shook his head, waited for her to enter the warmth of the kitchen, and then followed her in. "I know this is Misty Harbor, and a far cry from southern California, but you have to at least lock the doors, Liv."

Olivia liked the way he shortened her name. He made it sound all intimate and breathless. She also had liked the way she had felt in his arms moments before. She held up the keys she had put in her pocket when she had headed out the front door with Carol Ann earlier. "I locked the front door, does that count?"

"Only if you want to be half robbed." Ethan unzipped his coat, but didn't take it off. "Let me go check out the place to make sure no one got in while you and Carol Ann were out staggering in the streets."

"We weren't staggering." She stuck her tongue out at his back. ·

She might be in a wine-induced good mood, but she wasn't drunk. She would know the difference. Since Ethan obviously wasn't planning on staying, she stood in the middle of the kitchen and waited for his return. She heard him go upstairs and then there was the occasional squeak above her head marking his progress through the rooms. She tossed her coat and hat onto a chair. A moment later she could hear him coming back down the steps.

She didn't understand why he had been in such a rush to get her out of his house. She had been rude enough to ask for a tour, and he had been impolite enough to refuse. Strange, she had thought Ethan would be more than glad to experience some possibilities with her.

His comment the other day that sex with him wouldn't be casual had been her first clue. The second had been the knee-melting, toe-curling kiss they had shared earlier this evening when he had left her and Carol Ann alone to reminisce. She and Ethan had been alone in the foyer, and Carol Ann, the sneak, was supposed to be in the kitchen drying the last of the dessert plates. When he had pulled her into his arms, there hadn't been a moment's hesitation on her part. She had wanted that kiss as much as Ethan.

So why the sudden change of direction? Ethan didn't strike her as the kind of guy who got cold feet. Ethan didn't strike her as the kind of guy who got cold *anything*.

"You're all locked up," said Ethan as he entered the kitchen. "I turned off your front porch lights and checked on the fire." Ethan headed for the door.

She stepped in front of him and pressed her palms against his chest. "What, no kiss goodbye?"

"I don't think that's such a good idea right now."

"Why not?"

"Because there are three empty wine bottles sitting on the counter behind you." Ethan brushed his lips against her forehead. "I'll kiss you goodbye twice tomorrow night, okay?"

"No." She leaned forward and teased the corner of his mouth with her lips. "I'm not drunk, Ethan."

Ethan groaned as her lips slowly moved to the other corner of his mouth. "What do you think you're doing, Liv? I'm only human."

She could feel the rapid beat of his heart under her palm. "I know, I can feel your heartbeat." She trailed her mouth back over his lips. "The beat matches mine."

"Liv?" Ethan's arms wrapped around her waist and pulled her closer.

"Shhh. . . ." Her tongue outlined his lower lip, and her arms encircled his neck. The leather of his jacket felt cool beneath her fingers, but everything else was warm. "I'm experiencing some possibilities." She smiled as Ethan deepened the kiss and crushed her breasts against his chest.

Ethan released her mouth and trailed a moist path down the side of her neck to the valley below her throat. "I have no idea what you are talking about."

Olivia tilted her head back, to grant him further access. "I'm tasting possibilities." The back door pressed against her shoulders as Ethan continued his downward path with his mouth. Ethan's large warm hands cupped her bottom and tilted her hips forward. She gasped as his mouth brushed the front of her sweater, directly over an overly sensitive nipple. She had never felt this way with another man before. What was so special about Ethan that he could make her want so much with a simple kiss? On a sigh, she whispered, "Wonderful possibilities."

Ethan's hands caressed her hips and the indentation of her waist on their course upward. He raised his head and gazed into her face. "Tell me again you're not drunk."

"I'm not drunk." She caressed his rough jaw and read the heat and desire in his eyes. She also could see the doubt. Ethan didn't believe her.

She groaned out loud when Ethan released her and took a step back while shaking his head. Her empty arms fell to her sides. "You're leaving, aren't you?" She knew the answer, but wanted to hear him say it.

"Have dinner with me Saturday." Ethan's thumb caressed her lower lip. "We'll go someplace nice and have a real date."

"What? My cooking isn't nice enough?" she teased. "I'm all out of leftovers, so I won't be forcing you to eat everything in my refrigerator anymore." She was happy that he wanted to take her out, but it wasn't necessary. She'd much prefer the privacy of her own home when she was with Ethan. Just in case the temptation to explore a couple more of those possibilities arose.

"After dinner we'll go back to my place and you can help me decorate my tree." Ethan's fingers wove their way into her hair. "You did such a fine job decorating the one at the gallery, that I really could use your help at my house."

"You'll give me a tour of the house?"

"If you want." Ethan's gaze caressed her face. "I'll give you anything you want, Summer Breeze."

Olivia felt the softness of the Persian rug beneath her stocking-clad feet as she stretched to reach a higher branch to hang an ornament on Ethan's tree. Saturday night had finally come, and with it a wonderfully romantic dinner out with Ethan.

The past three nights she had seen Ethan, discussed the future sale of her house, and even watched some television with him. They had shared popcorn, opinions, and the most fabulous kisses in the world. Ethan was always the one to call a halt when things got too heated on the couch, on the porch, or in the kitchen. It didn't matter where they were—they always seemed to be kissing.

She liked that about Ethan. The man loved to kiss, and he was a world-class kisser.

Tonight there was something special in the air between them. Something hot and primitive. It had nothing to do with the seven-foot tree in Ethan's living room, and everything to do with the way he had looked at her over a candlelit dinner. Ethan had looked at her as if she were the only woman in the world for him.

Considering the heat that had been in her stomach and the rapid pounding of her heart, she was afraid she had been looking back with the same emotion burning in her eyes. She was pretty sure the dinner had been first class all the way, but she wouldn't swear to it. The only thing on her mind all night long had been the fact that they would be coming back to his place, and he had promised that he would give her anything she wanted tonight.

Tonight she wanted it all.

She had been thinking of nothing else since that first afternoon Ethan had showed up on the front porch ringing her grand-mother's doorbell. She didn't think it was possible to maintain a crush for ten years, without seeing the object of that infatuation. What she'd felt for Ethan ten years ago had been nothing compared to what she was feeling tonight.

She was still heading back to California at the beginning of January, as soon as a settlement took place. But she'd be going back with the precious memory of making love with Ethan. She wanted that memory.

Ten years ago out at Sunset Cove, one hot summer night, one of the local boys had tried to get a little fresh with her. At first she had thought she was handling the jerk pretty well. Then the jerk decided he didn't like no for an answer. The jerk wanted first base and beyond, and it didn't matter if she was letting him up to bat or not. It had been Ethan who had heard her protests and come to her aid.

Ethan had taken one look at her tear-streaked face, glanced down to make sure she was physically okay, and probably to check to see how far the boy had pushed it, and yelled at the top of his lungs for Carol Ann. Her best friend had ditched her boyfriend for the rest of the night and offered comfort, anger, and plans for retaliations. Payback hadn't been necessary. Ethan had handled it. Rumor had it that Ethan had dragged the boy home to his father and explained the situation, leaving her name out of the conversation. The father had taken care of the rest.

She had come away from that experience a little bit wiser about whom to kiss, and with a whole lot of embarrassment when it came to facing Ethan again. Carol Ann had been her rock, and with her sense of the absurd, the incident had been put into proper perspective and never had the chance to fester into some life-altering psychosis. She never saw Ethan as a hero. Her rescuer, her protector, yes. Hero, no. To her, a hero put his life in danger to perform a service to someone else. Ethan's life was never in jeopardy. He had outweighed the jerk by a good fifty pounds and was four years older. She might have had a crush on Ethan ten years ago, but she never hero-worshiped him.

Looking back on that night, she had been the young and foolish one to get into that situation in the first place.

"What's on your mind?" Ethan was standing next to her holding out another glittering Christmas ball.

She brought the tree back into focus and realized they were almost done decorating it. They probably hadn't said more than a few sentences to each other since Ethan had opened up the first box of decorations. "Sorry, I was just remembering something."

"Care to share?" Ethan handed her the ornament and reached into the box for the next one.

"I was thinking about a certain night, the last summer I was here. Out at the cove." She wondered if Ethan ever thought about it again.

Ethan appeared to be concentrating extra hard on hanging one simple ball. "What night was that? I was there a lot back then."

"You remember which night." She stepped away from the tree and looked at him. "I never got to personally thank you for coming to my rescue."

Ethan frowned. "You baked me a chocolate cake and left it with my parents the next day without an explanation. My mom thought it was cute, while Dad gave me a lecture on stringing along a young girl."

"Ouch." She tried not to smile as she took the last ornament from the box. "Sorry about that." She reached up and placed the ball in the only empty spot on the tree. She turned to Ethan and placed a kiss on his cheek. "Thank you."

Ethan looked surprised. "That's it?"

"What were you expecting? A parade?" She liked the way Ethan flushed. "That night was beginning to feel like an elephant around my neck. We both knew it was there, but neither one of us was willing to bring it out in the open."

"You're okay with it?"

"Okay, no. But it did propel me into taking some self-defense classes in college. It didn't leave any scars, if that's what you're asking. I'm not afraid of men, or forming a personal relationship, and I'm not frigid."

Ethan seemed to relax. "I'm glad I could help."

"You did, but Carol Ann helped more." She chuckled at the memory. "Do you know how many ways there are to castrate a sixteen-year-old male?"

Ethan cringed. "That sounds like the Carol Ann we all know and love." He reached out and captured her cheek with the palm of his hand. "Why are you telling me all of this now?"

"Because once we are in bed together, I don't want you thinking I'm doing it out of gratitude." She slowly smiled. "And just for the record, I no longer have a crush on you. You were replaced by

Robby Koznecki at my seventeenth birthday party. He had long hair and a motorcycle. My parents forbade me to see him. It ended tragically when he knocked up one of the cheerleaders at school."

His fingers trembled against her jaw. "I see." His gaze locked with hers. "When exactly is this event going to take place?"

"Tonight." She reached out and wrapped her arms around his neck. Once they had started to decorate the tree, Ethan had taken off his suit jacket and tie. His white shirt was crisp and bright against the strong column of his throat.

"Tonight?" Ethan's fingers skimmed her throat and teased the pounding pulse he found there. "Why tonight?"

"Because time is growing short. I've got to leave in a couple of weeks." She gently nipped at his lower lip. "I want to spend every moment I can with you, Ethan."

A rumble worked its way up Ethan's throat as he tugged her lower lip and sighed, "Thank God," into her mouth. The kiss started hot, and built toward desperation.

She broke the kiss and tried to catch her breath. "Ethan, I want that tour now." She playfully bit his chin. "Start with your bedroom."

Chapter Six

Ethan slowly lowered Olivia to her feet. His heart was ready to pound out of his chest. He wasn't sure if it was from anticipation or from carrying Olivia up the flight of stairs. Olivia had come right out and said she wanted to make love with him. What man's heart wouldn't have been thundering?

He brushed a kiss across her forehead and whispered, "This is my room."

Olivia's gaze never left his face. "Nice room."

He chuckled. The little minx hadn't even glanced around. "Did I tell you how beautiful you look tonight?" His fingers skimmed her arms and caressed the satiny smoothness of her long-sleeved dress. Olivia's demure black dress was seductive in its innocence. It concealed more than it showed, and that was probably the enticement. All through dinner she had been driving him out of his mind with her hungry glances and knowing smiles.

"Twice, but the third time might be the charm." Olivia's fingers toyed with the buttons on his shirt. "You look handsome, as always. But I already told you that." The first button slipped through the buttonhole.

His fingers trailed up Olivia's backbone, feeling the zipper as he went. He felt the second button on his shirt come undone, and slowly started to pull the tab of the zipper downward. Olivia smiled slowly and a third button was released. The zipper stopped its descent below her waist. He stroked his fingers back up her backbone. This time he felt nothing but warm silky skin and a very thin bra strap.

Olivia tugged his shirt from his pants, quickly unbuttoned the rest of the buttons, and then slowly pushed it off his shoulders. With hurried fingers, she quickly pulled his white T-shirt up and over his head. It landed without a sound somewhere over his right shoulder. He shuddered as Olivia's palms caressed his bare chest.

He closed his eyes and savored the feel of Olivia's hands rubbing his skin and her delicate fingers weaving their way through the dark curls splattered across his chest. How many nights had he been dreaming of this moment? Praying for this moment? Too many to stand there with his eyes closed, that was for sure.

With a gentle touch, he brushed her dress over her shoulders and down her arms. The black dress, which had driven him to distraction all night, pooled at Olivia's feet.

He hadn't bothered to turn on any of the bedroom lights. The hall light was lit, and there was plenty of light pouring in through the open doorway. Olivia stood before him, standing in a pool of golden light, looking like every one of his fantasies blended into one. A cloud of black hair framed her beautiful face, and a mouth begging for more than just kisses gazed back at him.

Olivia's skin was pale as moonlight and crying out for his touch. A lacy black bra cupped her generous breasts. A tiny waist and the gentle flare of female hips caused his breath to hitch. What caused his mouth to go dry as the Mojave Desert was the tiny black triangle she was wearing as underwear, and the lacy garter belt holding up sheer black stockings.

It was a darn good thing he hadn't known during dinner what she had been wearing under that dress, or he would never have been able to swallow. As it was, he was having a difficult time breathing. Maybe the flight of stairs had done him in after all. At the ripe old age of thirty he was going to suffer a heart attack.

"Ethan?" Olivia's voice sounded worried, and shy.

He forced himself to glance up from those incredibly long legs. Seeing the confusion in her eyes brought him back to the living. "You're beautiful." He stepped closer and tenderly took her mouth with his own.

Olivia melted against him as he swung her back up into his arms and then gently laid her on his bed. He smiled at the picture she made lying across his bed. Her pale skin contrasted with the dark comforter. Olivia looked like she belonged there.

He felt like a little boy on Christmas morning. He didn't know what to unwrap first. He started with unhooking those sheer black stockings and slowly rolling them down her silky legs. When the stockings floated to the floor, he kicked off his own shoes and socks. He brushed the garter belt and panties down as she reached for his belt and started to undo his pants. He captured her wandering fingers before he embarrassed himself, and completed the job himself.

Olivia lay before him wearing only a lacy black bra, with nothing covering her thatch of black curls. He stood there gazing at her for so long that she got to her knees and stared back at him. "Is there a problem, Ethan?"

"Yeah, you're perfection, and I'm scared to death that I might break you."

Olivia smiled and pulled down the thick comforter. A couple of the pillows fell off the bed, but Olivia didn't hide beneath the blankets. She sat in the middle of the bed and took off her bra. "There is no such thing as perfection, Ethan. I'm just a woman who wants you very much."

He reached into the nightstand and with shaking fingers he rolled on a condom. The bed dipped as he got on it and leaned over her. Olivia fell to her back and lay there staring up at him. "You will never be 'just a woman,' Liv." He reached out and traced a path over her moist lips, across her chin, and down her throat. His fingers stopped just short of her breasts. He smiled when she arched her back, silently begging for more. "Do you like it when I touch you, Liv?"

Olivia gasped with pleasure as his hands gently cupped her breasts and his thumbs brushed against her nipples. "Yes," she sighed as her nipples hardened more. Her hands reached up and pulled him down on top of her. She wanted to feel the weight of his body. She wanted Ethan's mouth on her. Night after night of frustrating kissing, which Ethan never let get out of control, had taken their toll. She wanted Ethan, and she wanted him now.

Ethan's mouth crushed hers as his tongue plundered and his hands stroked everywhere at once. Her breasts, her hips, her thighs. Heat spiraled and twisted as his fingers and mouth teased and tormented.

Her hands urged him on as her mouth answered his every demand. Her fingers stroked his back and gripped his hard buttocks. She opened her thighs wider and tried to encircle his waist, but he moved lower and tugged one of her nipples deep into his mouth. She nearly climaxed. "Ethan, please."

"Please what?" Ethan's mouth captured the other nipple and proceeded to torture her out of her mind. One of Ethan's fingers skimmed her inner thigh and entered her. His mouth left her breast and he stared up into her face. "Please this?"

She shook her head as she threaded her fingers into his hair and tugged his mouth toward hers. "Please more." She bit his lip a little harder than she had planned and then instantly stroked it with her tongue. "I want all of you."

Ethan growled as she wrapped her thighs around his waist and pressed herself against the head of his hard penis. With one heavy thrust he entered her and stilled.

Olivia wrapped her legs tighter and arched her hips. She felt him slip in a bit farther. She moaned and Ethan froze.

"Liv, sweetheart, am I hurting you?" Ethan's mouth was pressed against her shoulder.

"No, but if you don't start moving, I'm going to get extremely angry." She tried to arch her hips again, but this time Ethan wasn't moving.

Ethan chuckled against her collarbone as he slowly started to pull his way out of her. Just when she thought he was going to leave her, he slowly sank back in. He filled her to the limit. Only to start the whole process over again. "You mean like this." Ethan sounded like he had just run across the state of Maine.

"There's something called payback, Ethan." She bit his earlobe and she felt his movement increase, along with his breathing. The pressure inside was building, and she knew she was about to come. "Faster, Ethan."

He pumped faster, and she came apart in his arms, shouting his name. Sadly, his ear had the bad sense of timing to be directly in front of her mouth when she screamed.

Ethan's release started the same instant he felt her go over the edge and the ringing in his ear started. He at least was gentle-manly enough to shout her name into the pillow next to her head.

Olivia pulled the two hot cake pans from the oven and placed them on top of the counter. As soon as they cooled off a bit, she would tip the chocolate cake out and onto the cooling racks.

Ethan's arms slid around her waist as he sniffed the air. "Is that what I think it is?"

"Yes, your favorite." She snuggled deeper into his arms. "Chocolate cake from scratch." She turned in his arms, brushed her mouth over his chin, and wondered when she would ever get enough of Ethan. She feared the man was in her blood and in her heart. "My grandmother's recipe."

Ethan's lips wandered up the side of her neck and teased her ear. "You smell good enough to eat." His teeth nipped playfully at her lobe. "An enticing combination of brown sugar and vanilla."

She tilted her head and gave him better access. "That would be the Christmas cookies I baked earlier." She was visiting Carol Ann tomorrow morning and she wanted to bring the kids a spe-cial treat. Carol Ann swore that Christmas cookies came from the dairy section of Barley's Food Store in those cute little rolls you cut into slices.

"God, I love your cookies." Ethan's mouth grew hungrier.

Her laugh caused him to stop his exploration of her neck. "You are so easy." She grinned seductively. "All I've got to do is offer you food, and you're mine."

"I'm yours without the food. I just need all those calories to keep up my strength." Ethan eyed the cooling cake. "How soon before I can get a piece?"

"It's for after dinner, not before." She stepped out of his arms. "So, if you don't leave me alone so I can get dinner started, it will be even longer."

"Fine, what can I do to help?"

She liked that about Ethan. He never expected her to wait on him, and he was always willing to help. She liked a lot of things about Ethan. Too many things. "You can peel a couple of pota-toes and slice the cucumber for the salad. I'll do the rest."

Every night since they had become lovers, they had eaten dinner at her place, but spent the night in Ethan's queen-size bed. Ethan spent his days and a couple of evenings down at the gallery, while she had started the monumental job of going through her grandmother's things. The clothes had been the easy job. It was everything else in the house that was giving her problems. She didn't want to get rid of anything. Everything was too personal, too sentimental, or too meaningful.

A Hamilton had built this house back in the early eighteen hundreds. Amelia's bedroom set had been shipped over from England by the original builder. A Hamilton bride had slept in that bed for nearly two hundred years. How was she supposed to turn it over to some antique dealer, whose only thought would be to get the highest price possible for it?

She had spent the entire morning just going through the trunks in the attic. She hadn't seen a quarter of the treasures tucked away beneath the dormers before the tears had stopped her mental voyage into the past. Her grandmother always claimed that baking relieved stress. This afternoon she had put her grandmother's theory to a test, and she had been right. Decorating a couple dozen cookies and whipping up a cake for Ethan had made her feel better. Why didn't people bake more?

"Did you hear what I said?" Ethan gave her a funny look.

Olivia blinked and realized she was standing in front of the refrigerator with the door wide open. A package of chicken breasts was in her hand. She shook her head and closed the door. "Sorry, I was drifting again."

"You do that a lot lately." Ethan put down the peeler he had been using. "Anything I can help you with?"

"You said something about the gardens?" She glanced out the window above the sink. It was too dark to see anything out back.

"I was telling you about my trip to Karl James's place today."

"That's right. I forgot about that." Karl James was some local artist who had moved into the area about a year or so ago. Ethan was dying to carry some of his work, but it was too massive for the shop in town. "How did it go?"

"Great." Ethan resumed peeling. "He's got some pieces that blew me away. What that man can do with tree stumps and a chain saw and chisels should be classed as a miracle."

"What's that got to do with the gardens?" She seasoned the breasts and slid them into the oven.

"I'm probably going to have to call in a landscaper to change things around a little. I will need to showcase not only James's work throughout the yard and gardens, but other pieces as well."

She tried not to flinch as she stared into the oven's window at the chicken. Amelia's garden had been perfectly wonderful. Her grandmother, and her mother before her, and her mother before her, had never needed the services of a landscaper. The colorful chaos of flowers that bordered the picket fence had been planted with love, not with displaying artwork in mind.

Ethan's plans for turning the house into a gallery were wonderful. He was planning on leaving most of the house, and even some of the wallpapering, untouched. The integrity of the house would remain the same, but it would no longer be a home. It would be an art gallery. A distinguished gallery, but it would still be a shop.

The Hamiltons hadn't built this house to be a shop; they had built it to be a home. One filled with love, laughter, and the running footsteps of children. A home filled with the fragrance of bread baking in the oven and a riot of summer flowers blooming in the yard.

She realized now that was why her grandmother had left the house to her and not to her father. Amelia's son and his wife were settled in California and they were too old to have any more children. Amelia wanted Olivia to raise her family in the big wonderful home that overlooked the harbor.

She wanted the same thing as her grandmother. She had fallen back in love with the small coastal town. But how could she stay? Even with inheriting the house, she would still need an income to live on. Her heart would break every time she had to sell one of her grandmother's treasures to pay the bills. Constant repetitive heartbreak, or one quick break with the move back to California?

Where would her staying leave Ethan? He was planning on buying the house. She had already signed the contract for him to buy Amelia's house. Yellow legal pads filled with his ideas and plans were scattered all over his house, and this one. His dream was a larger gallery. Her returning home would give him that dream.

Where would her leaving leave them? Nowhere. There would be no "them." It would be her in California, miserable and lonely, and Ethan three thousand miles away. Something wonderful was happening between them, and she didn't think she had the willpower to walk away from it without discovering where it was all leading. She didn't want to leave. Not only for the house, but for Ethan. Most importantly, for Ethan.

She hadn't planned on it, but it happened anyway. She had fallen in love with Ethan. She was in love, and she now had one very big problem to solve.

Ethan stared at the woman he was falling in love with and wondered at her mood. In the past couple of days Olivia had changed. She had grown quieter, more prone to drift off into space, someplace he hadn't been able to reach her. The only time she seemed the same was when they were in bed together. Nothing had changed in that regard. She still responded to his touch. Still had the power to make him lose his control.

He never even imagined that making love with a woman could be like that. With Olivia it was more than two bodies coming together for mutual satisfaction. It was hotter, and growing almost desperate in its intensity.

Instant attraction had been his first reaction to Olivia's beauty, but it hadn't taken him long to realize there was a lot more to her than a pretty face and a killer body. He loved her laugh and the way her nose turned beet red whenever she was out in the cold. He loved the way she wasn't afraid to wear a ridiculous purple hat or spend an hour of her day down at Krup's General Store drinking hot chocolate and reminiscing with all the old timers. Olivia was generous with her time, and with her heart.

He knew she felt something for him. It was in her touch and in her eyes when she looked at him. It was in the extraspecial care she went through every morning making him breakfast, no matter how many times he told her cereal was fine. It was in the way she melted beneath his kisses and wrapped her legs around his waist every night.

He knew what he felt for her. He was afraid he was no longer just falling in love with Summer Breeze. He was actually in love with the woman who once had been the biggest pain in his bottom.

In less than four weeks she would be out of his life. He had no idea how he was going to manage to breathe, let alone live, once she got on that plane. He had no idea how he was going to ask her to stay in Misty Harbor.

To stay with him.

Chapter Seven

Olivia kissed Ethan goodbye and shooed him out the front door as fast as she could. Leave it to Ethan to want to dawdle this morning of all mornings. Didn't he realize it was Christmas Eve, and she had a hundred things that needed to be done? Ethan kept giving her strange looks all morning long, but she couldn't contain her excitement.

She had solved her problem. Or at least she hoped she had figured it all out. Tomorrow morning when Ethan opened up the small present she had gotten him, she would know her answer. One of the surprises was that Ethan's presents wouldn't be under the tree in his living room. They would be under the tree in her parlor.

The seven-foot spruce was out in the garage, waiting to be dragged into the house. Five boxes of decorations were at the top of the stairs, waiting to be dragged down and put up. Christmas would be coming to Amelia's house this year.

Wasn't Ethan going to be surprised.

Olivia hurried up the steps and started to drag down the boxes one by one. She had gone through the boxes yesterday, while Ethan was at work, and figured out what else she needed. The tangled strings of lights looked old and frayed, so she had stopped at Krup's General Store and bought new lights and about fifty dollars' worth of other decorations.

The second thing she did was pull a muscle dragging the tree in from the garage, where she had hidden it from Ethan. Getting it into the antique cast-iron stand she had found in the attic was a desperate act of brutal strength and curses. Lots of curses.

Olivia fortified herself with her fourth cup of coffee of the morning and then lit a blazing fire in the parlor fireplace. The tree branches needed to fall before she could start the decorating. With the caffeine rushing through her veins, she headed out front to drape pine garlands and red bows along the picket fence. By the time she came in from the cold, her hands were nearly frozen solid and it took a good twenty minutes standing in front of the fire to defrost them and to get feeling back into her toes.

The day was overcast and cold. Snow was once again predicted by nightfall. She turned on the porch lights and lit every candle she had bought yesterday. By late afternoon the tree was done, complete with a couple of brightly wrapped presents underneath for Ethan. The stack her parents had mailed her were neatly arranged next to Ethan's. A fire was burning brightly in both the parlor and the living room, and she had found a radio station that played continuous Christmas carols with no commercial interruptions.

The spirit of Christmas penetrated the house and filled her with hope.

All that was left was the food. Ethan was due home sometime after five. She wanted everything perfect for her surprise. She was staying in Misty Harbor.

It was nearly five-thirty when Ethan finally got to lock the doors of the Wycliffe Gallery. A couple of last minute shoppers had forced him to stay open later than he had planned. The customers had made it well worth his time, and had given him a chance to cool off. He no longer wanted to strangle Olivia.

The anger he had been feeling faded around four o'clock. Now he was hurt and confused. Sometime after two o'clock he had gotten a call from the secretary of Olivia's lawyer. The woman wanted to verify his address for a letter she was mailing to him. He hadn't thought anything about it at first, figuring it was about the sale of the house, but then the woman said something about legal ramifications. When he questioned what legal ramifications, the woman told him that Olivia was no longer selling the house.

Since Olivia had agreed in a legal contract to the sale, and she was the one breaking the contract, there obviously had to be some kind of ramifications. He couldn't remember what he had told the secretary before hanging up.

Ethan turned up his coat collar and headed for Olivia's. Snow had started to fall about an hour ago, but it wasn't sticking to the sidewalks and streets yet. By midnight he knew the worshipers at the late mass at the one and only Catholic church in town would have a hard time getting home.

How could Olivia do it? How could she sell someone else the house? It didn't make any sense. He had agreed to the price she was asking. She had sat there and listened to him as he had pointed out every improvement or change he wanted to do to the house. She had listened to his dreams for the house, and now she was selling it to someone else.

It didn't make any sense.

Olivia had been acting awfully strange and extremely happy for the past couple of days. It was as if she had a secret, a wonderful secret. He had chalked it up to Christmas and figured she had probably found him what she considered the perfect present. The only thing he had wanted from Olivia was her love. He didn't need any presents.

Now he didn't know what to think.

He slowly crossed the street, and headed up White Pine. Olivia's Christmas present lay heavy in his jacket pocket. Karen, his assistant, had come in about ten that morning and worked for a couple of hours so he could run into Bangor to pick up the gift. The tiny black velvet jeweler's box held all his hopes and dreams.

He was going to ask Olivia to become his wife and to stay in Misty Harbor with him. He loved her.

He would have sworn that Olivia loved him back. Now he wasn't too sure. How could she sell the house to someone else if she loved him? If she had wanted more money for it, all she had to do was ask. They could have worked something out.

The picket fence, with its fancy garlands and big red bows, caught his eye, but he wasn't in the mood to examine the fact that Olivia had decorated her fence. The bare porch from that morning now held a rocker piled high with foil-wrapped presents. An ancient pair of ice skates were draped across an antique sled that leaned against the siding. The most amazing decoration was the Christmas tree, fully decorated and lit, shining through the parlor's double windows.

What in the world was Olivia up to now? For weeks she had insisted she wasn't decorating her grandmother's house for the holiday. In less than nine hours she had the place looking like a magazine cover.

He opened the front door and stepped into a Norman Rockwell scene. The dark banister that soared to the second floor was wrapped in garlands and lights. Fires burned in both fireplaces, presents were under the tree, and candles were lit upon the mantels. There were even a dozen or so poinsettias scattered throughout the rooms. He could hear Christmas carols coming from the kitchen. Along with the clanging of pots and pans.

He kicked off his shoes and headed down the hallway to find Olivia. The entire house smelled of peppermint candles, pine cones, and muffins. Blueberry muffins if he wasn't mistaken. The closer he got to the kitchen, the more he smelled other fragrances. The smells of cinnamon, sizzling sausage, and French toast filled the air.

The sight of the kitchen stopped him in his tracks. It looked like the cabinetry had exploded. Pots, pans, and baking dishes were everywhere. Canisters of flour and sugar were on the counter, along with stacks of French toast, pancakes, and plates overflowing with muffins. A dozen blueberry muffins still sat in the baking tins.

Olivia, who had on a flower print apron over her demure black dress, looked like an elegant Betty Crocker standing in the midst of chaos. Baking ingredients were everywhere. The countertops and floor were dusted with flour. The sink was piled high with dirty dishes. A broken egg lay forgotten in front of the refrigerator door. Olivia stood in front of the stove flipping an omelet. She appeared to have more flour on her than in the canister.

Olivia gave him a radiant smile. "Oh, you're here." She slid the omelet onto a plate and pointed to a chair. "Quick, taste this and tell me what you think."

"What is it?" He hung his jacket on the back of a chair and sat. "What's going on, Liv?"

390 / *Marcia Evanick*

"It's a Western omelet." She slid the plate in front of him and handed him a fork. "Taste it before it gets cold."

The enticing aroma reminded him that he hadn't eaten anything since eleven-thirty. A fast-food hamburger and fries didn't even compare to what Olivia was serving him. He took a big bite and closed his eyes as he savored the taste of heaven. He opened his eyes and saw the look of anxiety on Olivia's face. She was acting as if she really cared what he thought. "It's delicious, Liv. Wonderful even." To prove his words, he took another bite.

Olivia's smile lit the room. "Do you think I can do it?" She crossed her fingers and held her breath.

"Do what?"

She glanced around the kitchen and for the first time realized what this must look like to Ethan. The man probably thought she was certifiable. Ethan would probably be right. Once she had started cooking up different breakfast ideas, she couldn't seem to stop. Even after she had gotten dressed, in what Ethan referred to as his favorite dress, she had to make one more batch of muffins. Blueberry muffins. Then when he had been late getting home, she had thought of a Western omelet. Thankfully he had walked in when he did. She had been contemplating Belgian wafffles.

She brushed a wayward curl away from her eye, and hurriedly tugged off the flour-smeared apron. She brushed at a streak or two of flour dusting the front of her dress and wondered why Ethan hadn't gone screaming out the front door. She must look a wreck. "This wasn't exactly how I planned on telling you." She had been planning something a lot more romantic than forcing him to eat an omelet.

"Telling me what?" Ethan's voice held a strange tone. One she couldn't place. Ethan stopped eating, and stared at her.

"I'm opening a bed-and-breakfast in my grandmother's house." She took a deep breath and blurted out the rest of it. "I'm staying in Misty Harbor."

Ethan's mouth dropped open and the fork dropped to the table.

"I'm sorry about the house, Ethan." She hurried from the room and practically sprinted to the parlor. Her fingers grabbed the small gold foil-wrapped present under the tree. Her stocking-clad feet skidded across the kitchen floor. She would have fallen on top of Ethan if he hadn't pulled her down onto his lap.

Ethan's mouth found hers in a kiss that threatened to burn down the house with its heat.

She was the one to break the kiss before it got totally out of control and she ended up making love with Ethan on the kitchen table. She shoved the present into his hands and demanded, "Open it. I was going to wait until morning, but I can't now that you know about the bed-and-breakfast." She reached up and wiped a streak of flour off Ethan's jaw. She had no idea how it had got there.

"I don't care about a present, Liv. You're staying, that's all that matters to me." He tried to pull her closer, but she held her ground.

"Open it now, or no muffins." She wiggled into a more comfortable position and couldn't help but feel the bulge in Ethan's pants. The man was definitely in the holiday spirit now.

"Fine." Ethan ripped the wrapping off the small box and lifted the lid. Buried in red tissue paper was a single sheet of paper, which he slowly unfolded. It was a real estate advertisement for the old marine supply building down by the docks, but positioned almost perfectly in the center of Misty Harbor. The building had been empty for three years, but the owners had been adamant, they weren't selling. By the price listed very discretely at the bottom of the paper, they not only were willing to sell the building now, but were going to be reasonable about it. He glanced from the paper to Olivia. "What's this?"

"Right now it's an old empty building, but it could be an art gallery. Your gallery." She watched his face, trying to gauge his reaction to this sudden change in events. "I know how important enlarging your gallery is to you, and I felt so bad about taking this house off the market. I went to the local real estate office a couple days ago. This listing came in that morning and I went to see it." She worried her lip until Ethan's finger stroked her mouth. "I don't know a lot about galleries, just what you have been telling me. But I've got to tell you, Ethan, this place is perfect. It has more square footage, and is closer to the shops and the docks. It needs a lot of work, but the asking price is lower than what you were willing to pay for this place."

Ethan chuckled and tossed the paper and the box onto the table. "Liv, relax. I'll look at it later, but right now I have more important things to do."

"Like what?" What could be more important than his dream of enlarging his gallery?

Ethan stood up with her in his arms and headed for the stairs. "Like loving you in that frilly pink bed upstairs."

She wrapped her arms around his neck and smiled. "I was willing to settle for the kitchen table."

Three hours later Ethan still held her in his arms. This time they were bundled up in blankets and sitting out on the second-floor balcony. They were watching the snow fall and the boats come into the harbor for the Festival of Lights parade. Every Christmas Eve a dozen or so boats outlined themselves in Christmas lights and in the darkness they sailed into the harbor. Most of the town lined the docks and the surrounding area for the glorious and moving sight of all those lights reflecting off the water. Ethan wasn't in the mood to share Olivia with anyone tonight.

Olivia snuggled deeper into his arms. "Lord, this is beautiful."

He placed a kiss on top of her head. "Are you warm enough?" She had changed into jeans, sweatshirt, and a pair of those men's socks she had bought when she first came to town.

Olivia chuckled. "After what we just did, I don't think I will ever be cold again." She took another sip of her hot chocolate. "Need a refill yet?"

"I'm fine." They had decided to snack on blueberry muffins and hot chocolate while watching the boats, since they both hadn't had time for dinner yet. They had been too busy making love in Olivia's pink frilly bed.

Olivia was staying in Misty Harbor. He could finally catch his breath. He placed his empty cup on the wooden deck. The last boat was slowly making its way into the harbor. "Since you gave me the best Christmas present ever, I think it's only fair that you get yours tonight too." There had been more than keeping warm to his purpose of wearing his jacket up to the balcony.

"I can wait 'til morning." Olivia brushed his jaw with a kiss and then turned back to watching the boat.

He took the small box from his pocket and chuckled. "I think not." He placed it in her hand. "You demanded that I open mine, now you've got to open yours."

By the pale light coming from Amelia's old bedroom behind them, he could see Olivia's fingers tremble. She glanced from the box in her hand to his face and back several times before lifting the lid.

Whatever light there was, it seemed to hit the diamond ring perfectly. There wouldn't be a doubt in her mind as to what she was holding in the palm of her hands. His heart.

"Will you, Olivia Summer Breeze Hamilton, do me the honor of becoming my wife?"

The tears slowly rolling their way down Olivia's cheeks tugged at his heart, but her smile was radiant and filled with love. "I thought you would never ask."

As the last boat pulled up to the dock, Olivia slipped on the ring, and out of her clothes. Underneath a small mountain of blankets, on a cold snowy Christmas Eve, Ethan unwrapped the best present he had ever received.